D0757436

BABY ZERO

EMER MARTIN is a Dubliner. She is a writer and artist who lives in Ireland. Her first book, *Breakfast in Babylon,* won Book of the Year at Listowel Writer's Week in 1996, and was published in the US in 1997. Her second book, *More Bread Or I'll Appear,* was published in 1999. Her short fiction has been broadly anthologised, and her non-fiction work has appeared in the *New York Times Magazine, Black Book Magazine,* and a selection of Irish newspapers. In 2000, Emer was awarded America's prestigious Guggenheim Fellowship.

EMER MARTIN

BABY
ZERO

BRANDON

A Brandon Original Paperback

First published in Britain and Ireland in 2007 by Brandon
an imprint of Mount Eagle Publications
Dingle, Co. Kerry, Ireland, and
Unit 3, Olympia Trading Estate, Coburg Road, London N22 6TZ, England

www.brandonbooks.com

Copyright © Emer Martin 2007

The right of Emer Martin to be identified as Author of this Work has been asserted by her
in accordance with the Copyright, Designs and Patents Act 1988.

ISBN 978-086322-365-5

Mount Eagle Publications receives support from
the Arts Council/An Chomhairle Ealaíon.

2 4 6 8 10 9 7 5 3 1

Cover design: Anú Design
Typesetting by Red Barn Publishing, Skeagh, Skibbereen
Printed in the UK

To Afshin, Jasmine and Jade

Story (stor'e), n. 1. A narrative, either true or fictitious. 2. A way of knowing and remembering information; a shape or pattern into which information can be arranged and experiences preserved. 3. An ancient, natural order of the mind. 4. Isolated and disconnected scraps of human experience, bound into a meaningful whole.

'Thus in the beginning all the world was America.' (John Locke)

PART I

THE COUNTRY OF ORAP

Chapter One

Dark Holes

My mother opened the door and pulled me inside. We had not seen each other in months, but the talk was not of homecoming.

'Did you come alone? You must play by the rules here, or they will have you flogged. Did you speak to immigration before you left? They've taken my passport. How can I get out without it? How will I get in anywhere without it?'

After a meal of plain rice, she told me, 'I have nothing else. I'm too afraid to go to the market by myself. I have no money. They won't allow us work.' The sack of rice was almost empty. I had always been afraid of my mother. More than my father. He was a dreamer. My mother Farah was a midwife and had done all the practical stuff: getting us out of the country, organising schools abroad. Now she hid in a one-bedroom apartment in a crumbling block, her hair grey and thin.

And she had shrunk. Her flesh was loose on her bones as if a strong wind could whip off her skin and leave her insides facing out. I tried to look out the window on to the narrow street. She had painted the windows black. 'If you cannot afford dark glass and you live on the ground floor, that is what you have to do. Another new law.' As my mother dozed off on the chair, I stared at the black and thought of the home the family once owned. Not far from here.

Across the city edge. We once had a three-storey house by the river. My father said that the river had another river inside it. A separate flowing. A contrary current. I never understood. I put my hands flat on the black window and felt the heat from the outside.

If I could not go outside by myself, why was I here? If my mother and I were stuck here without a man to escort us, what would we do in this dark, hot place with only a bit of rice left? I had made it from the airport in a taxi alone. Maybe I could call the taxi man and get back out of the country before she woke up.

I called the taxi driver and begged him to come over and take us shopping for food. He was not a relative, but he felt it would be a problem only if we were stopped. 'How likely is that?' I asked. And he laughed nervously and bitterly. I waited for him in the kitchen away from her. Roaches roamed like cattle across the counters. I put my little finger out to stroke one of them. It scurried away and waited under a plate. There was nothing to eat here. Poor starving cockroaches. There were cups and jugs and chipped bowls stacked up in three precarious towers. They looked like figures, individuals leaning aggressively toward one another. I decided that they were female, stuck like this in the kitchen. Crockery battling bitches. Every surface was glistening with grease. The old woman must be depressed not to clean up. Our house had always been immaculate, my mother the very picture of efficiency.

'Who were you calling?' Her eyes had red veins like blood-soaked tree branches.

'A taxi. He's going to pose as a brother and take us to the market.'

'They stoned a woman to death because she was with a man not her relative.'

'I'm an American citizen. They'll leave me alone. I'll just plead ignorance.'

She shrugged. Too worn out to fight. She was as hungry as her roaches.

'Your aunt still has a job. We can't go any more to the hospital, but they set up a separate one outside the town for us.'

'But she's a dentist.'

'She's everything now.'

'Maybe you could work there.'

My mother jumped in fright at the sound of the doorbell. The taxi man was reluctant to come in. As if it were a trap. Like a spider, I coaxed him into the hall. I told him I had dollars from America. He came inside. I struggled to get the voluminous black clothes over my head. My sneakers were white.

'You can't wear those,' my mother hissed.

'What? But I bought them specially. You told me to bring only quiet shoes.' I hadn't understood her at first. My shoes would hardly start singing in public. Sneakers were noiseless shoes. They did look so high-tech, with their air bubbles and fancy cushioning. My mother took some black paint from under the window and painted my very expensive shoes. I let her because she seemed to enjoy it so much. Glancing triumphantly at me as she did so. As if to say: 'Here are the rules I live by while you are driving your jeep under the palms on Sunset Boulevard.'

We were now alike, my mother and I—ageless, shapeless phantoms. The taxi man had a long nose with a bump on the bridge; he had an uneven moustache over a wide mouth. His eyebrows joined in the middle, and they were alive as caterpillars—moving up and down when he talked. It turned out that my mother had delivered three of his children. We told him that all the men in the family had left during the revolution. He shook his head and said they had abandoned my mother.

'But my father and brother can't come back. They would be shot or enlisted into the army. We were all in America at one stage, even my mother.'

'Why come back?' he asked.

'The new regime said the refugees could come back and get their property. She wanted to sell the house . . . that sort of stuff.'

'It was a lovely big house by the river,' my mother said. 'Many families live there now. They just took it over when we were away. I never got it back.'

All through the conversation, I was watching his face in the rearview mirror. It struck me that he could not see ours. We were stripped of expression. I turned to my mother, and she was facing me. I squeezed her hand and she stroked my palms. There was no air conditioning in the cab. My scalp was sweating under the veil, and my eyelashes kept scraping off the gauze rectangle in front of my eyes. Every time I blinked, I could feel an irritating scrape. This was new to me. Only poor people wore the veil when my family lived here.

The streets looked almost normal. A little bombed out, perhaps, but still bustling with people and lined with vendor stalls, and slogans written all over the walls. But the preponderance of black cloth in the heat was startling, as if these lives were angry paint strokes gashing through a bright canvas.

We were dark holes on the street. If you touched us, you would fall inside and disappear. We had eyes, but you could only imagine them. Our silence had the whole country tied up and despised. Then there was the fact that we had disappeared but were everywhere.

When we got home, we stacked the freezer with meat. Fruit in the bowl. A new bag bursting with rice. I dismantled the three crockery towers that had tottered aggressively on the counter since my arrival. There was something useless about the idea of rebelling crockery. When I took them apart, I couldn't help feeling that I was dismantling three totems. Then I washed up, scrubbed all the surfaces, and sprinkled poisonous powder for the roaches.

My mother sat on the couch with the TV blaring. She complained about everyone and everything in a tone and rhythm reminiscent of a prayer. First it was the government, the war, the revolution, US Immigration. Then, when she had exhausted the general, she moved on to specifics. My father the waster; the time they had been stuck in a refugee camp with a newborn baby and he had walked around boasting how he knew the king and queen, who he still referred as 'Your Majesty', even though they were a jumped-up military family with no aristocratic blood. My brother for running off to Silicon Valley, marrying a Chinese, and never calling; my uncle Mo for being Mo; my aunt for not helping her out, how she got to keep her job and be sent to the women's hospital while all the other women were forced to quit work; me for becoming too Americanised, forgetting my culture and roots.

'What culture is this?' I said as I lit the gas stove under a pan full of tomatoes and aubergines. But I was used to my parents' ability to hold two opposing viewpoints in their mind at once: loving America but not wanting to become American. Liking the stuff but looking down on the people. I cooked a big meal, but later I heard her get sick, and she was too embarrassed to catch my eye. 'Are you okay? Was it too much at one time? Too rich?' I asked. She looked at the black windows and rapped her knuckles off them. 'It's hard to tell if it's day or night,' she told me, as if in answer to my queries, 'but you can always check by the heat of the glass.'

That first night, I dreamt of the crockery wars. Womanly figures as stacked empty vessels, precariously lurching toward one another. Dark holes where their eyes should have been. I awoke sweating and sat bolt upright and naked. My mother was sitting in a chair at the end of the bed.

'Have you been watching me sleep?' I pulled the sheet up to cover my breasts.

'I've been alone a long time,' she told me in the darkness, and her face was so devoid of expression, she might still have been wearing a veil.

Chapter Two

The Deal

While I stood in the hall in the hot air of morning, I looked at all the photos my mother had put up of the family. None of us had ever been to this cramped, dreadful apartment, but she had our history pinned to the wall. Rows of faces pressed against small rectangles of glass. I gazed through my veil at the postage-stamp-sized faces of my grandparents.

'I must get some of these copied before I go back. I'd like to have them in the apartment in Los Angeles.'

'Copied?' my mother said. 'Where are you going to get them copied?'

She was also fully veiled, so I could not see her reaction. It struck me that it was going to be very hard to leave her here. She opened the front door and marched out. We met the taxi driver on the corner and got in quickly. Somebody might see us and report us.

My aunt embraced me at the hospital. At first, the building looked abandoned. Most of the windows were broken and painted black. There was electricity but no running water. There was no operating room. My aunt led me through the peeling corridors. There were a few beds with veiled figures lying inert under tattered blankets. I was afraid to go close and find their eyes through the cloth mesh. The wards were overflowing with women. Some were crouched on the ground with their hands over their heads. Leaning against walls. Rocking silently. My aunt informed me that many had gone mad. 'The suicide rate has skyrocketed. Most were widows because of the war and had no menfolk. They had been supporting children and elderly parents, so when they lost their jobs, they all starved. We have almost no medical supplies. There's no running water. Male doctors aren't allowed to see women patients, but there are no women surgeons. So they just come here to die while their children roam the streets hungry.' She waved her hand towards the beds with the women stretched out on them. 'They don't even move. They just lie there. We can't treat them.'

'The men's hospital is probably not much better,' my mother said.

'Yes, the West has imposed sanctions on the new regime because they've nationalised the oil. They punish us for having leaders who torture us.'

'Can I see your face?' I asked. We went into her office with my mother, and the three of us unveiled. My aunt and I smiled at each other and kissed. She was younger than my mother and always had been prettier. She did not appear so defeated and was even wearing light make-up.

'If we don't get some medicine and supplies soon, the staff have threatened to take all the women down to the government buildings and leave them there as a protest.'

I shrugged. 'Why not? They're dying here anyway.'

My mother looked worried. 'Don't risk yourself. You could be killed for that.'

'What can I do?'

'Did you ask about getting me a job here?'

'They say you are politically suspect because of your husband's ties with the royal family.'

Outside my aunt's office, two women waited. One had a two-year-old girl on her knee. The child's head was wrapped in an elasticised bonnet covering all her hair. She sat very still on her mother's knee. Glaring at us.

On Friday, we drove with my aunt and her family to the river. The sun roared and opened up the sky. Mountains folded back on to the horizon, cutting a clear line where the seamless blue sky met the rumpled fabric of land. The ground shimmered with heat as if the road and tree trunks were made of liquid. We were so sticky when we got out of the car that all the women ran shouting towards the riverbank. I wanted to strip off and dive into the crystal-clear water. But we halted like a herd reaching a precipice, and then someone pointed to the trees. We galloped under the trees into the shade and lay there, panting like dogs. The men were carrying picnic hampers, which the women took to prepare lunch. Then the men went to a section hidden by a canopy and stripped down to their shorts. We could hear them splash in the water. For every splash, my throat ached. We festered like black slugs under the trees and no one talked because the heat was roaring like a furnace. I felt like we had been buried.

'It is beautiful here in the mountains,' my aunt said, as we all lay side by side and murmured in acquiescence.

'Remember Baba used to say no one could swim to the middle of the river because there is another river inside this river with a different current?'

'Your father never knew what he was talking about. He couldn't even swim himself.'

'No, he was right,' my aunt said. 'I forget what it's called. They're dangerous because plumes can form. Polluting parts of the river if it's too close to the factory or a pollution source. I can't remember now, but there used to be a lot of stuff in the newspapers.'

'Why don't you try to get out of here?' I asked my aunt.

'This is my country. I'm not abandoning it now in its darkest time. What would all the women at the hospital do? The poor can't leave.'

'The poor!' My mother spat. 'The poor are always starting revolutions with their childish bias. It's all right for you. You have male relatives who live with you and can take you out. You have been allowed to work. You are living in your own home.'

'Why are we so passive?' I asked my aunt and mother. 'Like the

Jews going to the ghettos, then getting on the trains still hoping the authorities would let them live. It isn't as if we were always like this. Women used to have relative freedom in this country.'

'Ask your aunt. She's the activist. She has all the answers.'

My aunt stood up. I could tell by her curt movements that she was angry. I shushed my mother. 'Be nice. No wonder she doesn't come to visit you.'

'She lets me starve to death in that slum while she plays saviour to the poor. The poor, ha! You should see the house she lives in. She didn't have to lose her home.'

I fell asleep and dreamt that my mother, aunt and I were down by the river and stripping off layer after layer like small onions. As I was about to plunge into the delicious cool water, I woke up, frightened that I was naked.

I walked down to the river by myself. I had always been two different people in so many ways. East and West. Good daughter, bad daughter. I could not touch the water without falling in. I realised now that this had always been inside me—a river within a river. There was always the danger I might drift into the wrong river, the wrong part of me.

The men were crawling out of the river. Tiptoeing in bare feet across the stony ground. A strange, punctuated dance. Their bare arms flailing and dripping water. While they ate lunch, the women went behind the trees. My mother sighed and spoke to us. 'I don't see the point in this at all. All these retreats. Better to stay at home and socialise privately where we can eat and mix with the men.'

'But it's so beautiful here,' my aunt said. 'We can't let them take this country from us.'

'And what do you think, Miss America?' My mother turned to me.

'I was just thinking that it would be really easy to be a drag queen here.'

My mother laughed loudly. It was the first time I had heard her laugh since I had arrived. I wished I could have seen her smile. My aunt was puzzled. 'What's a drag queen?'

My mother sniffed. 'Abnormal people. Only in America would men want to be women.'

My mother and I sat side by side, day after day, sunk in silence.

I told her that I was leaving in a few days, and her face creased with fear. I told her I'd check on getting her a new green card, though that wasn't something I could do.

'But they took my passport, all my papers.'

'I'll leave you with all my money.'

'I can't leave the house to spend it.'

The phone rang, and I was glad to run and pick it up. My aunt needed me; she urged me to leave my mother at home and bring my US passport. She sent my cousin to pick me up. My mother cried when I left. When I was young, I never saw her cry.

In the dim light of the hospital, my aunt and two other women were standing in a circle, leaning toward each other. 'We need you. There's a truck outside. You're an American citizen, so you can pretend that you didn't know you were forbidden to drive. They won't touch you.'

'What do I have to do?' I could feel many eyes in the corridor on my back.

'We're taking the patients to the government building and leaving them there to die under the feet of their executioners. In full view of the city. They can no longer pretend that this is a hospital. This is a death camp.'

'I'm leaving in a day or two. I don't want to screw that up.'

'How can you walk away and leave us?' one of the women said. 'Look at your countrywomen.'

'This is not the country I grew up in. My countrywomen are not these black spectres, dying and mad in this filthy, shit-smelling place. I've been in America most of my life. My countrywomen are currently sipping cosmopolitans in bars and showing their belly buttons.'

'We had three suicides this morning.' Another woman grabbed me and came face to face so that I could see her eyes behind the mesh. 'Every day there are more and more. This is the end of the road. As you're an American, they'll let you be.'

'If I'm deported, I can't ever come back. Who will deal with my mother if anything happens?'

'I promise you I will.' My aunt sensed a bargain. 'We need to fight back for once. You said so yourself.'

'Will you let her live with you and your family?'

'Yes. If you do this, I will.'

'Okay, we'll make a deal. You take care of her, and I'll do this before I leave. I'll just drive.'

'So you'll do it.' The women were excited.

'I'll do it the day I'm flying back West. Then I'll drive straight to the airport.'

My mother was terrified I was going back home to America, but she knew I couldn't stay here.

'I will die here. I can't believe I will die alone.'

I wanted to let her know that she would be taken care of by my aunt's family now, that I had taken care of things, but I didn't dare let on that I was going to do something risky. The taxi driver drove me to the hospital.

Like giddy thieves, we loaded the patients on to stretchers and carried them to a waiting truck. Nurses stood on the truck and roughly dragged the very sick to the far corner. The patients expressed no surprise. None struggled. Most were catatonic. Wide open to fate. I had never imagined a human cargo so listless and passive. I raced around the ward like a demented sheepdog, herding the stragglers on to the truck. The women who were hunched by the walls I pulled by the arms and loaded on top of their sisters. I mashed them in together like livestock. I hurt some of them. Their discomfort and confusion was palpable, but any protest was paralysed by their fear.

Driving to the city, my aunt and I were the only ones in charge. She had sent her staff home to hide. The truck was huge. A man's truck. I'd never driven anything like it. At home, I had a jeep and thought I was tough. We had a patient beside us with stomach cancer. Her breath emanated from her clothes like something vile seeping from a rotten inner core. I would never see any of those women's faces. Never catch their eyes. They were objects to me.

They put my aunt in a sack and buried her up to her waist. Then they publicly stoned her. I sat on a chair in the interrogation room and watched them burn my passport. They told me I had no understanding of tradition.

I asked them why when they persecuted men for religion or colour, it was viewed by the world as oppression, and when they persecuted women, it was dismissed as tradition. I lay on the floor in a cell, bloody and bruised. The tiny cell was round and empty, but there was a window, a tiny slit in the wall, so high I could not reach it or look out.

Often I hear screaming behind the walls. Some nights, they come into my cell and hurt me. They always come in a group. I feel them exploring, tiny figures in a vast landscape. Fingers probe my crags to pull themselves up higher. I have to make sure they never stumble on the source of my second river.

I worry about my mother. I have not seen or heard from anyone. I'm not sure if they have even told her where I am. She must know my aunt is dead.

There are three layers of prison around me: the walls, my veil, and then the fact that I cannot see myself for the first time in my life. I have no mirror and I miss my face. It is the realisation that I might never see myself again that shocks me.

How far inside yourself do you have to go to be safe?

Imagination becomes my soul, and the past is my soul dreaming.

I recall one image from the cradle. My mother's face looming like a huge harvest moon above me, and when she smiles, her smile is a dark hole in her face.

Chapter Three

I Am an American

The government that had taken over during the revolution in Orap turned corrupt very fast. The Mercedes Mullahs, the peasants called them. They moved into the confiscated houses of the rich and became as complacent as we once were. They kept a war with the neighbours going interminably so they could keep the populace worked up and distracted. It was the poor who sent their sons and in the end their daughters, and the poor sons and daughters who died. The generals miraculously survived. All of them.

The poor had nothing but their children, and then they had no children. The government, in the name of God, had conscripted the remaining children, boys and girls as young as four, since the older ones had been slaughtered. It was the males out of these war-crazed children who eventually overthrew the government twenty-five years after the initial revolution. In the name of God. They said they would bring the true revolution. The government and its army now are made up of men between the ages of 14 and 25. Vicious, fanatical, shell-shocked children.

There has been no one here for days. Am I the only one here? I walk in circles. There is a can in the courtyard that blows about in the wind. It is the only sound, scraping the surface of the

world, as if it were the only thing left. I try to measure night and
day by the light, but I have not eaten, and I don't know how
many nights there have been. I am not organised enough. I think
of films I have seen where the prisoner keeps exercising. I don't
do that. For a while, I am so hungry I don't even remember anything. Then a 13-year-old prison guard opens up the door and
comes in with a tray of bread, feta cheese and rice and a mug of
water. He calls me the American. He wears a turban and beaded
wooden sandals with a slight heel. His flesh bulges slightly over
the leather straps. Sometimes his eyes are painted with the traditional black kohl. I ask can my mother visit me, and he says he
will find out if that is okay. I say that she will have to be escort-
ed: father, brother, husband, son. He tells me her cousin the taxi
driver can bring her. So the taxi driver is still in the picture. Every
day I ask to see my mother, and every day the guard says he will
convey my request. How long have I been here? He won't tell me.
He hesitates. I scrutinise him and see if he was one of the ones
who came in at the beginning and hurt me. I can't tell. He takes
my bucket out. He always looks inside and it makes me feel
ashamed. I ask him for a mattress.

There is a storm outside. Wind blows through the high slit of a
window. Shadows rattle over the roof like schizoid thought patterns.
In the hours-long monotony of the storm, the thunder snaps the
sky shut so hard, and so often, that the night is left in a shredded
pile. By the time day comes, I cannot clean up the night. All day, I
trip over fences of darkness, so that I cannot go from one side of the
cell to the other without falling. The door opens and the guard
comes again with food. I am lying in the middle of the cell. He is
surprised. I usually lie in the corner. He tells me that the storm has
flooded the bottom of the jail and that I might have a roommate. I
ask for a mattress.

No roommate, no mattress, and no mother. I wonder is my face
still bruised from the interrogation. How long ago was that? No
mirror.

I have another noise in my head. The noise has swelled to such a point that I wince when I try to remember. Trying to sort out voices, words and thoughts is too much of an effort. When I awoke this morning, I lay in the corner of my cell, on the cold ground, listening to the sound of a tin can being blown along cement ground. It is a small empty sound in a large place. The can rolls one way and stops. Peace for a minute and then the can scrapes across again. I shift about in expectation of the sound. I will the can to roll because the silent expectation has become worse than the noise.

I have to rely on memory to keep me connected with my humanity. I am afraid that by reaching into the past I am changing it. Rearranging it. Truth is a slippery, quickly evaporating entity, and truth is no match for time.

My veil was off my face when the guard came in today, and he stopped in shock. I don't think he expected that I had a face. I frowned at him, and he left my food and took my bucket. He glanced into the bucket.

'Were you sick?'

'The food was bad.'

'It is nearly winter. You need blankets.'

'There is a sound outside. You have to stop it. A can rolling across the ground.'

'You are expected to eat.'

'Can I see a lawyer? Does my family know where I am? Does my government? I want to contact the Embassy.'

'Embassy?'

'The American Embassy. Look, who's in charge here?'

He looks back into the bucket and leaves the cell.

Now I am alone, dozing. I had a recurring dream for years that doesn't come back to me at this time, but I'm waiting for it.

I am in a crowded car. I understand that I am a small bird. Someone has plucked all my feathers out. I don't remember who, but I know it was done aggressively and deliberately. I am contained in a small canvas bag. I'm half-dead.

I am a plucked bird in a bag.

The car is moving very fast. I realise who has the bag. My big brother, Zolo. I'm awash with relief because I think that he might have enough love for me to take me to safety. There might be just enough love to save me. But I'm not sure. It is the uncertainty that is the root of this nightmare.

The guard comes back and says that when I hear anyone at the door, I should put on my veil. 'You don't have to wear it when you are alone. The revolution asks this. Only if there is a man who is not your father, brother, husband, son.' I don't move to put on my veil. I stare at him. He is holding a mattress and blankets. I stand to take them and he steps back a bit. Is he afraid of me?

'Those other men who used to come at the beginning. Where are they?'

'You are allowed a mattress.'

'Are you one of them? They used to come at night . . .'

'Cover your face.'

'Are they coming back? I need a doctor. They hurt me.'

When he leaves, I pound at the door and scream.

'I want to see a doctor. I'm sick. I need a doctor. I am an American. You will be in trouble if anything happens to me. Send me a doctor.'

This night, maybe because of my shouting, two men come into my cell. They put my veil over my face, and they wrap all the material around my body tightly and face me to the wall. They spin me around and punch me in the face and on the breasts. They have a truncheon, and they rub it with chilli powder in front of me. They know they have used this before on me. Tonight they are lazy and do not end up doing anything with it. When they go, I lie swaddled in cloth that is damp with sweat. I don't think I am bleeding, but I don't dare put my hands to my skin to check.

I am a plucked bird in a bag. I might not get out of here. There is a possibility that this is the end. I pull the blankets over me and sleep with my face still in the veil, too afraid to uncover. Maybe they are still here in the cell. There is no light from outside tonight. No light through the slit of a window up high in the wall. Power cut.

I'm thinking of my brother Zolo. I was raised to worship him. My parents never stopped talking about him. About what a genius he was. But my dreams fell out of my soul when I bowed down before him.

Chapter Four

A Visit

When a guard comes in to take my food and bucket, I ask a few questions.

'Can I see a lawyer?'

'Is my family trying to contact me?'

'When will you allow visitors?'

'What's my release date?'

'What are the charges for which you are holding me?'

'I've been sick again. I need to see a doctor.'

This is all just to hear the sound of my own voice. I assume that my family has been working on the outside to get hold of me and effect my release That is an assumption. Knowing them, there will be the usual round of recriminations and accusations to get through before they will act positively. I worry about my mother. Why did she ever go back to Orap? Our family's lives were spent shuttling around the planet, always filling out forms and standing in queues for visas. It was a curse to be from here. We thought we were so privileged. We looked down on so many people.

This night, they come again. Marching in a gang. Glistening with group testosterone. Dragging me off the mattress and on to the floor.

I don't even know my crime. I drove a few patients to the steps of the government building. It was enough to stone my aunt for. I sense that more than a month has gone by. My breasts are sensitive; the nipples feel like open wounds. I'm waiting for my period, but it is taking for ever. I have stabbing pains in my lower belly, like menstrual cramps. Do I have internal injuries?

A miracle happens. They say I have a visitor. My mother. They lead me to a room and she comes in. Frightfully thin under her burka, she grabs me in her arms. She is wailing. I am too shaken to respond—it might be a mirage.

'Is this a good sign? Are they letting me go?'

'Oh, you foolish girl, listening to your stupid aunt. I should have known when you left . . . What are you doing in here?'

'What are you doing out there? Mother, my aunt was right. I still believe that. Can you get me a lawyer? Do you know how long I'll be held?'

'You haven't seen a lawyer? Where do you think you are? You foolish American. You have been so naïve. Everyone is afraid. It's getting worse outside. It took me a long time to get this visit. I can't travel by myself. Your cousins blame you for your aunt's death. They say you and your American ways caused it.'

'How come they let you visit?'

'Listen. You have to behave. They said you are difficult. You attacked another prisoner.'

'That's bullshit. What about Baba and Zolo? Can they come here and help? They're men.'

'No. No. They mustn't come. They'll be killed. One lost child is bad enough. Oh the shame. The way people looked at me when I came in here. Why can't you behave even in here?'

'Does Zolo know I'm here?' This isn't easy. I think she's going senile in her old age. She used to be such an organiser and hustler.

'You know Zolo and your father. They spend their time fighting and disagreeing on everything. How could you do this to us? What were you thinking . . . ?'

The visit ends there. They take me back. I never even saw her face. We were two masks facing each other because the guard was in the room all the time and I didn't dare raise my veil. It all happened so quickly that I had no time to collect my thoughts. For the next few days, I go over the things we should have said to each other. Nothing has been resolved; I had no information from her. One thing I noticed though. There was a calendar on the wall. The year is back to Zero. All the women in our family were born in the year Zero. The last three successive regimes have changed the calendar to suit their own story of the world. They have tried to start the world again. The past never stops beginning. We are always climbing on top of it. History rewinds each generation and, once playing, erases everything. But history is the present's waste matter: it can't be tidied up. It is the mess we leave behind.

Chapter Five

The Lawyer and the Doctor

The guard comes and takes me from my cell. My eyes are sore. I have not looked at anything beyond six feet in all the time I've been here. I am put in a room with eleven veiled women. When the lawyer comes in, he says he is the lawyer for us all. He instructs each one of us to unveil. We obey reluctantly. It can become a protection too.

None of the women have faces. One has some, but her nose is cut off. A flat hole sings wide under her mad eyes. I can see marrow pretending to be teeth in her second mouth. The lower mouth beneath grimly closed, easily mocked by the upper, that opened for a scream. But only snuffles.

There is much bad breathing in the room, as sinus passages have been dissolved and openings torn or melted shut. Most faces have been melted by acid. Their eyes peer through wads of skin.

The lawyer takes notes on each one without talking to them. He sketches them briefly and numbers the sketches.

These creatures do not look at me. I almost feel cruel when I unveil and have a face intact. The lawyer jolts when he looks at me.

'You're the American. You will get stiffer sentencing. Less pity.'

'They did other things to me,' I whisper.

'Who?'

'The guards.'

'The guards did not do this—their families did. They dishonoured their families.'

But I cannot resent these scraped spectres for their one triumph.

The women re-veil with relief. They will always wish to wear it now. It will be solace.

The lawyer says our trials will be in a week. We will all be tried together. The lawyer leaves the room.

A doctor enters.

'I want each of you to follow me for examination,' he says. Not looking at any one of us. 'You first.' He points to me.

The examination room is rudimentary. The wall has two colours. Blue on the bottom and white on the top. The paint peeled and blistered. It is very warm. After months without heat, I feel that my skull is about to hatch. I assume he is an educated man. My whole family are doctors. We revere the profession.

He tells me to strip completely.

'But you are a man.'

'You are a prisoner now. The laws don't apply.'

There is no curtain and he offers me no robe. I take off all the clothes I have not washed in months.

'I'm sorry,' I say, hoping to elicit his sympathy. 'I stink.'

He winces every time I speak to him, and I realise that he is not used to women addressing him. He motions me to lie on the leather bed. Naked, I lie as he probes and frowns. He writes things down.

'Your rectal passage is torn.'

I close my eyes. I have had pain there for weeks. Not ready to talk about that yet.

'Your uterus is fully enlarged. Wait.'

He comes back with a small hand-held machine, which he rubs on my belly.

I hear you for the first time. You make a noise in the world. A heart thumping like a mink in a trap.

'One hundred and fifty beats a minute,' he says. 'Your own heart is 80 beats. Everything slows down after we're born'

'I'm pregnant.'

He sighs. 'Most of you are.'

He walks to the wall. He picks at a blister and it cracks and bursts.

'Wait. I want to see a dentist. My teeth are falling out.'

Facing the wall, he sighs without turning. 'Babies need calcium.'

You build yourself inside me, and everything is for you and nothing for me. You are active while I wait, slumped and removed. You are coming through me, oblivious to me. I can't stop you. I have to tell you my story because it will be your story too.

Baby Zero, you are eight weeks old. Your face is changing: the ears, eyes, tip of the nose are appearing. Teeth develop under gums, intestines start to form. Leg buds begin to show feet; the toes are tiny notches.

I can't get too attached to this thing inside. Just because I know so many details of gestation doesn't mean I view them all with marvel. There is an element of dreaded inevitability in it all too. When I was a young girl, they told me that women are like water: their lives should flow into their family's desires, and a good woman should take on the shape of whatever container she is poured into. But there's always a river inside. I'm just not sure if it can help me this far along. Beware of me, Baby Zero. Everything gets brought back to the same moment, until there is no mystery in starting over.

I have a vision in my boredom. I see the prison open and one line of women march out. The town is sleeping, but more women creep from their houses and glide down the streets in silence. I see all the black-veiled women line up in twos. As they step closer, one woman is subsumed into the other until, in a flash, there is only one line of women. Woman minus woman. I see the mountain open and all the women go into the mountain. They turn, each one, as they enter. They look back.

Baby Zero, listen carefully, for this is your story too. Your messy inheritance. I know, I am baby zero too.

I remember the desert. The deep carved valley in the dry mountains. I remember her. Them. The lighted petrol-station signs on the road at night. Taller than anything else around. Shinning out one after the other by the highway. I even remember those. I almost remember those the best.

I dream of live pylons walking through black waters and greasy rushes still in oily swamps. And miles of cars, rusted, inanimate, gutted, graved, getting over their journey.

And truth?

Truths like aeroplane warnings needling into the sky. Always being the highest thing, saving what's beneath.

You are about to find out, baby. It all happened not so long ago. But I don't know if the distant past is more distant than the recent past. Neither is accessible except as stories.

The past is here with me now in the cell. I did it. Unleashed it. The past is here; it never goes away. It doesn't help.

My family was once the prominent and much esteemed Fatagagas family.

PART II

ESCAPING THE REVOLUTION— ORAP

Chapter Six

The Real Fatagagases

The real Fatagagases were two brothers who had a very prestigious second-generation practice in the capital. They were renowned throughout Orap for their elegant patients. In fact, they were celebrities themselves. They were ear, nose and throat surgeons, but mainly they performed cosmetic surgery, lopping the ends off the noses of the ruling class's daughters. The royal family were among their patients.

Ishmael Fatagagas and his younger brother Mo were just out of medical school. They were of no relation to the real Fatagagases. Ishmael and Mo had been born in Orap. Their father and mother had been goat herders in their native land but fled when communists annexed their country. Orapians were very tribal, and Mo and Ishmael were routinely stigmatised as foreigners and outsiders, despite the fact that they had been born here. Mo Fatagagas approached Ishmael and informed him that the bank would be willing to lend them the down payment for a surgery on the same street as the famous Fatagagas brothers. Ishmael at once saw his younger brother's brilliance, and the two started a state-of-the-art cosmetic surgery practice on the same street. Everyone confused them with the real Fatagagases and soon people forgot that they weren't going to the real Fatagagases.

For one brief moment, Orap had democracy. They elected a popular president who wanted to nationalise the oil and share the wealth among all the people. As a result of this, the CIA and MI5 funded a coup and chose a thuggish Orapian general to be king. This general king quickly married a real royal to legitimise his house and establish a monarchy. He gave the oil back to the British and the Americans. The allies of the old ruling class fled the country. The real Fatagagases, whose family had been practising on that beautiful tree-lined street for two generations, packed up and left for California. Mo and Ishmael stayed, as they had nothing to do with the old regime. In those heady days, when every beggar was changing places, they bided their time, and eventually the new royal family became their patients. Their prestige grew. It seemed as if Mo and Ishmael had been ministering to the rich and powerful for generations; in effect, they became the real Fatagagases.

Mo was irascible and bilious. His imperious manners frightened and awed the patients. The young women and their mothers were invariably bleached blondes, and he gave them new pert noses. Their men had long Semitic noses and jet-black hair. A visitor to Orap might have been forgiven for thinking that some genetic anomaly was taking place among the middle classes.

Mo insisted on choosing his patients selectively. Ishmael once witnessed him grabbing a man and his daughter by the scruff of their necks.

'Get out of here, peasants; you deserve those peasant noses.'

When the man and his daughter ran down the steps of the clinic, hiding their faces from curious onlookers, Mo roared, 'You are peasants and those are your noses.' Ishmael tried to calm his brother down. The awaiting patients stroked their own noses in terror.

The new queen preferred to deal with Ishmael directly. Ishmael was soft-spoken and bookish. He was tall and had a neatly trimmed moustache. Ishmael gave all her children tiny new noses. As much as it was proper, they became friends. She was 16 when she was married to the general. She gave legitimacy to the new throne, and he gave oil to her country. The queen's sister-in-law also sent her boys to Ishmael. This started a craze, and soon people were getting their sons clipped as well. Business was good. Ishmael married

Farah, a woman from the upper classes. Farah had her own mid-wifery clinic and had been trained abroad. Some of her family had been executed, and she was keen to change her name. They had a son and named him Zolo.

From birth, Zolo was marked to take over the family business.

The new king named the country Orap and changed the year to 0. That was part of his power, to state that time was subject to his authority. Time was under his control. A new name for a new age. Ishmael and Farah's second child, Leila, was born just as they changed the year.

Ishmael doted on his baby girl. He felt less pressure to mould her than he did his son, with whom he always felt obliged to be strict. Every evening, when he came home, Leila came running to him, and he would scoop her up and carry her around. He loved her smallness, her delicacy. The fact that she wanted to be held and cuddled all the time. He nuzzled into her neck, and she shrieked with joy. She said she had a special place and that it was sitting in his arms with her head on his left shoulder. She would touch his shoulder and say, 'Baba, that is my place. For me only.'

Zolo sneered. 'How can she own your shoulder?'

Ishmael would tousle his hair or offer to throw a ball with him. But he did not feel it was wise to hug or cuddle him lest he soften the boy. Zolo once tried to get on his knee when Leila was there and put his head on the other shoulder, but Ishmael let the five-year-old down gently.

'She's only two, Zolo. You're a big boy. I'll take you to our clinic. Would you like that?'

Zolo waited till Ishmael was gone, and he hammered Leila with a samovar until the servants pulled him off. Farah was unhappy that the samovar was one of her family heirlooms and now had a dent in it. The wailing Leila was soothed by her father. But it was Zolo who wept more and was inconsolable. So much so, his parents just raised their eyebrows and sent him to his room without admonishing him. Zolo was not a violent child or a fighter. He was rather soft in the beginning, and thoughtful. But the servants were at his beck and call; it was not their place to discipline him. He was given his own chauffeur when he was five. His mother was always busy in her clinic, or at social engagements; she wasn't raised to love or care for children. She herself had been raised by servants.

Ishmael doted on Leila. Leila was always turned out beautifully in designer dresses, bows, hats and bags. Ishmael found that he could get all the love and physical affection from his baby girl that his frosty wife was unable to provide him with. In turn, she adored her father and, once he came home, never left his side. Leila had her own set of servants to wait on her—a different set from Zolo's. Zolo began to identify with his uncle, when he discovered that Mo was immune to his cute little sister's charms. He also knew that it pushed his father's buttons when he followed Mo rather than Ishmael around the clinic. Zolo went from being a sensitive little boy to adopting a rather imperious manner. He was indulged and pampered without any tenderness.

Ishmael and Mo had more or less the same extraordinary nose, inherited from their father. It had a plateau on top so large that you could balance a bean, it dropped for a considerable length, and then, for a final flourish, it hooked inwards. Ishmael and Mo often talked of operating on each other, but in the end they decided that though they would do their children if such a nose appeared on any of them, they would keep their own giant flamboyant noses.

As outside got more chaotic, the royal family tried to go on with a semblance of normality. They threw lavish parties, and Ishmael went along to one of them. A select few were admitted into the private quarters to smoke hashish. Ishmael found himself in the queen's bedroom, and he walked into her closet and began to smell her clothes. Sequins, taffeta, silks, fur and linens. He held on to the world by these pieces of cloth. If he let go of that light chiffon scarf, he would tumble out of the closet through the lavish bedroom window, up past the manicured palms, through the blue desert sky, into the atmosphere and off beyond to a dark place unknown and of no interest. He nearly leapt off voluntarily when he was caught in the closet, nosing into a pile of jewelled slippers like a horse in feed. The queen raised her eyebrows; she was too well bred to comment.

'Doctor Fatagagas.' Stiffly, gracefully, she stood back into the bedroom to allow him out of the giant closet. 'I need to talk to you. I no longer trust my regular physician.'

'The people at the gate? The protesters?'

'You don't think there will be a revolution, do you?' She looked amused and worried at the same time. Such breeding, Ishmael thought.

'Your Majesty, they're poor, easily led by the fanatics.'

'And their own fantasies and deprivations, I'm afraid.'

'I can see you care deeply for your subjects,' he gushed sincerely.

'The trouble with fanatics,' she said in her tone of elegant resignation, 'is that they have more energy than the rest of us.'

Then the queen unbuttoned her blouse and turned her head to the side in shame.

'Doctor Fatagagas, you are the only one I trust. I have found a lump on my breast.'

When Ishmael was leaving the afternoon party, the queen gave him a large Chanel bag full of clothes. He was humiliated. He couldn't believe she would do a thing like this. Maybe her health worries had lowered her guard. She sensed his discomfort and tried to help him out. 'For your daughter. I just thought she would like some dress-up clothes.'

Dress-up clothes, he thought bitterly as his driver made his way through the mob at the gate. He could have given them to his wife, but if the queen saw her wearing them, he would feel stupid. These clothes were so exquisite. Even in the car, he plunged his hand into the myriad cloths, his fingers grasped like mouths at the textures.

When he arrived home, his wife was with their two children by the river. He stood on the roof with the bag in his hand, watching them with fond propriety. Then he spotted the gardener's 12-year old son hauling himself out of the river, and he grew irritated. His children had a perverse attachment to this particular child.

On the second floor of Ishmael's house, there was a small zoo in one of the rooms. One of the servants was from the country and missed animals. The children helped him tend them. There was a goose, a sheep, a hawk, a pig, a tortoise and a snake. Fearful that the neighbours might think he was a peasant, he insisted that the animals be kept indoors. Mo, who never married, brought a poodle back from London, and they called it Twinkle. Twinkle was deemed fit to parade in public. Ishmael desperately hoped that one day the queen would suggest that his daughter and son be allowed play at the palace with her children. Unfortunately, his daughter Leila and son Zolo seemed to prefer to play with Mehrdad the gardener's son. No matter how many times he forbade them and told them to amuse themselves in their zoo with their animals, he would come home and find that his servants had let them splash about in the river with Mehrdad.

When it was discovered that Zolo was a prodigy, Farah had been eager to push him ahead in school. He was always in classes where he was the youngest by four years. Still ahead in his studies, he could never mix socially. The other boys hated having this little know-it-all squirt in their midst and beat him up at every opportunity. Zolo was driven home by a rather resentful chauffeur, who seemed to smirk when he saw him arrive at the car with his shirt torn and scrapes on his face. Ishmael had thought that this was troublesome but would not dare overrule his wife.

Farah was from a good family in Orap and openly looked down on her husband because his parents were foreign. Ishmael, snob that he was, basked in her derision and loved her all the more.

Farah hated the zoo and complained of the smell on the second floor. She upset Leila and Zolo by ordering the cook to kill the goose and make soup, forcing the children to eat their pet before they realised it.

Mehrdad had slightly fuzzy hair, dark skin and a small training moustache. It was the family joke that he was in love with Leila. Though it was Zolo and Leila who sought him out. He lived in a two-roomed house, with his cousins and uncle and aunt, beside the Fatagagases' garden. His grandparents lived in a similar structure

with his cousins just opposite. It was the traditional Orapian compound set-up. A big brick wall sheltered them from the outside
world. The women rarely left the compound, and his mother, as the
daughter-in-law, worked for everybody inside. All the women who
had married into the family were servants for the men. Just as all
the women produced by them would be traded to other families to
work for them. That was why it was so devastating to have a girl.
She would not be there to look after you; she would eventually
belong to somebody else. If she did stay, she would have to be supported. It was the general understanding that those of the family
who didn't work were supported by those who did. In Mehrdad's
family, his grandparents were too old to work, and his uncle was
unemployed. His younger brothers caught birds and sold them as
pets and food at the market. His father took care of five gardens in
the neighbourhood. Mehrdad helped him after school. Weeding,
sweeping, pruning, he followed the slight frame of his father in the
heat of the afternoon.

Zolo would come to the house and ask him out to play. It
always sounded like an order. There was not much time to play, but
Mehrdad went anyway. Leila, as always, waited to tag along. Cowboys and Indians. Zolo would be the Indian and Leila and Mehrdad
the unsuspecting couple riding the plains in the stagecoach.

Mehrdad loved their second-floor zoo. Zolo examined the animals each day, marching up and down with his white poodle Twinkle tucked under his arm. General Zolo making a tour of inspection.

'Ears intact?'

Mehrdad bent to check out the sheep.

'Yes, sir. All two of them.'

'Any distinguishing features worth mentioning?'

'Very woolly, sir,' Mehrdad would say after a moment's thought.

'Male or female?' Zola would bark.

Leila and Mehrdad would drop to their knees and look under
the pig's legs.

'Female,' they would say in unison as Zolo marched on, Twinkle's tail wagging back and forth furiously.

Zolo and Leila wore private school uniforms. Blue skirt and shorts and white top. Red tie. Mehrdad went to the national school and was barefoot year round. The private Christian school taught all the lessons in English. The upper class went there along with children of ambassadors and diplomats. English had become the language the middle and upper classes spoke in Orap to distinguish themselves from the rabble. Leila and Zolo taught Mehrdad English, and they conversed only in that language. Mehrdad was a quick learner. This was the reason why, despite his father's pleadings, his mother turned a blind eye to his fraternising with the boss's children. Mehrdad made sure to come back with tales of the hours he spent on Zolo's computer. She knew how useful it was to him.

They had a big globe in their living room. Leila covered Mehrdad's eyes while Zolo spun. Mehrdad blindly reached to slow the globe down, feeling her cool hands cupped against his skin. Zolo would stop and look at the part where Mehrdad's fingers stalled the ball.

Leila was lovely. Bright, sharp, funny and goofy. She craved affection from Zolo, and Mehrdad craved attention from her. She was as good as Zolo was cruel and mischievous. He trusted her. He was half-afraid of Zolo. A little bit in awe of both. But he loved to play here more than anywhere else, and all his father's pleading wouldn't keep him away. The three were inseparable. Zolo disdained boys of his class for Mehrdad. Mehrdad didn't understand why, but he liked it.

'One day, I will play with the prince. My father has promised,' Zolo said, posing on the balcony of the second floor with a blindfolded hawk on his gloved arm. 'We'll go together and play tennis with him.'

'Me too,' Leila said.

'Not you, Frog.' Zolo flung his skinny arm about Mehrdad's shoulder. Mehrdad eyed the bird nervously. Zolo didn't seem quite in control. He had had the bird only a day.

'I could be the ball boy,' Mehrdad said to Zolo. 'I've seen them on TV. They run so fast.'

'Ball boy?' Zolo shook his head. 'You have to set your sights higher than that. They have people at the palace to pick up the balls. We'll just play. We're not there to kiss ass. They're no better than us, just luckier. Like we're luckier than you.'

Invariably, Zolo wanted to get rid of Leila. Mehrdad loved having Leila around. Zolo sensed this and tolerated her, content to ridicule and bully her while Mehrdad stood by helplessly. Relief came when Zolo was in hospital with meningitis. Mehrdad would meet Leila after school, and they would go to the zoo. Her parents were always at the hospital, so they had the place to themselves. Without Zolo, there was less jostling and competitiveness. Leila did not have to be on the defensive and strong and defiant all the time. She could just be Leila. Instead of conducting inspections, they took brushes and combed the animals. They looked for Orap on the globe, but it was an old one, and Orap was swallowed by somewhere else. So Leila took a marker and they drew it in themselves.

'Do you think we got it exactly in the right place?' Mehrdad put his nose to the globe and squinted.

'Thereabouts.' Leila shrugged. 'Who cares where we are anyway? It's what happened that's important.'

'So history is more important than geography?' Mehrdad always had fun following Leila's convolutions.

'Mmm! I guess what happened happened because of where we were.'

'Not who we were?' Mehrdad said.

Leila and he giggled at the knots they were tying in the conversations.

Leila was not interested in all the statistics like Zolo was. She had history books and read parts of those to him. Most of the library had books in English. Their uncle Mo had got the lot from a British professor who was leaving the country. Ishmael was very taken with the collection and had bought it immediately from his brother, globe and all.

Leila showed him all the books with pictures. *The Water Babies* by Charles Kingsley had the most intriguing colour ones. A beautiful, long-haired woman sitting at the bottom of the ocean surrounded by adoring naked babies. Miss Doasyouwouldbedoneby. They were titillated by the nudity of the children.

Inspired, Mehrdad and Leila agreed to sneak out at night and meet by the river. This was especially difficult for Mehrdad as he lived with all his family in one room. However, he would say that he was going to his grandparents' across the way. Leila's parents were too frantic about Zolo even to look in on her at night. The children stripped and lay in the rushes. Breathless and moonlit. The river was cold and the current was strong.

'Have you ever touched the river inside the river?'

'I don't think so,' he said.

'Could we sit at the bottom like the water babies?'

'I don't think so.'

'Would we drown?'

'In real life, we would.'

Real life returned with Zolo back from the hospital. Pale and imperious. A recovering little prince of his own limited domain. Hungry for power and action.

'I asked for you in the hospital, my friend. Why didn't you come?'

'They never told me.'

'They wouldn't let him come,' Leila said.

'Shut up, Frog,' Zolo rasped. 'What would you know?'

'I heard them speak about it. Maman and Baba.'

Zolo was too weak to fight her. He turned his back. 'I was dying. They would have given me anything.'

They did give him a flying saucer. Uncle Mo brought it to the hospital. That night, it rose and flew about the room, hovering above his bed with the lights flashing. When Zolo came home, he insisted that it was capable of doing that. He searched for the switch. He could make the lights flash on and off, but it did not fly. He swore he had seen it fly. They told him it was the fever. Zolo put the flying saucer in with the tortoise. They were about the same size and shape. He told Mehrdad what he had seen and was relieved to see that Mehrdad believed him.

Uncle Mo was the most frightening and ludicrous individual Mehrdad had ever encountered. He had nightmares about him. Mo had marched up to his father when Mehrdad was eight years old and dragged him off to do errands and work in his house. House was not really the word; palace was more like it. There was marble everywhere: marble floors, walls, ceilings, counter-tops, pillars, swimming pool and fountain.

'Build me a dome. I want a dome.' Mo had been screaming at a cowering architect who was clutching blueprints and stammering all sorts of anti-dome excuses. There was only one bedroom in the whole house; everything else was stuffed with arts and artefacts from Europe and covered in paperwork. Mo did not harbour the notion of guests. He did not harbour the notion even of chairs. There were tables but nowhere to sit at them. Traditional Orapians sat on the floor on carpets. Westernised Orapians like Farah and Ishmael insisted on chairs and tables. Mo never sat and, since he never thought of others, they would not sit either. Over the years of his childhood, Mehrdad planted myriad orchids in pots. There was no grass or flowerbeds. Just pots everywhere. Pots Mo kept rearranging to his eternal dissatisfaction. He loved orchids.

'They are the beautiful, difficult, anorexic ballerina girlfriends you never wanted,' he told the boy, as he stroked a petal showing slight signs of deterioration. 'And they always let you down,' he added admiringly.

At the time, Mo smoked, and he offered the boy cigarettes as they stood together and surveyed the multitude of potted exotic plants. Mehrdad took the cigarettes and put them behind his ear to bring home to his uncle. Zolo always manoeuvred to come around when his friend was working. Zolo was 12 now but short for his age and so thin from his most recent bout of illness that in this raw light you could almost see right through him.

'You will always be able to say that you worked for the great Moses, a poet, philosopher, scientist, physician,' Mo said dreamily to the potted palm trees by the pool. Zolo stood at the pool with a snorkel and fins. He shuffled backwards until he was level with

Mehrdad, making sure he was out of his formidable uncle's earshot.

'He means he's a nose-chopper, fat sucker, mother fucker.'

'The Great Moses needs his cars cleaned today.' When addressing Mehrdad, Mo always referred to himself in the third person. He called himself Moses even though his name was short for Mohammad.

Mehrdad wished Leila would come too, but Mo had eyes only for Zolo as the heir apparent. He would never have children of his own. If there were to be no chairs, there would be no woman.

One time, Leila did come with her parents. Mo and Ishmael played tennis on the court while Farah floated in the pool on an inflatable silver bed. Leila wore a blue bikini with pink spots and a yellow frill. She had a straw hat with a red ribbon and red sunglasses shaped like strawberries. She lay on a towel, reading a big book in English. It was getting too hot, so she put on a mask and snorkel, and joined Zolo at the bottom of the shallow end of the pool. An underwater scuffle broke out. Farah sighed and paddled with her hands up to where her children twisted beneath the surface like one uncontrollable animal. Leila came up gasping.

'Maman, he doesn't own the pool. Tell him to let me play.'

'Leila,' Farah stroked her daughter's black hair, 'leave your brother alone. Go back to your book. It was lovely and quiet.'

Zolo was pulling himself up the marble steps. He clambered out clumsily in his fins, lifting his legs high and slamming them down.

'It's you who looks like a frog now,' Leila shouted from the water.

Farah grabbed her by the shoulder and hissed, 'I'm warning you, Leila. Your brother was very ill. He doesn't need to be bothered.'

Zolo took Leila's big green book from the lounge chair. 'The collected works of Oscar Wilde,' he read out loud, flicking through the thin small-print pages. With a quick motion of his hand, he chucked the book into the pool, without turning to look at it when it splashed.

Mehrdad was watering the plants. He had erected a 'For Sale' sign today and was cleaning the place up for the expected onslaught of visitors. He saw Leila pound furiously towards the sinking book. She couldn't swim. Later, he saw her with the soggy book in the sun. She had it open in the middle and was squinting at the sky. Zolo was with his father and uncle on the tennis court. He wore his snorkel and goggles still and, barefoot, was holding a racket and practising backstroke as Ishmael gently lobbed balls towards him and Mo stood by him, correcting his grip. Farah was asleep, her inflatable bed dangerously drifting toward the deep end. She couldn't swim either. She wore a black bikini and gold jewellery. Her toenails were painted red, and her flat stomach was brown and glistening with oil.

'Be careful—you'll tear the pages,' Leila said, on the point of tears, when Mehrdad tested one wet page.

'They'll get all stuck.' He examined the book.

'It's my favourite book.'

'I'll buy you another one,' Mehrdad said firmly. Their heads almost touched as they hunkered together.

'It was from the library at home. You can't get it in the shop,' Leila pouted.

'You are so smart. I could never read a big book like this with words so small.'

'I read the plays and the fairytales.' Her eyes lit up behind the strawberries.

'I'll order it online to be shipped.'

Leila laughed out loud. 'You need a credit card and a computer for that.'

Mehrdad glanced about nervously. Farah still slept uninterrupted.

'I got all As on my report yesterday.' Leila mournfully poked the soggy book.

'Wow. Your maman and baba must be happy.'

'They notice only if there's Bs, and then they complain. They expect As from Zolo and me.'

'I got an A in maths,' Mehrdad told her. 'And English. I'm the best in English.' He hesitated shyly. 'In my school, that is.'

'Will I help you wash the cars?'

'No, I'll do it.'

'I'll tell them I wanted to.'

'They wouldn't like that. You'd get me in trouble. It's not your place.'

Zolo spotted Mehrdad and Leila talking, and he called to Mehrdad deliberately so his parents would see them together. Farah called immediately to Leila.

'Do you want to sneak out and meet by the river tonight?' Leila whispered as she walked over to her mother.

'Are you going to bring Zolo?'

'No, I hate him.'

Zolo sat behind the wheel of the Mercedes while Mehrdad hosed the outside. Zolo still wore his snorkel and mask. Twinkle stood on his knee, her paws on the wheel. Ishmael and Mo looked on.

'You're asking too little for the house.'

'Do you see who's building next door?'

'Who?'

Next door, for months, a huge house had been under construction. It was a storey higher than Mo's two-storey house.

'Some famous mullah's coming back from exile. He's on all the posters down at the bazaar. They're distributing his speeches on the black market. You know what that'll be like. We won't be able to use the pool. They'll want the women shrouded or they'll start harassing us. No more cocktail parties and barbecues. I'm selling before he moves in.'

'But why can't you just buy somewhere else? You're leaving everything we worked so hard for. I can't manage the practice on my own. You have loyal patients.'

'You fool. Haven't you noticed that all the loyal patients are buggering off to California and the French Riviera?'

'They'll be back when things settle down.'

'You stay here if you like and ruin the future for your kids. Look at Zolo; at least get him out. There's talk of war with our dear neighbours, and he'll be conscripted in a year or two, along with his little friend there.'

'I don't like them to play together.'

Mo shrugged. 'They're not playing. Mehrdad is being paid to wash my cars, and Zolo is sitting on his wet ass on my leather seats.'

Mo was selling his cars too.

'It's the only friend he has. He's almost perverse about it,' Ishmael complained. 'He's such a difficult boy.'

'He reminds me of me.'

Ishmael raised his eyebrows. 'You had no friends, my dear brother.'

Mo nodded and put his arm about Ishmael, squeezing him too tightly. 'I wasn't going to be conned by people pretending to be nice to me. What did I want from them? Nothing I couldn't get myself. You are a dope, brother. You worry too much about the wrong things. Zolo is recovering well. He still looks terrible and a bit stunted, but the boy is brilliant; that much we all know.'

'It's that that makes me all the more careful. He needs guidance.'

'I'm here for him.'

'Thank you, Mo.' Ishmael looked genuinely relieved. This would have been a pretty pad to inherit, he thought.

'He'll grow out of his friendship with the other boy, what's his name?'

'Mehrdad.'

'Yes, yes. He'll soon realise they're not cut from the same cloth. It will happen naturally. Right now, he's just doing it because it's the one thing that'll drive you crazy.'

'You don't help matters. Why do you have to have Mehrdad around here?'

'I've borrowed your other servants and it didn't work out. That fellow came with a parrot on his shoulder, and it shit all over my marble halls. I kicked him in the ass and knocked his head off the wall. The great Moses demands a higher class of person to serve him.'

'Oh God: Abdul. He loves animals. The kids love him, and the zoo is a fixture now. He's worked out well for us, and his wife does all the cooking and cleaning.'

'A zoo in your house. On the second floor. You never had much sophistication, my dear brother. Once a peasant always a peasant. We may have been born inauspiciously, but we escaped and we don't have anything to do with the rest of our rabble. We left our family in the mud where they belong. Don't forget you are a Fatagagas.'

'But I was a Fatagagas then.'

'Yes, but now you are a famous Fatagagas.'

'Only because the real Fatagagases left.'

'And you let your servants walk all over you.'

'I suppose that's why I have servants and you don't,' Ishmael said morosely. His younger brother always kept him in thrall but had been a burden. 'You keep borrowing mine and beating them up.'

'That Mehrdad boy works harder than all of them combined. I was thinking of offering him a full-time position. He's polite and he can read and write. But I spoke to his father and his father refused. Can you imagine? I offered good money, but his father said he had to stay in school and pass exams. Such notions!'

Mo stepped back and stumbled over Leila sitting cross-legged in her polka-dot bikini.

'What is that spoilt brat doing with that book? Is that from the library I gave you?'

'Library you sold us, oh Great One,' Leila said.

Ishmael laughed and leant down and kissed his daughter's forehead.

'You do look splendid in those strawberry glasses. The epitome of summer and dark as a berry. But those books are not toys. You can't destroy them like that or I won't allow you into the library any more.' Ishmael didn't sound like he meant it. He never personally used the library and had given the books no more than a cursory glance since purchasing them.

Leila was putting stones between the pages so they wouldn't dry together. 'I'm drying it. Zolo—'

But her father and uncle had walked over to inspect the Mercedes, so she stuck her tongue out at them and went on watching the book dry. Suddenly, she jumped up and went to Mehrdad.

'Meet me at midnight tonight by the river.'

Leila's small brown feet sank into the mud by the river. There was no moon or stars. Power cuts were in effect, so the city was as dark as an empty mountain. Their clothes were in a bundle in the rushes.

'If I had a key, I'd open the night.'

'What does that mean?' Mehrdad lay by her side, their arms touching.

'I'd find the light inside the night.'

'But nights are dark. You'd find only the dark.' Mehrdad reached and found her tiny wrist. He held it as if he were taking her pulse.

'I had a dream,' Leila said, 'that I was sitting by the river on a lawn chair, and Zolo and Baba and Maman and Mo were stuffing the darkness down my throat. They were wrenching it out of the sky and shoving it down me.'

'What was left?'

'What?' Leila took her hand away from him and sat up.

'What was left after they pulled the darkness from the sky? What was in the sky?'

'I don't know, Mehrdad.' Leila sighed. 'Mehrdad?'

'Yes?' Mehrdad sat up too. Her back was curved. She was much lighter skinned than he, and her vertebrae lay like little stones beneath the skin.

'Teach me how to swim.'

'Tonight?' Mehrdad peered at her. She was looking intently at the water, and he was feeling bad for her.

'We can't do it in the day. I'm not allowed play with you or swim in the river, so now is fine by me. If you have a problem, then . . .' Leila leant forward and fell into the river. Mehrdad jumped in. The water was icy cold and he could not see even her shape. He groped and swished his hands and legs around. He twisted and turned in panic, rising to the surface when he was out of breath. He thought he saw her swept away. A small limb shooting out of the water. But it could have been a stick. He swam into the centre.

'Leila. Leila,' he roared.

In the centre, the current changed, the water was warmer. He was electrified, oddly powerful. He saw her all the way on the other bank, clinging to a rock. He dived under the water and, holding his breath, swam over to her.

'I can't let go,' Leila said. 'Get help.'

Mehrdad felt the slippery rock and tried to get a grip. Her fingers were white with the strain of holding on. He looked back up into the dome of the sky. 'Hold on to my back.'

'No,' Leila cried. 'I'll tell them it's my fault—that you were just passing by. Please go and get Baba.'

'I can't leave you.' The current was making it impossible to swim on the spot. He was drifting away.

'I can't hold on,' Leila gasped. Her legs were thrown about the rock. Mehrdad reached for her and she put her arms about his neck. He turned to the far bank. He swam with her riding his back. They pulled themselves up by the rushes. Her legs and arms were bleeding heavily. Mehrdad looked at the house on the other bank. It was stoic and unresponsive. There was no bridge. In all the years they had grown up here, he had never made it to the far bank and did not know how to get back.

'We'll walk a bit and it will get narrow just above the turn, and then you can hold on to me like we did and we'll swim back.'

Leila was weeping. 'I'm not going back in.'

'Did you feel it? The river in the river?'

'No.'

She ran over the ridge, and he ran after her. They wandered naked into a group of mud houses. The unpaved maze of narrow alleys was flanked by clay walls that had windows with no glass. Rats scurried by in the gutters. It was so dark that the children reached their hands out and groped along the walls to guide themselves. They turned right and left and walked further and further with no mind to where they were going except away from the river and their lives and their little bundle of clothes. They came to an opening, a square. Mehrdad stood and frowned. Leila hid around a corner and peered out.

'I've been here before,' Mehrdad told her. 'The bazaar starts over there. Look, there are lights.'

'We can't let the bazaari catch us with no clothes. They'd send us to prison.'

It was true. The bazaari were the most conservative and power-ful of groups. It was they who were pushing for a revolution.

'If only Zolo were here, he'd know what to do,' Leila snuffled. Mehrdad felt a pang of jealousy. Leila began to laugh. She pointed between his legs. 'Your thing is up.' Mehrdad glanced down in hor-ror. It was true. Here he was with his father's boss's naked and bleeding 9-year-old daughter, and he 12 years old, without a stitch on himself, stumbling into the night market, with an erection. They'd hang him for sure. By his thing. Leila was poking her head into a window. She put her hands up and grabbed the curtain and tugged. It came off and they ran back down the alley and around a corner.

'You can cover yourself,' Mehrdad said.

'Tear it and we both can.' Leila offered him the material. They tugged and tugged but it wouldn't tear. Leila wrapped it about her-self until there was a yard to spare. Mehrdad wrapped himself in that and, entwined, they shuffled as one unit back to the market square. They edged about the periphery towards the lights in the bazaar. The bazaar consisted of more endless mud streets but with a cover-ing over the alleys making it all the more suffocating and inter-minable. Having existed for 500 years in a nomadic culture, it was the oldest human place in Orap; the prison was the second oldest. Most countries in that region had bazaars dating back millennia.

'I never knew it went on this late.' Mehrdad stared as men lay about their carpet shops, smoking hubbly bubbly, drinking Turkish coffee and talking in low and excited tones.

'Mo said they're plotting the revolution here,' Leila whispered.

'Mo is leaving soon. I've been packing his stuff for weeks.'

'My baba says the international community won't allow the royal family to be toppled. There'll be no revolution.'

There was one shop in particular that sold spices, medicines and rare foods. Mehrdad knew it well.

'I was here last week for your uncle Mo. I bought him yak's penis and caterpillar fungus from China.'

'Ugh! Mo never talks to me. He likes only Zolo. Zolo will be a nose-chopper too.'

'He's smart enough to be a great sturgeon.'

Leila giggled. 'Sturgeon is a kind of fish.'

Mehrdad sighed. 'You speak English all day in school. I speak it only with you and Zolo.'

The children turned a corner, and there was a group of twenty men sitting cross-legged outside the entrance to a small mosque. They had long beards and turbans. They were all yelling at once. More people were joining them and crouching in silence to listen. The bazaari, merchants to the bone, were taking the opportunity to sell pistachio nuts and tea to those gathered. The children slid down against a wall and watched the proceedings. More and more came. There were no women, and all the men were either merchants or poor. Mehrdad saw his unemployed uncle who lived with them among the bunch. He was lounging against a wall, smoking the cigarettes that Mehrdad had got from Mo. Country peasants with donkeys loitered about, their toothless mouths open like the glass-less windows from where Leila had stolen the curtain. Some were there to sell stuff for the morning; some men had fire in their eyes.

'Can we go home?' Leila was scared.

'I don't know how to get home except for the bus. We don't have any money, so we'll have to sneak on. We could get the first one and be home by 5.20, and no one is up by then.'

They shuffled away, backing down the labyrinthine intestine of shuttered alleys. Passing by one window, they saw a white horse. His bones were sticking through his skin, his rib cage jutted out.

'Why do they have a horse in their house?'

'How do I know?' Mehrdad snapped. He was disorientated.

Leila began to cry. People were sleeping on the floor around the horse. The starved horse was still as a statue but looked at them with the same fire Leila had seen in the eyes of the mullahs. Mehrdad felt guilty for snapping. He reached his one free arm across his front and patted her.

'It will be morning soon.'

They found a way of walking that was easier. Like in the three-legged race, they wrapped their legs about each other and walked in sync. Mehrdad wouldn't tell her but he was lost.

'We're lost, aren't we?' Leila said as they reached yet another fork. Some of the shutters were crashing up. Light was eking in about the edges of the street canopy. The mournful static cry of the mosque rang out, calling for prayers. For the first time, they saw women. The women were shrouded in black. Only their eyes were visible. They looked through the children as if they were ghosts. These were figures Leila had previously glanced only at a distance. A world apart from her cosmopolitan one. They had been so mysterious. Up close, they retained their mystery. Leila dragged Mehrdad up a narrow set of steps to a roof where they unwrapped. Finally they could see the city. Mehrdad climbed up on the wall to get a better look. Glass embedded in the cement cut his hands. He saw the mosque and tried to get his bearings. Leila unpegged a bunch of black clothes hanging on the line. The two children exited in burkas, fully shrouded. A grill hiding their eyes. The cloth trailing on the dusty ground. They followed all the scuttling yawning people to the mosque and found their way to the market square. Already it was a different world. Stalls were set up and food laid out. A truck pulled up; men shouted and banged crates. Disguised as women, they could hold hands without attracting attention. Mehrdad's hand was bleeding profusely. A fully veiled woman sat at a loom in a side room of a shop. She beckoned to them. Nervously they approached her. She took a wet cloth and wiped Leila's hand. She was puzzled to see no cut. Mehrdad held his dripping hand out to show her the blood was all his. She took some raw wool from a bucket and wrapped it about Mehrdad's hands. Mehrdad could not see her face, and she could not see his. He nodded thanks. When they left, Leila inspected his hand.

'You'll probably get lockjaw.'

'No. Don't say that.'

'That wool must be filthy.'

'Look, Leila.' Mehrdad pointed as he led her to the bus depot.

There was a barefoot peasant in rags hunkered on the ground beneath the one tree in the square. His cataract eyes were glazed and oozing puss. A rope kept his trousers up. He had come to town with only one thing to sell. Before him was a pair of horse's legs, hacked off just beneath the knee. They were tied together and standing upright. Flies were already buzzing about the hooves.

Leila and Mehrdad stopped in front of him and absorbed the image for a second. As they hurried away, Leila kept looking back.

'Who would want that?'

'That's not the point.'

'What's the point?'

'The point is it's all he has.'

'Well, if no one wants all you have, what's the point in selling it?'

'He has no choice.'

Chapter Seven

Degenerate Feathers

Mo sold the marble house with the out-of-place dome to the next-door mullah's organisation. He sold it, potted plants, imitation Louis XIV furniture, chairlessness, Mercedes, BMW and all. Mehrdad carried his suitcases to the taxi. There were a few boxes of paperwork and clothes to be shipped when he arrived. Mehrdad was entrusted with this duty too. Mo paid Mehrdad well, but Mehrdad was relieved that he was gone and he was free of his tyranny. Mo had been an unpredictable and verbally abusive boss, and Mehrdad needed to concentrate on his upcoming entrance exams.

Zolo had fond memories of Orap. During the summers, his maternal grandparents would stay with them. Everyone would sleep on mats on the roof because the rooms were so hot. He loved this. Sleeping outside. And the river. That river was special. There was a part you could swim to where the current and temperature changed dramatically. It was electrifying to make it through that part. Ishmael had one other brother, Darius, who was not estranged. Darius had a family—older teenage boys who were like uncles to Zolo. They took him to fairgrounds and skiing. They had leisure time that his parents never had, and they never hated him for his brilliance like the kids in school. Their two little sisters were babies, and Leila played with them, so delighted that, for once in her life, she was not the youngest. Farah also had siblings who came over, and they had lots of parties in the house. Farah's brothers and sisters were aristocratic and glamorous and teased Farah for working so hard. While Zolo had trouble getting on with his own parents, he found great comfort in his extended family. Life had privilege, solidity and joy. Zolo had almost everything in Orap

One night, they turned on the TV to drown out the sounds of revolution on the street. It was summer and they were sleeping on the roof, listening to the rushing river water below. In the chaos, schools had been shut down for a month, and Zolo had been demonstrating on the street with his uncles, against the king. Ishmael didn't know that. Zolo would go to the universities and protest. His mother's sister was a dentist. She was very pretty, and Zolo loved her more than any of his own family. She loved him too. She spoiled and pampered him and was so young and fashionable. She was softer than his mother, and her elegance was natural where his mother's was calculated.

Then they looked over the roof of the house and saw a man hanging from a newly erected barricade, his feet cut off and flies cupping the stumps. Ishmael told Zolo that he was of a different religion. Chasing the wrong God. Ishmael said it was a foolish thing in life to chase any God, for none will listen, but the wrong God is a curse, and, with that, he signalled to Farah to get Leila and Zolo downstairs. The servants told Ishmael that they had been warned not to work for him any more.

Farah's brother was arrested and, when her other brother went to the police station, they handed him a bundle of neatly folded clothes and told them he had been executed. Then this brother disappeared too, and they were afraid to go to the police and ask about him.

Ishmael had to go out with his brother Darius and go to the university barricades to carry the body of his teenage son home. The same boy who had taught Zolo how to ski.

When they saw the footage that night of the queen and her family leaving the country, finally Ishmael listened to Farah, and they packed the Mercedes and drove to the nearest border. Orap was a tiny place, and the drive took them all of two hours. Leila and Zolo sang songs in the back seat to pass the time.

Zolo had wanted to stay; as a 13-year-old boy, he had found it all so thrilling. But now, leaving, he was caught up in the excitement of that adventure. At the border, there was a checkpoint of revolutionary guards. They asked for ID. Ishmael gave passports and birth certificates for the whole family, and driving licences for his wife and himself. Farah cursed him as she sat in the front seat watching him shuffle all his paperwork. The guards went into a huddle and then ordered the family out of the car. Farah grabbed all the suitcases from the trunk and the back seat. She knew what was happening. The guards said they wanted to check the suitcases. Farah shouted at them. They shoved a gun into her face and she pushed it aside. There was a traffic jam building behind them. Ishmael tried to assure the guards that he was a well-connected person. He tried to offer them money. They took his money, his car and all his documents. Zolo decided his mother was right when she cursed his father as they made their way on foot with several peasant families to the refugee camp across the mountains. They were walking for two days, and Leila kept asking to be carried because her feet were blistered. Farah kept telling her, 'You're not a baby any more.'

Farah carried her big, black handbag with the deed of the house in it. It was the only document they had left.

In the refugee camp, the Fatagagas family had to share a tent with another family. There were old train carriages at one end with people living in them. They had brought so little out, just what they could put in the car, and then the car had been taken from them, and so they had only what they could carry. It would have been a nice touch if Ishmael had still had the bag of precious clothes that the queen had given him. But this was not the place for such nice touches. There was nothing to do all day but stand in queues: queues for water, queues for food, queues to see a Red Cross doctor. There was an abandoned oil source on the slopes near by; the hill was always on fire. Baby flames covered the ground in small patches. The people in the camp prophesied that they would return home only when the flames went out. The Red Cross claimed that the hill had been burning for decades.

Ishmael was standing in line for water when Mehrdad, the gardener's son, came running up to him. Ishmael was so taken aback to see him there that he patted the 13-year-old on the head. Mehrdad eagerly took Ishmael's container and offered to wait for him. Mehrdad hauled the water to his tent every day after that. Ishmael was delighted; his own children refused to budge for anything. Zolo was sulking. Leila lay on her bunk and cried for Twinkle. Twinkle had been left behind with the snake, the tortoise, the sheep, the pig and the new goose.

Farah spent every day haranguing the authorities for placement in host countries and writing letters to Mo to get him to send tickets to the USA. Farah gave the children maths problems every day. She made them write essays and corrected their spelling and grammar. Ishmael was sure to tell the other family with whom they shared the tent that he had been the doctor to the royal family. He went to the Red Cross every day to enquire about the queen. Where was she? Did she get out?

Mehrdad came one day with a stack of *National Geographic* magazines, and Farah instructed Ishmael to read to the children to improve their English. In truth, she wanted to give her husband a duty because he was lost in his dreams and harboured a strange predilection towards melancholy, which she attributed to a flaw in his family line. Ishmael read to them about whales. The other family in the tent listened in, and Farah resented them profiting from instruction meant for her own children. Her children had learnt English in their private schools and also with home tutors. Zolo had been diagnosed as being gifted; his IQ was 160. The other family was not of their class; in fact, no one in the camp appeared to be. Most of the middle class had got out weeks before and taken all their money with them. Ishmael had refused to look disloyal to the queen.

By the time they decided to leave, the banks had been shut down, and they could not access their money. All they had in terms of capital was Farah's jewellery.

The other family kept stopping the lesson and asking for a translation. Farah bade Leila and Zolo to do the translating; at least that would force them to concentrate. But when they were huddled in bed at night, sharing the one bunk, Farah and Ishmael whispered their annoyance at having to contribute to this other family's education. What did the other family do for them? It was take, take, take.

'A whale leaves an imprint on the water above. The surface is different. You can track a whale in this way, spot where he is. This is commonly known as a whale's footprint,' Ishmael would read, and Zolo would translate for the parents, grandparents and children of the other family. Ten of them in all. Then the other family would have to discuss this phenomenon and slow the whole process down.

Mehrdad came every day with water and more magazines, and sometimes he would be able to get them precious thread and ceramic mugs, and once a supply of tea. Where he was getting such treasures from, Ishmael did not know, but he was a peasant's child and wily as such. The other family drank most of the tea. Soon, Mehrdad's father, their old gardener, came to the tent and asked permission to enter. Humbly with bent head, he gave Ishmael all respect due, as if he were still an employer and not a fellow refugee shacked up in this crowded tent. He requested that his son, Mehrdad, partake in the lessons too. Farah was furious when she heard.

'What could I do?' Ishmael threw his arms up in exasperation.

'You could have said no.'

'Farah . . . My love.'

'Everyone is getting things from us. What are we getting? You'd give everything away. Everything we have. I've been standing trying to get places out of here, contact everyone at home, and write to Mo for help. And you, you . . .'

That night, Ishmael read to everyone, including Mehrdad, about a Victorian woman who kept a travel diary. She had commented on a hornbill bird that actually had eyelashes. She was aghast at a bird having such a mammalian feature. She would not acknowledge them as eyelashes. Degenerate feathers, she called them. Even Zolo had great difficulty translating this. Leila started giggling, and soon everyone was laughing. Mehrdad's eyes were shining as he sat beside her.

In the bunk in the middle of the night, Farah was awake and burning with cold anger. Ishmael tried to touch her, to stroke her neck, to put his finger under her cardigan and stroke her nipple. She pushed him away. 'Leila and Zolo are picking up bad habits from all these peasants, and you used to be so careful keeping them with their own class. Now you give away all we have got left, all that's ours.'

Ishmael heaved a lordly sigh. 'Degenerate feathers, whale foot-prints. For God's sake, is that so much to give away?'

That was always how it was with the family. Always nervous that people were getting things from them. Draining them in some way. What is that person getting from you? Why do they come around all the time? Why did you take that from him? Don't you know he'll want something now? Look at your cousin: he is a good boy; he has no friends; he does his study and is never distracted. There was no such thing as friends in the family. Ishmael and Farah and Mo simply didn't believe in them.

Winter came in the camp. The gulls carried it in under their wings. Evenings collapsed into wind-blown puddles that swelled between the tents like a rash. Everything was mud, and everyone was wearing all their clothes at once. Suddenly the burning hill was a good place to play. Children ran around the flames for warmth. Ishmael had become an involuntary English teacher. He read from his *National Geographic* in a large bare space in the centre of the camp, and adults and children wrote things down. Then it snowed.

The snow covered everything. Reports from Orap were bad: the neighbouring country had declared war, and there was fighting on the border. Now there were three families in Ishmael's tent, and he was losing hope. Farah was more determined than ever to get the children out. The Red Cross was building more permanent-looking structures. Mobile-home housing that they were told had been ordered from a Canadian company that specialised in emergency housing. Ishmael did not want to move into one of these rectangular creatures; he thought they looked too permanent. Farah stood in queues in the snow to put her name down for a move.

Leila and Zolo played with Mehrdad. Mehrdad was only 13, but he helped out at the hospital in the camp. He invited them to a party for a 25-year-old man who was celebrating the arrival of his prosthesis. The new refugees' stories were getting worse. There were mass executions at home, and all the young men were being recruited for the new war. Mehrdad asked the man to tell his story to Leila and Zolo when the party was over. He asked Leila what age she was, and she told him that she was 10, and Zolo was 13.

'We travelled at night only because we did not have papers. There were twenty of us, and we had all paid the guide. The children were more expensive because they would have to be carried at some points. The group had to cross the mountain pass. I was the oldest in the group at 25, and the guide was 15 years old. We walked for days and nights and once slept with nomads in a tent.'

Zolo was excited by the story. The young man smiled at him.

'We came by car,' Zolo said glumly. 'Then they took the car off of us, and we walked over the same pass. We walked for four days to get here, didn't we?'

Leila nodded. 'There was no snow then though.'

'Still,' Zolo said. 'Four days. And they took our papers and passports and everything.'

'Maman still has our family photos and the deed to our house,' Leila said.

'Some use they are,' Zolo scoffed. 'All of our feet had to be painted with iodine when we got to the camp.'

'Everyone was like that,' Leila agreed. 'We all sat around with our purple feet waiting for tents to be put up.'

Mehrdad put his finger to his lips. 'Let him tell his story.'

'What took you four days took us two weeks because of the snow. We were not allowed talk or even smoke, and we could go only at night. We had to sleep on the frozen snow.'

'Why did you do that?' Leila asked.

'Why? There was no shelter. The snow buried our food. It was waist deep, and we had to keep walking. Then it came up to my chest, and the children had to be carried.'

'Still, how did it take you two weeks?' Zolo was sceptical, jealous of this man's obviously superior adventure.

'We were lost. I was carrying a little girl on my back. She was four or five. Younger than you. She had no adults along with her. Just a sister who was even younger. I realised after a while that she had frozen on my back. I left her body in the snow.'

'How did you lose your legs?' Zolo asked.

'We got to a house and we stayed for a while. Two boys died in the house. My toes had fallen off. I could see my bone.'

'What did you do with your toes?' Leila asked and Zolo thumped her.

'First my little toes fell off and then my big toe. My skin fell from my ankle.'

'All the children died,' Mehrdad told them when they left the man with his new plastic legs at the hospital. 'All of them who started out froze. Only the grown-ups made it and only four of them.'

'Did the guide make it?' Zolo asked.

'Yes.'

'Well, he was 15. That's officially still a child.' Zolo stood up straight, and wagged his finger authoritatively. 'So, you can't say all of the children didn't make it.'

'I suppose not.' Mehrdad would never dare to contradict Zolo.

The fatal snow on the mountains kept falling, and soon the flood of new refugees became a trickle, and then it stopped completely. Ishmael would stand outside their tent and stare at the mountain, wondering what was happening to the people behind it. In November, they made contact with Uncle Mo. He could arrange to get Zolo and Leila out of the camp and over to America on visas if he declared them his children. There was no hesitation.

Ishmael and Farah packed one suitcase for the two children. They had a farewell dinner of beans and canned tomatoes. Ishmael could not let Leila go. He was teary-eyed and clung to her as ferociously as Farah had clung to the deed of the house. An official came to the camp in the morning with their new papers. Farah wore her Chanel suit and string of real pearls so they would understand that they were respectable people and not like the rest of the camp. The official barely looked at the children, swaddled as they were in layers of clothing. They got into his jeep, and Ishmael told Zolo to look after Leila and never let her out of his sight.

'Tell him not to keep calling me a frog,' Leila said to her father. Ishmael leant into the jeep and grabbed her hands in his and kissed them.

'Zolo.' Farah looked worried and stern. 'Zolo, take care of her. Mo can be . . .'

'Frog, tell him not . . .'

'Shh.' Ishmael handed the case to the official, who put it into the jeep. 'We'll join you as soon as Mo gets something worked out for us.'

'Zolo, I'm trusting you now. Remember, boys are like diamonds and girls are like cotton.'

'What does that mean?' Leila asked.

Ishmael laughed out loud. 'She means, if boys get dirty, they can be washed clean.'

'And,' Zolo looked at his sister in disdain. '. . . if you do dirty things, Frog, you stay dirty.'

Farah hugged her two children, who were no longer legally hers. The jeep pulled out.

As they drove away, Leila cried and cried and waved to her maman and baba as they held on to each other in the camp.

Zolo sighed. 'I always wanted to travel in a jeep. Would you hush up, Frog. You're interfering with the thrill of world travel already.'

Later, Ishmael would tell Leila and Zolo in a letter that he had found out that his brother, Darius, had been executed with his wife back in Orap. His two remaining sons, who were such good friends with Zolo, had been conscripted and eventually were killed in the war. Before they had left for the front, they had paid a guide to get their baby sisters over the mountains and to the refugee camp. Ishmael's brother's two little girls had been part of that same group that the young man had described. If one of them had been frozen on the man's back, he was unable to pinpoint where the youngest died.

PART III

LOS ANGELES

Chapter Eight

Zolo and Leila Arrive in America

The two children sat in the sky, immaculate, blameless, not in control. When they touched down, winter just fell away. They were as stunned as if the world had started turning the other way. Los Angeles sunshine. Pure. Golden. Banging off walls and sending the sky up even higher. Zolo and Leila saw their uncle Mo at the airport. They ran to him and he threw his arms about them. He took their one suitcase and led them towards his car.

'I'm setting up a clinic here. So I'm very busy. You two are old enough to entertain yourselves and get yourselves organised. What age are you now, Zolo? Seventeen? When I was 17, I was already putting myself through college. My parents gave me nothing. They were still beating me with a stick, and my grandmother was beating them with the same implement. They say you are gifted, Zolo. You will do medicine, no doubt. Follow me into my clinic. Cosmetic surgery is the way to go here. These Americans are so stupid, and the Orapians who made it over here are even dumber and richer than the Americans.

Leila was trailing behind, blinking in the sunshine, very hot in all her layers of clothes. Zolo stopped in irritation to wait for her. Mo walked on ahead at a brisk pace.

'Come on, Zolo.' He threw the suitcase into the trunk of his Lincoln. 'You'll go to USC. University of Spoilt Children. You'll fit right in. You must get the forms and all that. I don't have time. I remember your father used to bring you into the surgery and stand you on a crate to watch the operations, ha!'

Leila was removing her coat and her sweaters. Mo appraised her for the first time.

'She's pretty, your sister. We'll find her a good husband. A doctor. Bit flat-chested, ha! They don't like that over here. We can fix that, you and I, can't we, Zolo?'

Zolo frowned. 'I'm 13, Uncle Mo. Leila is 10.'

Mo was already in the car, searching all his pockets for the key.

Leila and Zolo climbed in. Zolo was in the front seat. Mo was lost in thought, then he said almost to himself. 'Ten. My mother was married at 10. A mother at 13. That's nature's way.'

Leila was looking at her chest. Zolo shrugged.

Leila bit her lip and touched her finger to its soft moist swell. The city outside was full of blank spaces and one-storey buildings. *National Geographic* had somehow given her the impression that the whole foreign world outside would be under water. She felt oddly betrayed to be driving and not looking at strange fish and coral.

'If your father had listened to me, he wouldn't be in the mess he's in now. He's ruined you all, running around after queens and princes. They were just a jumped-up military family with no royal blood. Idiots, all of them. Thugs. American and British puppets. And this new bunch will be worse, no doubt. Orap has always had governments that went out of their way to kill their own people.'

'Uncle Mo.' Leila leaned in between the seats nervously. 'When will you get Maman and Baba over?' She knew he heard her because he flexed his hands on the wheel in irritation.

Mo grabbed Zolo's nose suddenly and pulled it hard. Zolo flew forward, his arms flapping and his hands trying to peel his uncle's hairy fingers away. 'This is becoming quite a konk. I'll take the end off of it next week if I've time.' Then he glanced at Leila. 'God knows what will be appearing on her face in a few years.'

Mo left them off at his beach-front house in Malibu. To Leila and Zolo, it looked like a blue wooden shack. They walked inside in a disappointed daze. He had owned a mansion in Orap. There was only one bedroom and a living room with a kitchen counter in the middle. Zolo went on to the deck with Mo to look at the Pacific Ocean. The deck was bigger than the house. Unlike all the neighbouring decks, it had no table and chairs, no plants.

'I'm tired,' Leila complained, lingering at the French doors, cupping her hands over her eyes to see the two floating human shapes in the intense sunlight.

'You have jet lag,' Zolo was delighted to inform her.

'Will I get better?'

'No. It's fatal.'

'Uncle, why is your house so small?'

Mo twisted about in a rage. 'Small? This is fucking Malibu! Do you know how much this costs? Do you have any idea where you are?'

'No, she doesn't,' Zolo laughed. 'She's just a little frog.'

Leila slunk away from the doors and sat on the big black leather L-shaped couch. Mo drew his nephew into an embrace. 'Zolo, you have great things ahead of you. There are opportunities here that you never dreamed of. This lousy revolution was the best thing that could ever happen to you. Mark my words.'

The doorbell rang. Mo swept into the front room and opened the door. Suddenly, a woman with blond hair and a red leather jacket stood framed in the light.

'We had a zoo in our old house,' Leila said resentfully to Zolo when he sprawled on the couch and nudged her hip with his foot.

'Yes, but we didn't have the Pacific Ocean.'

'We had a river. And that river had a river inside it.'

The woman smiled nervously at the children. Mo was opening drawers in the kitchen part of the room. In a frenzy, he was throwing boxes on the counter and putting on white gloves.

'Zolo, come and observe. You can learn a thing or two.' He beamed at the woman. 'Rita, this is my young apprentice. When I have my surgery up and running, he will be the heir to it all. We will work side by side, as I did with his dear father.'

Rita took off her jacket. She was very tanned and wore a tank top. She knew where to sit and what to do. Obviously, she had done it many times before. When she was sitting firmly on a stool by the counter, Mo came with a needle and injected it straight into her forehead.

'What is it?' Zolo was standing entranced by his uncle.

'Botox. A form of toxin that causes botulism. Technically it's a poison.'

Leila looked over when she realised this woman was being killed. A frost formed beneath her skin.

'It paralyses the facial muscles so you don't use your face, and as a result you don't get wrinkles.'

'You don't get old,' Rita managed to say to Zolo as she clasped a cool compressor to her head.

'Oh, you get old all right, Rita.' Mo winked. 'But your forehead stays young.'

'I wanted to ask you about AlloDerm, Mo.'

'Mo. Mo. We are past the stage of formalities, are we not? Sure. But I have earned my title, and I'd rather we stick to it.'

'Whatever, Doctor Fatagagas. AlloDerm, tell me about it.'

'I can do that too. It's permanent though.'

'I won't have to keep coming back every two months then?'

'Look, Rita, I'll have the surgery up and running soon. These injectables are not the answer. You can't beat a good facelift. AlloDerm is taken from corpses, and I can fold it, roll it and stack it so it fits into your face. It will even become you, become your own tissue, but five years from now, when your jaw drops . . .' He patted her jaw and slid his finger down her neck. '. . . and your neck becomes a real turkey gobbler, then, when I'm pulling your skin during the operation, the filler will still be in it, and it won't be moving anywhere. You might be left with a big lump somewhere. Other doctors will do it, but I have scruples, Rita. Just keep getting the Botox every two months, and even after the surgery, we'll use it to fill out any lines.'

Then he kissed her. She smiled at him, and then he touched her lips.

'I need some more bovine collagen, don't I?' Rita said eagerly.

Rita wrote a cheque, and Mo saw her to her car. She had a red Corvette that matched her jacket. Her red leather sandals had straps that wound around her legs like snakes. Zolo stared at them in wonder.

Zolo whispered to Leila, 'He doesn't have a clinic. The old bastard.'

Mo showed Zolo how to clear the counter. He then took some pasta from a plastic takeaway container and microwaved it. There was a Tupperware box with a white sticker that read, 'Larks' Tongues.' He shook some on to the pasta. He ate it by himself while talking in a stream of consciousness to Zolo. He was unused to eating in company; he never thought to offer any.

'Rita is addicted to this stuff. I charge only $300. Till I get my surgery, word of mouth, I do it here. Easy money, Zolo. I might marry Rita. I need an American passport. You have to find a born-again Christian. That's what she is. They're the most stupid people in America. LA is the good life, Zolo; you'll like it here: 80-year-olds on bicycles and roller blades. The Americans don't believe they can die. They don't even like to think they use the toilet. They call it restroom, bathroom, powder room. It's best to stick to the edges of this country. As a foreigner, it is wise not to go too far into the middle. Deep inside the country is a place called the Midwest, and the real piggy Americans live there. They actually have faces like pigs. Their bodies are pink and hairy.'

Mo went to the bathroom. He stayed in there a long time and left the beach house in a cloud of aftershave. Zolo and Leila were not sure where to sleep. They were too afraid to go into the bedroom and use his bed. Zolo tested it out. He fell into it and rolled around.

'Water. This bed is water.'

Leila dive-bombed the bed, and she and Zolo rolled about wrestling. Zolo easily overpowered his sister. He pinned her to the bed, his eyes glinting with inevitable and easy triumph. They lay beside each other, panting.

'We can sleep outside. We used to sleep on the roof at home.'

'Only when it was too hot,' Zolo said. 'They have air conditioning here.'

Leila yawned and was afraid that she was going to fall asleep on Mo's bed and he would come home and find her and inject her with all sorts of stuff. She went out to the deck and took a bundle of clothes with her. She placed her coat down on the wood and lay on top of it, covering herself with sweaters and leggings and shirts. Zolo followed her example. There was a sunset such as they had never seen before. A giant red ball gliding down a hazy, smog sky, the sea glowing like the burning hill. As darkness pulled over them, the tide came right in under the deck. They rolled over on their stomachs and pressed their noses between the wooden planks. The bottom of their world was fluid running back and forth in a silky rhythm.

'This is better than a stupid river. Even if it had a river inside it.' Zolo's voice was muffled between the boards. They tensed as they heard a car pull up outside. The front door opened and Mo came in. They heard voices, glasses clinking. Then the bedroom door slam and no more noise. Zolo crept over and peered in the French windows to Mo's bedroom.

'Who's there?' Leila whispered.

'His favourite person.' Zolo sighed.

'That woman, Rita?'

'He's alone,' Zolo giggled. 'Must have been talking to himself.'

'I want to go back to the camp, Zolo.'

'We're not going back. There was a war going on there, remember? It might spill over, and then the soldiers would come to the camp.'

'What would they do?'

'Undoubtedly kill everyone.'

'What about Maman and Baba? Will they come tomorrow?'

'They're gonners.'

'I miss Twinkle.'

'She's just a dog.'

Leila's eyes welled with tears. Zolo sighed. 'Will I tell you a bedtime story?'

'Like Baba does?'

'While we were in the camp for all those months, the sheep got hungry and ate the tortoise. Then the snake ate the goose, and the hawk ate the sheep, and the snake ate the hawk. Then Twinkle ate the snake after a massive struggle in which she outwitted him with her poodle savoir faire.'

'So she wouldn't be hungry?'

'No. Because the revolutionary guards would have eaten her anyway when they came to our house.'

'Why would they eat her?'

'Because dogs are considered unclean, and only decadent Western-leaning degenerates own dogs.'

Leila contemplated all this information. Zolo closed his eyes. He was smiling.

'Zolo?'

'Yesso?'

'Are there people like pigs in the middle of this country?'

'Yes.'

'We should stick to the edge then.'

'Yes.'

'We should never lose sight of the Specific Ocean.'

'Shut up, Frog. Go to sleep.'

Leila closed her eyes and dreamed that the sea was on fire and all the fish beneath were scrambling to lower depths away from the heat.

At daybreak, Mo came tearing on to the deck. He stopped short on discovering two tramps sleeping on his property. The children stirred in their mountainous heap of clothes.

'Get up! Get out!' Mo began tearing at the mounds of clothes. 'You can't lie there like peasants. Like refugees. I have a reputation in the neighbourhood.'

Suddenly he stood still and put his hands up in surrender. He breathed deeply and composed himself. 'Come on. Come on inside.'

They stumbled after their uncle, and he showed them the couch.

'Haven't you ever seen a fold-out couch? Good lord. What am I going to do? This isn't going to work out.'

The doorbell chimed.

'That's my patient. Quick. Into the bedroom. And don't touch anything.'

At lunchtime, Mo came into the room. The children were sleeping on the floor.

'Why didn't you use my bed? I never said you couldn't use my bed.'

'She's hungry.' Zolo pointed disdainfully at Leila.

'I have nothing but larks' tongues, and they're hard to get. I have to have them delivered from Chinatown in San Francisco.'

'I think she was thinking about rice and stuff.'

Mo, Zolo and Leila sat on a wooden bench in a restaurant by the sea. The waitress came with a tray of oysters. Leila wouldn't eat them.

'They look like melted eyeballs.'

Zolo wasn't too keen either, but his sister's disgust spurred him on.

'This is grown-up food,' she whined.

'Look at your brother.' Mo ruffled the boy's hair.

'I AM TEN YEARS OLD!' Leila pounded her fists on a pile of oysters, sending them flying. Zolo looked at his sister with interest and then at Mo. Mo was lighting a cigarette and sitting back as if scrutinising the sea. He drummed his fingers lightly off the table. Leila stood in front of the sea with her arms folded and her back to them.

'Zolo, you are going to have to teach your sister manners. I'm afraid no man will have such a wilful little animal.'

'I don't want a stupid man,' Leila wailed.

Zolo nodded. 'Thanks for the oysters, Uncle Mo. They were delicious. I think Leila should go back on the next plane to Ishmael and Farah.'

'And you?' Mo asked Zolo.

'I shall return to Orap.'

'Orap?'

'This is the greatest moment in history, and I should be there.'

'What?' Mo snorted. 'You want to go back and fight the revolutionaries?'

'No, Uncle. I want to join them.' Then Zolo took out from his pocket a picture of the revolutionary leader and unfolded it. Leila came back to the table. The leader was an old man with black eyebrows and a long grey beard. He had a red turban and a red-and-white robe. His face was gaunt and his eyes were shadowed. One eye was almost pure white. The other was swollen in its socket. His face was without wrinkles except for four lines, two down from his mouth and two from his nose. Leila noted this and pointed to the picture.

'He needs injections there and there, Uncle Mo. And . . .' she made a scissors motion with her fingers. '. . . the end of his nose needs clipping.'

Mo roared with laughter.

'Maybe it's you who will be my surgeon. Your brother is an idiot.'

Zolo focused a fanatical glare on Mo as if to reduce the man to ashes. Mo was implacable. Derisively, he waved his manicured hand at all the other customers eating seafood, talking on phones and sipping mineral water and white wine.

'Take a good look at these people, Zolo. These Californians. Do you think any one of them knows where Orap is? Have they heard of it? A small news item before the sports section? Between the *Hollywood Minutes*? Do you think when they have 200 channels that they even watch the news when it by chance lights on our poor nation? And if perchance they do deign to alight for a second on us, what would they glimpse? Endless lines of badly dressed, rumpled refugees spilling unwanted over borders because they can't keep their leaders under control. People with nothing left but big plastic bags of clothes and a few mementos.

'Your beloved leader with his cataract eyes and red hat, who is he? Another Santa Claus of the atomic age? Beliefs? What are beliefs? Can you touch them? Drive them? Live in them? Eat them? These folk want to live in huge houses, big enough to be schools or hospitals or hotels at home; they want to lie on beaches that are not filled with land mines; they want to eat fresh food that they don't stand hours in long lines for; they want to stay young for as long as possible, or at least to look young.

'Are they better than we are? Maybe. We do want to look like them. Blond. And we want their noses. Sure, they have their miseries, their cancers, their car crashes, and they all end up rotted in the ground, or as piles of ash, and their children resent them and blame them for their own petty failures; but, and this is the fatal difference, but they do not get carried away by ideas. That is the rub. These people are animals, but they know it more than we do. Food, shelter, prestige, sex—like the tribe of apes we are. Leave ideas and ideals to the fanatics. Live your life here like the animal you are and understand it. Enjoy it.

'You want to go back and get a plastic gold key made in Taiwan that will unlock the gates of heaven? That's what they give to their child soldiers who run over the minefields ahead of a rabble army. There is no heaven. This is as close as it gets. Oysters on the half-shelf on a warm sunny Californian day in early December.'

They left the restaurant and got into his car. Zolo searched through all the music selection in frustration.

'Beethoven, Beethoven, Beethoven. All you have is Beethoven.'

'I was told that Beethoven was the best. Why should I listen to anything but the best?' Mo rooted around in his pocket and found a card.

'By the way, I know Orapians don't have middle names. But you need one. Get yourself one that means something.'

Mo gave Zolo his business card with a flourish. Zolo and Leila read it.

Does the mirror make you miserable?
Time can and will be reversed.
Dr Mohammad Ludwig Van Fatagagas, plastic surgeon
I exist to recapture splendour.

Chapter Nine

The Motel by the Freeway

Mo had had enough. He stuck his nephew and niece in a budget motel by the freeway. The window was facing the first-floor walkway, and they didn't want strangers looking in and discovering that they were alone, so they kept the curtains closed. They didn't hang their clothes but left them rumpled in the suitcase.

Zolo put up the picture of the leader, balancing it on a framed picture of Yosemite. Leila looked on. 'Why are you putting him up here?'

'Didn't you hear what I said?'

'I thought you were just doing it to drive him crazy. Where did you get that picture? We had to leave Orap because of him.'

'I'm experimenting, Frog. Trying to feel what it would be like to have beliefs. See how long I can sustain the abstraction.'

'You're just doing it to annoy everyone. I don't want to look at him. He's scary. He's the reason we lost everything.'

'No. The corrupt monarchy were puppets of the West. They were giving our oil away, and that was the reason for the revolution. This guy just filled a gap. Orapians have been devoid of politics so long we don't have alternatives.'

'Was that where you were when you said you were at school?'

'Yes. I was in the streets with my uncle Ali. We were throwing stones at the military. Building barricades. Now I'm here.'

'I hate it here too.'

'I don't hate it here, Frog. It's a pity you're so simple-minded.'

Zolo wore a brown polyester T-shirt with a collar and a picture of a racing car, and a pair of long slacks. His hair was a fuzz that grew out instead of down, until his face was haloed by a jet-black Afro. His nose was becoming the Fatagagas nose. A prominent piece of architecture on his face.

Leila was as skinny as her brother was. Her hair was straight and in a bob. Long lashes flickered over big brown eyes. There were small half-moons of darkness under her eyes. Still jet lagged when Mo dropped them off at the motel, they rolled into the beds, closed the curtains and slept. In the dead of night, Zolo turned on the TV. There was one ad that played all through the breaks. A local car dealership. Tig the Tiger, he called himself. This man with a chain around his neck who drove into the screen in a car shaped and coloured like a tiger. Leila said they should go to him and ask where the school was. Come on Down, he said. Zolo pointed the remote at her and tried to switch her off. They fell back to sleep with the TV on. The tiger driving in and out of their dreams, zooming into one of their ears, pummelling through one brain, and out along the headboard and into the other sibling's ear and out and in and out and in.

During the day, they stood in the parking lot. The motel was on a freeway. They looked up and down but could see nothing but the road on either side and a gas station opposite.

Leila and Zolo stood beside each other, not touching. The sky was a blank blue, the ground was warm, cars zoomed and zimmed blindly past them. The ground began to shake. The motel sign was swinging, and a woman in a yellow dress ran from the office screaming but not spilling her coffee, which she held out in front of her. The people at the garage were dashing from their cars. Cans of stacked oil tumbled down. A bin toppled over. Cars stopped and skidded; a blue BMW smashed into a VW. The horn went off. The men in the cars got out and spun around while looking at the damage. They leaned towards each other, bewildered, unsteady, and not angry yet. A palm tree cracked in half and nose-dived on to the road.

Zolo and Leila felt a jolt and then nothing. The sky was empty. Leila glanced at her bare feet where the ground had stopped moving. She and Zolo sat down quickly, very close but not touching each other. They watched all the people start their cars up and drive off. The woman in the yellow dress went back into the office, holding one hand to her heart and smiling. The garage man came outside and indicated the rolling cans to a Mexican worker. The two men with crashed cars wrote things down. The charged air fizzled and the hairs on their arms stood up.

'Wow, Frog, did you feel that?' Zolo was thrilled.

'I didn't know America would have earthquakes.' Leila patted the ground. 'I thought it was just for poor countries.'

Zolo and Leila dressed up in their best clothes and combed their hair. Zolo placed pens in a row in his shirt pocket. They took what fake identification they had and walked down to the reception to wait for the taxi. Zolo had found the number of the taxi in the yellow pages. He had been reading the yellow pages all week to improve his English. Leila had watched television.

'We'll buy some books,' Zolo said.

'There's no shops around here.'

'Uncle Mo has given us money.'

'What if he doesn't come back and it runs out?'

'He said to call him when it runs out.'

'He said he would come and take us to the movies, but he didn't.'

'He's busy setting up the clinic.'

Leila and Zolo looked at each other for a minute. Sometimes Zolo would complain about Mo and Leila would stick up for him. They took turns in comforting each other. A week had passed by in the motel, and their uncle had not called once. Not even after the earthquake.

The motel reception was closed for the first time since they had been there, so they stood outside and watched the taxi pull up. Zolo opened the door and slipped in and Leila followed. She had trouble closing the door since it was so heavy.

'Where to? You going to a family dinner?'

'We want the nearest school.'

The taxi driver shrugged and started to drive.

'Any school?'

'A high school.'

'You kids look too young for high school.'

'No, we need high school.'

Zolo wasn't going to be slowed down in America. He was always years ahead in all his classes. The taxi driver dropped them off at a big school. He seemed reluctant to leave them.

'Should I wait?'

'No. This will take a while. Go.' Zolo sounded more imperious than he meant to, and the taxi driver, annoyed at his tone, drove off.

'He just wanted to charge us for the wait and get as much money out of us as he could,' Zolo told Leila as she followed him over the open lawn.

'You sound like Maman,' Leila said, jogging to keep up.

Zolo laughed. They walked around the school. It was empty. They looked in the windows and saw no one. It was a huge prefab building with picnic benches and tall trees.

'Not very snazzy, huh?' Zolo peered in a window at the language lab. 'Just like the dumps back in Orap.'

'Where is everyone?' Leila strained on tiptoes but couldn't reach the windows.

'I don't know. It's a weekday.'

The two children sat under a tree. Zolo pulled his knees up and rested his chin on them. Leila stretched her legs out and plucked at the grass with her hands. A man in a security uniform came walking towards them.

'What are you two kids up to?' he asked suspiciously.

Zolo stood up quickly. 'We're here to enrol in school, sir.'

'Today?' The man scratched his head. He shifted his belt with his two hands. Then he laughed. 'Do you know what day it is?'

'It's a weekday. And we thought the school was open.'

'You kids are just off the boat, eh? Where are your folks?'

Zolo took their papers out of his pocket. 'Can you sign us up for school, sir?'

The man was smiling and shaking his head. 'It's Christmas Day, son.'

Leila slumped in front of the TV. She jumped when she heard a hammering on the motel door. She glanced around the room. What a mess! Leila went to the window and peered through the curtain. Mo rapped on the window.

'It is I. For God's sake, child. Open the bloody door.'

Rita was with him. She was wearing a tight zebra-pattern dress from the Extinct clothing line and a cross around her neck. Mo and Rita sat on what had been Zolo's bed.

'Where's your brother?'

'He started school.'

'Good boy. Good boy. Hear that, Rita? What did I tell you? The boy has put himself into school.'

'It's Sunday, Mo,' Rita drawled. 'School's closed.'

'Indeed. So it is.' Mo glared at Leila.

'Faz's mother got him into a programme. He stays in a dorm room.'

'Faz? Who is he?'

'He's from Orap.'

Rita leaned over and stroked Leila's hair. 'My! This hasn't been brushed in some time.' She took a brush out of her bag. Mo grabbed her hand at the wrist and squeezed.

'These kids were in camps. They could have anything crawling on them.'

Rita shot Mo an angry glance and then moved over to Leila and began checking her for lice.

'You look like two monkeys.' Mo smiled.

'Tell her why we came, Mo.'

'I came to take you for a drive. Rita here said it's her treat. Since when has Zolo lived in a dorm?'

'Since a month.'

Rita raised Leila's head by her chin. 'Have you been on your own?'

'He and Faz come by after school.'

'Every day.'

'No.'

Mo paced, throwing his arms above his head. 'I'll kill the little fucker,' he boomed.

'He's only 14.' Rita combed Leila's hair. 'What do you expect?'

Mo swung around and yelled up close, right into her face, his spit beading her mascara, 'I never wanted brats. I warned my brother to get out but he wouldn't. I wasn't made for children, so I had the god-given sense never to have any. I know what kind of man I am.'

Rita looked as if she were about to cry, but she composed herself in a split second. A smile wobbled on to her face, unsure of its presence, anything but radiant. 'Well, Leila, you're already dressed.'

Leila nodded—glad she had done something right by sleeping in her clothes.

'We'll get your brother and go to church and then take a drive up Highway 1.'

'We can skip the damned church. These little soft-brained fools are brainwashed enough.'

Rita uncrossed her legs and stood up. In front of the mirror, she adjusted her dress, reaching into the top of it and resetting her baseball breasts so that they pointed directly in front of her like car headlights.

Zolo was unimpressed to find his Sunday plans so dramatically altered. He sulked for the first part of the journey until Mo placated him with ice cream and beef jerky.

'Leila was staying with Faz's mother for a week, and she went back to the motel by herself.'

'How does an 11-year-old all of a sudden decide where she can live?'

'How indeed?' Rita glared at Mo, applying a thick layer of gloss

to her lips while driving. Mo grabbed the gloss from her hand and
threw it out the window. She gave him a look but said nothing.

'What am I meant to tell your parents?'

'They haven't even written.'

'I may have some letters. Remind me to give them to you before
I drop you off.'

'When are they coming?' Leila asked.

Mo made Rita drive without stop all the way up to Monterey. For
seven hours in the car, he played only Beethoven. 'Only the best for
your uncle.'

Rita said very little. She seemed in awe of Mo. He was a despot
whose tyranny gave a shape to her. His rage was hygiene for both
their spirits. She would breathlessly freeze in his wash of fury and,
when it was over, she radiated a martyr-like serenity and he a distracted numbness. She had a lot of money from dead husbands; it
was apparent from her demeanour that she didn't make it on her
own or come from a rich family. She never overruled Mo, and her
masochism was proof to him of her ardour. He needed her for more
than sex and a green card. He needed her absolute subjugation. He
was practically autistic in his relationship toward others, seeing them
only as objects that existed for him. An ego like his demanded its
human sacrifices as nourishment. Mo had no separation of the
world and his ego. There was no point of demarcation where he
could accept that his life and influence ceased to exist in the world.
Rather, his being melted out over everything he saw and touched,
and all things related back to him. He filtered everything through
his own vision of himself. All that entered into his world was there
to service him. Even Beethoven.

At the Monterey Aquarium, they were able to pet stingrays. Leila
put her hand in the tank and the creature flapped up to her like a
submerged bird. Rita looked around vacantly. She caught a glimpse
of herself in one of the tanks, and sucked her stomach in. When the
others looked at the fish, she was looking at her reflection in every

glass display, with the water glugging behind her face, and a brain stuffed with plankton.

The jellyfish room was an eerie blue, dark place with wall-to-wall tanks. Huge jellyfish pulsated through the water. Each mushroom orange translucent body had a trail of tentacles dragging after it, like escaped atom-bomb clouds.

'I mean, is that it?' Mo glared at Zolo, his eyebrows joining over his nose. 'Do you want your sister to go out whoring herself?'

Leila didn't understand this new development but thought it best not to enquire as to its significance.

'Well? Would you allow that? Your mother and sister to go out whoring themselves?'

'Where does Farah come into this?' Zolo rolled his eyes. 'And if that's what they want to do—go out whoring themselves—well, that's up to them.'

Mo turned to Leila in shock. 'Did you hear that? He wants you and your mother to go out whoring yourselves?'

Leila began to cry.

'What's wrong with your sister? Jellyfish make her cry?' Mo was already marching to the next room. Zolo took Leila away from the glass and asked what the matter was.

'Baba would know about these fish.'

'You're kidding, aren't you?' Zolo laughed. 'He only read all that stuff in magazines. He didn't know it.'

'Everyone wanted to listen.'

'Good God. Talk about a captive audience. They were only peasants. They'd listen to goats fart in the hills for a bit of diversion.'

'I want Baba.'

Zolo dragged his sister to the next room. People were staring.

Rita tried to push Leila's hair out of her eyes. Leila shoved her hand away roughly. Mo grabbed the child. He kept his voice low.

'If you behave, I'll give you letters from your mother tonight. Okay?'

'Tonight?' Rita was aghast. 'I can't drive all the way back tonight.'

'I have school,' Zolo barked at her. 'I have to go back to the dorm. If you don't bring me, I'll go out on the road and hitch a ride.'

A giant sunfish floated up behind Leila, and Mo drew back startled.

'What is that?' Zolo's hands dropped to his side, and even Rita was stupefied. Leila turned her head slowly and encountered the fish eye to eye. It was the size of a refrigerator. There was no tail. Just a big crude box of a fish with stupid lifeless eyes. The sunfish turned and floated off among giant tuna and sharks. The four of them watched this blank being fade into the back of the gloom.

'Sweetie, this place is giving me the creeps. Let's you and me go and do some shopping. I'll see you boys at Bubba Gumps in an hour.' Rita took Leila by the hand and dragged her out. Leila turned to catch a last glimpse of the monster ugly fish.

Leila arrived at Bubba Gumps with leopard-skin leggings and a pink halter-neck top that exposed her belly button. Her shoulder-length hair was bunched up in a sparkling scrunchie, and Rita had sprinkled glitter on her face. She wore pink lipstick and blue eye shadow and high white zebra shoes.

'What kind of fish are you?' Zolo hooted.

'Doesn't she look amazing? They had the Extinct clothing line for kids too.'

Mo talked at length. It was of no concern to him that the children were too intimidated ever to reply or contribute.

'Do you miss your parents?' Rita chirped at one point.

'Rita, don't talk to them about their parents. It's hard enough as it is.'

Rita looked at Mo and tears filled her eyes. 'Oh honey, of course. You are so right.' She reached out and touched him with stick-on fingernails that were longer than her fingers. A blue sparkling stone was fixed in each one like an eye. They glittered like minnows. When the fruit salad came along, she speared the cubes of melon with her nails and popped them into her mouth.

That night, they drove for five hours, and Leila was dropped off first at the motel. They waited in the car as she walked up the stairs and along the balcony to her door, taking pigeon steps on the cement in her new high heels. Clutching her old clothes, she waved awkwardly with one swoop of her hand so as not to drop anything as she unlocked her door. She watched out the window as the red car pulled off.

Alone. She reached for the remote and lay on the newly made bed. The maid had been here. Flicking up and down the channels, she saw women in work-out clothes with strange new equipment, Dollars and Sense stock market news, a preacher, a comedian, a woman running through a forest with a man chasing her, movies, guns, car chases, shopping, a woman getting slapped by a man, slapped again, Chinatown it said as it went to ads, a man wrestling a crocodile, miniature Victorian shoes for sale on the Home Shopping Network. Narrow Escapes. Finally, she settled on Engineering Disasters. The History Channel. The *Thresher:* nuclear submarine. America had enough fire power on one submarine to wipe out any country on the face of the earth. The *Thresher* sinking to the bottom of the ocean; the other submarine, the *Skylark,* listening as they hear it bottom out at 8,400 feet. Leila switched back to the Chinatown movie; police killed the woman. She woke with the light on in the middle of the night, Tig the Tiger driving his tiger car, Come on Down. She got under the covers with her new high heels.

Zolo had made a friend. Faz. Tall, heavy-set, a round child's face, a training moustache, 16 years old, and three years in the United States. He was Zolo's roommate at the high school and fully instrumental in getting Zolo accepted into the dorms. His mother Mina helped get the forms and write a recommendation. She introduced Zolo to a Persian forger in Westwood who would prove to be the most valuable contact Zolo ever made in the US. Faz was an only child, and his mother had taken him from Orap before the revolution to get a good western education. His father was dead.

Faz walked strangely. At first Leila asked Zolo if the boy was spastic, but Zolo said that was the cool way to walk. Faz swaggered with his arms hanging down by his side. His super-baggy pants hung off his ass, and he always wore what looked like black panty-hose on his head.

Leila spent the whole next day in the motel watching TV and washing her clothes in shampoo in the bathroom sink. Occasionally, Zolo would come to ignore her. Now he brought Faz with him too.

Zolo took a pile of letters out of a plastic bag.

'I made Mo give these up. After we left you off last night.'

Leila took them.

'They're from Ishmael and Farah.'

'What do they say? Are they coming?'

'I barely read them. They disowned us, Leila, said we were Mo's kids and he hates kids. Don't count on those losers. Make your own luck.'

Leila looked stung.

'Right. We'll be back. Don't go anywhere.' Faz swaggered out the door and Zolo followed.

The letters were full of enquiries as to Zolo's education. It was imperative that he did not have a break in his studies. He had to prepare for medical school. Their parents were hoping that once the spring came, they would be able to join them. There was a chance that they could sign up as refugees and get placed in a western country. They hoped, of course, for the United States. The war in Orap had got closer. You could hear shelling and bombs rumbling through the empty middle of the nights. The days were quiet, but the snow was relentless. Had Zolo settled in to his studies? Was he looking after Leila?

There was her name in her father's handwriting. Leila was waiting for a letter for her, but they were all to Mo and Zolo.

Zolo was the first-born, and only son. He slept in his parents' bed until he was 10 years old. When he was three, he saw his newborn sister lying on her stomach in the cot with her arms and legs splayed. Unimpressed, he said she looked like a frog.

Five years old on an upturned crate in his father's surgery. Green mask, green gown flowing over the crate. Once a patient turned and saw him, and screamed, thinking he was the surgeon. Little demon doctor. Playing at his mother's feet while women splayed themselves in stirrups. He was raised in clinics and always sick from something.

Twelve years old with meningitis. In the hospital, surrounded by his toys. Brought back to life by vigils. When he left the hospital, he had every toy available and came to that awful realisation in the toyshop. Scouring the shelves, his face bunching in panic, he turned to his mother and demanded an electric shaver. Said he would need it some day. She got her demanding 12-year-old an electric shaver that day in a country where most people had barely enough to eat. No wonder there was a revolution!

All his life sneaking games with Mehrdad, the gardener's son. Mehrdad once naked in the river. They were exactly the same age. Nine years old. Mehrdad was good-looking and athletic. Zolo was not. Mehrdad's head bobbed over the surface and Zolo stood at the bank. Mehrdad taught him how to swim. Zolo peeled off his clothes and dipped into the cold river. The reeds brushed off him as he slithered away from the bank into the middle. He and Mehrdad took turns standing on each other's shoulders and fainting into the water. A servant saw him play naked with the gardener's son and reported this to both fathers, who were aghast. Zolo was admonished but never punished. Mehrdad was ordered to be whipped by his own father.

Zolo excelled in maths and science. Shooting ahead in school year after year until he was 11 in a class of 15-year-olds and bullied unmercifully. The bullying served only to cement his pitiless disdain for others, and he remained an imperious little monster. Finally, and much to his relief, they sent him to a school for the exceptionally gifted.

When his father and uncle bought a cinema, Zolo was there every night with a bag of pistachios, sitting in the centre of the back row, his usual seat, the boss's son, watching kung-fu movies. The cinema was sold after a few disastrous months. When he was 12, his father told him he didn't need a crate for surgery. He donned his green robes, reaching the floor but not dragging off of it. A woman's breast implants had gone rock hard, and Ishmael had to break them up. Ishmael smashed and pounded and kneaded those breasts. The lifeless body almost fell off the table. The nurses held it down. Zolo was stunned. The woman's skin was turning blue and black and yellow. He grabbed his father and begged him to stop. Everyone looked in shock at the boy.

'Get him out of here,' Ishmael said. Sweat pouring from under his elasticised green mask. Zolo would not speak to his father for a week and declared that he would never go near the hospital again.

In Orap, Zolo was brilliant, brimming with possibilities, ambition and promise. Cunning, kingly, cruel; he was imperious to his parents and his teachers, all of whom adored him and tripped over each other to sing his praises. If Ishmael ever worried that they were creating a tyrant like his own little brother Mo, he reasoned to himself that Mo was an extremely successful man with wealth and prestige, feared but respected.

Zolo in California was a refugee, and a nerd, a skinny little brainy boy with an Afro, from a Middle Eastern country so small that no one had heard of it. Orap was not on the news, unless you caught a snippet on the BBC news on channel 21. CNN forget it. Mathematical whiz, genius, geek, he sat in the classroom drawing pictures of tanks and guns and dreaming of the revolution. Meanwhile, his classmates talked about football or the prom. Faz took him to the Persian forger he knew, and Zolo now had a forged driving licence that said he was 16. Faz was teaching him how to drive. In their shared room in the dorm for foreign students, Zolo put up the picture of the revolutionary leader. He was now 14 years on the planet.

'Take that moron down,' Faz said lazily.

Zolo shook his head.

'We'll never get chicks with an Islamic fundamentalist on the wall.'

Zolo wasn't sure. 'I never get chicks anyway.'

He was streets ahead of everyone and had applied for college for the coming fall. He did his own work and Faz's also. He filled in college forms for Faz. They would both study science, he decided. When his parents came, they would get Leila into a school. The frog could wait.

Faz decided that Zolo needed some de-nerding. Faz spiked his Coke with LSD one afternoon, and he finally woke to his new surroundings. The long-legged blondes, the swimming pools, the mission-style houses with lawns, pink bougainvillea and red tile roofs, and security systems, the white shiny malls, the endless highway, surfers walking the glimmering sea. He took down the picture of the leader. It would be the last time he would form an abstract allegiance. From then on, he decided that this was better than Orap anyway and he wasn't going back.

That night, after reading the letters, Leila lay on the top of the covers and closed her eyes. Among the pile of letters she had found three from Mehrdad, addressed just to her. They were lovely letters, full of news and stories about his family. He told her he missed her more that anything else in Orap. She could now give him the address of the motel and ask him to write every week and she would write back. There was a dog barking. It sounded far off and empty, as if it were guarding a sealed hollow.

Chapter Ten

The House With No Anus

The private college Zolo and Faz got accepted to was in the desert between Las Vegas and Los Angeles. The fees were high, but Zolo again went to the Persian forger and got all the papers necessary. His grades were so extraordinary that he was granted a full scholarship; the forger was so brilliant that he was able to take out loans for the rest of his expenses. Zolo and Faz shared a room in the dorm. The first week, Jack Clancy swept regally into the cafeteria clad in a tuxedo, his roommate trailing him, haplessly clutching a large silver candelabrum. His roommate stood behind Jack with a tea towel draped on his arm and watched him eat. Jack solemnly rose, and his roommate took the plate and glass and left them over at the counter before following him out the door. Rumour had it that the roommate had lost a bet. Jack had been chasing a girl whose biology project entailed extracting the fluid out of cockroaches' spines. The roommate had scoffed, saying cockroaches didn't have spines. Jack wagered him to be his servant for a month, and the roommate lost.

'Chordate,' Jack would say. 'All chordates have spines.'

Impressed, Zolo proposed that they kidnap Jack, dose him with acid and dump him in a lake. Faz agreed. Jack was duly grabbed and bustled into Faz's mother's Volvo and driven to a lake. He took the acid willingly, though he admitted he had done nothing heavier than grass in high school. They threw him fully clothed into a lake. He trod water and grinned at them.

'Do you guys know where the hot springs are?'

'No.' Zolo was about to get into the car and drive off.

'All the college girls go skinny dipping there.'

Faz and Zolo fished their new friend from the lake. Jack in turn introduced them to his sister Desiree, who dealt pot.

Zolo stood on Mo's deck as his uncle arranged pots of orchids.

'Your sister can't stay alone in the motel.'

'That's my plan. I'll move her to my friend's house if you give me the motel rent money as my college spending money.'

'I hope you are on track to do medicine. Science is all right as a foundation, I suppose, but . . .'

'Do we have a deal?'

'Half the rent for the motel and make sure you visit her and keep an eye on her until your parents are over.'

'Deal.' Zolo was relieved to find a source of income that would free him to study. He almost felt affection for his uncle that went beyond his dependence on him. 'I'm glad you got your orchids again.'

'I'm glad too.' Mo put his arm around Zolo and he stroked a purple petal. 'I've discovered how to take care of them finally.'

'How's that?' Zolo asked.

'Neglect,' Mo mused. 'They thrive on neglect.'

Zolo went to the motel and drove with Faz, Jack and Leila to Jack's parents' house in the desert.

'Welcome to the House With No Anus,' Desiree said. 'Everything goes in and nothing comes out.'

A forest of empty shampoo bottles in the bathroom. Forty toothbrushes with smushed yellow bristles, overgrown hedges of newspapers in the corridors. War rations, cans and packages avalanching from the cupboards. Jars with strange green liquids in the fridge door, Uncle Peter's gallstones, every closet spilling out into trails on the floor. Paths beaten through each room constantly in danger of overgrowing with shoes, one-handed clocks, rock-hard bagels, pots, pizza cartons. Desiree's brother Jack slowly picked his way through the rooms, giving Leila, Zolo and Faz the grand tour, pausing for effect at moments of particular chaotic horror.

Jack pointed his foot to a large bag of cat food that was split down the middle, allowing the red pellets to overflow on to the floor. A giant, fuzzy grey cat was sampling the wares. 'Saves feeding them yourself. That was getting to be a problem.' Dirty saucers with hardened pieces of cat food lay about the kitchen floor like lily pads on a filthy linoleum pond. Desiree came up behind them and in a low voice said, 'Show them your room, Jack.'

Jack's room was an oasis of neatness. He had his watch collection, his skull collection and his old camera collection neatly presented on a huge plywood desk. The pictures on the wall were not the pictures one would expect from a 19-year-old. No declarations of musical affiliations, rather there were photos in identical brown frames of various tribes and freaks. One such frame contained a photo of an entire African tribe with elephantiasis of the scrotum. There were several photos of Carnie freaks. 'My great-great-grandfather grew up in Jersey City. He went to all the freak shows. He knew them all.'

'Then he married my not-so-great-great-grandmother,' Desiree declared dryly. She was 18, born exactly a year later than her brother Jack; Jack was born a year after Ernie, same hour same day. Irish triplets, their mother called them.

'Since I'm in the dorms, you can use this room,' Jack told Leila. Leila liked how he talked to her as if she were an adult.

'What will your parents say?' Zolo asked.

'They won't mind, I assure you. They're always adopting people.'

'Adoption by default,' Desiree said. 'There's this guy Patterson. I think he's about 40. He came to fix the roof a year ago, and now he comes around every day and just sits in the living room for hours reading the newspaper and watching TV. He leaves shortly after my father comes in in the evening. They discuss football for a few minutes, and then he gets off the chair and disappears. We don't know where he lives. Certainly my mother has never commented on it.'

Jack Clancy opened a wooden cigar box and took out some grass. He set up a bong, and the assembled sat cross-legged on the floor and passed it from one to another. Desiree handed it to Leila. Leila instinctively looked at her brother to gauge his reaction. He seemed otherwise absorbed, so she took a puff and coughed hard and long. They all laughed.

'You'll get used to it,' Desiree comforted her.

Faz took the bong. 'Don't your folks say nothing about you smoking in the house? My old lady would sniff it in a second.'

'Technically they disapprove,' Desiree drawled. 'I used to go out on the roof and smoke. One time I was out there with a friend and she started freaking out. "Come in, come in, I know what you're up to." So I came in protesting my innocence. I said, "How do you know what I'm doing out there?' So she says, "Because your bong is missing from your dressing table." After that, I didn't even bother to hide. We just smoke inside.'

'We gotta bounce,' Faz said.

Zolo got up to leave. Leila walked with him through the house, and when they were outside, she reached out and held his hand. He was stunned. Not sure if she was being affectionate or trying to pull him back.

'Sup?'

'I don't know where I am.'

Zolo was puzzled and then relaxed. 'Oh, it's the high desert.'

'How far away will you be?'

'About 35 miles. Not far.'

'Does Mo know I'm going to be living here?'

'Frankly, Mo doesn't care. He wants to save on motel rates, so he'll be fine. I made a deal with him because I needed pocket money in college. He's giving me half the money he would have spent on the motel, and I'm putting you with friends.'

'Why are you getting all the money?'

'She has a point.' Jack laughed.

'What am I going to do for money?'

'Look, when Ishmael and Farah come over, they can take you, put you in school, whatever. For now, just stay put and behave. You're safe here. They're crazy but harmless.'

'Zolo, I don't know where I am.'

'It was you who said you didn't want to live in the motel any more. Hey, Ishmael and Farah would approve: their dad's a doctor. They think doctors are sacred beings beyond reproach.'

'Will you visit me every day after school?'

'No. I'm not in high school. I'm in college. Desiree comes to sell pot all the time on campus. Drive in with her if you must.'

'Zolo . . .'

Zolo stamped his foot. 'Do you think your life is so precious?'

Faz and Jack strolled outside and stretched in the evening sun. Jack draped his arm around Leila. 'On further consideration, your brother tells me you are a bit of a slob and, while that is nothing new in this household, my own domain is a tranquil place of scientific study, so here's a key to my brother's room.'

'Your brother?' Leila took the key and looked at it in consternation.

'Ernie. He has a room at the end of the corridor, adjacent to my own, but he never usually goes there.'

Desiree nodded. 'He sleeps either in his car or in front of the TV.'

'Oh yeah?' Faz grinned. 'Where does he work?'

'The local tax office,' Jack said.

'You guys are all freaks,' Zolo said and got into Jack's jeepster. 'Relax, Leila. You're in California.'

'This is about all you need here.' Desiree threw Leila a pair of sunglasses.

Leila found the room at the end of the hall. The lock turned with a jolt. She pushed the door open in trepidation. Inside, the floor was covered in tiny white feathers. A layer of dust coated everything. In one corner stood a children's miniature boxing ring with two dusty robots facing each other, arms held up defensively. On a shelf over the bed there was a small clay statue. It was a home-made piece that looked like it had been first rolled into a sausage and then squeezed three times with a small fist. Eyes and mouth were scraped with fingernails into the top, a fingernail scrape down the bottom third to signify legs. Scrawled in the base were the words 'The Idiot'. She cupped her own small hand, and her fingers fit exactly into the grooves. A child had made it. There was a picture of Ronald Reagan over the bed and an oil painting on one wall of a stern-looking eighteenth-century woman with many chins, a pug nose and a red face. A typed sign stuck with scotch tape on to the canvas: 'Benjamin Franklin as a young woman'. The window had an American flag nailed over it. Leila pulled the flag aside; the view of the desert, a scattering of low, sprawling ranch-style houses with many old cars piled in the yards and the bare mountain rising far away. The single bed was soft and springless. Leila lay on the bed and put on her sunglasses.

Chapter Eleven

A Trip to Mexico

Desiree came down the corridor pounding her feet flat on each step. 'O Tannenbaum, O Tannenbaum,' she sang vigorously. The whole house shook. Leila locked the door.

The mother of the house, Mrs Clancy, was a German immigrant. There were photos about the house to attest to her considerable beauty. She lived for three things: her garden, the visiting nurses' sale and her skewed ambitions for her children. At most times of the day, she could be found on her hands and knees in a flowerbed trowelling at weeds. That the garden never responded to her ministrations was never commented on. There was not so much as a flower. A few wild cacti and weeds were all that eked out a life under her un-green thumb. She spent an inordinate amount of time moving piles of clay from one side of the drive to the other. Like an earthworm. Too much digging and no watering.

The visiting nurses' sale was once a year at the Veterans' Hospital. The house would swell with junk. Desiree and Jack responded genetically to such training and bought up a storm at their mother's side. Desiree bought a big iron wheat thresher with sword-sharp prongs, and put it on the dining table. Jack bought watches, old camera equipment, obsolete computers, shields, swords and parts of military uniforms. Mrs Clancy bought everything, even two urinals: 'you never know vot you might need.'

Her ambitions for her children were closely linked to an idea she had that they were aristocrats. This was gleaned from an old family photo of a nebulous German ancestor who 'had an aristocratic bearing'. Ernie, the eldest, was a delicate child who hovered mutely on the unhinged periphery; Jack was a nineteenth-century dude and raised as such; Desiree was a Monstre Sacre. Her mother hoped she would go to LA and get on *Wheel of Fortune*. That it had been off the air for years did not deter her. Desiree, or Katrinka the Powerful as her father nicknamed her, was a force of nature. Carnivorous, attractive, witty, avaricious, loud, bouncy and insecure.

The family lived entirely in the present. That was why it was easy to move in with them. It was against their nature to question the sequence of events that led up to your arrival. When something changed in their environment, they accepted it as a condition and never tried to alter anything. There was no past to dwell on, no future to strive towards, just the bright glare of the present and the satisfaction of appetites.

In Ernie's room, Leila found a tomblike solace. Nothing to do with childhood or games. Ernie never came upstairs any more. He kept his clothes in the back seat of his car and slept on the couch downstairs. Mrs Clancy acted as if it were natural for an 11-year-old refugee to move into her eldest son's bedroom. Leila did not eat with the family. Only Mr and Mrs Clancy ate together. Leila would wait till no one was around and rummage through the jumble of food in the refrigerator. Zolo had left her no money, and so she felt she shouldn't be discovered taking too many liberties in this family. She did not mind being here so she wanted to stay. Underneath the bed in Ernie's room, she found scrapbooks of clippings, compiled seemingly at random.

> The World Church of the Creator is a religious organization devoted to white supremacy and hatred of all nonwhites, defined as including, but not limited to, Jews, blacks, Asian, and Latinos. It refers to these people as 'mud races'. The World Church of the Creator was founded in 1973 by a former Florida State legislator and

the man who invented the electric can opener, Ben Klassen. He committed suicide in 1993.

Followed immediately by another clipping:

> Although biologically a canid, the fox's doglike features are melded with felinity, as though the old antagonists, dog and cat, seem magically blended. It's feline adaptations—lithe body, whiskers, movements, mouse chasing, tree climbing—contrast to its doggish bushy tail, hole living, pointed muzzle, barking, and trotting.

Leila liked Ernie's home-made books, and she decided to adopt them and continue them with her own clippings and notes. They needed a theme. A story. She would work on that.

She liked Ernie, and everyone in the house liked and respected her. She was happier and more free here than when she had been in Orap. She had found a place where no one judged her, where all the world's discarded things had equal value and were cherished. Not only was everyone in the family eccentric and entertaining, but Mrs Clancy was kind. However, in Ernie she found a friend.

Small strange smiles landed on Ernie's face like alien ships when the two crossed paths in the gloom of the corridors. The inside of this house was musty and chilled while the desert sun grilled the land outside. Going into the house from the outside was plunging to bottomless depths. Downstairs, Ernie asked her her name the first time he saw her, when she was painting her nails on the couch with a bottle found in the bathroom.

'Leila.'

'Hi, Leila. I'm Ernie.'

'I know.'

'How do you know?'

'I live in your bedroom.'

'That's not my bedroom.'

'No?' She stopped polishing her nails and stared at him. 'Whose is it then?'

'Ernie's.'

'You're Ernie.'

'That Ernie is dead.'

'What did he die of?'

'I live downstairs.'

Desiree came pounding in, her red hair flaming around her face like a glorious mane. She had a weighing scales under her arm, and she put it in the centre of the living room.

'I got this at a yard sale.' She stood with her flat Fred Flintstone feet on the plastic scales. Her toes were like blocks and far apart. 'I ate only an egg today, so I hope I've lost a couple of pounds.'

Leila stood up and weighed herself. Desiree stared at the results enviously. 'Jesus, you barely exist. I wish I were 11 again. Mother said she'll buy me a whole new wardrobe if I lose weight.'

Leila looked at Desiree; she was broad-shouldered but lean and muscled from scouring around like a desert rat. Mrs Clancy came home from her first-aid class, clutching a four-foot-tall, smelly teddy bear. Desiree looked appalled. 'What are you doing with Mr Biggles, Mother?'

'I had to perform mouth-to-mouth resuscitation on him. And the rest of it. Vee needed a model.'

Mrs Clancy lit up when she spied the scales. 'I bet I'm lighter than you,' she said to Desiree. She was. Desiree looked crushed. No one acknowledged Ernie.

'What did you learn today?' Leila asked Mrs Clancy. Mrs Clancy opened her mouth, about to launch into a full description of her day's events when Desiree snatched Mr Biggles and snorted. 'She learned how to bring a stuffed toy to life.'

In the evening, Leila found herself alone with Ernie again. He was watching football.

'Can you tell me where I am?' Leila asked.

'In relation to what?'

'My brother is at your brother's college. How far away is that?'

'Two hundred miles probably.'

'Two hundred?' Leila's mouth opened wide, but she could say no more. 'How close are we to LA, to Malibu?'

Ernie contemplated this. 'I'm not quite sure. One hundred miles maybe. I've never been.'

'In all your life, you've never been to LA, and it's the nearest city?'

'There's talk of the train line extending out here. When it does, maybe. . . . You don't know where you are, do you?' Ernie never took his eyes off the TV, but his voice was gentle and patient. He rose stiffly out of his seat. He always walked straight up without moving his spine or neck, his legs awkwardly pawing their way before him, and when he turned, he never swivelled his head, but turned his whole body. He had great big eyes. He was like a lone fish in a bowl. Staring out on to the world without connections. Circling and circling, alone.

He entered the room with a big coffee-table book, with a discount sticker, *The Illustrated History of the West*. Not bending down, he squatted slightly and held it out in front of her. She accepted it.

'That will explain where you are,' he said.

'Thank you.'

'And it has pictures.' He was already lowered back on to the couch and watching the football.

This book changed everything for Leila. The story fell into place.

Leila saw a map in her history book from 1688. California was an island. She did not know what year it was now, but this map gave her a clearer picture of where she was.

She hitched a ride with Desiree to see Zolo. The journey was long, and Desiree opened the windows and turned on the AC.

'I hated being a child. I had no control over anything. I used to sit and sulk and dream of being an adult where no one could say 'No' to me. When I wanted two Cokes, I could just get two Cokes. I used to dream of driving with the windows down and the AC on. That to me was the definition of growing up.'

'Where do you get all this?' Leila opened the glove compartment and was looking at all the bags. Desiree shut it quickly.

'At the end of our road, behind the rocks, there's a mobile-home camp. You know it? We were always forbidden to go there. Full of freaks. Especially out here in the desert. There's an old guy about 40, my brother calls him a stocky mesomorph, he's short and fat that means, but you know my brother. Anyway, he has hair growing on his ears, not out of them understand, but ON his ears. All around the lobes and the rubbery part. He's a paedophile too.'

'What's that?'

'He likes them real young, so maybe I won't introduce you. He spends part of the year in Cambodia screwing little girls, and he even fell in love with one and took her home. Her name is Lan; she's real cool. She's 16 now, so he doesn't do her any more, so she does everyone else in town for money, but she still lives with him in his trailer and cooks and shit. She's terrified he'll bring home another little girl and she'll be sent back to Cambodia.'

Desiree drove in silence for a while and then said, 'He's known as the Ick-Man after an old John Cooper Clarke song.'

'The Ick-Man.'

'It's what we always called him. Underneath that yellow shirt, beats a heart of solid dirt, the most disgusting man on earth, is the Ick-Man baby. Actually, I think the song is the It-Man but Ick suited better.'

'He's more icky than itty?'

'Yep.'

Trees and parks surrounded the college built on the grounds of an old Spanish mission. The buildings had plenty of steps and columns. Leila liked the place instantly. Desiree led her to the dorms. Zolo, Jack and Faz proudly showed them a couch settled surreally halfway up a tree. They had thrown it out the window, and it had landed perfectly.

'Let's go to Mexico,' Desiree said. 'We could go down to Ensenada and stay in the Motel California.'

'I don't have a passport,' Zolo said.

'They only look at your driver's licence on the way back across.'

The five of them went to Mexico in Desiree's car. Leila made sure she was sitting next to her brother so she could feel close to him. Their arms pressed together all the way south, and she knew he didn't care. At the border, there was a sign saying that no firearms were allowed into Mexico.

'We Americans are gun crazy,' Jack said. 'We still think it's the Wild West.'

'Isn't it?'

'You do know that this part of the world is called the West only because its recent conquerors came from the East. To the Spanish it was the North, to the Russians it was the East, and of course to the Brits and the Frogs who were firmly ensconced in Canada, it was the South.'

'Jack, if you don't stop lecturing, it'll be the end. I hate Mexico. It's so tacky. So third world. Let's go to Vegas. Vegas is class.' Faz sat in the front as they smoked a joint while waiting in line to get through. They passed over the border in a haze of pot smoke.

'Vegas, alas poor Vegas,' Jack said. 'We're always in Vegas. It's time to get cultural.'

Over the border there were lines of Mexicans waiting to get through. Stalls sold big plaster Virgins of Guadeloupe, bleeding Jesuses, giant plaster Bart Simpsons and South Park characters.

'I want a poncho and a hat. We have to do this properly,' Desiree said.

They all chose ponchos. Zolo bought one for Leila. Faz bought an ugly one with a turtleneck. Desiree turned up her nose.

'A turtleneck poncho! That guy's such a dork.'

Leila rolled a joint in the car. She found that rolling joints kept her busy when they were all talking, and everyone liked the joint roller. It was a good role to have if social skills were lacking. A police car followed them for a bit but then pulled away. They were edgy and went into Tijuana and had cocktails. Zolo wanted to get food, but Desiree wasn't interested.

'Liquids! Liquids!' she chanted.

They settled on tacos from the street. 'As good as a laxative,' Desiree gloated.

In the bar, she showed Leila how to induce a good vomit.

'You do this after you eat something you don't want.'

'I did want that taco.' Leila was content just to watch and marvel.

'You're only 11. Wait till you start getting breasts and periods.' Desiree ripped some sheets of toilet paper off the roll and laid them on the surface of the toilet water and on the seat. 'This is to prevent back-splashing.'

'I thought women paid to get breasts.' Leila had no idea they grew by themselves.

'You'll fit right in.' Desiree choked and gagged on her fingers. She roared, 'Uuughhhghhhtuh.' Whoosh, a stream strung out from her mouth and hit the side of the bowl. Desiree stood and clapped her hands. 'You should start with ice cream. As good on the way up as it is on the way down.'

The boys were amused when they came out of the toilet.

'Thanks for sharing that experience with us all.'

Desiree guzzled a margarita, wiping the salt off with her unwashed finger.

'Bulimics are meant to be sneaky and secretive, Desiree,' Faz said in disgust.

'I am the proud bulimic.' Desiree sucked her drink dry and grabbed Jack's.

'Why do you do it?' Faz asked.

'Mother has promised me a whole wardrobe.'

'You are thin,' Zolo said.

Desiree shrugged.

'Mother was a beauty when Father met her in Germany,' Jack said. 'She was tall, long-legged and rake thin. Father thought at least he'd have good-looking children.'

'Yep.' Desiree nodded. 'Instead we all look like him, and Mother has never done a day's work in her life, let alone vacuumed the house once.'

'Bummer,' Faz said.

'She won't buy me any underwear either,' Desiree said. 'She'll pay for the best designer stuff, but she won't buy underwear. She doesn't believe in it.'

'Well, you can't see it,' Jack said. 'She believes only in what she sees.'

'I've been reduced to stealing underwear from friends' houses when I go to visit.'

It was dark by the time they tottered to the car.

'Let Jack drive. He's a good drunk driver,' Zolo told Desiree.

'Iz my car.' Desiree shoved him and fumbled with the keys.

By the border walls, rows of men perched furtively with plastic bags, waiting to make a run. A spotlight scoured and they bent over, willing themselves invisible. Leila craned her neck to see them; their faces were flat and half-hidden. The people on the wall looked like the Indians in her book and not like the Europeans. As if in tune with her thoughts, Jack pontificated to no one in particular. Leila decided that he must have memorised the book. She had heard that he read obscure books and memorised whole passages to use at parties. Anything could trigger him off. Leila found him gentlemanly and courteous; she felt protective over him: he was decent to the core. But Zolo and Faz liked to bring him along, and set him loose among the crowd, and watch him pin people down with talk and ruin their evenings. It was a source of endless amusement to see the hapless victims' expressions pass from mild interest, to surprise that the flow of talk had no end, to anger, to numbness and then to sheer despair. 'Hernan Cortes, conqueror of the Aztecs, he took Mexico and with it riches that had never been witnessed before. Of course, as you know I'm sure, when the Europeans landed in Mexico, the cities here were bigger than any city in Europe. As the conquistador said, "We came here to serve God and his Majesty, to give light to those who were in darkness and to get rich, as all men desire to do."'

'Now we just come to get rich,' Zolo muttered.

'I knew we should have gone to Vegas,' Faz countered.

Leila spoke up: 'We find ourselves threatened by hordes of immigrants, who have already begun to flock into our country, and whose progress we cannot arrest.'

Everyone turned to Leila in astonishment, as if she had spoken in a voice not her own.

'What was that about?' Desiree said.

'It was the voice of Pio Pico,' Leila said.

'Oh and who is he?'

'Pio Pico . . .' Jack had regained his composure and was ready to display his own erudition. '. . . was the governor of California when California was Mexico. He was talking about the white Americans spilling over the borders illegally on top of the Mexicans.'

'Times have changed.' Desiree nodded sagely. 'Strange times, always strange.'

Zolo was smiling at Leila and she almost felt afraid. The others were impressed with her speaking-in-tongues historical outburst.

There was an enormous line of cars waiting to get through to the US. Desiree and Jack sat in front in their ponchos, their sombreros banging off each other. Faz still wore his ugly turtleneck poncho. Zolo fell into a deep sleep over Leila's knee. She cherished this proximity, and stroked his hair because she knew he was in a semi-coma and would not object. He was the first person she had touched in a long time. When they got to the checkpoint finally, the guard sat in his box and asked them, 'Which nationality?'

'US,' Desiree said, trying not to breathe on him.

'US,' Jack said.

'US,' Faz said.

'Say that again.' The guard looked at Faz suspiciously.

'US,' Faz said nervously.

'US,' Leila said.

'And him, wake him up.' The guard pointed to the crashed-out Zolo sprawled over Leila's legs.

'He's US,' Jack said.

'I want to hear him say it.'

'Zolo, Zolo.' Leila shook him.

'Wha'? Wha' the fuck?'

Desiree swung around and punched him.

'Which nationality?' the guard asked, scrutinising the young Orapian in a sombrero and poncho.

'I'm a Mexican,' Zolo said, waving his hand at the guard dismissively and lying back down. They all burst out laughing.

'He's US.' Desiree wiped her eyes.

'What nationality ARE you?' the guard shouted at Zolo through the window.

Leila shook him and Zolo sat up in a rage.

'I'm a FUCKING MEXICAN!'

The guard jumped out of his box and pulled the door open. Leila grabbed Zolo's wallet and showed him the fake US driving licence.

'This could be easy or this could be the worst day of your life,' he growled. 'Have you kids been drinking?'

Everyone hesitated. The car smelt like a brewery. Even Leila was drunk. Jack said in his most aristocratic manner, 'Admittedly, we have imbibed some libations, sir. We have feted ourselves not wisely but well. However, my sister here is our designated driver.'

They held their breath. A designated driver going down to Tijuana was something of a stretch. Desiree did not look like anyone's designated anything.

The guard glared at Zolo, and Zolo snatched his licence back. The guard for some unfathomable reason waved them through. Desiree was shaking so much she had to pull immediately over to the side.

'What the fuck did you do that for, Zolo? I could have got a drunk driving; Faz and you have fake IDs and aren't citizens. Leila has no ID and is a drunken 11-year-old in our charge. You idiot.'

Zolo made a face. 'I thought we were trying to get into a club.'

'A club?' Faz rolled his eyes.

'A club?' Desiree was incredulous. 'No, not a club, just the United States of America.'

'Indeed.' Jack raised his eyebrows. 'I suppose you could call the United States of America a kind of club.'

'I need a joint.' Desiree signalled Leila.

It was the middle of the night when they arrived at the college. Leila and Desiree slept together in Zolo's bed. Zolo slept on the floor.

'I need a glass of water. I'm thirsty,' Desiree whined.

Zolo got up and stumbled to get water.

'And not tap water either,' she shouted.

Zolo gave her tap water and said, 'Out of curiosity, what do you want carved on your tombstone?'

Desiree guzzled the water and handed him the glass. 'I want more.'

'A fitting epitaph.' Zolo nodded and declined to get her another glass.

'Good night,' Desiree said.

'Good night, Zolo,' Leila said.

Zolo grinned at her. 'Good night, Pio Pico,' he said, and actually ruffled her hair.

Chapter Twelve

The Ick-Man

Yellow maps changing page by page until they realised that California was not an island. Land streaked with spidery rivers: the Colorado, Columbia, Missouri, Mississippi, the Dismal, the Big Sandy, the Little Sandy, Sand Creek and the Greasy Grass, The River That Scolds All Others, the River of Disappointment and the River of No Return. Tribes, painted faces, bejewelled, feathers, skins, patterns, wooden masks, peaceful friendly tribes, unwelcoming fierce tribes, one that 'cast away their daughters at birth; the dogs eat them. They do this because all the nations of the region are their enemies, with whom they war ceaselessly; and because if they were to marry off their daughters, the daughters would multiply their enemies.'

Leila was contentedly walking the long road, holding the book that finally told her where she was, when she spotted Lan. Lan was standing outside the 7/11 in her bare feet. She was 16 but looked younger. Her Cambodian eyes were shaped like lemons, and her skin was coffee brown. She wore a pink halter-neck top and tiny shorts, and a red baseball cap turned backwards on her head. Her breasts were like small buds inside her top, and her body was narrow, firm and childlike. Her hair was shoulder length and shiny brown with a blond streak flashing through it like a skunk marking. She had had the map of Cambodia tattooed on her thigh by a local guy who didn't know what shape Cambodia was. She had showed him an atlas, an old one. The shape had probably already changed, but she wasn't going back. She had two shopping bags with no handles, and Leila ran up and offered to carry one for her. Lan drove Leila home in an old truck with no pads on the pedals, her dusty bare feet pressing on the steel sticks. Lan was a terrible driver; the old car jolted all over the place and sounded like a typewriter. She passed other cars by closing her eyes for a few seconds and swallowing her breath. Apples rolled out of the bag across the floor. Leila scooped them back in when they arrived at the trailer park.

'Is the Ick-Man home?' Leila asked, staring at the trailer. It had cacti growing outside, and Lan had put little polka-dot curtains up over the windows. Inside it was immaculately tidy, and there were little cacti perched everywhere. Lan shrieked with laughter. Leila had known her fifteen minutes, and she had laughed from the belly easily three times. The rest of the time, she beamed. Lan made some lemonade for Leila. Leila had not smiled so much in months. She smiled now, and felt like she would split in two.

Ernie had taken to calling her Little Misericord. Not because she was miserable, he pointed out, but because she was a hidden precious thing that only God saw. And that's what she was, hidden away amid the collecting mania of the Clancy family. Dr Clancy had his collection of decoy ducks; Mrs Clancy collected old cans without labels and everything else in the world that came within reach of her sticky web; Jack collected knives, swords, military uniforms, cameras, watches; and Ernie collected soda cups. His car was overflowing with them. Only Desiree was a rejecter, not a collector. She had sent Leila to find Lan, to get the grass, to sell at the college. She had managed by sheer force of will to get her diet down to one egg a day and a diet bar. Now she lay about the house listless with her red wavy hair moulting over the furniture. Dr and Mrs Clancy were delighted with the way she looked, and she was suddenly taken to the mall all the way in LA on a regular basis. Leila agreed to go to Lan.

Misericord also meant pity and heart.

Lan had forgotten to pick up her laundry so Leila came with her to help. Leila insisted on carrying the big black bag full of skimpy slut clothes. When she swung it on her shoulder, the hot air puffed out of it, breathing on her neck like a strangely comforting detergent-breath beast. Leila wanted to do things for Lan because she wanted to learn things from her. Like how to keep smiling like a Cambodian.

'The Ick-Man is back in Cambodia,' Lan said. 'He spends half the year there. He teach English. Guns, girls and ganja. Thas what the white men say about Cambodia.'

She showed Leila a postcard the Ick-Man had sent her, instructing her to send him more of her money. She grew pot out the back, but she also fucked guys in the trailer park and their friends and charged them. 'I send him the money because I want him to stay longer,' Lan confided.

The Ick-Man was 5ft 3in, fat and bald, with hair growing on his back and on his ears. The only place hair didn't grow was on the palm of his hands and on top of his head. He had a face that looked like boiled mutton, pierced by two red cracks of eyes and upturned nostrils. If you stood close to him, as a child would, and only a child would be smaller than him, you could see his brain up his nostril. There was one photo of him as a child. He was ugly then too. 'Pig-heart' was written under the childhood photo by some unknown person, presumably not himself. All the trailer park kids sang the same song about him and stayed away.

Underneath that yellow shirt
Beats a heart of solid dirt
The most disgusting man on earth
Is the Ick-Man baby.

Lan had no pictures of her family. 'I come from North Cambodia by the Vietnam border. My father and mother had eight children and sold me and my sister to a brothel in Phnom Penh called Kiddy Corner when I was 11. Same age as you are. They swapped me for a motorbike and my sister for a television. They got no money. We sent them money, my sister still does. I stop. What they do for me? Sell me is all.'

The Ick-Man liked only children's bodies and liked children for their bodies only. Phnom Penh was an easy place to find child prostitutes. First, it had been Bangkok, the brothels in Chinatown, but one of them burnt down, and all the 12-year-old girls suffocated because they were chained to the beds. The Ick-Man grew wary of the ensuing publicity. In a bar in Patpong, morosely he sat and watched over-the-hill teenagers fire ping-pong balls from their cunts. A fellow westerner with similar appetites told him of the cornucopia that was Cambodia. Cambodia was much more innocent in a way, the brothels more open, less mercenary, less commercialised. Cambodia, land of plenty. He was in heaven. It was a different culture; American standards didn't apply. It was racist to impose the same standards across the board. And it was cheap. Only a few dollars a fuck for a sexy little thing that had no titties and no body hair.

'He take me to America because he afraid if he no have me here he would not be able to stop going for a little girl here.' Lan combed Leila's hair and then braided it. 'He like you, I bet. You 11.'

'I look older than 11. Desiree says I look 13 or even 14.'

'Why you want to grow up so fast?'

'Desiree says it's better to be grown up because you can order as many Cokes as you want in a restaurant and you can ride in the car with the air conditioner on and the windows down.'

'I no wanna be old and ugly.'

'My grandmother was married at 10. Same as you.'

'I no married. Never.' Lan was vehement.

Again Leila looked at childhood photos of the Ick-Man all over the trailer. He really had never been cute. Always podgy and menacing, even at three in front of a birthday cake on a chair that looked like a throne, surrounded by sullen friends. There are not many ugly children, but the Ick-Man was a pig-hearted baby.

Lan bit her bottom lip and said, 'I grow old here, and now I am just maid for the Ick-Man, and I like that better because he was always on top of me and breathing beef. But I don't want him bring new children back 'cos I don' wanna to go back to Cambodia. It's nice and quiet here in the American desert. No one bother me.'

'I have to go now, Lan. Have you the grass for Desiree? I'll be collecting it in future.'

'Ah, I wonder when Desiree get tired of doing so little, but she never do. Now you work for her for no pay, right?'

'I'm just collecting it as a favour. I live in their house. I eat food from their fridge.'

'You come to me for food. Come any time you want, you hear?'

Leila ran errands for Lan, and Lan gave her pocket money. Leila was able to buy food for herself and was saved from foraging in the fridge in the Clancys'. Mrs Clancy didn't seem to mind her eating in the house, but Desiree moaned about the food she bought. 'It's easy to have an eating disorder in this house. Mother buys rotten fruit because it's cheaper.'

Mrs Clancy unpacked the shopping erratically. One time, Ernie found himself sitting on a stack of newspapers, and underneath that there was a plastic bag of sliced ham she had forgotten to take out and put in the fridge.

On witnessing this, Mrs Clancy lamented bitterly, 'Nobody eats the food I buy.'

'Mother,' Desiree drawled, 'you buy cold cuts and leave them on the chair, and then they get buried under an avalanche of newspapers. But besides all those hazards, you never match the food up. What are we going to do with cold cuts when you don't buy bread? We can't just roll them up and pop them into our bellies. Cold cuts/bread. Cold cuts/bread. Just think next time.'

Leila laughed aloud and Mrs Clancy winked at her. She missed her Baba Ishmael because he was the one person in her life to cuddle her and hug her. Her Maman Farah had been cold. In the Clancys', no one touched either. But they did like each other, and there was no mention of school, to her great relief, so she read through Ernie's scrapbooks and his book on the West, and anything else she could lay her hands on. Besides, Lan hugged her every day and kissed her cheeks and combed her hair. She was a great cook and loved to feed people.

Lan cooked rice and stews with pineapples and peanuts. Leila rolled joints.

'You make perfect,' Lan said admiringly. 'Mine always look like a snake just swallowed a pig. Shh! He play it again.'

'What is it?'

'I dunno, but is beautiful.'

There was a Native American man who lived in the next trailer. They said he was from the Kickapoo tribe in the East. His people were shoved to Oklahoma last century, and he came out West when he was a child. His name was Joseph Smith, but the kids decided to give him an Indian-sounding name, so he was widely known as Sleeps Too Much. When he said he was from the East, he pronounced it with a deep eeeee, as if dredging that e out of the depths. He didn't talk to them much, but Leila did his laundry and he gave her a few dollars a time. He played the one Little Jimmy Scott CD over and over again. 'This land is mine; God gave this land to me.' Lan thought it was 'This land is mined.' It reminded her of home. Lan sang all her own words to songs: 'ill never be your pizza burning', 'Every time you go away you take a piece of meat with you.'

'Next time you do his wash, you go and see who sings so nice. Then we buy her CD for us and play it when we want.'

So take my hand and walk this way with me.

Though I am just a man.

Leila and Lan painted each other's fingernails and toenails, gave each other massages, did each other's hairstyles. They fed each other strawberries and shrimps at the table. Sometimes they dozed together in the hot afternoons. They spooned, with Lan always putting her arm around Leila. Leila settled comfortably into her embrace. She was the little one, the one to be cherished.

So take my hand and walk this way with me

Leila wished Lan would stop making money by fucking the trailer-park guys and the high-school guys who hung around the 7/11. Lan even gave Sleeps Too Much blowjobs when Leila did his laundry. All of this frightened Leila, and when she got a hint of a male presence in the trailer, she would sprint back up the dusty road out of the park and all the way over to Clancys', where she buried herself in the rubble at the thought of growing as old as Lan and having to do things.

Lan took care of Leila and always acted pleased to see her. She encouraged her to come around and tell stories about the American West. The desert breathed hot from the inside of the ground; the heat came up under the floor of the trailer and kept their bare feet warm. Lan had fans on all over the room, and they would lounge in front of them and drink homemade lemonade.

Lan said Leila was her teacher, since Lan never went to school. Leila took her responsibility seriously. She began to teach her to read and showed Lan a photo in the book, of Abraham Lincoln's wife, Mrs Lincoln, and some white women with six Indian chiefs in Washington. All the chiefs would be dead within 18 months of the photo, by a white man's disease, and the others were murdered. She kept coming back to that image; she would trail her finger across the white women with Mrs Lincoln in their bonnets and fussy dresses. Strange costumes. The Indians in native dress looked strong, fierce and resilient, but they weren't. And to think it was those whites that won. And won only because of their sheer savagery. Their methodical cruelty and violence was beyond what the Indians could comprehend. Lincoln had received the chiefs and told them that the white man would win because they were not as prone to fighting and killing each other as their 'red brethren'. And this was during the Civil War.

Leila was beginning to realise that the West was a special place. She felt lucky to have ended up here. The history was more sweeping, extreme and close than the haphazard ancient shifting history of Orap, which she could never follow. Over there, it was all turbaned tribes pushing each other this way and that. Here, good and evil were raw and magnified like the light on the mountains.

Lan joined the Clancys for Christmas Day. The Clancys opened their doors typically to all the flotsam that was washed in with the desert wind. Faz, Zolo, Leila, Lan and Patterson, the middle-aged mysterious intruder who watched TV in the house during the day and never explained himself. All gathered around the table with the Clancy family, Ernie, Jack and Desiree. The father, Dr Clancy, a distant and abstract man, seemed slightly bemused, as if he had an inclination that all was not apple pie in his half-German cluttered desert home.

Desiree was on all fours, staring at the cat's ass in the kitchen. She suddenly shuddered and shook her head.

'No. No. No.'

'What?' Zolo asked.

'That cat has a worm on its ass. Can you see it?'

Zolo and Leila bent to see a white worm wriggle on the cat's ass.

'I saw that and had a sudden urge to scoop up the worm with my fingernail and pop it into my mouth.' Desiree walked back to the living room with the tray of roast potatoes. At the table, she raised a toast. 'Fuck Weight Watchers! Here's to a worm off a cat's ass.' They all clinked their glasses. Dr Clancy busied himself with the turkey carving. Mrs Clancy leaned over to Lan and Leila.

'Dr Clancy and I met two Danish homo-sex-you-als in Morocco. Very interesting people.'

'Really, Mother, not all homosexuals are interesting,' Jack said.

'Yes, but these vere Danish,' Mrs. Clancy said.

'Mrs Clancy,' Zolo said, 'now that I've met you, I understand Jack and Desiree so much more.'

Ernie quietly and without fanfare removed himself from the table.

'Why is Ernie so stiff?' Faz asked Jack.

'We were all brought up in quite a formal manner befitting children who were descended from European aristocracy.'

'No. He's literally stiff, I mean.'

'He had some kind of accident ten years ago,' Desiree shrugged. 'Fell off a ladder looking at the gutters.'

'I can't imagine him doing anything so practical as look at the gutters,' Zolo marvelled.

'Hey, Ernie,' Faz asked him just before he left the room. 'What gets you up in the morning? What's your passion?'

Ernie looked serenely through Faz as if he were made of glass. 'Reading the newspapers.'

'Don't you ever want to go out? Get married.'

'Oh, well, I would like eventually to do that. I need someone to cook and clean.'

'What gave you the impression women do that, Ernie?' Jack sighed. 'Certainly not Mother or Desiree.'

Dr Clancy rose without a word and lumbered in after his son to watch TV.

'Tell us more about the Wild West,' Lan demanded.

Leila was in the throes of obsession and didn't need prompting. 'Once upon a time, Black Kettle was given assurance by the government that he was protected, but he wasn't.'

'You're giving the story away by saying that,' Zolo snapped.

'What?' Lan glared.

'By saying he wasn't, you know what's coming next.'

'No, leave her tell story.' Lan banged her fork off her glass. The note rang through the dining room. 'Leila tell good story.'

Leila looked from one to the other, smiling shyly. She adored them both. 'Colonel Chivington wanted to be governor of Colorado and he wanted to do it by killing all the Indians. At Sand Creek, the Indians huddled under an American flag for protection, and Black Kettle said they would be all right because he was promised they would be, but the Cowboys shot them all anyway. There were women hiding in a hole, and they sent a six-year-old girl out waving a white flag. The Cowboys shot the girl and killed all the squaws. One Cowboy cut off a woman's cunt and put it on a stick. Other men put cut-off cunts over their hats while riding in ranks.'

'Where did you learn that word?' Zolo asked, shocked. Then he looked at Lan and raised his eyebrows. 'Oh boy!'

'Charming,' Jack said. 'I don't know if Mother and Father would care to hear your history of the West.'

'Cunt on a stick,' Desiree said. 'Sounds like something you might buy at the 7/11.'

Leila's eyes burned with outrage for all past crimes. 'Chivington went back to Denver, claiming to have killed warriors in a great battle, but it was only women and children and old men who they caught sleeping.'

'Well, I'm sure they were punished, dear.' Mrs Clancy smiled and laid her hand on the young zealot's arm.

'One night, at the Denver opera, they put one hundred of the Indian scalps on display, and the orchestra played, and the audience stood and applauded.'

'They mightn't have applauded the cunts.' Jack rolled his eyes. 'Leila, you are the smartest child I have ever met. You scare me sometimes. But has it ever occurred to you that you're not an Indian? You too are here in the West on their old land.'

'You are so smart, Leila.' Mrs Clancy sighed. 'Vot vill become of you? Don't your parents vant to come rushing over and take care of you? Make sure you live to your potential?'

Leila then told the story of how 30 million buffalo were wiped out. 'The Kiowa Indians were not vegetarians. They ate buffalo. They lived in tepees made of buffalo. They wore buffalo. Their containers were buffalo hides, bladders, stomachs. They worshipped the buffalo.'

'We get it,' Jack said. 'Living in and consuming their gods but never diminishing them. Granted, it is sad about the Indians, but it was so long ago, and we all inhabit this space courtesy of that genocide.'

'What's with the buffalo? You're not a vegetarian now?'

'No.'

'I consider vegetarianism an eating disorder.' Zolo speared some turkey with a fork.

Baby Zero, listen to the story Leila then told at Christmas dinner. They all listened. You should, too. It is a story that keeps happening. A loop in history. A story I think about. When Leila told the story, she had the power. She had cut out the story and put it in her scrapbooks, with handwritten notes at the side margins. She had begun writing parts of a diary in the scrapbooks as well as notes on clippings.

The Grand Duke Alexis Alexandrovitch of Russia came to join in the new white craze of buffalo hunting. The whites thought the buffalo was the stupidest game animal in the world. They were so easy to kill. Hard to miss with their big sweeping herds carpeting the planes. Custer, the general who liked to kill sleeping Indians on reservations, and Buffalo Bill, who claimed to have killed 4,000 beasts, were to be the Grand Duke's escorts. They were instructed to make sure he got at least one buffalo as a trophy.

First kill was reserved for the Grand Duke, of course. The big Cheese himself, mounted upon a horse, and armed with a custom-made Smith and Wesson rifle.

And of course the buffalo came.

The Grand Duke of Russia fired six shots at one buffalo and missed completely. He turned his attentions to another buffalo and emptied his revolver in the general direction. No joy. The buffalo cruised on implacably. Buffalo Bill, sensing this was going to be harder than he thought, gave the now bulletless Grand Duke his own rifle and whipped the Grand Duke's horse so that it ran right up to the buffalo. Point blank range. Alexis did not hesitate. One buffalo fell dead. They drank champagne.

'Strange trio on the Plains,' Leila wrote in the margins. 'The Grand Duke, Custer and Buffalo Bill.'

Strange trio on the plains, Baby Zero.

On the last day, Custer told the Grand Duke that they should play a game. They pretended the buffalo were Indians. With the immortal and searing words of Custer, 'Boys, here's a chance for a great victory over that bunch of redskins on the other side of the hill!' the trio launched their attack and galloped, guns blazing, into the massive herd of giant beasts. Custer's golden ringlets were flying behind him. He was such a dandy. The Grand Duke adored this game, and managed to shoot a dozen himself. All in all, they killed

50 buffalo, and as usual took only one or two as a trophy and left the rest to rot. The Grand Duke Alexis Alexandrovitch kissed Custer in all the excitement.

Kissed him, Baby Zero. Imagine.

The next time Custer led a charge on real Indians, he and all his battalion were killed. Indian squaws found his corpse among the dead, and they stuck sharp awls into each of his ears and right through his dead brain into the centre of his head.

('Why did they do that?' Zolo asked suspiciously.

'They did this to improve his hearing because he had not listened to them when they told him that if he broke his peace promise and started fighting them again, the Everywhere Spirit would cause him to be killed.'

'In a way, the Everywhere Spirit got the kissing Grand Duke Alexis Alexandrovitch, too.' Ernie winked. 'Peasants who had had enough of his ilk shot what must have been his nephew, years later, and his entire family.

'Sometimes, only sometimes,' Jack agreed, 'and rarely at that, there is such a thing as comeuppance in history.)

The Everywhere Spirit could not help the buffalo.

When the railroads were built, the whites would spot buffalo herds from the trains, and all the males would get their guns and hang out the windows, shooting for fun.

Then someone discovered that if you spotted the leader and you didn't kill her but wounded her, the rest of the herd would not leave her, but mill about her. So you could wipe out the entire herd in one go without even moving your horse about too much.

'It shoots today, and kills tomorrow,' one person said of the efficient new rifles. You could kill a buffalo from half a mile away with them. Now one hunter could kill two hundred buffalo from a single spot, stopping only to piss on his rifle to cool it down, and then continuing to shoot.

Orlando A. Bond, AKA Brick, killed 300 beasts in one day and 5,855 in one outing. Brick was deafened permanently by the sound of his own rifle.

They said the very air itself stank with dead buffalo.

Then the plains were quiet.

The buffalo were gone.

The Kiowa Indians said that the buffalo knew they could no longer protect their people, so they had a buffalo council, and the few surviving buffalo were spotted by an Indian woman one morning, walking into the mountain that opened up before the last herd. She said she caught a glimpse of the world inside the mountain, and it was the past. The old days. Before the settlers and hunters came. She said, 'The rivers ran clear, not red. The wild plums were in blossom, chasing the red buds up the inside slopes.'

That's the story, Baby Zero.

They all sat at the dinner table and listened to Leila; even Zolo listened. She felt the storytelling was making her powerful. These stories were the first power of her life. Leila was having a great Christmas.

Mrs Clancy shook her head and said to Desiree, 'And you say the brother is the genius. This child, tsk, tsk.'

'You have your own extinctions,' Jack said. 'Your own slaughtering. Your own trail of dead things. Yet you can sit at Christmas dinner with no passport, no money, no parents, and worry about the buffalo.'

'There was always something wrong with her,' Zolo said, but he listened.

Not only did Zolo listen to Leila but he came to her later when they were all dozing by the fire.

'Does Desiree ever talk about me? You know, when you two are alone.'

'Yes.'

'What does she say?' And he looked so pleadingly at his little sister that she was momentarily speechless. 'She says you are cool.'

Zolo was so pleased that he got up and took up one of her scrapbooks off the floor and gave it into her hands. 'Happy Christmas, Frog.'

'Happy Christmas, Zolo.'

The Everywhere Spirit was not there when Leila knocked on the trailer door and walked in.

'Lan?'

'Hello.'

She turned, her flesh creeping in slow ripples across her body. The Ick-Man was back. He brightened up when he saw her, but it wasn't much like brightening up—more like his flesh resettled in a manner that made him look more aware, cautious, predatory. His face was an old baby face: wrinkleless but aged. The top of his head shone red reflecting the red roof of the trailer.

'I was looking for Lan,' Leila blurted out and pawed blindly behind her for the door handle. The Ick-Man smiled a hideous smile. He had no shirt on and freckled breasts sat like fat sleeping seals on his round rock of a stomach. He stood and his breasts jiggled. Leila fled.

Desiree was rooting through the fridge. Her hair brushing over the piled masses of unidentifiable produces. Leila was breathless. 'The Ick-Man is back.'

Desiree's face contorted in disgust. She reached for a jar way at the back and pulled it out. It was clear with green liquid, and two stones floated inside.

'Whoa! I think these are Uncle Peter's gallstones from years ago. What are they doing here? Hey, they're kind of beautiful. Golden. We could make jewellery out of them. Never go near there again. While the Ick-Man is there. Let me handle business now, okay?'

Lan came knocking on the door. Desiree and she conferred for a bit. Lan came in and gave Desiree a big bag of grass.

'Where's Leila?' Lan asked.

'She told me he's back. I told her not to go near him.'

Lan sighed. She had three small half-moon bruises on her slim upper arm.

'He thinks he can come back and be my pimp, but I'm not young any more.'

Desiree nodded sympathetically but distractedly.

'Can I stay here?'

Desiree jolted. 'I don't know, Lan . . .'

Leila was listening from the kitchen. There had been no issue about her staying. She was surprised. She could share a room with Lan. The room with all the small white goose feathers on the floor. She had lived in it so quietly that she had not even disturbed the dust. Lan left and Desiree came into the kitchen. She knew Leila had heard.

'You don't shit on your own doorstep.'

'She could share Ernie's room.'

'Forget about it.' Desiree tore open the fridge and resumed her fruitless aimless search. There was some whipped cream in the door, and she pulled it out and bent the spray nozzle backwards, inhaling the gas. Her pupils shook for a moment and she beamed.

'A day without a buzz is a day that never wuz!'

'I can tell you about the Ghost Dance.'

'Okay, but let me get stoned first; otherwise you'd be unbearable. Let me get this straight, you have become the foremost 12-year-old authority on the West through reading one book that was a companion to a TV series.'

'Yes.'

'That's so uncool, it's cool.' Desiree laughed and handed her a bag and some rolling papers. 'Hey, kiddo. Earn your right to tell the story.'

'We once lived in a house in Orap and it was on a river. This river had a river inside. I know what that was now.'

'What? Is this the Ghost Dance?'

'No, not yet. The river inside the river is the story. There is your life, and then there is the story of your life.'

'I need to smoke more before you go on.'

Lan came up to Leila at the 7/11.

'Teeny Weenie Leila! You don't come around any more. I see you do Sleeps Too Much's laundry but not mine.'

'Desiree told me to stay away from the Ick-Man. It's not you.'

'I miss you.'

'I miss you too.'

Lan laughed loudly, but she looked tired. She had her hair up and her neck was red. She confided in Leila. 'Do you see me? I'm always covered in marks now. Like he's writing all over me.'

'The Ick-Man?'

'He takes my money and threatens me with police and immigration if I say no. It's always like this when he's at home, but now I'm 16, he finds me old and is worse because he doesn't love me any more.'

'Can't Lan come and live with us?' Leila asked Desiree that night.

'No. I'm away most of the time. I'm in the dorms. I'm going out with Zolo. He's a wild man, your brother. And he drives the professors crazy because he sails through their classes without showing up. He's a genius on the computer. He's become a hacker. How cool is that?'

'Why can't she move there and go to school?' Leila did not want to talk about Zolo since he hadn't contacted her in two months and Desiree never invited her along on sales trips any more.

'She can't. Lan . . . oh Jesus. We can't have her up there. She's a whore, Leila. I like her, but she's such a whore. She'll never stop. She doesn't know anything else. She doesn't even see anything strange about it.'

'Women are like cotton,' Leila said.

Leila drove with Desiree up to the college and asked Zolo could Lan stay with him. Zolo said no. Leila asked him could she herself stay with him. He said no.

'You and Desiree have fun in the desert.'

'Yeah, but she's up here most of the time now.'

'You have Lan to keep you company.'

'A Cambodian in the Wild West.'

They all laughed.

'Hey,' Zolo grinned. 'At least everyone has heard of Cambodia. I've yet to meet an American who's heard of Orap.'

'Any more letters from Maman and Baba?'

'I've heard you get letters every week at the House With No Anus.'

'They're from Mehrdad.'

'What?'

'He writes every week. I gave Maman and Baba my new address and wrote to them, but they keep writing to Mo instead.'

'Mehrdad was *my* friend!'

'Do you write to him? I'm sure he'd write back.'

'Writing is for girls.'

'Mehrdad writes.'

'Yeah, well, he was always a bit of a girl.'

'Can Lan . . .'

'NO. NO. NO.'

The Everywhere Spirit was nowhere to be found.

Leila awoke in the soft bed feeling soggy. There was a moist hot feeling between her legs. She moved slowly and felt herself leak. She put her hand down and felt about. Everything was thick and wet. She took her hand out from under the covers and saw blood—smelling it instinctively. There was a dark red clot on her finger. This was a short life, she thought. I am twelve, almost thirteen. Gone.

In the bathroom, she hung her head down and saw that blood was smeared all over her thighs. She sat on the toilet seat, streaking it with blood. The stained sheets were in the bath on top of the thousand empty shampoo bottles. A string of dark red goo came out when she pissed. It came out behind the streel of piss. From somewhere else. She couldn't imagine where. She couldn't go to Dr Clancy because of where it was coming from. She raced down the desert road in horror.

Lan opened the door and starred at Leila in consternation.

'You have to take me to a hospital.'

'Who's that?' the Ick-Man said in a gruff voice.

'No one.'

The Ick-Man came to the door. A slobber of a smile manifested on the lower part of his face, but his eyes remained piggy and inexpressive.

'Come in.'

'Lan!' Leila screamed.

Lan stepped out of the trailer and soon she was laughing.

'Oh.' She slapped Leila on the face and hugged her.

'Why did you do that?'

'That's what my mother—not my real mother, but the woman who ran the Kiddy Corner—that's what she did to me when I got it.'

'Got what.'

'Your period. So early for you. You only 12. I was 14 thank-god. Not good for business.'

'I'm not in business. How long will I bleed?'

'Until you're almost 50.'

'Will it not kill me? How can I bleed for that long and not die?'

'It's for babies.' Lan laughed again. 'Now you can make them.'

'I don't want this baby.'

'You have a baby?' Lan looked at Leila, holding her shoulders.

'I'm bleeding.'

'No, that doesn't mean. You have to be with someone. Come in for lemonade.' The Ick-Man appeared at the door with his shirt off. He was holding a glass jug of yellow lemonade up to his chest. His freckled breasts were magnified.

'Na, na.' Lan waved dismissively at him. 'We go to 7/11. Leila need stuff.'

Lan visited Leila. They sat in the living room. Patterson had the TV on to the sports channel.

'Is there any sport you don't like?' Lan asked him.

Patterson was silent.

'Leila, come over. I want to bring you somewhere special.'

'Why?'

'To honour you.'

Patterson grunted and then said, 'Synchronised swimming.'

'Oh,' Lan said. 'That's the only one I like. Come now.'

'Why now?'

'Leila, why you so difficult?' Lan was shouting. Leila was scared. Lan's eye was black and her lip was swollen.

'Okay.'

'Okay?' Lan slumped almost disappointed to get her way. 'Okay. Good.'

'You don't look happy.' Leila was confused.

'Les go, kiddo.'

They drove in silence around the back of the trailer park. There was a few acres of used cars, gutted, burnt, their journey done. Leila never went there. Not even to explore. It was endless. She looked out the window. So many crashed cars. Airbags blown out.

'What are they for?'

'I dunno.' Lan sighed. 'Junkyard. For men. You so little, Leila. You ask so many question.'

They came to a clearing in the cars. Far away from the trailer park. There was an inflatable kiddy pool full of water. Leila was delighted.

'You did this for me?'

'To celebrate you.'

Leila's eyes were downcast. 'It stopped. I can't have babies now.'

'What?'

'It's over. No more blood. After a few days, it just went.'

'It come back.'

'But you said I would have it till I'm 50.'

'Not all at once.'

Leila was baffled. She resolved to ask Desiree. True, Desiree was brutal, but she was more pragmatic than Lan and explained things better.

'You want to swim?'

'I didn't bring a suit.'

'No one here but us.' Lan took off all her clothes and Leila did too. She was shyer about her body than Lan. She had never taken her clothes off before in front of anyone except Mehrdad. Lan's body was covered in bruises and burns. The water was up to their shins. It was nice and cold. Leila sat down. Lan splashed her. They goofed around.

Leila started. There was a noise from a car.

The Ick-Man baby.

Leila jumped out of the pool and grabbed her clothes in fright.

The Ick-Man came from the car. He grabbed her.

'Lan. Lan.'

Lan stood naked and said, 'You only supposed to watch. You promise no touch.'

'Lan. No. Lan. Help me. No. Lan,' Leila screamed in a crescendo of fear and horror. 'Help me. NOOOO.'

The Ick-Man took her to a car and lay down on top of her. His breath was beef. She could hear Lan sobbing. He stroked her and would not stop his probing. His fingers shoved into her mouth made her sick and the vomit swirled in her throat; her eyes watered. He had her legs pressed wide apart and was shoving inside her, sweating. A shadow came behind him. It was Sleeps Too Much. He tore at the Ick-Man. The Ick-Man covered his head with his hands as Sleeps Too Much punched him. The punches hit him with such ferocity that his skull sounded wet. Leila scrunched up into a ball. Lan was gone. Sleeps Too Much reached into the car and pulled Leila out. She slithered into his arms, and he carried her to his car. He gave her his shirt. They drove home.

'Are you an Indian?' she asked him, wearing his giant shirt and biting her knuckles.

'No. All the kids think I look like one though. I guess it's the long hair.'

'I thought you were an Indian.'

'I'm Greek. From New Jersey.'

Leila said. 'I thought you were an Indian.'

'So you said. You want an Indian? That guy Patterson who hangs around your house, he's full blood. Ask him.'

'Where are we going?'

'To the police.'

'I can't. Zolo would kill me. I don't have the papers for the country. All my stuff is made up. They can't see it.'

'We have to stop that guy. He never gets caught. He usually goes out of the country to do his stuff. He knew you had no one.'

'I can't go to the police,' Leila screamed and pulled at the car doors. Sleeps Too Much leant over and pulled her hands away from the locks. 'My parents are in a camp and there is a war and a revolution . . .' As she spoke, Leila heard the words. They weighed in heavier that she had thought they were. War, revolution.

Sleeps Too Much shook his head. 'Up to you. One day I'll just go in and kill him.'

'How did you know I was there?'

'You're very chatty for a little kid who's just been attacked.'

Leila was ashamed. She felt giddy. Blindly disoriented. She was bleeding again over his shirt. There would be no end to this blood once it had started.

'Your friend Patterson came looking for you at Ick-Man's trailer.'

'Patterson?'

'He had thought about how Lan had come for you. We put two and two together. I seen them prepare all day. Bringing water back and forth. It took a while to find you. You have to stay away from that whore, Lan. Don't come to the park no more. I'll get someone else to do my laundry. You escaped with your life, kid. You were lucky, believe it or not.'

'He was going to kill me?' Short life, Leila thought.

'He got AIDS. Full-blown. Lan got a dose of HIV, but he keeps all the medication for himself, and she won't go to a doctor. I might have it too from her. I just might have. And every other sucker around the fucking park. I always used a condom with the little whore; boy am I glad now. But I bet some of them didn't and she's greedy; she don't care. Was keeping it to myself, but I'll tell you what, kid. If you don't go to the police, I'll let everyone know and those sickos will be lynched anyway.'

'Will Lan be okay?' Leila was losing blood and she passed out in the car.

Underneath that yellow shirt.

Beats a heart of solid dirt.

That story had an end. Not one of those that went on for ever.

Leila told no one.

Sleeps Too Much told no one.

Patterson told no one.

Leila would have liked to ask him what tribe he was from, but she was ashamed to catch his eye. Now she possessed her own dirty secret. But it didn't change anything at the Clancys'. Every night, Dr Clancy would get up from the table after ingesting whatever atrocious concoction his wife had conjured up for him. He would open a bottle of wine and pour it into a giant glass, almost the size of a fish bowl.

'I'll just have a glass of wine, and go in and listen to some opera,' he would say and close the living-room door, sit on a chair and blast his stereo, slurping his wine, his eyes watering from the music or the liquor. Mrs Clancy would talk to Leila, or Ernie, without expecting responses. Desiree would pull herself out of bed, emerge disgruntled, stomp around demanding something, smoke dope and disappear in the car. She explained in raw detail every aspect of sex education. Leila was not impressed. She decided there was not too much joy to be got from all of that. Desiree grimly agreed and advised her to rely on more solid sources of pleasure like drugs and booze. Leila had bad dreams. And stopped looking down there. It was a source of pain and great gulping shame. Best to be erased. The Ick-Man went to Cambodia for ever. He carried the plague with him to all the new little fresh Lans in the Kiddy Corner outside Phnom Penh. Their fathers riding the motorcycles they'd swapped for their daughters, the mothers and brothers watching the televisions. Better they'd have killed them at birth like the nasty Indian tribe. Lan was run out of the trailer park when news of her disease got out. No one heard from her again. Rumour had it she went to Las Vegas.

Sniffing around the West for a clean place to die.

Sleeps Too Much went back to sleeping and listening to Little Jimmy Scott.

This land is mine. God gave this land to me.

Leila dreamed of joining Lan in Vegas and helping her to die. She did not want her best friend to be alone. In the end, she knew that Lan was just a lonely child.

Baby Zero, if Leila was left all alone, she never blamed anyone. She knew only parents have any interest in looking after their own children and sometimes they can't. If no letters were given to her, she knew that it was her uncle who held them back. There was no malice on his part, just carelessness. She was well trained at even a decade on this earth to accept the self-obsession and unwieldy sense of entitlement that the men in her family felt. She did not harbour resentment at that point. She had the understanding that events had taken over, that history was pushing them around, that she had no more significance as an individual than a leaf on a tree in a forest. She had the story in her head of her cousins who had died in the snow. She knew their deaths did not matter since their parents were also dead. At least she was somewhere warm. At least she had Mehrdad's letters to stick into the scrapbooks and make him part of the story she wove. What happened with the Ick-Man couldn't fade. The nightmares would never go away. His shadow stretching beyond hers on the sandy road, his watching face outside every window. He had taken something from her that she was unaware she possessed.

PART IV

REFUGEE CAMP TO IRELAND

Chapter Thirteen

Gone to Gondwana

It was a bad time for girls. The news came over the mountains. The revolutionaries in Orap were using girl soldiers, and their distaste for them was illustrated by the fact that they were putting them in the most danger. Poor as goats, scrawny, fingers of straw, and inside as alone as caves. The new Orapian regime scooped them up. Trained them to run ahead of the regular forces. Slim-hipped child warriors. Brains turned at the edges, curled with bad ideas paraded as truths. Little girls shedding coloured tribal cloth for universal khaki death. Hiding henna-tinted hair under black veils. Bleeding secrets away from their commanders. They slept outside in huddles. Bad years for girls in the mountains. Folded into each other, limbs entwined, a sleeping carpet of ruin.

When the UN collected bodies in the trenches and the live ones were patched up in the camp hospital, they brought in a reporter from the *New York Times*. 'Look, child soldiers.' They pointed. And the girls spat borrowed dogmas and demanded to go back to the war, the ugliness of their dreams shocking even the most seasoned war men. No one could tell what age the dead ones really were. A tangle of bodies pried apart, ripening quickly. Mehrdad helped to bury them side by side. Not even names for the graves.

Bad years for girls, running beyond the mountain, barefoot in scabrous fields, unyielding hard snow-packed earth, no bellies grown soft or huge, and no hand to push back a strand of hair from a radiant face. Ishmael hung around the hospital and tried to help out in a doctor's capacity. They were not sure of his qualifications, so they offered him jobs an orderly would take. He refused, but stood and saw the putrefied forms that doctors would not comment on to the *New York Times* reporter. Could not professionally say. He overheard one hospital worker tell the reporter, 'They were all young: 6, 8, 12, 22. It was hard to tell what ages they were. They were small-made.'

'What do you mean, small-made?' the reporter asked.

'They were all so tiny and slight. Like Asians.'

Ishmael brought the paper to his wife. 'Mehrdad showed me this article about girl child soldiers. The world is finally paying attention. "Child Warriors in Former Tiny Principality of Orap." Page eight. We're not even front page,' he shouted. For the first time, he admitted he was scared for his 10-year-old girl.

'At least she is out of here,' his wife said, putting on her reading glasses and taking the paper. 'We got her out. Your brother will take care of her and Zolo. She is safe. Unlike these girls left behind.'

'Small-made,' he said, quoting from the paper. 'Small-made.'

Ishmael was too depressed to read much more of the paper. The world could go on without him. In his current state of mind, he preferred reading the ancient magazines. He prepared a piece to present to his audience today. It was a piece in his *National Geographic* about Gondwanaland. South America, Africa, Antarctica, Australia and India were once one land mass known as Gondwanaland. North America, Europe and Asia were another super continent, Laurasia. At the end of the Palaeozoic, both these land areas joined into one colossal continent called Pangaea. Then this whopping continent fractured, and the separate pieces floated away to their present positions. It was hard from the drawing to tell where land-locked Orap had been. Orap had always been disappearing.

'I've signed us up for moving. We're leaving,' Farah told him.

'We got a place?'

'Not yet, but we'll take the first one that comes up.'

'The US?' He stood up, excited.

'That would be ideal, of course.' Farah spoke as if she was speaking to an idiot child. 'We'll go wherever is available, but we have to move soon.'

Ishmael looked at the map on the page, but the world was stuck together in one awful clump. 'Gondwanaland.'

One more interminable day, Ishmael and Farah walked side by side through the camp. Farah kicked a hardened piece of snow. First with one foot and then with the other. Anger focused on to the snowball. She frowned and repeated the words, 'I can't believe this is happening.' They waited in line for the food parcel for two hours and she held his hand, Farah's green eyes catching his momentarily. Her hair was shoulder length and dyed blond at the ends. The roots had grown so long it was half-and-half. Her lips were full and sensual, and he suppressed the urge to kiss them.

'It will be all right. We will sort it out. It's a new beginning. A good omen. A sign of hope.'

Farah looked at her husband as if he were mad. Ishmael's hair was thinning on the top but not grey; he was tall and broad-shouldered. The weight he had lost in the camp suited him. She thought he looked younger than she did now, even though he was years older.

Her family had never liked him, but that was not unusual. As soon as the wedding was arranged, the complaints traditionally began. The way Farah saw it, no Orapian was liked by their in-laws. The custom was that the woman married into the man's family and acted as their servant. Her only hope of power was to produce sons and lord it over them. Then the sons would get married, and she could exact revenge on the sons' wives. That way, even though the perpetrators never got punished, the victim got revenge. Farah had chosen Ishmael because he had been estranged from his mad family, and his brother Mo was not interested in custom, only in money and prestige.

Farah had fair skin and green eyes. She dyed her hair blond like all Orapian middle-class and upper-class women. Mo had the embarrassing habit of telling patients and colleagues that she was American. He thought it gave them status. She never knew how to react when confronted. She was grateful to Mo for taking care of her children and getting them out of the camp and into school in California. He was not an ordinary man, but when the chips came down, he had proved to be compassionate and family-minded.

With their food parcel, Farah and Ishmael walked hand in hand back towards the tent they shared with a large annoying peasant family. When the children had left, they had been forced to give up their module housing and return to one bed. In their old life, they would not have walked like this—like courting teenagers. But camp life was nothing if not infantilising, and they had nothing but each other.

Ishmael noted that when they reached the spot where the terrain had forced Farah to abandon her snowball, her foot found it again and she gave it a good kick.

'You are a loyal person.' He squeezed her hand. She was surprised, not understanding the reasoning behind his comment.

'What else would I be?' she replied curtly.

'Do you remember when His Majesty changed the calendar?'

'Yes,' Farah sighed. Ishmael was still so attached to the old Orap. He genuinely seemed to have been invested in the lies that were spun so crudely.

'Leila was born in the year zero. Her birth date was always 0.'

Farah laughed; she liked to talk about the children, to feel connected and closer. 'We called her Baby Zero.'

'Baby Zero.' Ishmael smiled. 'Well, if you read the newspapers, the new government has changed the official name of the country to Orapistan. . . .'

'Such nonsense. What rabble we'll be associated with—all those countries that end in "stan". What was their contribution to humanity? Your family went to a lot of trouble to flee from one of them only to end up in one of them.'

'Yesterday they announced that this is no longer the year 10. They are starting from scratch. This is the year zero again.'

Farah sat on a snow bank. 'I feel dizzy.'

Ishmael sat beside her. 'Mehrdad told me he would get iron tablets from the clinic for you. You're probably anaemic.'

'I can't believe this has happened to me.'

'To us.'

'No. To me.' Farah looked at the blue sky and the snowy mountains. There was a patch where the snow had melted. The burning hill. Still burning.

'I don't want this baby to be born in a refugee camp. That's no start for a child. Ishmael, I'm 43. I'm not up for this. Two children were enough for me. We should have been more careful.'

'Takes two. I thought you were past it.'

'We were like irresponsible children fooling under a blanket, with another family in the room.'

Ishmael opened the parcel and tore a piece of dry bread, then opened a can of sardines. He stuck a boneless sardine into the bread and handed it to his wife.

'There was nothing else to do.' Ishmael suppressed a grin. He was delighted with the news. Farah pushed the crude sandwich away. 'I'm not eating in public sitting at the side of the road. We must maintain our dignity.'

'My point is . . .' Ishmael munched the sandwich, speaking with his mouth full of little fish. '. . . we're going to have another Baby Zero.'

Farah had forgotten how mired in the physical she became when she was pregnant. How the mind was belittled in the presence of the growing belly. The belly that knew how to make a human being and the mind that could only dream. She hated sharing a tent with another family. The family knew she had conceived amongst them and that irked her. It poked holes in her aloofness, and she felt they were smirking at her when really they were only smiling. She threw up beside the bed, and they complained immediately about the smell before she had a chance to fetch water and clean it up. Ishmael laughed heartily when the family shook their heads and said, 'At your age, really.' He liked people knowing he still had some last vestiges of potency, even basic animal ones. Farah's anger simmered in her until the baby was cooking in a cauldron of bitterness. She did not cry in front of Ishmael because she didn't want to admit to any more vulnerability. It was bad enough waddling about in the mud and ice, suspecting people snickering, first at her swollen belly and then at her old face.

'Forty-three won't be old in America,' Ishmael told her.

'It's old here.'

There was opium in the camp. Ishmael got some for her, but she refused it. All the young men were developing nasty habits, and she was grateful every day that Zolo was out of harm's way. He was so wilful. They never had any success in taming him as a child. As a teenager, he would be twice as bad. When he was a toddler, he used to punch her and Ishmael. They did not want to break his spirit, so they never punished him. She regretted that now. On his, own as a foreigner, he would need more discipline than they had ever instilled in him. They had spoilt him because they thought he would be part of the generation that would inherit power in Orap. He had not been raised to have the patience of a refugee. And worse, Farah thought as she lay awake at night feeling the child hiccup in her stomach: he was not raised to be responsible for his sister. In other boys, that was ingrained and taken for granted. They had put no such burden or expectations on him because it had not seemed necessary. Farah would never say it to Ishmael since it would anger him, but she did not think that Mo would be capable of looking out for Leila either. Leila, her second child. When the midwife had pulled her out head first, she was white and grasping, with both hands outstretched. The midwife slapped Farah on the face before she had even time to hold her child. Slapped when her arms were outstretched for her newborn. She had been stunned. Then the midwife had hugged her and explained, 'It's a girl. We do that in my village for women who have girls. Takes the bad luck out of it.'

Incensed, Farah had the woman fired. There was no place for peasant superstition in the modern Orap. She herself had a university degree, and her own mother had gone to school in Germany. She considered herself a modern, emancipated woman.

Her child should be raised to be an educated subject, whether male or female. But Farah saw in the camp all roles revert. Abrasive women battled the mud, trying to heat unmarked canned food on camping gas rings, standing in queues for water because the men were too proud. The daughters were as shrill and embattled as their mothers, the feckless sons smoking opium and strutting around, aggressively bored. In extreme times, roles revert and any tiny gains disappear overnight. Even if the men felt powerless, they had one power left. The power over women.

The camp women were workhorses for the camp men. That way a man always had a servant, was never quite at the very bottom. The women had their children, but there was an innate servitude in that dynamic. They did everything for their children, more for the sons who would take them over and less for the daughters who would become them. Some camp girls were becoming fundamentalist and joining the child soldiers, running off to join the enemy's ranks, claiming they would be respected for their fight and not looked at as objects for men's pleasure. But Farah thought that they got it wrong. The veils they were wearing were saying just that— that their whole existence was sexualised, while the men's was not. But it was a myth that the veils made women submissive, Farah noted. Every Orapian women seemed to be a force, even if it was to secure their children's future and not their own.

But Farah did not worry about other people. She knew what was coming. The eighth month of her pregnancy was in the autumn. Women were naturally different from men because there was a situation in which they found themselves that was completely intractable. The eighth month. Knowing where it has to come out. Knowing there is nowhere large enough. Almost every woman she saw, no matter how ordinary, had been through the same terror. She was 43, living in a refugee camp, a registered nurse and midwife herself, pregnant. Her husband spent his time smoking opium and reading *National Geographics*—as damp and yellow-spined as himself—to a bunch of peasants who sneered behind his back. Ishmael bragged to everyone that he had connections to the royal family; he hinted that he was related, though he was only their doctor. Farah implored him to stop his boasting. She knew that the other refugees cared little for the royal family. They had been spied on by the secret police, subjected to random disappearances of kin, and the tiny upper class had flaunted its wealth in a time of economic desperation. Oppression was a given; they expected nothing more. For the general population in Orap, bad government was as natural and inevitable as bad weather.

'I have something to tell you that I haven't told a soul,' Ishmael proudly told his wife one night as they lay beside each other on the bottom bunk. 'Her Majesty, the queen, has breast cancer.'

'How do you know that?'

'She let me examine her and do the tests in private.'

'She showed you her breasts?'

'I'm her doctor.'

'You were her plastic surgeon.'

'She couldn't trust her real doctor.'

'Ishmael, we have to leave here. Get out. The war is getting closer. I don't want my child born in a refugee camp. It's not good for his future. It would always be a black mark against him.'

'He won't be born here, I promise.'

'So you keep saying, but what are you going to do about it?'

'I know people in the camp. The UN people. They know I was high up. A famous surgeon. A Fatagagas. Our family has not been forgotten. We are influential people. I'll talk to them. Just leave it to me.'

The next morning, she saw her husband walking along the burning hill, looking at the little flames as if they were rodents. He was kicking through them with his scuffed designer shoes. She walked up the hill to him. He started when he saw her.

'Did you do anything?'

'What?'

'I just spent the last two hours waiting in line, getting water. I thought you were going to the UN office. I hear they are assigning places in host countries.'

'If the fundamentalists lose, we can go back to our house by the river.'

'And if not? And how long do we wait? Our child will be born soon. Do you want this to be his birthplace? You didn't go anywhere, did you? You're useless.'

'Yes, Farah.' Ishmael stood on one of the flames. 'I am useless. I had everything and now I'm nothing. I'm ruined. He will be born here and he will be ruined too.'

He took his foot away, and the exasperating flame still burned on.

Farah felt the first pain rip through her, later that day.

'He's early,' was all she said to the woman in the tent with her.

The woman stood up and nodded. 'I will get Doctor Fatagagas.'

Farah told her, 'Tell him he will be born here. It's too late.'

Farah sat with a watch, timing her contractions. Ishmael massaged her shoulders, her lower back. Despite themselves, they felt a strange euphoria at the very beginning. The thing was finally happening. Outside, they walked up and down at intervals.

'Five minutes,' Farah said.

'That's it. Let's go.' Ishmael had been trying to convince her to get to the clinic earlier, but she stuck to the rules of labour as if there were a good hospital waiting for the birth.

They slouched through the refugee camp on foot.

There was only one doctor on duty at the clinic. The baby hadn't turned; its cord was around its neck and under its arms.

'He doesn't want to be born,' Farah shouted at Ishmael, who looked helplessly at the doctor.

'You have to assist me,' the doctor told Ishmael. They bent Farah over, stripping her naked, and put a needle in her spine. Ishmael cut her open, and he and the other doctor put their hands into her belly. Ishmael was sweating underneath a green mask. It had been a long time since he had performed non-cosmetic surgery. His fingers groped around, and he let himself be guided by the other doctor. He sliced through the womb and felt his child's head. They pulled. Farah felt a huge force dragging her insides out; she couldn't breathe. The baby came, covered in a white coating, fright flailing and grasping. She heard a pitiful screech.

'I can hear him,' she gasped.

'It's a girl. A girl.' Ishmael's voice was breaking in excitement.

The nurse immediately took the baby to the side to wash her off and wrap her.

'What colour is she?' Farah asked.

The dark-skinned UN nurse laughed as she sponged the baby. 'All the Orapian mothers ask that in the first seconds. Don't worry— under all this, white seems to be more white.'

'We Orapians are Aryans. Like the Persians.'

'That's what you think.' The nurse smiled. 'Wait, this one is dark after all.'

Farah stayed in the clinic for the rest of the week. She lay in bed unable to sit up or stand straight.

'We will give her an American name because that is where we want to go. She will have to fit in.'

'Mary?'

'No, no, too Christian.'

'Marguerite?'

'Are you sure the Americans will understand that one. It sounds strange.'

Ishmael took credit for getting them to Ireland, but it was 14-year-old Mehrdad who came and told him how to do it, stood in queues for him and told him where to go and what to bring. The UN were disbanding the camp because the fundamentalists were securing power in Orap and mobilising their army to cross the mountains and take the territory.

Farah could not walk. She lay in bed and had to call for the nurse to take her to the toilet.

'Why can't you bring the bed pan? I can't bear the pain.'

'Farah . . .'

'My name is Madame Fatagagas.'

'Madame Fatagagas, you must get up and go to the toilet. The more you move about, the quicker you will heal. The old-fashioned way of letting patients lie in bed to recover is out the window. Doctor's orders.'

The toilet was a hole in the ground, and the nurse held her while she pissed. She could have only liquid until she farted. Every day the nurse and doctor asked her had she passed wind. Ishmael would stare at her clear soup and tea and ask the same. 'Haven't you farted yet?' Her insides had literally stopped in shock because they had been touched.

'If you eat now, the pain will be unbearable,' the nurse explained.

'The pain is unbearable, and I'm so hungry and weak. Even my shoulders are sore,' Farah whined.

'That's the gas. The operation has trapped air in your insides where no air has ever been let in before. Your body needs to expel it.'

'Nothing works. Thank God there's no mirror.'

The baby cried. Farah groaned. The nurse sighed.

She had never breastfed before, but now, with supplies low and bottle sterilisation an impossibility, it was mandatory. The nurse squeezed poor Farah's cracked and bruised nipples; the baby was sucking furiously on the wrong part and blackening the red aureole. The baby needed to eat every hour. Farah squeezed her fists tightly and scrunched her face in pain as the infant sucked. It always felt as if nothing were coming. With Zolo and Leila, she had had a nanny, a cook and a maid, and had bottle-fed both. She was instructed to smear some of her own milk on her nipples and sit with her breasts exposed to the air to aid the healing. Just because she had been a midwife and in charge of thousands of women in her position didn't mean she felt in control. If the nurse had told her to stand on her head and sing the new Orapstanian national anthem, she would have done it. Her body was a public thing now, a place where the baby had built and sustained itself. Her teeth ached and the doctor took a look.

'Two of your teeth have fallen apart. One is rotting quite badly. We have no dentist in the camp. You'll just have to wait.'

The child who had built her bones off her teeth lay swaddled and sleeping. Its head was flaky under a wool hat, and the sticky eyes were an indefinable colour. Ishmael sat with it in his arms, afraid to catch its eye in case he would have to apologise for allowing it to be born in this camp.

'We're going to Ireland. I've arranged it all.'

'Where is that? Is it in America?'

'I wish! There are no places in America.'

'So where is it?'

'Somewhere in Europe. I think between England and France. Or else it is part of the island of England. Or once was.'

'Or once was?'

'Gondwanaland land.'

'Are there places in Gandwana land?'

'No more.'

'I have a brother in London.'

'I know, but those places are gone. Their quota is full.'

Ishmael went to find Mehrdad. He was helping to dismantle tents, and Ishmael noted that the UN had allowed him to drive one of their jeeps for errands. Capable boy.

Mehrdad waved at him. Ishmael strolled over with the air of a surveyor and stood watching the young men work.

'Mehrdad, where is this country we are off to? I've checked in my pile of magazines, and I don't see even a mention.'

'Mustn't have any tribes with hoops around their necks or strange burial rituals,' Mehrdad smiled.

Ishmael straightened up before the boy; he detected a slight hint of mockery. Or maybe he was getting as paranoid as his wife. Mehrdad was a good boy. 'Don't you know where we're going, boy?'

'West of Britain, Doctor Fatagagas. It is an island.'

Farah was sitting with her breasts pointing downwards. The

baby lay on her lap like a bloated tic. Ishmael took the child from his wife.

'She's light as a feather. Do you remember the others being so tiny?'

'They won't give me any painkillers because they're afraid I'll pass it to her through my milk.'

'I can get you opium.'

'Who gets you that? Mehrdad?'

'No. Mehrdad must never know about that.' Ishmael placed the baby over his shoulder without looking at it and rubbed its back. 'I've found out where Ireland is. Beside Britain.'

They had few choices in host countries, and the revolution in Orap was complete. The new religious fundamentalist regime was already entrenched and busy lining dissenters up against walls. Mehrdad's family chose this small island at the edge of Europe because his father researched the options and found that the island had good schools where English was spoken. Mehrdad wanted to be an engineer. Ishmael thought that becoming a doctor was the only thing good enough for his own children but appreciated that the gardener's son was bright and had a possible future.

'I want to go with the boy. I've grown fond of him. He's been so helpful.'

'You want to go with a family who remembers they were your servants.'

'You think you see right through me. You think you are the only one suffering.'

'Are the people white?'

'Yes, of course.'

Farah seemed somewhat comforted.

'Maybe we should have kept Leila here with us. Zolo had to go to school. Leila could have waited. She could have helped me out with the baby.'

'Do you think my brother is taking care of her?'

'Do you think your son Zolo is? We should have kept her.'

'No. She'd then be a refugee in the US. Now she's an immigrant.'

'She's now Mo's child,' Farah said.

'Mo with children. That's a frightening thought.'

Farah's eyes fluttered closed and she dozed off. Ishmael pulled up her gown to cover her bare chest, placed the baby back in the bassinet and crept away.

The ground was muddy, so plywood boards formed rough pathways from the clinic. Farah was so exhausted that she slept through all the outside noise of a camp being dismantled. Some were taking their chances and returning to Orap. The very poor who did not care who stood over them as long as they were not physically hurt or directly harassed. Expectations were low. But low expectations had eternally been the poor's key to happiness.

The nurse woke Farah to hand her the wailing child. Farah wasn't even sure that she had been sleeping, but the nurse assured her that she had.

'Sleeping hard enough to sleep through the crying of your baby.' The nurse's tone was fringed with disapproval. Or so Farah thought. Actually, the nurse had always been kind.

'I'm too old for this.' Farah took the child and twisted her around in a football hold so the child could feed without touching her wounded stomach.

'Not too old to do it though,' the nurse chided, taking Farah's breast in her hand and, with a painted-nailed finger, shoving the bruised nipple into the child's bawling mouth. Tiny hard gums clamped and suctioned furiously. The baby's forehead creased in concentration. Farah held on to the side of the chair and strained her head back, wincing.

'The milk won't let down when you tense up like that. You're only making it worse for both of you.'

The UN people came in to start packing the clinic. Farah watched as they hauled cardboard boxes in and everything around her started to disappear.

'Are you going home?' one man asked her.

'To Ireland.'

'That's where I'm from. Do you like the rain?'

'What is it like?'

'Green. But then most places are.'

Farah studied the man closely to distract her from the pain of the feeding. He had brown hair and a freckled face. His eyes were blue, and the bridge of his nose had several broken veins. He whistled as he worked.

'Is it close to America?'

'Right next door. Nothing between us and them but a lot of water. Stand out on the cliffs in the west and the next parish is Boston.'

'My two children are there.'

'Boston? Really?'

'No. Los Angeles.'

'Far from Boston.'

'I know that,' Farah answered sharply. Did everyone think she was an idiot just because she was a mother?

The nurse came in and put her hands on her hips.

'Farah, she's been long enough on that breast. You have to change over.'

The man kept working and whistling. Farah blushed—nurses were so crass.

'She won't take the other one. I put her to it, and she just screams and pounds her fists off it.'

'Feisty little thing. Good, I'm glad. She'll need a strong personality.' The nurse pushed the nipple away and switched the baby.

'I can't walk. How do you expect me to carry it?'

'She's not an it any more; she's a she. We'll bring you out in the wheelchair. You have to get dressed now. As of tonight, everyone is gone from the camp. Soldiers are taking over this territory in two days.'

'Orapians?'

'Yes. We talked to some of them arriving already. They're all about 14 years old, with big guns. There's something grotesque about it all,' the nurse said, as the baby's face reddened and eyes flashed in anger at the offending new nipple. 'You'll have to put her on that one first when she's really hungry; otherwise it's no good and she'll want another feeding in half an hour.'

Farah didn't look at the baby as she handed it back to the nurse. 'You'll have to help me get dressed. I can't bend down.'

'I'm busy now, Farah. Lots more patients, in much worse condition than you, to pack up and send off to God knows where. I have a footless man, would you believe? What lies ahead for him, I can't imagine. Where's your husband?'

Ishmael stood on the burning hill, cursing his fate.

Mehrdad arrived to take down the tent that was the clinic. It had seemed so permanent, but now it just fell away to the open mountain. He saw Farah among the boxes with her breasts exposed and her hands holding to the side of the chair. Her eyes were closed, but though she was sleeping, she did not look peaceful. Her mouth quivered and hung open and her forehead creased. Her hair was half-grey. He remembered it bleached blond when she was in Orap. She had been a glamorous slim woman who always wore gold jewellery and diamond earrings to her practice. She had never been an easy person, nor particularly warm to him or his family, but they had all known their places, and she had never been cruel or rude either. He talked to the nurse and she woke Farah. Mehrdad was standing with the baby in his arms, smelling its head. Farah started awake and immediately covered herself.

'Madame Fatagagas,' Mehrdad said. 'With your permission, I thought I would help you to the jeeps.'

'I have to get into a jeep?'

'The jeeps will bring you over the rough terrain to the airstrip,' the nurse confirmed. 'It's only a few miles. I'm going to give you some painkillers. A little won't harm the baby, just this once.'

The nurse pulled her out of the chair. Farah felt her stomach rip. 'Lean on me. Put all your weight on me. Pull on me.' The nurse grunted. Mehrdad put the baby down and came to the other side to push Farah out of the chair. Farah was standing now but doubled over. She straightened slowly and it felt as if a hot poker had been shoved inside her belly. Blood began to gush out of her, down her legs.

'If you give us a little privacy, I'll dress her, and then you can come back and wheel her and the baby out,' the nurse told Mehrdad, who slipped away. The nurse washed the blood off Farah's legs.

'He's a good boy,' the nurse said as she crouched on the ground, holding Farah's underwear. 'Everyone loves that kid.' Farah's toe crept towards the leg opening, and she winced as she lifted her foot a few centimetres off the ground.

'Now the other leg,' the nurse said.

'He was the son of our gardener. We know him since he was born. I delivered him.' Farah held on to a tent pole as she edged her toes towards the other leg hole.

'You had a gardener? I've heard the gardens are beautiful in your culture.' The nurse pulled the panties over her foot.

'We had a big one, with a river running by the end. The river had a separate river running inside it.'

'How could that be?' The nurse carefully pulled the panties up her legs.

'I don't really know. Just something they said.' Farah closed her eyes in anticipation of the underwear being pulled over her raw belly.

'Shit.' The nurse actually looked upset for the first time.

'What?'

'I've put them on back to front.'

Farah sat in a wheelchair on a muddy plywood board and watched as the clinic finally collapsed. The Irishman made a fuss of the baby as he gave it to Farah.

'She'll be an Irishwoman, so.' He had a strange lilting way of talking. What kind of accent was that? Farah wondered. It was not normal. His good cheer seemed out of place. She hoped she was not going to a nation of dimwits. She took the baby from him, without looking at him. Farah had never cried in front of anyone in her life since she was a little girl, but now she was alarmed to feel tears squeezing out of her eyes. She put her head down and concentrated on not making a fool of herself. The baby was asleep but would wake soon and need yet more feeding. The nurse kissed her on the cheek.

'Good luck, Farah.' Then kissed the baby. 'Poor human. Good luck, Marguerite. Have a great life. Be strong.'

She squeezed Farah's shoulder and then rushed off to help her other patients.

'My bag! My bag!' Farah signalled for her bag, and Mehrdad put it on her lap. 'I have the deed to our house in here. It's all I have left.'

Farah kept her head down. She concentrated on deflecting the sharp pains at every bump at the end of every board.

'Sorry, Madame Fatagagas,' Mehrdad said at all the bumps.

The baby's eyes were flickering. Its head began to swivel, the tiny face scrunched up. Not here, Farah thought, please, not here.

'Maybe Marguerite is hungry,' Mehrdad whispered tentatively as they waited in a big crowd for a jeep. The baby was turning purple with the ferocity of its own yells. Farah pulled up her blouse, trying to be discreet. The nurse had always helped her get its mouth latched on. She shoved the baby at the nipple, but the baby was too hysterical at that point to close its mouth and suck. It screamed into her breasts. People were staring. A veiled woman came forward. Most of the women who were returning to Orap were wearing veils. The government said that it would not punish those who returned, but they sent messages that the women were to arrive with faces covered. Only eyes could be revealed. Since garments such as these were expensive, the UN reluctantly distributed them.

The woman took the baby, put her finger in the little mouth, and rocked it until the crying abated. Then she knelt in front of Farah. Farah and she locked eyes as the woman took Farah's breast in her calloused hand. A worker, Farah thought involuntarily. When the baby's mouth was wide open, like a baby bird's, she popped the nipple in. The baby ferociously suckled. Farah gasped.

'It will get easier,' was all the woman said to Farah, having mauled her. Farah noticed her accent was coarse, a lower-class, city accent. To think she let strangers come and handle her so intimately in the middle of a crowd. There seemed to be nothing left.

'Here he is, at last,' Mehrdad cried. Ishmael was making his way through the crowd. His hands were black. 'I have to go, Madame. I have to help my family.'

'Mehrdad!' Ishmael cried out, too loud. 'There's a good boy. All our suitcases are outside the tent. Bring them here.'

Mehrdad hesitated. 'Yes, Doctor Fatagagas.'

Mehrdad ran off.

Farah looked at her husband. His eyes were pinned and his mouth was crooked. He never even looked at the baby. 'Why are your hands black?'

'I was on the hill, burning magazines.'

'You're stoned. I was all alone.'

Ishmael surveyed the crowd. 'You call this alone?'

'I hate you.'

'I hope that boy hurries with our stuff. I can get a jeep quickly here. They know who I am.'

Exhausted by its earlier fit of crying, the baby now fell asleep. Milk dribbled down its cheek. Farah removed the head and covered her breast quickly. It would be hungry again soon. She was so sick of her own body and all the physicality. There was no end in sight. The child was only five days old.

The Irishman came looking for Farah. 'I have you a jeep. Come with me. We'll get you on the first plane we can. You'll have to walk.' He took the child and put his hand out.

'I can't,' Farah said.

Two women beside her pulled her out of the chair. She groaned. 'Careful, careful, not so fast. I'm so sore.' Farah grabbed the Irishman and they shuffled through the crowd. Ishmael followed.

'Who is this?' the Irishman asked when they arrived at the jeep.

'My husband.'

The man turned to Ishmael. 'Get her into the jeep and look after her.'

Farah balked when she saw the high step into the vehicle. The baby began to cry. Ishmael got in first and slowly pulled her up backwards into the front seat. Mehrdad arrived with their luggage. He handed Farah a jar of cream. 'This is for you from the nurse. She said its antibiotic cream for the infection that has set in where the tape of your bandage was. She said to rub it over the blisters every few hours.'

Farah grabbed it gruffly, wishing the nurse wouldn't give everyone details of her condition. She would have had her fired before.

'See you in Ireland.' Ishmael smiled sleepily.

'You can't take all that shit.' The driver was staring at five huge suitcases. 'The jeep will take only one more bag.'

'It's all we have in the world,' Farah protested.

'Lady, that's not my problem. We have thousands of people to evacuate in three days before the soldiers come over the mountain. And there's one other passenger I have to take.' A stretcher came carrying the young man who had lost both feet to frostbite. Mehrdad ran to his aid. Ishmael was delighted.

'He has no bags. Nothing. Excellent.'

One suitcase fitted in the back of the jeep. They put another one on the back seat.

'Mehrdad, your family has probably very little. We had a car when we left, you see. Take the other three to Ireland, and I'll make it worth your while.' He slipped two of Farah's diamond earrings into Mehrdad's hands. He had been keeping them for an opium trade. Mehrdad pocketed the earrings in embarrassment. Ishmael got into the back with his suitcase. The medics pushed the young man behind the seat. Ishmael pulled him into the car almost on to his own lap. The baby cried.

'Hungry again, little fellah? That's what life's about, eh?' The driver winked at Farah. 'Are we right?'

They all nodded. Ishmael was beaming with excitement to be leaving the burning hill camp.

'I won't miss this place,' he said to the young man. The young man's eyes were pinned and glazed. Ishmael took note.

'Didn't my children meet you when you had just come over the mountain?'

'They were the kids who used to play with Mehrdad?'

'Play with Mehrdad. It's hard to imagine that boy ever played.'

Mehrdad stood and waved as the jeep pulled off. In empathy with Farah, he sucked in air sharply as he watched it bounce over every hole and ridge in the field. Then, in disbelief, he took the diamonds out of his pocket and watched them sparkle.

It was on this journey that Ishmael learned that his brother and his sister-in-law had been executed and that the two little girls who had died in the snow were his nieces.

Small-made.

Chapter Fourteen

Ishmael's Trip to France

When Ishmael arrived in Ireland, he went first thing to the US Embassy to try to get a visa. He had pinned a yarmulke to his head.

'I'll say I'm a Jew,' he told his wife. 'They love the Jews.'

'Just get us out of here and over to Zolo and Leila.'

Ishmael sighed. 'I'm so tired.'

'Your body is dreaming of opium.'

'Listen to me.' Ishmael darkened. 'Whatever you do, don't tell anyone about that. I don't want it to be known that I had a dependency. Especially not by Mehrdad.'

'You care more about Mehrdad than anyone else in the world. He's just a servant's son. Think more about your own children. We have to get the family back together. I worry about what might happen if we don't.'

Heather, their assigned, overextended, 24-year-old Australian social worker, called Mo's Malibu number for them, but they only ever got the answering machine, and he never called back. 'I was busy,' he would say later. 'It's not my fault you ruined your life. I warned you years ago.'

Ishmael left Farah. The vindication he had felt when the queen had tracked him down and asked him to come to France had been enormous. Farah forbade him to go without her. But only he was granted a special visa through the queen's connections. 'Her Majesty needs me,' was all he said. Farah noticed her jewellery gone and knew that he had had to pay for his own ticket. Farah despised Ishmael. Everything was wrong with him. He was no good. His reason had vanished with his prestige. She told Ishmael never to come back. He told her there was nothing to come back to.

When Ishmael packed his leather case, he would not catch her eye. He did not kiss the baby goodbye.

'Mehrdad will look after you.'

'How could you leave me here in this country with all these Unwashed Asses?'

'The queen has breast cancer. She hunted me down.'

'But you're a plastic surgeon.'

'My theory is that she doesn't trust any of those foreign doctors. She doesn't want the news leaking to the press, so she has summoned me. I know all kinds of medicine, not just the one. I am a renaissance man.'

'You sound just like your brother.'

'Don't bad-mouth Mo. He's taking care of our children.'

'Something their own father failed to do.'

'It's not like you haven't been with me all along. You know what happened.'

'I know all you have is my jewellery.'

Ishmael rose off the bed and balled his fist near to her face. 'Who gave you all that jewellery? Huh? Who gave it to you?'

'Actually, my mother passed most of it down to me. We could be together as a family if we wanted to. We gave our children away too easily. At least all those other women have their children.'

'The darkies? Now you want to be like the darkies? Yes, my children are not here. It was you who was so insistent to get them out of the camp.'

'And what's that?' Farah pointed to the baby on the bed. 'That's not your child?'

'I have no idea whose child that is,' Ishmael hissed. 'For all I know, you were screwing all over the place to get favours. A man can't watch his wife in those circumstances. I wouldn't put anything by you and your lousy pushiness.'

'Go, go. My mother warned me you were weak. She said you were all nose and no backbone.'

'Where's your mother now? Huh? Or any of your family?'

Farah's family had managed to get themselves killed by two successive Orapian governments.

Farah hissed, 'It was your fault we stayed too long in Orap. Your fault that you handed all our documents and money over to the border guards.'

In the new host country, when Farah was left alone with the baby, she could not stop thinking that she might hurt it. She imagined eating it. A circle of red veins and bones where the neck was. The baby headless. When she changed the nappy, she looked at its slits and folds and imagined a future where it might be hurt. Girls were beyond protection. The room was a dark hole. She rarely opened the blinds on the window. The grim view was a red-brick wall and a partial view of another window. More refugees. Blacks. Moving about their rooms like olives in a jar. The suspended way refugees were kept alive was very little to do with living, more like pickling.

The blacks had told Farah that they didn't like the streets. Too much hostility. The black women were tall and slender; they wore bright colours in the yard where their children played on swings. They stood close together and reserved their few smiles for each other.

The light in Ireland went at four o'clock. There was no sunset because there was no sun. During the day, grey clouds were densely mashed into the sky. By evening, a tidal darkness collapsed behind the clouds. When Farah fed the child, she sat on the bed and imagined herself falling and cracking the baby's head off the hard tile floor. She let the night come lapping around her like a liquid phobia. She talked about this to Heather, the social worker. Heather pursed her lips and said she should consider getting anti-depressants from a doctor. She was a new mother yet an old mother. Forty-three and functioning on three hours of fractured sleep. Plus she was recovering from an operation, major abdominal surgery. Her husband had left her. Had she ever heard of post-partum depression?

Then the social worker told her that the island of Ireland was the first stop for all the westerly winds blowing off the Atlantic, that the clouds were always low lying and rain producing, that the ancient people who lived here had had a fear that the sky would fall on their heads.

The baby was losing weight. It had jaundice. Farah tried to put on her Chanel suit, but it no longer fitted, so she had to wear her pregnancy clothes that had been given to her by fellow refugees in the camp. She had no buggy, so the blacks lent her a multicoloured sling for the child. It was embarrassing, but otherwise she could not carry the child far on her own. She looked and felt like a peasant when she took a bus to Tallaght Hospital and waited in the A&E. Her nipples had leaked on the bus when a baby was crying on the back seat. Someone else's baby. Farah felt betrayed that her body was connecting to other people's babies by mistake. Her blouse sported two big incriminating damp patches.

The doctor was an attractive woman, with long red hair.

'May I take your photo?' She spoke slowly and clearly. Farah was relieved because often she had difficulty understanding the Irish accent. 'I'm making a presentation on refugees and hospital services. We're trying to get a separate clinic set up to deal with your special needs.'

'I speak English. I don't have special needs, and I certainly don't want my picture taken.'

'Of course. Entirely up to you. I'm sorry if I offended you. She's a dote! What's her name?'

'Marguerite.' Farah so rarely said the name aloud. She had never said it to the baby. It was such a foreign name.

'Are you breastfeeding?' the doctor asked. The doctor wore earrings that had flashing lights on them. Paediatricians always accessorised strangely.

'Yes.'

'How many minutes each side?' The doctor pressed the baby's stomach and peered into its eyes, then its ears.

'I was only doing one breast, but then I was told to get her to the other one when she was hungry and do ten minutes on either side, but she just falls asleep, and doesn't feed and she doesn't like the right breast at all.'

'If she is only feeding ten minutes on each. then she is only getting the fore milk to quench her thirst and not the nourishing hind milk which is higher in calories. Would you consider supplementing with formula?'

Farah nodded miserably. 'I can't buy it at the moment.'

'Your baby needs to regain her birth weight. We need to flush out the jaundice. How many dirty nappies is she having a day, and what colour are the faeces?'

'Black like oil.'

'That's not good at four weeks old. That's meconium—'

'I know what it is, young lady. For your information, I was a midwife with my own clinic back in Orap.'

'Orap? You're the first person I've met from Orap. Geography was never my strong point. Where exactly is it? The Middle East?'

'I didn't know where your country was either. I never heard of it myself until we got here. I don't particularly care to end up in your paper,' Farah said coldly.

The doctor raised her eyebrows. 'Fair enough. Anyway, she's not getting enough food from you. She's dehydrated as you can tell from her little head. The fontanel is caved in. . . .'

Farah shuffled back to the bus stop with her new baby. She looked at the baby on the bus. The baby cried. She had to unbutton the jacket and slip her baby under. The doctor had given her a can of powdered formula and had told her she would contact the authorities in charge of them to make sure she could always get some more. Special needs, Farah thought. Maybe she was just an ordinary refugee. No better than the Romanian gypsies who made so much noise and showed off their gold teeth to the doctor as she was leaving, or the black faces who wore such bright colours yet were afraid to step out. The bus journey took her through a maze of housing estates with identical houses; she hadn't seen much green since she'd got here. Just a sprawling cement provincial city with neither skyscrapers pointing to a future, nor glorious architecture left over from the past. The drizzle on the bus window merged with the grey outside; already the day was losing its light. The people were so pale and unhealthy looking. At the bus stops, their faces were luminous, staring out from the hoods of giant black coats.

The blacks undid the sling and took it back when she came from the hospital. She had been under the impression they had given it to her to keep, but obviously not. They shook their head over the baby. Yellow, caved in and doomed. She knew what they were babbling about in their primitive tongue. Her baby would not make it. Born a refugee. Each day, it was getting smaller and smaller, and darker and darker.

Every night, Farah lay with the shrinking baby beside her to pull her to her breast when she awoke for food. They had no cradle. She reminded herself of the pig the servant had kept in the house in the children's zoo. Lying on its side, multi-titted, all its piglets taken away but one. Invariably, she woke in a sweat, sometime in the early hours, thinking she had rolled on top of the child and smothered it, or else a pillow had slid over its face, or it had ended up wedged between the headboard and the mattress. Tonight, after the long trip to the hospital, she took two towels and folded them inside her suitcase before placing the infant in the open case. When the baby slept uninterrupted for the first time for three straight hours, Farah awoke with a start. There was a strange new silence in the room. Stiffly, she swung her legs out of bed. Her stomach still so sore after a month. She hung over the child in the dark. There was no sound. No breathing.

'Ishmael, Ishmael,' Farah croaked. 'Ishmael,' she said louder. 'The child has stopped breathing.' But Ishmael wasn't there. Ishmael was far away, serving his queen without a country.

Farah slithered through the sheets away from the inert child that lay in the suitcase. It was better to wait till morning and pretend she had discovered only then. That way she could exist a few more hours, pretending nothing was amiss. But she would have to cope with it eventually, so she might as well find out now. Then whom could she go to in the middle of the night with a dead baby? Its birth date would be zero to zero, as if it never existed. Farah crawled back over and poked the baby lightly in the stomach. The baby was still as stone. She picked it up. The skin was cold. It was dead.

She shook it gently. The baby scrunched her face up. Her tiny lips quivered. Farah sat back on the bed and listened to the long wail. It was simple but it was extraordinary, and it changed everything; for the first time, she realised that she did not want the child to die.

It was at this very moment that Farah decided that since she had lost power over everything else, she would make securing her youngest daughter's future the primary purpose of her life.

Heather the social worker came to Farah's room with some books.

'These are nursery rhymes for the baby. If you can't talk to her, you could try reading to her. It's easier sometimes. You feel less self-conscious, and she needs to hear your voice, not sit in silence in this room.'

But Farah, to Heather's surprise, was holding the baby and kissing her cheeks and blowing on her feet.

'What happened here? You bonded at last, huh?'

Farah took the books and looked at them suspiciously. They were second-hand.

'Oh, and I've found you some compatriots. A boy, Mehrdad, asked would it be all right if he comes to see you. He was worried when I told him that your husband had left.'

'My husband, Doctor Fatagagas, will be back. He is attending the Queen of Orap, who is terminally ill, if you must know, and I'll thank you not to let others know my business. That's very unprofessional.'

Heather stammered, 'God, I'm sorry, Farah . . .'

'Madame Fatagagas.'

'Madame Fatagagas, of course.' Heather left without sitting down. 'I was just worried about you and Marguerite.'

Farah closed the door after her. 'Nosy bitch,' she said to Marguerite. Marguerite gave a windy smile. Farah put her over her shoulder. 'But if young Mehrdad comes, I can get him to go out and get us more formula.'

Later, she read the nursery rhymes to the tiny baby who lay beside her on the bed. Nonsensical things but good for learning English. *Ladybird, ladybird, fly away home, your house is on fire, your children all gone.*

All except one.

Ishmael sat by a swimming pool in the south of France. The pool was a deep blue, the exact same colour as the sky. It was as if a perfect rectangle had been cut from the sky and rolled out on the ground like a rug. The dying queen swam in this liquid slice of fallen sky. Her thin white arms shot out of the water and dipped back in, barely breaking the surface. Her head was covered in a swimming cap. She had no hair but could not bear to swim bald. The future king, her 14-year-old son, was the same age as Mehrdad and Zolo. He sat on a lounge chair like a fat monster and ate from a big bag of pistachio nuts. The boy had always been chubby, but Ishmael was shocked to see him so obese—all rumpled and folded. There was a bag on his left side for the shells. The nuts were to stop him eating sweets. He looked like a miniature Emperor Nero, even in his tight green Speedos. Almond-shaped eyes set far back in his head glared at the doctor. His nose was hooked and crooked. It was hard to tell what noses children would have. Mostly it was genetic and geographical. Ishmael maintained that the world had a nose gauge. Small noses in the West, then rising, getting larger by the time you hit Italy and Greece, larger still in Turkey, rising to immense proportions in the Middle East, a peak, then shrinking in India, before getting tiny again in China.

Ishmael had known as soon as he was ushered in by a servant and introduced to the family why he had been summoned. If this ugly little man still had to make a play to be king, he was going to have to be somewhat appealing to his supporters.

'The poor boy is eating himself to death,' the queen confided in private. 'All this upheaval and pressure.' Ishmael looked out the window at the boy by the pool underneath the palms. The view swept down to the Mediterranean. Bodyguards lounged about the tiled patio, watching action movies on a tiny laptop TV. Ishmael observed the young prince; he had neither the brilliance of Zolo nor the cunning of Mehrdad. What he had was blood, royal blood. If Ishmael had been able to hold on to his wealth, he might have caught the queen in a moment of weakness and married Leila off to the fat prince. Ishmael indulged in his fantasy of genuinely royal grandchildren while the queen answered her mobile phone. Her husband was in Algeria. France had not granted him a visa.

'How is your family?'

'Great. We were lucky. My two children are in America. Doing very well there. My wife and I are currently in Ireland. We have a few servants with us. A family we rescued and brought out of the country. I'm trying to use my influence to get them visas for the US. The young boy, Mehrdad, is very bright.'

'You were lucky to keep your Orapian servants. We find the French so arrogant and expensive.'

'In the effort to save our servants, we overlooked our own visas. We really need to get to the United States. Maybe you could put in a word with the Americans for us . . .'

'I'm afraid we don't have any influence. The French police are watching us. They say they are protecting us, but I feel like a prisoner.'

'Not a bad prison.'

'A prison is a prison.' She smiled sadly as she surveyed the huge white villa. 'These few remaining luxuries are not equitable with freedom, alas.'

'It's the nose, isn't it?'

The queen smiled conspiratorially. 'Yes. The nose, of course.'

'Of course.' Ishmael sighed. 'He's rather young. I'd have waited personally. Can I have access to a local operating theatre?'

'I can arrange that. It has to look like the noses of his sisters. You've done them all. Your style.'

'A family resemblance.' Ishmael brightened. 'My trademark bridge and delicate nostrils.'

'You have two children? Yes?'

'Yes.' Technically, that was true. He had three now but also two if you thought of it like that, and it was wise not to mention the new baby in case the details of the birth would have to be revealed. Best to avoid lies. 'My visa is for one month. It has to be done in that time.'

'It can be done this week, Doctor, but of course you are welcome to stay on with us at the villa.'

Ishmael bowed and smiled.

The bald queen threaded her way gracefully through the pool. The doctor sweated in the sun. Plish plash of water soft against his brain. The abominable prince glared at him, his pistachio breath sweet and sickly. Ten royal repulsive toes squirmed in a puddle of Coca-Cola on the tiles. A French servant approached with a mop, spitting vitriol at the plump dictator wannabe. *'Quel méchant! Vous êtes gâté, Monsieur, pas gentil.'*

Ishmael fell asleep on the chair.

He was spiralling towards a black point. Closer and closer, speed rising. When he hits, he will either break through on impact into an infinite hole of darkness or smash into tiny pieces. His eyes fluttered open. Water, all over him, in drops. The fat prince was in the shallow end, yawning, and splashing water over his back with his sallow thick arms like elephant trunks. Ishmael squinted at him. He had forgotten which nose he had given his two sisters. Perhaps he should ask for a photo. Where were the sisters? Where was everybody?

Baby Zero. At the same time, Farah was singing to her little baby.

The king was in the counting house, counting all the money,
The queen was in the parlour, eating bread and honey,
The maid was in the garden, hanging out the clothes,

The imposter's servant. Kind father fool. He might have been charming and harmless in less interesting times.

When along came a blackbird and pecked off her nose.

There are three Baby Zeroes.

One was born the daughter of a surgeon. One was born in a refugee camp. One will be born in a prison. Servants raised the first. Refugees raised the second. A prisoner will raise you.

Abomination. Perfectly formed. Always this—the quiet reception. Unjubilant regard.

Zero minus zero minus zero.

Chapter Fifteen

The Good Son

Mehrdad's father had a look of horror on his face for one whole month after they arrived in Ireland. He lay in a hospital bed with his face turned away from the ward and towards the window. His mouth was open. His wife sat beside him. She could not bear his expression. It was disturbing the youngest children.

'We will be all right, Baba,' she urged him resentfully. 'Just go on and do what you have to do.'

There were seven children and Mehrdad, at 14, was the eldest. They had nothing to do but sit around him and absorb his horror.

Mehrdad's father was unconvinced.

Mehrdad assured him that he would take care of everyone.

Mehrdad's mother grunted in agreement. 'He's a good boy.' She wore a headscarf and a long grey coat. The two girls over the age of 9 wore headscarves.

There was a smell from stomach cancer.

'Baba,' Mehrdad said nervously, 'tell Maman we are decided about the earrings. Tell her what you said to me last night.'

Mehrdad's father's eyes shone with love. He loved his eldest son more than anything else in the whole world.

'Trust not in fortune, vain deluded charm!
Whom wise men shun, and only fools adore,

Oft, whilst she smiles, Fate sounds the dread alarm
Round flies her wheel; you sink to rise no more.'

'Poems are nice things for the rich,' Mehrdad's mother sniffed.

'I have contacted Madame Fatagagas's social worker,' Mehrdad said. 'I'm going to give back the earrings when I see her. I've discussed it with Baba, and he says if I feel uncomfortable about such a lavish gift for carrying a few suitcases, I should do as my conscience sees fit.'

'Your father doesn't like owing anybody anything, but you don't owe them. We had nine of us, and we took their three suitcases as well. It was a lot of trouble. Now is not the time for grand and noble gestures. Give them to me.'

Mehrdad looked at his father imploringly.

'That's an order,' his mother said.

'Good boy, good boy,' his father whispered.

Mehrdad had kept them on him at all times. Never in his life had he ever possessed anything of such luxury. He was as relieved to give them up, as if they had been burning a hole in his pocket. His mother inspected them.

'Diamonds. Probably real ones too. We'll use them to bury you,' she said.

The children watched their mother as she squinted up at the jewels in the light. The baby grabbed for them. Her eldest daughter Sakina got up and walked quickly through the ward. The others looked after her and then back to their father. The look of horror remained set, but he was dead. Mehrdad's mother sniffed his head. He still wore the tight black wool skullcap he always had worn. She glared at him, as if he had just got away with something.

The state paid for his burial. There was no funeral, but the family made a trip to the mosque in Clonsilla for prayers. His wife had known for many months that he was dying. She knew he had clung on till they were out of the camp and secure in this new place. Programmed refugees, not like those who came in on trucks or smuggled themselves in containers. There was an infrastructure in place, and they had been invited. This is what Mehrdad found himself explaining to Madame Fatagagas when he visited her in the hostel.

'We have work permits. You and Dr Fatagagas can work. Many other refugees cannot.'

Mehrdad knew this only too well. Some of Mehrdad's extended family had begun to find their way over. They paid agents big money to get them to Ireland's shores only to arrive broke. This seemed baffling to the host country—but walking down the street worried about being arrested and sent back to be shot was better than being arrested and shot. Mehrdad helped them to establish contact with the authorities and translated for them. He was used to a busy life; now he was in charge of his whole extended family. He was 14 years old.

'How many Orapians came?' Madame Fatagagas was writing a shopping list for Mehrdad.

'Only our two families as programmed refugees. And Ali. My cousins heard we were here and now some have arrived . . .'

'Who's Ali?' Farah asked sharply.

'Ali? He was with us for the journey.' Mehrdad was surprised she did not remember.

'Oh, the footless one. Well, he doesn't count. What can he do anywhere?' Farah waved her hand dismissively.

'He's in this hostel,' Mehrdad said.

'He is? I've never seen him. What are you going to do now, Mehrdad?'

'I'll get your groceries, Madame.'

'No, I mean now your father is dead and you are head of a large family. Your mother speaks no English.'

'I've enrolled all of us in schools, and I have a job in Abrakebabra. My mother cleans houses for three hours in the evening, six days a week, when my sisters come home from school to take the little ones.' He wanted to let her know he wrote to Leila, but he didn't dare.

As if sensing something, Madame Fatagagas handed him the list and said, 'Zolo is gifted, as you know. He has got himself into medical school at age 14.' Madame Fatagagas was taken aback by her own lie. She was becoming as bad as her useless husband. In truth, she had not heard from either of the children or Mo in months.

Mehrdad glanced at the list. He didn't know if he should wait around for money or just buy it out of his own. 'Leila's just as smart as Zolo,' he said. 'I hope she's doing well.'

'As smart as Zolo? Perhaps. I never thought of that. We got Zolo tested when he was young, but Leila didn't cause so many disturbances, so we never thought of it.' Madame Fatagagas smiled indulgently. She gave him her Gucci purse. A real on, not a fake. None of her designer clothes fitted her, so she clung to this one status symbol. 'I've counted the money, and bring me a receipt with the change.'

'Of course.' Mehrdad took the purse in relief.

Farah was hanging out some washing to dry in the courtyard of the hostel. The African women had taken up most of the line space with their voluminous, wildly coloured clothes. They inspected Marguerite and oohed and aahed.

'Much better, Madame.' One of the women squeezed Marguerite's legs. 'Nice and fat now.'

'Not yellow any more.' Another smiled gaily. They picked her up and swung her around. 'Such a pretty baby. Look at all the hair.'

'I will be looking for a job soon.' Farah watched them with the child. 'Maybe you could look after her when I'm at work.'

The two African women stopped and said, 'We'd love to. We cannot get work here. Not allowed. We wait and wait for the permission to stay, but our cases never seem to reach anyone, and if they do, no one believe us where we came from and what we must not go back to.'

'Why can't you go back?'

'Why do you not go back?' they asked her.

'There was a revolution. My family had ties with the royal family. Anyone who stayed seems to have been executed. There's a war with the neighbouring country, and all the men and boys are enlisted. There's no question of going back until it changes.'

'Same with us. War, Madame. Bad government. We're on the wrong side.'

Farah was amazed they were talking to her so easily. This was a first. She was uncomfortable all of a sudden. They were actually looking at her as a peer. She stood up straight.

'I'm a programmed refugee. I'm here on invitation. Legally. I can work.' She parroted what she had just heard from Mehrdad. 'I certainly would not have put my family at such risk to just arrive uninvited. How did you get past customs?'

'We came on a truck, Madame. We pay all our savings and he takes us. An agent in Togo arranged it all. We give all our money to come here for our children.'

'Hiding on a truck? With your children? You must have known what reception you would get. How could you expect anything else? Are you that naïve? It's just irresponsible to come to a country without proper documentation and expect to live off charity.'

The Africans' eyes flashed sorrow. 'Yes, we are not welcome here after all that.'

'I'm not surprised,' Farah said. She took her child away from those dreadful people and left them fighting the wind to gather their damp, savage, print clothes.

The Africans came banging on Farah's door, interrupting her reading nursery rhymes to her baby.

Tom, Tom, the piper's son, stole a pig and away he run.

She was perplexed at this as it seemed to be as foolish as all the others but grammatically incorrect.

'Madame, Madame!'

The pig got eat, Tom got beat

Farah reluctantly opened the door.

'Come, Madame. It's Ali. Your countryman. He's out on the road in all the cars.'

'Who's Ali?'

'The man with the no feet.' One of the women grabbed her and began pulling her. 'We look after baby. Go! Go!'

Farah followed one of them out on to the street. A small crowd had gathered to witness the spectacle of a young dishevelled man on his hands and knees in the middle of the road. It was the Orapian. He had no legs beneath the knee. One of his crutches had rolled away. He managed to stand on one crutch, and then he slammed down again. The police were stopping traffic. He had already been swiped by one car, and his shoulder looked crooked and dislocated. Every time the police went near him, he would slither away, squealing. Farah had a gut instinct not to get involved, but the African was firmly propelling her along by a flat hand in the middle of her back.

One of the police came over to her.

'Do you speak English?'

'Of course I speak English,' Farah said haughtily. 'I don't know this man.'

'But he's from your country.'

'I think so.' Farah knew so.

The African woman said, tapping her head with a long finger, 'Ali has been in the hospital. They were meant to give him feet, but instead he said they operated on him and removed his heart.'

The police stood baffled. 'We can't hold up traffic for ever. Go and talk to him.'

Ali saw Farah and a flash of recognition crept into his dementia.

'Ali, Come in off the road. You are making a fool of yourself. You are letting down the Orapians. What will they think of us?' Farah scolded him. Ali lay on the ground limply. Farah supposed that he had once been an ordinary young man. Now he didn't look human. Suddenly subdued, he stared up at her. The police scooped him up. They carried him back to the hostel.

'May I go now?' Farah said. Ali was shouting again. He was shouting that he was turning into a fish. Farah saw Mehrdad come running down the road with Heather, the social worker who was dealing with all the Orapians, so she discretely slipped away. She picked up where she had left off with the baby.

All the king's horses and all the king's men, couldn't put Ali together again.

Mehrdad was worried about Ali. Heather was worried too. They talked to the gardaí as they carried him into his room in the hostel.

'It's all this gross stuff going on in the Irish hospitals.'

'What's going on?' the garda asked.

'Weird stuff. They were taking organs from dead bodies without the families' permission and using them for research. Highly unethical, but I suppose they figured what they didn't know didn't harm them. Sometimes they were burying miscarried foetuses with other corpses. You know, just chucking them into the coffins because they had nowhere else to shove them. Tucking them in under the feet. Most hospital workers just didn't think it was a biggie.'

'To get buried with a dead baby at your feet,' Mehrdad marvelled.

'Well, you'd be dead too.' Heather laughed. 'My friend, another Aussie social worker, was dealing with all the aftermath now the cat is out of the bag.'

'Or the baby out of the bag.' The police laughed.

'Yeah, or the baby.' Heather shook her head as if in disbelief. 'My friend was freaking out, and we were just commiserating with each other about the system over here. She had just got a phone call from a set of parents, and she had to tell them that the hospital had their 12-year-old daughter's brain in the lab for the last few years. They had no idea.'

'Ali overheard all this?' Mehrdad said.

'Poor bugger! He thinks they nicked his heart.' Heather took a breath and changed tack. 'You know, your voice is breaking? You sound hilarious.'

Mehrdad blushed.

'You're turning into a fine young thing,' she joked. Mehrdad was becoming handsome and tall. He blushed more.

Mehrdad told Heather and the gardaí that he would take care of Ali. Check in on him and bring him food in the evenings.

Mehrdad helped his siblings with their homework and their English. He had been closer to his father than his mother. His father only reluctantly beat him for fraternising with the employer's children; his mother lashed out for everything. Now that his father was dead, his mother treated him with respect. He was the only man in her life. She'd never take a stick to him again. He would protect her honour and his sisters' honour.

Mehrdad dreaded his sister Sakina's arrival home. When his mother was this angry, she kept tweaking the hairs on her chin until they curled like tiny springs. Mehrdad had been at school all day and soon he had to work in the fast-food kebab restaurant. He was trying to do his homework, but the younger kids were leaping about like wild animals. Aisha, the 11-year-old, had ratted on Sakina, her 13-year-old sister. Aisha was guiltily sitting on one of the plastic chairs they had got from the thrift shop. She regretted her betrayal. Mehrdad was pissed off with her for causing trouble. He was hoping he'd have to go to work before Sakina came home from school, but the flat door opened and she came in. Her mother leapt up and boxed her in the ear.

'Whore.'

Mehrdad was up like a light and broke it up before it could go any further.

'Sakina, come and sit down and explain.' He steered her to a chair. She glared at Aisha as if she knew. Aisha cowered.

'Sakina, it has come to our notice that you have not been wearing your headscarf, and Maman would prefer if you did.'

'It makes no sense here.' She pouted, eyeing her mother nervously, placating Mehrdad because she knew he'd protect her.

'Why?' Mehrdad asked.

'If we wear it in Orap so no man will look at us, then wearing it here makes everyone stare at us. So it's silly.'

Mehrdad looked at his mother. 'She has a point.'

'Besides. . .' Sakina was emboldened. 'I was drinking water from a paper cup, and a man walked by and put money into my water.'

'What?' Their mother clenched her fists.

'Calm down.' Mehrdad gestured to his mother. He was smiling. 'He thought she was Romanian.'

'He thought I was begging.' Sakina, knowing nothing was going to happen to her, went to the window. She placed her hand on the scratched glass. Her fingernails were painted blue. 'Why is it always raining here? Why can't we go somewhere else? My friend in the camp went to Paris.'

'You need to get her married off,' his mother hissed at him. 'Find someone as soon as possible. Go to the mosque and ask the mullah.'

Mehrdad worked in the fast-food restaurant in a state of hyper-awareness. That state in which one is so preoccupied by an overriding notion that everything seems to be of relevance. He was 14, and this was the first time he had felt so deeply. He missed Leila so much it felt like physical pain. Every evening, on his break, he would walk to Temple Bar and sit and eat his kebab on the curb of the road. This shift, he had burnt his hand in the deep-fat fryer. The Chinese manager had held his arm under cold water, but it hadn't helped much. He had burnt it right over the scar he had from cutting his hand on the glass on the roof, a couple of years ago, when he and Leila had gone on their naked escapade through the mud walls of Orap. There was a busker who would take up position in the old stone walkway leading to the river Liffey. The stone walkway, Mehrdad read on a plaque, was a part left of the old walls that once ringed the city almost a thousand years ago. The busker had a limited repertoire and, to Mehrdad, she always seemed to be singing the same song.

My young love said to me,
My mother won't mind
And my father won't slight you
For your lack of kind.
She stepped away from me
And this she did say,
'It will not be long love
Till our wedding day.

Mehrdad was electrified by the song. It sustained him throughout the day.

One night, Mehrdad's mother prepared to go out to her cleaning jobs. She stopped and looked at her son in his silly fast-food outfit.

'Did you get your homework done?'

'Yes,' Mehrdad said. He was used to working and studying since he was nine.

'Good boy,' she said. Rare praise indeed. Sakina and Aisha were feeding the little ones. Mehrdad walked his mother to the bus stop on his way to work.

'I told Sakina you would take her to the mosque soon. Remember what I told you. Don't tell her anything,' his mother said as he walked off.

He looked back at her. She was the only woman at the bus stop with a headscarf. She was short and round and her face was a bit puffy. He could take a guess about what the Irish thought of her. They were none too pleased to have her stand amongst them.

His mother had always seemed an immutable force of nature. Housebound with only one trip twice a week to the market with the girls to get food, and Mehrdad to carry the bags. Pregnant and breast-feeding, steering all the kids through the drudgeries of the Orapian system. She loved them with a stoic, hard, ruthless, pragmatic love. He had never seen her do anything just for herself. Everything had been for her husband and children. She was a maternal machine.

On the little downtime they had at weekends, Mehrdad, Sakina and Aisha would play games with the little ones, while his mother finished the cooking and cleaning. Mehrdad saw a television in the St Vincent de Paul shop and bought it. His mother disapproved but let them keep it as they were cooped up in the one-bedroom apartment all week. When the work was absolutely done and the kids sat in front of the TV, his mother would sit to the side. Her hands resting on her thighs. The Koran open on her lap. She would stare ahead, not at the book. She did not know how to read or write. He invited her to watch the programme with them, but she had no interest. The great chore of a day was over. It was as if she was switched off. His mother was empty.

Mehrdad's voice was breaking. His sisters and brothers snickered when he spoke. Mehrdad made a date with Sakina to take her to the mosque. Sakina squeezed his pimples and told him she would go shopping for clothes.

'We're not going to the St Vincent de Paul. Let's go to the Ilac Centre or Grafton Street and find some cool clothes. I know what's in fashion. You have to trust me.'

Mehrdad soon learned what a good shoplifter Sakina was. She tried to get him in on the action, but he was terrified even to walk into a shop with her. Instead, he opted to wait outside. It wasn't the first time he had been to a city with a female thief.

'Get me one thing, Sakina,' he said as they walked down Grafton Street. Sakina marched beside him, her eyes shining with adrenaline. Suddenly, Mehrdad spotted someone he knew. He grew excited as if encountering an old friend.

'That's my singer. My singer. She sings here too.'

The busker seemed to recognise him. She winked as Mehrdad gave her some money to impress Sakina. He had never given anything before.

She stepped away from me,
And she moved through the fair
And fondly I watched her move here
And move there.
And she went her way homeward
With one star awake,
As the swan in the evening
Moved over the lake.

'That's a creepy song,' Sakina said when it was over.

'No, it's not,' Mehrdad said emphatically.

A few minutes later, they were in Waterstone's.

'I don't know where to find it.' He had never been in a bookshop before. There were so many books.

'We'll ask at the counter. What's it called?'

'We can't ask and then take it. That's too obvious.'

'Why don't you ask and we'll find it and I'll come another day.'

'When will you be back here?'

'I'm in town all the time with my friends.'

Mehrdad was struck that Sakina had friends. His mother had always disapproved of friendship unless it could get you something. It was the Orapian attitude, born from centuries of betrayal, spies, fighting and disloyalty. Trust only your immediate family.

The book on the shelf looked identical to the one he had seen before. *The Complete Works of Oscar Wilde.* He picked it up and removed the jacket to stroke the green cloth cover. He liked the weight of it in his hand. Sakina took it and shoved it in her jacket. He felt ill and his legs started to wobble. They left the shop and walked quickly into Trinity College through a side entrance.

'You do know your way around.' Mehrdad kept looking over his shoulder in terror. As the boy, he was the one who was allowed all the freedom. But all he did was work and study and bring groceries to Farah and Ali. Sakina lied to her mother all the time. As her eldest brother, he was responsible for her and should keep her at home out of trouble. Anything could happen.

'Isn't this lovely in here? Look how old it is. Nothing was this old and well kept up in Orap.'

'Yes, it is. I never even guessed it was here. Reminds me of home.'

'Orap? Are you mad?'

'It's like a paradise. Inside the city. Like the enclosed gardens at home.'

'I'll be going to this college as soon as I finish school,' Sakina stated.

'We'll be back in Orap by then.'

'After you, dear brother. I'm not going back,' Sakina said. 'I'm staying here. I hated it at first, but I've changed my mind. I've talked to the career guidance teacher in school, and she said she'd help me when the time comes. My English is getting better. I've Irish friends. The girls in school like me. I'm popular.'

'You were telling Maman that you were playing hockey after school. You're 13. Maman was married and pregnant with me when she was your age.'

'Maman's not too bright; she's just a workhorse peasant. That's what they programmed her for.' They sat on a bench. 'I hate being stuck in that flat. And now our cousins have come over too. We're as squashed as we were in Orap. I'm expected to look after their little ones as well.'

'Everyone has to work. They are at great risk as their status as refugees is not official. You must put the family first. I won't have you talk about Maman like that either. Not in front of me. Everything she does, she does for us.'

'At least you get paid for working. I mind the kids every night for free.'

Mehrdad was genuinely shocked. 'You're their sister.'

'I'm going to be a lawyer. I'm going to make lots of money.'

'Then maybe you'll stop stealing,' Mehrdad said.

'Spare the lecture, brother.' Sakina took his hand. 'That's a nasty burn. You should sue them. What I learnt about the West is that here you exist for yourself, not for your family. You are an individual, not a group. Progress, dear brother, not stasis. That's what my teacher said.'

Mehrdad studied his hand. 'The planet could do with a bit of stasis and less progress. Progress has gobbled everything up,' he said. The burn was at the bottom of his thumb. The skin around it had become tight and red and wrinkled. The burn was deep and green and glistening. The centre skin had been stripped by a few layers. It looked weird—scaly almost. He thought of Ali, who thought he was turning into a fish. What if all the Orapians were mutating once out of their homeland?

Humans had come from fish when the world was fresh and new.

Students walked by with books and bags. They talked to each other excitedly and laughed aloud. The women were as confident as the men.

Sakina smiled at him. 'Brother, you're going to look so cool in all those new clothes I got you. If you wear them, you can come and meet me and my girlfriends sometime. They think you're hot. They all want your number. If you open your eyes . . .' Sakina babbled on about her secret life, safe in the knowledge that Mehrdad would never betray her. 'I even have a friend from Nigeria. She's an unaccompanied minor. Came over on a truck on her own. She's escaping Sha'ria laws, she said. They were going to give her a hundred lashes. I met her in Virgin Megastore. She came up and started talking to me. She guessed where I was from. The only person ever to have heard of Orap. She's 17. She's pregnant. That's why she had to leave. She's going to sell her baby on the Internet and make some money and. . . .'

The word money brought him to his senses. 'We didn't spend much money. We can give some back to Maman. She'll be happy. You have to tell her I took you to the mosque after we got clothes. It's hard for her here.'

'Mehrdad, you're such a Good Son,' Sakina sneered. 'Good boy. Good Son. Well I'm going to use that money and go to McDonald's for dinner before we go home. If I have one more meal with rice, I'll puke.'

Mehrdad acquiesced; he was having a good time and seeing parts of the city he never saw. It was nice in the square in Trinity College. There were grand old statues and trees and grass. He hadn't seen a patch of grass since he had arrived in Dublin. They had a ground-floor flat off Parnell Street, where everyone had bars on their windows, and the natives were hostile. It had seemed such a grey, mournful city, he had shut it out and soaked himself in memories. But the parts his little sister was showing him were beautiful. He began for the first time to look about him at the people. Up till now they had been ghosts. Sakina gave him the book and he held it in both hands.

'You going to read that?' Sakina asked. She rested her head on his shoulder.

'No. I'm going to send it to Leila in America.'

'Are you in love with her? She's younger than me, and the Fatagagases will never allow it. She's not our class.'

'There's been a revolution. That stuff doesn't matter, does it? She's nearly 12 now. If we go back to Orap, I could marry her.'

'Mehrdad's in love,' Sakina said in a singsong voice. 'How are you going to get it to her?'

'She's with her uncle Mo. I once told Farah that I needed to send him a letter about his affairs in Orap and that way I have his address. I've been writing even in the camp. Now I have her direct address.'

'Has she written back?'

Mehrdad nodded his head and tapped the book. 'All the time.'

Mehrdad left the fast-food place after midnight. He wanted to go straight home after work. He was tired. But he had promised Farah and Ali that he would deliver their groceries for the upcoming week. Wearily, he served the populace kebabs of two shapes and sizes. They never looked at him nor he at them. Dark holes bored into his brain, and at the bottom of each one, Leila swam in a dark pool and her eyes were dark holes in her head, and in these dark holes he felt himself slipping as if down a tunnel to the end of something, and the end of something was down by the river, and the nights they spent there were the most magical and special of his whole worried life.

He slunk along cobblestone streets full of drunks. A group of Scots with painted faces bent over and flipped their kilts up, mooning at a shrieking gaggle of skin-tight sparkling women. Shrivelled boys with pale sunken faces pulled rickshaws, straining with a cargo of hefty inebriated revellers. It was obvious to Mehrdad that unlike their Asian counterparts, they were unused to such work. Blasts of music breathed from pub doors. Bald bouncers in cheap suits pushed people away. A young man, naked from the waist up, had a bottle broken over his head. He was spinning and screaming, the blood churning into his eyes. Mehrdad turned down a side street, and a girl was pissing between cars. She stuck her tongue out at him as he walked by. The streets got quieter and darker as he walked away from the forlorn mayhem of the Friday-night centre. He climbed the worn stone steps of the red-brick hostel and walked the corridor to Farah's room. He didn't want to knock so late, but he hesitated to hang the groceries on the door handle, as thieving was rife in the city. Farah opened the door.

'I thought it was you. Come in, child.'

Farah was wearing a black silk dressing gown with a dragon on the back. Mehrdad went immediately to Marguerite, who lay awake on the bed.

'She's getting so big.'

Farah gushed proudly. 'She smiled today. A real smile. Not a windy one.'

Mehrdad picked her up. He was well used to babies. 'I'm sorry I'm so late. The other guy didn't show up for his shift. So I had to stay on.'

'Aren't there labour laws here? Aren't you too young to work?'

'They think I'm older.'

'How can your mother survive on what the government gives her with all those children?'

'I work. She cleans houses.'

'You know, I don't think I've ever seen your mother,' Farah said.

Mehrdad knew she had. They had all been together on the flight over and waited in immigration offices for hours to get processed. 'We were on the journey together.'

'I forget the journey. I just kept taking the painkillers that dreadful nurse gave me.'

'Any more news about Ali?'

'No.'

'Has he got out on the road again?'

'I don't know, Mehrdad. I've nothing to do with him.'

'I remember him in the camp. I remember the day his group arrived. He wasn't crazy then. He seemed to be so relieved to be alive that the feet didn't matter.'

'On reflection, I'm sure he realised that he would need feet.' Farah sat on the bed. She wore a silk negligée beneath the gown. She still wore all her gold necklaces. 'Marguerite has been up all night. I'm too old for this. There's a reason you shouldn't have kids in your forties. I don't have the energy.'

'When is Doctor Fatagagas back?'

'Who knows? He's off with the royal family in the south of France. The queen needed him. She's got cancer.'

She had repeated this information so often.

'If you need to work, Madame Fatagagas,' Mehrdad said nervously, 'Sakina and Aisha could look after Marguerite. They wouldn't notice another baby.'

'I'm a registered nurse and a midwife. But I don't have any certificates or paperwork to prove that. What can I do?'

'My mother says that cleaning people are always in demand as the Irish don't want to do that work themselves. My restaurant has all foreign workers.'

Farah pulled her gown tightly closed. 'I am not going to do that kind of work. I had my own clinic. Everyone in my family is a professional.'

Mehrdad kissed Marguerite's feet. She smiled crookedly at him. He laughed. 'She does smile now. That's incredible.'

'Zolo smiled when he was one month old. He was holding his own bottle at eight weeks. He never crawled but pulled himself up and walked at eight months. He was speaking words at ten months. By the time he was two, he could read. I wasn't around many children after they were born. I took it all for granted.'

'And Leila?'

'Leila? Now that you mention it, she wasn't much further behind. I thought all babies progressed like that.'

'Zolo and Leila were the smartest kids I ever knew,' Mehrdad marvelled.

'What age is your mother, Mehrdad?'

'She's 28.'

'Twenty-eight? I thought she looked older than me.'

Farah must have noticed his mother after all. Mehrdad didn't say anything. Farah was looking pretty old to him, too.

When he left her room, he went upstairs to Ali. There was a burnt spoon with a bent handle on the bedside table. Mehrdad saw a syringe in Ali's hand. Ali wanted Mehrdad to get him drugs.

Instead, Mehrdad got him everything else he could. Ali always needed money. Mehrdad couldn't afford to keep giving, so he bought his groceries as a gesture. Ali had confided in him that his skin was becoming scaly. He kept touching his cheeks and saying that he was about to grow gills. The social worker was trying to keep him to his hospital appointments for his prosthetic-leg fittings. Ali distrusted hospitals, believing that they had secretly operated on him and taken his heart. Mehrdad had asked him what they had done with it. Ali had told them that they were using it in experiments.

The room smelt bad, like water left too long in a vase of rotting flowers. Ali sat on the bed; he had been given feet by the government. They were strapped on the bottom of his legs. The polite, hopeful young man that Mehrdad had first seen had metamorphosed not into a fish but into a foul-smelling deranged skeleton with synthetic feet.

'Ali, you got feet!' Mehrdad exclaimed.

Ali had black half-moons beneath his eyes. His hair was stale and sticky. He put a syringe to Mehrdad's throat. His breath smelt of all the chewed-up corpses that waited inside him. It smelt of all he had to become. His eyes were small and vicious. His skin was slippery and pale.

'I know you got paid tonight.'

Mehrdad shook his head and felt the syringe scrape his throat. 'Okay. Okay.'

'You think you're better than me, don't you? You think you do all the right things? A right little goody-goody-two-shoes.'

Mehrdad cringed as Ali groped into his jeans pockets. They were the new jeans Sakina had got for him. All this could be revenge for his own criminality. Ali slipped his hand up Mehrdad's shirt and found his money pouch. He emptied it out on to the floor. The notes fell in a neatly folded bundle at Mehrdad's new Nike shoes.

'Give me those shoes.'

Mehrdad flung the shoes across the room and ran.

As he fled the room, he ran in his socks from the hostel. He couldn't bear to go to home after what had happened. He didn't want to see any more Orapians ever. Shame came swinging out of the sky like a sack of cement on a rope and hit him full blast; he stumbled, falling face forward on the pavement. As he pulled himself off the ground, people watched from across the road. He wanted to tear off the stolen clothes and run naked through the city. He had to forget about Orap. He had to face life on this remote island that was painfully metamorphosing into the world. They hated him. Maybe they were right about who all his people were. Bad strangers on foreign shores, coming in ragged droves. Sending out the word. Flooding in from unheard-of places. Thieves. Scammers. Deranged drug-addled wards of the state. Uninvited guests. Unaccompanied minors. Liars. Calculating children.

What were they now? Only refugees. Hiding from the mess. Unsung wars, bad kings, bad gods, bad bad luck. Growing darker and darker as they got further and further away from home.

Once there was a time. And that was all he had. Down by the river. His memories of Leila. A time when they could babble about the nature of the night. A time before they had to stand out on the heartless road in an alien land, terrified of turning into something they were not.

Chapter Sixteen

Ishmael Returns to Ireland

A coin will be unearthed in thousands of years. It shows the profile of a king. Ishmael is not a king, but he is the creator of a king's profile. Ishmael cut into the nose and began dreaming. He felt genuine grandeur as he reshaped a small part of the inert, porky body of the anaesthetised crown prince. That the country no longer existed, and that the knocked-out fat child that lay on the table was the grandson of a son of a conniving military despot, no longer of any political relevance, had no effect on his spirits. He hummed as he worked. He practically danced about the operating table, flexing his nimble fingers, and believed he was in the privileged position of carving a nose that would belong to history.

After the operation, he scrubbed up and prepared himself to go home to the queen. He imagined a candlelight dinner, just the two of them, and some discreet bodyguards outside the door, as her son recovered in the hospital. He would, with his long fingers, trace the outline of the new nose in the air. The queen would lower her eyes and smile. Instead, he returned to the residence to find the gate swinging open and all the bodyguards vanished. He walked into the villa, loudly pounding his feet, clearing his throat to announce his presence. He dozed in the living room for an hour as a phone rang and rang. He was exhausted from his exertions in the theatre. He was out of practice, he regretted—before, he could perform seven routine surgeries a day. A cook arrived for the evening shift and ran screaming back through the house. She did not notice Ishmael sitting there. Ishmael went out to the patio from where she had come. The queen's daughters and one bodyguard were lying by the pool face down. They had all been shot. He contemplated running but instead went to look at the three bodies. The cook called the police as he squatted down by the princess and put his jacket over her. He had nothing with which to cover the other princess, so he took off his shirt and placed it over her. The bodyguard was not royal, and he just nudged him with his foot. Then he thought of the police arriving and finding him shirtless by three murdered bodies. Ishmael took his bloody shirt back and put it on.

He went running from the house down to the village to hail a taxi. It was up to him, Doctor Ishmael Fatagagas, to protect the prince. Of course they had wanted the prince as last heir to the throne. The police picked him up as he was huffing and puffing down the long winding road. He tried to tell them what he was doing, but they spoke no English and handcuffed him and left him locked in the back seat of the car.

He had an alibi, of course. He had been at the hospital. The prince would have been killed if he had been at home. In a way, Ishmael's rhinoplasty had saved his life. But the autopsy reported that the younger princess had bled to death. Ishmael had arrived shortly after the assassins had left. He might have saved her if he had not stopped to doze in an armchair. The queen, who had been at the hospital with her son, was told this.

That was his part in a footnote of history. He was a footnote of a footnote. And was it worth it?

For him, I think it was.

Ishmael returned to Ireland shaken. Comforted, though, that the prince had a nose fit for a king, and was alive and ripe for succession. Ishmael promised the prince that he would look out for him. That he, Ishmael, would take special interest in his life. He assured him that he would one day return to the throne. The prince seemed not to pay attention to his doctor. To this average, unimaginative young man, the throne seemed more like a seat on a roller coaster. He had had to attend the funeral with a bandage on his nose. People saw the pictures in the newspapers and assumed he had only just survived the attack.

It was hard to come back to the grim Victorian red-brick hostel in Dublin after the villa in France. It was hard to look at his venomous wife and mewling baby all cooped up in one room after he had just been to the funeral of his murdered royal family. And he, Doctor Ishmael Fatagagas, had stood in the third row around a royal grave.

'You need to lose weight. You are so fat now,' he said to his wife only five minutes after returning. 'It was never a problem with the other babies. You still look pregnant.'

'I was not in my forties then,' Farah hissed bitterly. 'Your hair has all fallen out on top. You are no prize. It makes your nose bigger than ever.'

'Your hair is getting thin too. I think you're going bald. And you're a woman.'

Farah put her hand up to her head in horror. She had been finding clumps of hair on the pillow in the morning. When she brushed her hair, locks just fell away on to the floor.

Ishmael picked up Marguerite and looked closely at her face. 'I think she has not got the family nose. Perhaps she won't need surgery. Who knows what we can afford when she is 16.'

'Is that it? Do you intend to give up just like that?' Farah took her baby away from him. 'We must get to America.'

'We are the garbage of the world. No one wants us.' Ishmael shrugged.

'You have to go get a job. I've been relying on Mehrdad to feed me and bring me groceries.'

'Mehrdad?' Ishmael brightened at the sound of his former servant's son's name. 'I knew he'd come by. He's a good boy.'

'Mehrdad says that we can work since we are programmed refugees, not like the others.'

'How can I be a doctor here? I'll have to pass exams. I've forgotten everything. It's been a long time since I was in school.'

'Perhaps you could be a non-practising consultant.'

Mehrdad got Ishmael a job as a night security man in an office building on the quays. Ishmael was grateful that it was a lonesome job, and that no one saw him there. Ishmael had based his personality on impressing others. He had gone to medical school, not because he wanted to be a doctor but because it was the most prestigious degree in Orap in his day. He dressed impeccably, not to please himself but to make an impression. He bought a house by the river, not because he liked to be beside the water but because it was the most upmarket property he could find. He purchased a library, not because he liked books but because it would make him look learned. He loved the royal family, not because of who they were but because of what they were.

That was Ishmael—inadequate, blind, vain.

Maybe the family should have loved Ishmael more. They would have loved him more if he had all the vestiges of success still around him. His surgery, his borrowed fame, his royal connections, his big house by the river. But in their eyes, he was damned as a refugee, pared down to just the essence of a human. He was a tamed animal, dependent on others for support and security. He was at the whim of every visa office and immigration officer. His manner both beseeching and resentful.

There was nothing to inherit. His legacy was only that: resentment and forgery. Lies and exaggerations. Distrust of officials. The ability to wait for hours in any government office, holding a number, daydreaming about royalty.

Did those official men and women know that Ishmael was doctor to a queen?

And his bald queen—did she care that he stayed loyal? Perhaps her one loyal subject. As she ran from villa to villa, Riviera to Riviera, with her cells multiplying in all those swimming pools under all those plush suns, her daughters dead, and the servants whispering, the cafés buzzing, hints of ridicule for one fallen, cells exploding, the news of her dropping from the back pages and finally off the paper on to the train-station floor, where Ishmael walked over her image in Dublin as he got a shoeshine just to have someone at his feet, someone to look down on. That was how he discovered she was dead; he had his foot on her obituary while getting the shoeshine.

Ishmael disengaged from the present; he permitted himself one folly—a subscription to *National Geographic*. In essence, he got trapped in geological measurements, and could no longer fathom the insignificance of human-scale time. He retreated into a world of flora and fauna, of animal facts and geological facts picked out of magazines.

Baby Zero, that is the comfort for my baba. If we are judged geographically, his life amounts to the same as every other life. Beethoven and Ishmael are equal in this. There is no failure and success for individuals. Millions of years pass in short sentences.

All his money was lost, the currency collapsed, the houses confiscated. Ishmael was still in shock. Most of the other wealthy or middle-class Orapians had seen it coming and got their money out. His brother had warned him. He didn't do it, and now he was here with his wife and his new daughter.

In Orap, Ishmael was robust and jolly, with Western manners. Now, here in the West, he was gaunt. A refugee, shrinking in his old good suits grown tatty, less Western than he fancied, darkening by the minute, black eyes throwing shadows in half-circles beneath. He was once in the queen's bedroom, and she confided in him. She gave him a bag of her clothes. He could never believe a country could disappear. He never knew you could grow darker and more foreign without a country, smaller as the world expands, seething because your life felt over. He kept the TV on all day as if its noise could fill his exile. On the nights he didn't work, he left it mute but slept in front of it, as if its noiseless flickering could pace him, illuminate him, sex him, and rock him through the nights when he knew that his queen was dead and his land undone.

Ishmael stood at nights on the fifth floor of the office block, looking through the glass at the black river Liffey flanked by high grey stone walls. When it rained, the river filled to the brim, shuddering and sloppy. This night, it was dry, and the river was so low that he could smell it from behind the glass. A city river that reminded him of the other river in Orap, and then the river inside the river. This dirty river had all the mystery of every river. Origins in high clean mountains, its deliberation, its unfriendliness, and its disbelief that it was one day to be part of the sea.

Reading the *National Geographic* at work, he learnt about early man. Yes, Farah said, when he was foolish enough to try to engage her in conversation on the topic, yes you should get on with the cavemen. That is what you have brought us to. She would talk only about visas, passports or immigration. She carried a big leather handbag everywhere she went, with all their current documents. The only thing he ever saw Farah read in all those years was the deed to her house in Orap. She read it time and time again.

Ishmael would tell the polite Mehrdad, 'At the very beginning, animals began to be aware of each other on the Savannah, the hunter and the hunted. Humans developed words for animals first. The words for everything were like markers, and words were signs. Now we use stamps and visas to mark territories. Our mind was full of awareness of animals that we don't need now. Animals had given us language and made us human. So you see the consequences to us of losing all the wild animals on the planet that could challenge us. Sure, there are still squirrels and raccoons, but are there lions?'

Mehrdad would nod and take his leave. Ishmael would be left to look out the window. That river that he starred at each night. As the tiger marked with urine, we mark it with a word—Liffey. He couldn't think why this was important, but it did seem to be. What did animals matter to us now? He saw from his dark window a few seagulls cut in and out of the night sky, and once in a while he heard a mouse scratch behind a desk. Did they make him human? He was lonely. He would ask Mehrdad if he thought it was important. It would be good for Mehrdad to see that Ishmael thought of other things besides visas like Farah and money like Mehrdad's mother. Ishmael would be there to show him that other things must be contemplated to be a distinguished, fully rounded gentleman. Ishmael tried to think of what he was thinking, but he had forgotten it already. In truth, he couldn't really grasp what the article had been getting at, but Mehrdad wouldn't delve, and Mehrdad would think he knew, and that's what counted.

Ishmael always wore a karakul hat, a football-shaped fez-like hat with ripply, baby-soft fur. All the rich nobles wore such hats in Orap. It had taken him a long time in Orap to work up the courage to wear the hat. He started once he graduated from medical school, and he wasn't going to give it up. It was rather kingly, and it served the dual purpose of reminding him of his own rank and covering his baldness. He suspected that it made him stand out here and look more foreign, but he hoped it signalled to the Irish that he was a man of stature. The hat he would take off and stroke for comfort. It was this soft because shepherds in Orap killed pregnant ewes to get the foetuses' fur. The fur had a special quality—innocence, never being exposed to light or air. It took a whole foetus to make one hat. This man, who had lost his profession, two of his children and his country, strolled around the empty, dimly lit building in a security guard's uniform and his whole-foetus hat.

Marguerite was often sick, and they always brought her to the A&E together. These were their only outings, he and Farah together. Farah said he dragged his feet when he walked; she said his shirts were wrinkled; she said his pants were worn; she said he spat when he talked; she said he snored; she said his breath smelled when he crawled on top of her at nights; she said he ejaculated too quickly and she no longer had an orgasm with him, his belly was growing too big and pressed on her unpleasantly when he lay on top; she said he breathed too loudly, made whistling sounds through his nose; she said that hairs were growing out of his nose and ears that she found repulsive; she said he was sloppy when he made the formula for the baby, he spilled the powder on the counter; she said he left his cups around with tea in them, and left teabags in the sink, and tissues in his trousers pockets that came apart in the laundry. She said he was like all other Orapian men when he got up and pushed her. He had never done that before. He pushed her against the door handle. Then he tried to strangle her. Her legs buckled and her face turned red. He was yelling while kneeing her in the chest. The African women came running down the corridor and opened the door and pulled him off. He had never done that before. His father had done it to his mother, and his brothers had done it to their wives, and even the king had done it to the queen.

But Ishmael believed he was justified, as it was Farah who would goad him and goad him, pointing out all the myriad proofs of his uselessness until he would have to shut her up. Then when he sat contrite and hateful, she would goad him again: look at you; at age 55, you become a wife-beater; is that all you can think of?

When Mehrdad had found him this job and taken him along for the interview, he had admired the way in which Mehrdad knew his way around the city. They had stopped to listen to a busker sing a sad song. Ishmael felt his old self with Mehrdad. Mehrdad showed him deference. Farah nagged him to study and become a doctor all over again, but he was 55 and, frankly, almost happy here alone in the building at night, walking the floors, through the offices and booths, looking at other people's family photos and reading the cartoon strips they put on their cubicles. Being part of the building but not part of the people. He actually liked this job. His visits to the American Embassy filled his day. Down there, he wore a skullcap and told them he was a Jew and had been persecuted in Orap. They were getting tired of him; they told him there was little they could do for him. He was lucky to be out and should make his life here. They didn't know he had two children in the States that he had to get back to. He couldn't tell the truth because Farah had been so quick to get Mo to say they were his children to get them out of the camp. All their papers had been taken from of them when they were fleeing Orap. Farah brought that up every day. She blamed him for that too. Ishmael had spent his whole life in Orap inventing himself, and now the struggle to reinvent was too much.

Mehrdad said that programmed refugees were often offered legal status in the country after a number of years. Like the wily peasants they were, Mehrdad and his family were thriving. They were all speaking English in the funny Irish way. They all did well in school and worked jobs after their studies. Their mother cleaned houses relentlessly. Mehrdad found Ishmael and Farah a small flat in Parnell Street, away from the hostel, and they moved and were more comfortable. Again, Mehrdad made the mistake of telling Farah that she could clean houses too. Farah told Ishmael to keep him away from the house.

'Has that insolent boy forgotten who we are? You have done too much for him, been too familiar. How dare he! I had my own clinic.'

'He was only trying to help. Of course he knows we are his betters. He always treats me with respect.'

But Farah discovered to her irritation that she needed Mehrdad. She could order him around. He did all the painting in the new flat for free. He even supplied the paint from leftovers from his own flat. He did the grocery shopping for her. He walked Marguerite up and down when she was grumpy and restless. He got them furniture from the St Vincent de Paul. He was the only visitor.

Farah never left the flat once they moved in, except to go to the hospital with Marguerite, the Embassy or any government office she could think of. She was always at government offices trying to extract things from them. The doctor with the long red hair, at the hospital, tried to explain to her that she shouldn't be using the A&E for general care, but she ignored her. She trusted only this doctor and wanted to be in a big hospital, not a small surgery.

This was their life in Ireland: embassies, A&E, empty buildings, river-gazing, wife-beating, blaming each other for everything.

'The children could have been with us,' Ishmael said.

'Thank God they are in America and not this place. What would become of them in this place?'

'Mehrdad is doing well. It's Europe after all. It's not so bad. Leila is only 12. We should have her with us.'

Farah sat at the bay window and looked down the street. 'I don't know if this is Europe. There are so many black people here. I feel I'm in Africa.'

'There are black people in America too,' Ishmael said.

'Yes, but they live in separate places. I don't think they live with the whites.'

'Mehrdad says we look black to them,' Ishmael said. 'The Irish.'

'You do with that hat of yours. You don't blend in. I think I pass for Italian or Spanish.'

'In your dreams,' Ishmael snorted.

'The Irish are ignorant. They are not Americans. Americans know the difference.'

'I saw Mehrdad's sister with an Irishman in a café. Sakina, I think her name is. The pushy ugly one who never wears a veil.'

'They are all whores, those girls.' Farah perked up, folded her arms and shook her head.

'And they're all pretty ugly too. Not like our little Leila. She is lovely. Remember her in her little bikini by the pool. Do we have any photos from then?'

Farah nodded, smiling, and went to get the photos. This was a pleasant conversation between them. As long as they were both criticising everybody, they got along just fine.

Farah scrutinised the people who walked past the window. 'There are no good-looking people here in Ireland.'

'I hear the women are all blonde and tall in California,' Ishmael said.

Farah smiled longingly. 'Yes, that is what they are.'

Marguerite, their dark daughter, stirred in her sleep.

The next day, Mehrdad came to the apartment. He gave Farah a Tupperware container of Orapian stew from his mother. Farah took it grudgingly.

'Your mother is lucky she has time to do such things,' Farah said. Farah and Ishmael had a tiny kitchen and did not cook much except rice and canned food.

'My cousin has been killed. His was one of the families to come over hiding in a ship's container. He was walking home alone, and some men spotted him as a foreigner and beat him to death. They were living with us. My mother is very shocked and scared. I took this to you because I was hoping you'd visit her, Madame Fatagagas. A visit from someone from home would mean a lot.'

'Where are the boy's parents? Are you all living together in one flat?'

'His parents are still in Orap, trying to get out.'

Farah sighed. 'We have found ourselves in a savage place. I'm frightened to go out. When Ishmael comes home from the American Embassy, I will ask him to escort me.'

'Why is he always at the Embassy?' Mehrdad asked.

'Doctor Fatagagas, his brother, has great influence, and we are preparing to get our visas and join Zolo and Leila.'

'I will miss you,' Mehrdad said shyly.

Farah was shocked.

When Ishmael arrived back, she told him, 'We may be from home, but we are not of their class. I don't know if we should pay a visit. It might be giving the wrong signal. We would never have gone to their compound in Orap.'

'Are you asking my advice or telling me you won't visit?' Ishmael said.

'Why does everything have to be a challenge?' Farah shouted.

'You started it,' Ishmael said, raising his voice.

And so they started yelling and shouting at each other again, and no one went to see Mehrdad's mother. Heather the social worker made an unexpected visit that night.

'There is a service in the mosque in Clonskeagh. It's in honour of Mehrdad's cousin Parvese who was murdered. I can drive you there tomorrow, if you'd like. I know public transport in Dublin is a pain. Hey, I heard Ishmael is working. That's fantastic.' Heather was sitting with the baby in her arms. 'Marguerite's looking great— so much better.'

Heather arrived the following morning in a beat-up tiny car with magazines and books scattered all over the back seat. Ali, with his new feet, was sitting in the back. Heather had got a baby seat for the day, and they all squeezed into her car and took off towards the mosque.

'I must buy a car,' Ishmael said, turning to Farah in the back seat. 'It feels funny to be in a car after all this time. Doesn't it feel funny, Farah?'

Farah replied, 'Don't be foolish.' She looked at Heather. 'We both had Mercedes cars in Orap. They are good cars.'

'Wow!' said Heather. 'On a social worker's salary, this is all I get. Second-hand at that. I know a friend who's selling a car. Maybe I could hook you up.'

Ishmael brightened up. 'Yes. Yes. Now that I'm working, I could possibly afford one. It would be nice to get out of the city at weekends. We've seen nothing of this country.'

'We are not buying a car. We are going to America,' Farah said.

Ishmael shrugged at Ali and winked in male complicity. 'She's the boss.'

Ali shook a rattle in the baby's face, and the baby smiled at him.

Ishmael glanced at the gaunt Ali and said, 'She smiles at me all the time. She just doesn't respond to her mother.'

'That's not true. She smiles at me too,' Farah pouted.

'I'm so glad you two are coming.' Heather beamed. 'Mehrdad's mum is in a really bad way. She needs all your support.'

The mosque was crowded. The building had been newly rebuilt after an arson attack. It was a splendid mosque now, with a magnificent gold dome and intricate tile work donated and paid for by a worldwide Muslim effort to restore Dublin's historical first and premier mosque. All of Dublin's Muslim community had turned up for the funeral. The Lord Mayor of Dublin was present, and so too were several members of the Catholic hierarchy. There were TV cameras outside and photographers. Ishmael was impressed.

'See, this is a big deal,' he said to Farah. 'I'm glad we came.'

'Now I feel bad I didn't visit Mehrdad's mother,' Farah said, nodding.

Mehrdad's family was outside. The mullahs were leaning forward and talking to his mother. Farah approached and the mother saw her. They squeezed hands. Mehrdad's mother had been crying. Mehrdad was supporting her. His arm was around her. She leant on her son. Her six other children sat forlorn and grieving. The murdered boy's sister was shaking with sobs. All the women were in veils. Farah had brought a headscarf with her to put on before entering the mosque. She was giving her condolences to the family when she saw Sakina, Mehrdad's eldest sister. Though she wore a veil, she was heavily made up, and diamond earrings glittered on her ears. Farah got close to her and embraced her so that she could get a better look. Farah's face flushed. An electric current coursed through her body. Everyone was picking up Marguerite and admiring her. Farah went to the side and grabbed Ishmael.

'What is it, woman?' Ishmael was irritated. He wanted to enjoy himself here. For the first time, he was seeing other men and had some status as Mehrdad's only elder from Orap. 'I should talk to the mayor. Do you know the mayor of the city is here?'

'Ishmael, look at Mehrdad's sister, the tallest one. Look at her earrings.'

'What are you talking about? Everyone is going inside. We must go. I want to be with Mehrdad's family. I think the head mullah is talking to him now.'

'Hush. They are my earrings. Mine. I recognise them. They are from my mother. Mehrdad must have stolen them on one of his visits. I knew he was too good to be true. He was just using all that help as a pretext to rob us blind.'

'There must be a mistake,' Ishmael said.

'No mistake.' Farah was triumphant. 'They are my earrings. You want to buy a car? You could buy several cars with those earrings.'

'Really?' Ishmael turned to look. 'Which one is she?'

Farah and Ishmael told Heather. Heather said she would look into it. 'If he stole them, why would she wear them in front of you? I don't think Mehrdad would steal anything.'

'Ask them,' Farah said.

Heather said, 'Not now.'

'If you don't ask them now, I will call the police.'

Heather took Mehrdad aside and they talked frantically. He went to his sister and pleaded for the earrings. Sakina refused. 'They gave them to you for taking their suitcases. We had to leave most of our stuff behind just to take all their suitcases. There were five suitcases.' He told Heather. Heather said, 'I'm sorry. I'll tell them to lay off. This is not the time.'

Heather went to Farah and told her as much.

Mehrdad's mother kept glancing at Farah during the ceremony. The grief on her face had been replaced by a look of worry.

Farah asked Ishmael, 'Did you give my diamond earrings that my mother gave me to Mehrdad in exchange for taking our suitcases from the refugee camp to Ireland?'

'I don't think so,' Ishmael said. 'I wouldn't do a thing like that.'

'You gave away much of my jewellery for opium.'

'No. No, I didn't give your stupid earrings to Mehrdad.'

Farah went up to one of the many gardaí and told him.

'I remember you. Your friend with no legs was out on the road, and you came to get him back.'

'He is not my friend. We are from the same country but not the same class,' Farah said. 'And those are my earrings, and they have been stolen.'

Heather came running up, flustered. 'Farah, there has been a misunderstanding. We'll sort it out.' Heather looked at the garda who was only too happy not to interfere. Farah was led away by Ishmael. A rumpled man with a red face and a cravat came up to Farah a few minutes later and said, 'I heard you reported a theft.'

Farah said, 'I most certainly did. That family has hijacked my earrings. They were in my family for two generations. My mother gave them to me. Those earrings I thought were lost. I was most upset to have lost them. That young man was my gardener's son in Orap. He pretended to help me when my husband was performing surgery on the queen's son. Instead, he was stealing my jewellery. And they sit and weep and look so innocent. That family is trouble.

Those girls pretending to be so modest in their veils. My husband spotted them hanging out with boys and with no veils on. Not that I agree with the veil. But still . . .'

The man was writing it all down in a notebook, with a stubby blunt pencil.

'Officer, I do not want trouble. I know it is terrible what happened to their family, but I do want my earrings back. They are all I have left.'

The man smiled slyly. He had patches of egg on his tweed jacket, and his eyebrows were shaggy and wiry. 'I'm not an officer. I'm a reporter for the *Irish Globe*.' Brusquely, he signalled for a photographer beside him to take Farah's photo. Farah smiled into the camera.

The next day, Ishmael was holding the newspaper, screaming at her. 'They say we are from Iraq. Didn't you say Orap?'

'I just wanted my earrings back.' Farah's face reddened.

A CLOSER LOOK AT A REFUGEE TRAGEDY

Refugee woman claims that fellow refugee stole all she had left, while her husband was off performing vital surgery on the Queen of Iraq, to save her life after she had been brutally butchered by extreme fundamentalists. This man's cousin is murdered and the Irish Establishment has the decency to extend their sympathy at a Muslim funeral, but the thief's family have the nerve to show up draped in a stolen heirloom necklace. The murdered man paid smugglers to get him into the country illegally. Two bishops were there to pander to these illegals. If one of our own dies, does he get this kind of attention?

Heather sat with Mehrdad's family in the tiny one-bedroom apartment. The family was huddled together, united in a siege mentality. All of them, even the youngest of the children, looked haggard and exhausted. They had stayed up all night grieving, and a frantic and distraught Mehrdad had called Heather in the morning when a neighbour had showed them the newspaper. Heather tried to find the words as she nursed a glass full of hot tea. Mehrdad's mother always gave her tea in a glass that burnt her fingers slightly. And there was always too much sugar in it. Even in her bewildered state, Mehrdad's mother laid a tray of biscuits out for the guest. 'No one reads this trash. They are always inciting people about refugees and immigrants.'

'I heard it was the biggest circulating newspaper,' Sakina said.

'Can't you just give the earrings back before there's trouble?' Heather wrapped a napkin around the glass so she could pick up the tea.

'I never wanted those earrings,' Mehrdad said. 'My father said to give them back. It was too much just for a few suitcases.'

'We had to leave most of our stuff behind to carry the Fatagagases' suitcases because Mehrdad and Baba said we should. We deserve the earrings.' Sakina scowled. 'I propose we get a lawyer and sue them for talking about us like that. The thief's family. Tell her to prove it. That bitch. My friend's father said we could sue them for defamation.'

'What's defamation? How do you even think like that, Sakina? Everyone at work read it.' Mehrdad was trembling with shame. Heather put her arm around him. To the shock and horror of all the family, Mehrdad began to cry. His mother yanked him by the arm and pushed him into the bedroom. Heather was tired and had another appointment. She made her excuses and left.

Mehrdad came that night to where Ishmael worked. Ishmael let him inside the dark empty building. They stood on the fourth floor overlooking the cold, murky river Liffey. There were shouts from the drunks below, and a soft rain was beginning to pattern the brown pavement like spots of ink.

'Doctor Fatagagas, I apologise. I knew it was too much at the time but I took it. There was so much confusion, and the camp was breaking up. You must tell the newspapers that it was an exchange.'

Ishmael adjusted his wool hat, and his face was creased with worry. 'Mehrdad, I don't remember. Did I exchange such valuable diamonds for porter services? I can't see that I did. There was, as you say, too much confusion. Perhaps you took them out of the suitcases. Just give them back and we'll let the matter rest. I won't press charges out of deference to your family's recent tragedy. Your mother must be upset enough with you. Unless she told you to take them. Did she?'

Mehrdad was incredulous. 'Doctor Fatagagas, you gave them to me. I didn't steal them. I will give them back. But I never stole them.'

Mehrdad stood in a tourist shop in Temple Bar, trying to choose a present for his mother. There was a song piped over the speaker. *If you're Irish come into the parlour, there's a welcome there for you.* Mehrdad bought a tin whistle with a set of songs and decided to teach himself to play like the busker he liked. He asked the red-headed woman in the shop if she had a tape with the song he liked. He didn't know the name so he sang a bit to her.

She crept close to me and this she did say,
Oh it will not be long love till our wedding day.

The woman was delighted with him and found him a tape with the song on it: 'She Moved through the Fair'. They sang it together in the shop. Some South Americans stopped to listen and they clapped. He finally got his mother a cushion with an old Gaelic prayer embroidered on it.

He took the cushion home and his mother hugged him. She couldn't read, so he read and translated it for her. *Deep peace of the running waves to you. Deep peace of the flowing air to you. Deep peace of the smiling stars to you. Deep peace of the quiet earth to you.*

She looked at him with tears and said, 'You are a good boy. The only one who remembered my birthday. Mehrdad, did you take those earrings?'

Mehrdad said that he did not. Sakina took the cushion and hit Aisha over the head with it.

'Maman, of course he's innocent. He's Mehrdad. How can you doubt him? Look at him. He's such a dork, buying a cushion for his mother. Look at the little cottage embroidered on it. Tacky!'

Mehrdad's mother took her cushion back. 'I would like to live in such a house. I want you to get all of us out of this city.'

Sakina snorted. 'You'd have to lose the veil for once and for all, or we'd get lynched.'

Aisha found the tin whistle in a plastic bag and they gathered round. 'Teach me, Mehrdad. Teach me!'

Mehrdad took it back, annoyed. Sakina was laughing at him. They were all afraid of Sakina. She had such Orapian female ferocity. Even his mother let her off all duties and chores. She was allowed do her study and hang out with her friends. She did as she pleased. Sakina now took the tin whistle out of the package and danced around the room, the children following her like the Pied Piper. Mehrdad's mother laughed for the first time since they had left Orap. Mehrdad did not intervene because he was happy to see his mother enjoy herself.

'This is the new Riverdance,' Sakina shouted breathlessly. 'Mullahdance!'

When the family of eight, plus two cousins, slept in the tiny flat that night, Mehrdad went to Sakina's bag and took the earrings. Sakina followed him out of the house in her pyjamas. He stopped at the street corner and let her catch up. He was wearing pyjamas too, under his jacket.

'Now you are a thief. If these stupid things are worth so much, let's sell them and get a small house somewhere.'

'Even Maman thinks I stole them,' Mehrdad said.

'I know you didn't. I know that Doctor Fatass was doing opium with all the men. I heard all the talk about him giving away everything his wife had for it. I know he would have just given them to you in his lordly fashion.'

'You're only 13 years old, Sakina. What do you know?' Mehrdad said, but he was relieved she was here talking to him.

'What do you care what the newspapers say? They got everything wrong. They said we were from Iraq not Orap. One of the other newspapers said we were Afghanis.'

'No one even knows where Orap is.'

'That's our lot in life. No one who doesn't come from Orap knows of its existence. Hey, before we got here, did we know Ireland existed? Anyway, they said it was a necklace and Doctor Fatass was operating on the queen. None of them bothered to get the truth, and now it's forgotten. The earrings are real and worth a fortune. Think of our family.'

Mehrdad shook his head. 'They were from Madame Fatagagas's mother. It is all she has left of her family. They are special to her. Worth more than money. I was thinking of the Fatagagases today when I was buying Maman a present. Their children are far away. Leila is lonely. Zolo doesn't write to them. They have no one. I have all my brothers and sisters and I have my mother. We are lucky.'

The pyjama-clad brother and sister walked all the way through the town to the big empty office building. Ishmael opened the door with many keys.

He didn't let them in. He was holding a magazine and looked distracted.

'Did you know that three-quarters of known animals are no bigger than a shoe?'

'No,' Sakina said, raising her eyebrows. Mehrdad put his hand firmly on her arm before she said something insolent. 'Are you okay, Doctor Fatagagas? You look worried.'

'I have had such bad news. Terrible news.'

'Are Leila and Zolo okay?'

Ishmael's face became guarded. 'I have things to think about. The geological truce between our restless planet and us may be coming to an end. Nature is impervious to our needs. I'm reading about the Hawaii seam. Everything could fall apart, and a tidal wave could wash over the west coast of America.'

'Leila and Zolo should come here maybe,' Zolo suggested.

'What's the difference? Everywhere is in peril. The polar caps are melting. India and China are converging at two inches a year. The geological quiescence isn't going to last. We are living on this planet by geological assent.'

'Did you read that in the magazine?'

'No. I have a small portable TV. I was watching the Discovery Channel. In some places, only four miles separates us and the magma.'

'The magma?'

'Intolerable heat.'

'I've brought the earrings,' Mehrdad said.

Ishmael took the earrings and pocketed them without looking at them.

'Good boy. We can put this behind us. Good boy.'

'He is,' Sakina said. 'He's better than all of us. And I think you should quit this job. It would make anyone demented.'

Ishmael went back inside to look at the earrings. Cataclysms momentarily forgotten.

Mehrdad pulled Sakina away and she was laughing. They broke into a sprint across the arch of the Halfpenny Bridge.

'His eyes were all red. Do you think he's on drugs again?' Sakina said.

Mehrdad shook his head. 'I don't know. I didn't know he was ever on drugs. That was just Orapian gossip. Orapians might have been jealous of him because most of the people in the camp were poor or servants like us. The Fatagagases were almost the only upper class that didn't get out on time. They were unlucky.'

'Stupid, more like it.' Sakina shrugged without an ounce of compassion. 'The bollocks looked like he was crying.'

On the way home, Ishmael told Sakina of the time that he and Leila had walked through Orap with no clothes.

'That's why you're leaving the earrings back. So they'll let you marry her. Dream on. I hate that family. No one likes them.'

'Not really. I was thinking of Madame Fatagagas and her mother.'

Sakina put her arm around her older brother. 'You probably were, you idiot.'

'Leila writes lonely things in the letters,' Mehrdad said. 'We are lucky.'

Ishmael sold the diamond earrings the following week, bought a car and opened a bank account in his name only.

Mehrdad moved his family to County Wicklow outside Dublin. His mother no longer wanted to live in the city because the incidents of harassment were adding up and her nephew was dead. There were only two bedrooms, but the living room and kitchen were big, and a picture of the Virgin Mary hung over the huge fireplace. The kids raced around the overgrown garden and climbed the stone walls. The man renting it was a farmer; he carried a blackthorn stick and wore a cap. Mehrdad thought with satisfaction that he looked like the men in the posters in the tourist shops. The farmer slapped the walls and said, 'This is an old place. Used to belong to my grandmother. There's no heat, but you can light a fire. The toilet is outside. This house is built from limestone. We rent it out as a holiday cottage from time to time, but I'd rather have ye in it all year round.'

'What's limestone?' Sakina asked. She glanced around in horror—to be stuck here and not in the city.

'Look, she's wearing a veil too.' Aisha pointed to the picture of the Virgin.

The farmer inspected the picture and looked closely at his new foreign tenants. Suddenly he relaxed. 'Indeed, you're right!'

Mehrdad wrote that in his next letter to Leila. But Leila had abruptly stopped writing back. Mehrdad summoned the courage to go to Ishmael and ask about her. Ishmael had missed Mehrdad.

'She's fine. Just busy. She's going to be a doctor.'

'But she's only 12.'

'She must concentrate on her studies. I had no idea you were writing to her. Where are your family now?'

'We live in a cottage in Wicklow. It's called Limestone Cottage. I take the bus into the city to work, but all the kids are going to school out there. The farmer we rent it from said he could give me a job. I won't be in Dublin much any more.'

'Limestone Cottage?'

'Its walls are made of limestone.'

'Do you know what limestone is?' Ishmael puffed his chest out and frowned at Mehrdad.

'It's just the white stone walls.'

Ishmael lowered his voice with some reverence and said, 'Shells, corals, bones, teeth, and sea lilies from the tropical sea that used to cover Ireland.'

'A tropical sea covered this country?' Mehrdad asked him in disbelief. 'When was that?'

'Two hundred and seventy million years ago,' Ishmael said.

'Should I visit Madame Fatagagas?'

'No,' Ishmael said. 'It's better you don't visit. It's better you don't write to Leila any more. She's no longer at the address you're writing to.'

'Could I have her new address?' Mehrdad felt panic rise in his throat. He felt his world slip away.

'No, you can't write to her any more.' Ishmael marched away to the door and signalled for Mehrdad to leave the building.

That was the last time Mehrdad saw Ishmael until he turned up almost a quarter of a century later at the Fatagagas apartment in Westwood, Los Angeles. He was 40 years old and he felt 15 again.

PART V

LOS ANGELES

Chapter Seventeen

A Day Without a Buzz

Clip, clip, clip! Leila cut a rectangle of words from a Balinese guidebook and rubbed the glue on the back. Mrs Clancy had stumbled on a box of out-of-date *Rough Guides* from various countries and had purchased it for a mere five dollars. She had placed the box outside Leila's room and promptly forgotten it. Leila was looting it for her scrapbooks. Now she was learning the history of the world through guidebooks; while also skimming valuable information about flora, fauna, visa requirements and what to pack.

> When the Dutch invaded and took over Bali, there were other portents at the time, such as the huge Banyan tree in front of Pura Taman Sari bursting out into strange golden flowers, sightings of comets, beached whales and mudslides. These were taken as a sign that Klungkung's time was up. Around 200 members of the Balinese royal household committed suicide that day; the remainder were exiled and did not return for many years.

She stuck this new piece into the scrapbook. She was beginning to have the outline of something. The same Cowboy and Indian story over and over again in different costumes, in different locations, and somehow she thought that led to what they said was happening to the animals, the speciocide. Everyone knew species were dying out, but no one was doing enough to stop it. The human brain was big but not logical. Leila saw the human addiction to stories, stories through TV, movies; all religion was worship of a particular story: Mohammad, Jesus, Moses, the Ramayana. The bibles were made sacred because they contained the story. These stories caused trouble and had people hating. On the front of the scrapbook, she had glued a dictionary explanation of her endeavours. The definition of a story:

> Story (stor'e), n. 1. A narrative, either true or fictitious.
> 2. A way of knowing and remembering information; a shape or pattern into which information can be arranged and experiences preserved. 3. An ancient, natural order of the mind. 4. Isolated and disconnected scraps of human experience, bound into a meaningful whole.

Under it she wrote this observation: Our brain is big but not good for thought, swollen through a series of extinctions. Arrived bloated with fantasy. Not thinkers but storytellers. Unstoppable.

She found another quote to glue on the cover.

'Thus in the beginning all the world was America.' John Locke.

Dr and Mrs Clancy were going on holidays for a month. Mrs Clancy had wanted Morocco. Dr Clancy had wanted London. They compromised on Ireland—English speaking yet still primitive enough to retain some sort of exoticism. At the last minute, they were going over details with Ernie, giving him the number to dial to get pizzas delivered. Dr Clancy took Desiree aside and beseeched her to throw out as much junk as she could before Mrs Clancy returned.

'Last time I did that, Mother wept,' Desiree protested. 'She said there were articles that she had been saving in all those newspapers that she wanted to read.'

'I'm selecting you for your ruthlessness, Desiree,' her father said, handing her a large sum of cash.

Desiree nodded. She understood. Dr Clancy shuddered as he looked at the wall-length kitchen cupboard. The doors were no longer able to close. It looked like an abstract painting in its jumble of intricacy. Yet on approach each item was recognisable. He was somewhat awed by his wife's ability to create something like that. Dr Clancy mounted the stairs to pack; it was a modern house, open plan, and as such had no banisters. Something that had been a problem when the kids were babies and again now that he was old. Desiree watched him, realising for the first time that her father was an old man. It occurred to her that if he died, there would be no one to give her money. Her mother was too cheap.

Dr Clancy paused on the landing and rested against the wall.

'The child,' he said.

Desiree was counting the money.

'We can't just leave the child here.'

'What child?' Mrs Clancy came into the kitchen with shopping bags.

'The little one.'

'Leila,' Desiree said.

Mrs Clancy frowned. 'Does she have anywhere to go? She has been here such a long time now that I think of it. She's a real, live refugee, you know.'

'Yeah, but not as long as Patterson.' Desiree nodded at the bearded man sitting in their living room watching ice-skating on TV.

'She has a brother, Jack's friend; call him,' Dr Clancy said, taking a deep breath before attempting the second leg of the stairs. 'Isn't she registered with any refugee centres? What do they do with these people? We can't leave her alone here when we're gone. I'd be liable if anything happened. She's a minor and we have, like it or not, assumed responsibility.'

'All right, all right. Animals are disappearing. The world is full of refugees. Ve vere doing our bit.' Mrs Clancy was irritated. 'Poor child. Vot can ve do?'

Zolo drove with Faz to LA to see Mo.

'She can't stay with me, Uncle Mo. I'm in the dorms.'

Mo was looking at Faz. 'What's with your friend? What has he done with himself?'

Faz had dyed his hair purple. He had a T-shirt that read: 'I am a Fed.'

Zolo turned to Faz as if contemplating him for the first time in a long time. 'He's shed the home-boy image, and now he's a cyber punk.'

'Better groupies,' Faz explained.

'What does the shirt mean?' Mo had taken chairs outside, and they all sat on the deck of his Malibu home, with the ocean creeping in under them.

'We went to a big hackers' conference in Las Vegas,' Zolo explained. 'And if someone thinks you are a Fed, they point you out, and by law you have to admit you are a Fed; then you have to wear the T-shirt.'

'You are working for a law enforcement agency now?' Mo was perplexed.

'No, but I swapped the T-shirt with someone who was.' Faz grinned.

'This hacking thing is clever, boys. I'm impressed. Tell me, I don't understand the motivation. Is it the challenge?'

'It's like joyriding as opposed to car stealing.' Zolo sipped a beer. 'The car thief sells the car. The joyrider sets it on fire.'

'Fine. Fine.' Mo didn't care to understand. 'When all this undergraduate messing about is done, you have to get into a good medical school and buckle down.'

'I came here to talk about Leila. The Clancys are leaving—'

'By the way, I have a whole pile of letters from Ireland. I'm away from here quite a bit, and when I come back they are clogging up my mailbox. They've got much more frequent. One was a package. I had to go all the way to the post office to collect it. I don't have time for this nonsense. Can't they afford to call you on the telephone at the dorm or get email? Really, nobody writes letters any more.'

'Can Leila stay here? Or maybe back in the motel? Just for a month. The Clancys are going away on vacation.'

The telephone rang, and Mo fumbled in all his pockets and shuffled it from one hand to another like a hot coal before answering it. When he finished, he said, 'I might have a client coming over. You boys stay on the deck.'

'You still don't have a clinic?'

'I do now, but I still do simple stuff here like injections for select Malibu clients. I'm telling everyone that I'm Persian, not Orapian. So if you bump into this lady, just remember that.'

'Why Persian?'

'This is Los Angeles; some call it Teherangeles. They have a presence here and are respected. They had the Persian Empire, and cats, and the hostage crisis, and the Ayatollah, and carpets. What are we known for?'

'We're not.'

'Precisely. You boys should do the same. Just tell everyone you are Iranian.'

'What happens when you meet an Iranian?'

'Say you're Turkish.'

'What does Turkey have?' Faz asked.

'Delight,' Zolo said.

'Believe me, boys, Iranian is a step up from Orapian. And even the Iranians are always trying to hide themselves. Do you see how many Persian restaurants pass themselves off as Mediterranean cuisine? They all say that these days. Iran is nowhere near the Mediterranean.'

Zolo and Faz sat on the balcony with their laptops on their knees, clicking away. Zolo had written a program whereby he could insert addresses automatically into a thousand websites and request catalogues. He typed in Mo's details and set it off running.

Faz sniggered. 'Dude! Can you imagine getting a thousand catalogues delivered in a week?'

Zolo sighed and put his head back. He looked at the clear blue sky. Mo came out and threw him a bunch of letters.

'Oh God, can I stand more of the saga of the wandering fake Jews?' Zolo let the envelopes fall on the wooden deck.

'I can't believe your old lady had a baby. I'd puke thinking of my mom having sex. She's so out of shape.' Faz spat on the ground.

'It doesn't bear thinking of.' Zolo peered at the letters.

Faz was peering into the apartment. 'What's your uncle up to? He's injecting a needle right into a woman's forehead?'

'The prophet Ludwig Van Strangelove? Why, I do believe you are witnessing him restoring the world's splendour.'

'Man! They're heading into the bedroom.'

'Maybe he's screwing half of his patients. Exchanging sex for botulism.'

'Nope.' Faz was peering inside, getting his grubby handprints all over the French windows. 'They're back in the living room.'

'Figures!' Zolo leaned back on his chair and looked at the cloudless smoggy sky. 'Mo's kick is not sex; he's just showing off his beach house.'

'I'm happy here. This is my home.'

'You have to move out while the Clancys are away.'

'I want to stay with you,' Leila sulked.

'You can't. I'm in a dorm,' Zolo said. 'How bad can one month in a Malibu beach house be?'

'Desiree is always up there with you in college.'

'Yes, and that's painful enough, but she provides a service,' Faz said, hoisting his trousers up and looking around, bored. 'Zolo, just get her in the car.'

Zolo nodded. 'Come on, Leila. I'll help you throw a few things in your suitcase.'

'No.' Leila flopped in a chair and covered her head with her arms.

Leila sat in the back of the car on the way to Los Angeles. She was holding the *Greatest Works of Oscar Wilde* on her knee; Mehrdad had sent the book to her. She left her scrapbooks in Ernie's room. As they approached Malibu and saw the shimmering Pacific, Faz stretched his arms wide, steering with his thigh.

'Ah, California! We should move to San Diego after we finish college.'

'Why?' Zolo asked.

'San Diego still has that southern Californian paradise feeling that LA has lost.'

'Okay. Let's do it.'

'Maybe.' Faz grabbed the wheel and leaned towards the window. He yawned sharply, as if needing air.

'Why not? You just said you wanted to.'

'Nah, on second thoughts . . .'

'Why?' Zolo said. 'What changed in the last few seconds from when you made the statement?'

'It's just . . .' Faz shook his head. He strained to articulate his thoughts. 'I have a feeling that the babes there might be shallow.'

Zolo laughed. 'Yeah, Faz, and you're about as deep as a plate.'

Faz scratched his newly shaved head and wiped his trousers as if scraping off the insult and discarding it without absorbing it.

Faz was in a petrol station buying some beers, leaving Leila and Zolo alone in the car.

'Is Desiree your girlfriend now?' Leila asked.

'No. She's a monster. A sacred one, but a monster nonetheless. She's busy joining the Young Republican Party so as to date rich guys because they buy her stuff. Desiree would trample her own grandmother to get what she wants, even if she didn't want it that bad.'

'A day without a buzz is a day that never wuz.'

'That's her motto.'

'Jack doesn't come to visit the house much any more. Mrs Clancy was complaining.'

'He's busy boring into people's heads in college. He just got a car that he swapped for a burrito. It doesn't work. Surprise, surprise. But he won't give it up. He's obsessed with the thing. He has to stay around campus to push it from one side of the street to the other for parking regulations. I think he's got about ten tickets already. So, up he gets in the morning, trying to rope us into pushing this pile of shit around the corner . . . He's an idiot.'

'A sacred one?'

'Not even.'

'Does Faz think he's an idiot?'

'Faz is a bigger idiot.'

'Do you hate all your friends?'

'If you can't hate your friends, who else can you hate? Hating anyone else would be petty.'

'Why do you have to hang out with Faz?'

'You don't like Faz? He doesn't like you either.'

'He's not nice.'

'Nice? Nice? Nice people are two a penny. Who cares about nice? I care about interesting.'

'Faz is interesting?'

'Jack likes you.' Zolo smiled. 'But then he is insane.'

'I know. Mrs Clancy told me he was diagnosed with Asperger's Syndrome when he was six. I looked it up, and that's why he can't stop talking even when people aren't listening.'

'Really?' Zolo was actually interested in something she was saying.

'It's why he fixes old watches and has collections in his bedroom.'

Faz came racing back to the car.

'Let's go to Vegas. I've got that Vegas feeling.'

Zolo shrugged. 'I have to drop Leila off at Mo's, and I told Desiree and Jack that I'd pick them up at the Lava Lounge at seven to drive them back to school.'

'Then can we go?'

'Sure.' Zolo was the boss.

Faz beamed and sat behind the wheel and stuck a beef jerky into his mouth.

Leila found herself that evening in the back of the car with Jack and Desiree, heading for Las Vegas. Zolo was driving and shaving with an electrical shaver. Faz was dozing with his feet up on the dashboard. He had a pack of cards in his hands, which he shuffled in his sleep. Jack was lecturing about glass blowing in ninth-century China.

'Do you know, and this is beside the point, but I came across a tribe in BAR—'

'What's bar?' Leila asked. Was she the only one listening?

'*Biblical Archaeological Review,*' Jack said quickly, amazed some-one was listening. 'A tribe who like to hang upside down on tree branches and insert magic mushroom enemas.'

'I was looking at enemas the other day . . .' Desiree perked up.

'Why were you looking at enemas?' Zolo asked.

'I thought if I pulled the food out quicker, I could still eat it without vomiting, and lose weight all the same. It was just a thought. But one of these enemas had a 10-year warrantee. I mean, can you imagine? Going back to the shop in year 8 and saying that your trusty enema had finally broken down.'

They crossed the California border into Nevada. The casino sat in front of a prison. Zolo pulled into the parking lot.

'I'm not getting stuck here.' Desiree stomped her feet. 'Last time, we didn't get any further. This place sucks. I want Vegas.'

'I have to get back by eight tomorrow to college to move the Burritoville.' Jack yawned and stretched. He wore his usual outfit of khaki pants and safari shirt and camouflage cloth hat. He never changed. Occasionally he would take a shower and bring the clothes into the shower with him and stomp on them. If he used any kind of soap, his body came out in red blotches.

'I want a bagel with butter. Lightly toasted but not so hot that the butter melts all over the place. I hate that.' Desiree was march-ing into the casino on a mission.

Faz was already mentally at the blackjack table.

'We're not stopping long. I just need a bite to eat,' Zolo warned him.

Zolo, Jack, Desiree and Leila sat at the casino restaurant while Faz played the tables. The waiter eyed them suspiciously.

'Where are your parents?'

'They're playing,' Zolo said, not taking his eyes off the menu. 'I'll have a cheeseburger. Medium.'

Desiree was difficult in restaurants. Somehow she felt entitled to torture anyone who found themselves in the unfortunate position of her server. She suffered from Momentaryslavedriver Syndrome.

'Can I have a cup of your mole sauce to taste?'

The waiter looked stunned. 'Okay.' He shrugged.

'I think I'll have a salad,' Desiree said. 'A cobb salad.' Then she leaned forward, lowering her voice and looking around from side to side. 'Say, what kind of dressing do you guys have?'

Jack rolled his eyes. 'Desiree, you're not trying to score drugs. Dressing is legal in the state of Nevada.'

The hapless waiter listed his selection. Desiree, unimpressed, looked back at the menu.

'This menu lacks imagination,' she grumbled.

'What do you want?' Zolo said. 'Dragon soup?'

'Mmmm. I think I'll have a Monte Cristo Sandwich.'

'As well as the Chicken Mole?' the waiter asked.

'Chicken Mole?'

'You wanted to try the sauce.'

'Oh yes. Yes I did.'

'So you want Chicken Mole?'

'Maybe I'll have a Caesar salad. How do you make your dressing?'

'I beg your pardon?'

'Well, is it made here or is it a mixture?'

'We make it here.'

'Mmm! Really. That's good. Who makes it?'

'I beg your pardon?'

'Well, one time I was in this restaurant and I, by mistake of course, went into the kitchen, looking for the bathroom, and there was this old guy in a dirty coat making the Caesar salad dressing. It was gross. I don't want that to happen again. I never really got over that.'

'You're just a shadow of your former self,' Zolo suggested.

'That's right,' Desiree nodded vigorously. 'Absolutely. Nothing was ever the same again.'

The waiter froze, unsure what to do. All his brain circuits had ground to a halt. The others put in their orders to bring him back to life while Desiree scanned the menu.

'It's like trying to choose a horse.'

'Just have a cheeseburger like the rest of us,' Zolo said.

'Aw, all right.'

The waiter ran before she changed her mind.

As soon as he was out of sight, Desiree said. 'Hell's bells! I forgot I wanted a buttered bagel.'

'They don't have bagels here,' Jack said firmly.

'Who on earth says Hell's bells any more!' Zolo said. 'I can tell you two were raised by a foreigner.'

'Our mother's not a foreigner; she's our mother. I think I'll have oyster and lobster bisque instead of a salad.' She got up and went in search of the waiter.

'Desiree said she'll marry me for my green card tomorrow in Vegas,' Zolo told Jack.

'Congratulations.' Jack raised his eyebrows. 'I guess I should stick around to give her away. I did have to move the car though.'

'Then I can get a passport after a few years. My papers are in a mess because everything is a sham. I'm listed as Mo's son and I'm not. My entire ID has me at 20 years old and I'm just 15. An Orapian passport doesn't exist any more now that Orap is Orapistan, and the government doesn't even have a consulate here.'

'I can't believe that they don't just give you an honorary citizenship,' Jack said. 'You are the essence of an American—a materialistic, anarchist drunkard. You, my good man, are the cheese melting on the burger.'

'I think you're right,' Zolo agreed.

The bride-to-be came back. 'I'm going to go look for a hot buttered bagel. I really have a craving for one.'

The waiter arrived with their cheeseburgers and Desiree's oyster and lobster bisque. It went uneaten. She returned only at the end, to decide on a dessert.

'Don't take too long on this; we have to get to Vegas,' Zolo said.

'It has only minutes in my stomach before it's out in the world again anyway.' Desiree winked. 'All I need is a good meal and a bucket,' she told the terrified waiter.

Zolo took his portable shaver from his top pocket and started shaving again.

'Why do you always do that?' Desiree said. 'You barely have any beard.'

Jack looked at Zolo with great affection. 'He's got rid of the stubble. It's his face he can't stand.'

Leila walked to the back of the casino after dinner. She gazed at the prison. She imagined the prisoners longingly looking out every night and seeing the ant-black shapes of people entering the place of light.

Leaving a shoddy chapel in Las Vegas—a bunch of children. They all had those shoes, except for Leila. Those shoes with tiny removable wheels built in. They glided out of the chapel and Leila followed them. Somehow she was always excluded by something.

One child is insatiable.

One child is unshutuppable.

One is a purple-headed gambling cyber galoot.

One is her beloved brother.

Three are from Orapistan. It is so new a country that it does not exist in the dictionary. When they type in Orapistan in the computer, spell-check tries to substitute the word Rapist for it.

Leila is thinking of rape. She told Desiree about the Ick-Man. Will Desiree tell her brother? What will her brother do? Boys are diamonds, girls are cotton. The physical pain went after a couple of days, but months later she feels things rattling around inside. And then there is the disease. Desiree said she could have it now. Desiree said she will take her to be tested. Eighteen-year-old Desiree is now her sister-in-law.

'Leila is lovely,' Jack told Zolo in the motel the night before the wedding. 'Such a serious, thoughtful little thing, so fairy-like. She seems wise beyond her years.'

'Give me a break, you pervert,' Zolo said. 'She's only ten.'

'No. She told me she's 12. Filius Nullius.'

'What does that mean?'

'Child of no one. It's Latin.'

'Latin, for God's sake. You and your sister. Hellus Bellus.'

'Poor Leila having to stay with Mo. He's not the kind of a man that I would entrust my offspring to.'

'I wish my parents would stop dicking around in Ireland and send for her. She's their child. I never wanted siblings. They forced her on me from the beginning. She can't live in your house for ever.'

'Why don't they just get her to Ireland?'

'It's a visa thing. They're trying to get over here to the US. My father was in France for a while, but he's back in Dublin now. My mother says he spends all his time in the US Embassy, making petitions, wearing a little skullcap, pretending to be a Jew.'

'What are his chances of getting over here?'

'Zero. Absolutely zero,' Zolo said. 'We have no history, no prior existence. All our papers were confiscated by Orapian rebels when we left. Confiscated is too kind a word for it. We arrived in the camp with no evidence of our past or ourselves except our bodily existence. I'm just afraid that they'll fuck it all up for me. I'm registered as Mo's son. I don't want them alerting the authorities to any abnormalities in my status.'

'Don't worry.' Jack patted him on the back. 'I told you. You are the cheese melting on the burger.'

'They managed to call me up at the college. I have no idea how they even knew where I was. Maybe Mo told them. But he never returns their calls either; he's busy with his clinic. Even if they wanted her with them, she's nowhere on record as their daughter; she's Mo's. I told them Leila was staying with you lot. They were impressed your dad was a doctor.'

'We should have got them to hook up when my folks are in Ireland,' Jack said brightly. 'My mother loves meeting in-ter-est-ing people.' Jack said the last part in his mother's thick German accent.

'Yeah, right,' Zolo said. 'They told me they would be over in the US as soon as possible. They're broke. I told them not to rush over. I mean, what would I do with them here? They'd all want to live together like a bunch of immigrants, helping each other out and all that good shit.'

'That's not your style, is it?'

'Fuck no.'

Leila was lovely then. There are no photos to prove it, but everyone remembered years later. In a butterfly print dress that had once belonged to Lan, with her hair down to her shoulders and her dark eyes shining and full mouth almost smiling. Her wiry limbs are held awkwardly by her side, yet even still she has the poise of a dancer. Desiree wears a wedding dress of red-checked material with suspenders and fishnets and big combat boots. She has her red hair loose like a lion's mane, and her face is glowing and savage. Zolo holds her hand tentatively, a geeky Middle Eastern boy with an Afro and big tinted glasses. Jack is the best man in safari attire. Faz the impatient, lounging, vaguely disgusted, itching to be at the green baize tables. Faz is fuming because Jack is best man, not he. But Leila, she was lovely. Her delicate and questioning stare, looking intent and dreamy all at once. Leila is the only one who has read the companion book to the *Wild West* TV series. She is the only one who knows exactly where they are and exactly at which point in the larger narrative of history. She knows in the whole wide, wild history of the West that this coming together is nothing unusual in its strangeness. The West has always been strange, always wild.

If people are animals,
Leila is a caterpillar,
Desiree is a tiger,
Zolo is a unicorn,
Jack is a sloth,
Faz is a boar.
Some are legendary. All are extinct.

On the way from the chapel, Zolo drove the car. They were looking for the Barbary Coast Casino. It was a worn-out, ancient casino, but they still had double-deck blackjack, and Faz and Zolo liked to count cards.

'There it is; we passed it.'

'No, that's the Mirage.'

'Do a U-ee.'

Zolo did a U-turn right on the strip. A siren wailed.

'Shit.'

'Busted.'

'Pull to the right,' the cops barked from a loudspeaker.

'Oh my God!' Desiree screamed.

'Hush, do be calm,' Jack said.

'I'll endeavour to try, brother dear,' she snarled, 'but I have pot on me.'

'I have a warrant out for me here,' Zolo said. 'For an illegal right turn I made six months ago.'

'Great,' Faz groaned.

'I'm going to say I'm you. Everyone thinks we look alike.'

Faz threw him his licence.

Zolo stepped out of the car. The cop sized him up.

'Licence.'

Zolo handed the cop Faz's licence. 'I was pickpocketed, Officer. I just realised it, and that's why I did a U-turn. I was in shock and needed to get back to the casino to report it. I'm awfully sorry. I just got married.'

'What's your name?'

'Faz Haighaghi.'

'I'll run a check.' The cop walked back to the car, studying the licence. He returned, somewhat placated. 'Okay, lover boy. It's your wedding day, is it? I'm going to write you a ticket.'

'Okay, Officer. I'm sorry, sir.'

The officer handed him a ticket, but then started shouting. 'Freeze, hands up on the car. What the fuck is that?' Zolo put his hands on the car, and the cop grabbed his wallet from Zolo's back pocket.

'That's my friend's wallet, sir.'

'What friend?'

'He's in the car.'

The officer was baffled. He peered into the back of the car at Faz and looked at Zolo's photo on the licence. Desiree jumped out of the front seat and threw herself melodramatically at the cop.

'Oh, Officer, Officer. We just got married. Let him go.'

'Who is this?' the cop said.

'My wife,' Zolo said.

'Your wife?' The cop scratched his head and addressed Desiree. 'This is your husband? What's his name?'

Desiree looked at Zolo and then at Faz. She faltered. 'Whatever he said.'

Desiree on her wedding day fumbled in the Mirage fountain for coins. She retrieved some and passed them to Jack. Jack polished them dry on his shirt and handed them to Faz. Faz took a pile and went to play the slots. He made five bucks and took it to a table. He doubled up the money into bail.

Zolo spent his wedding day in Vegas Jail. The other guys who were in there were down-and-outs who needed food and jumped up and down naked in front of the police station until they were thrown in the slammer and fed. They allowed him one phone call. As he dialled, a drunk was screaming and crazy, and the cops pushed his head into the wall. He called Mo, got the answering machine and held the phone out.

'Hi, I'm in Vegas Jail. Just got married. At a great party. Listen to this.' He recorded several shouts and punches before hanging up.

Leila was barred from the casino and so curled up at the entrance, working on the one scrapbook she had taken. She always carried a scissors when she read. Two white Siberian tigers prowled behind the glass as she cut out a piece of the book. Long ago, two performers had brought the Siberian beasts to the American desert. The tigers were the last remaining two on the planet, and they were both female.

Woman minus woman.

Jack, who was no gambler, pounced on her, grabbed the scrapbook and began to read it.

'What are you cutting out?'

'I'm adding to your brother's scrapbooks.'

'What scrapbooks?'

'Or should you say what brother?'

'What does that mean?'

'Do you ever even think about Ernie?'

'I make it a point to think of Ernie at least once a day.' Jack was uncomfortable with the grilling. He read the front clipping definition of story.

'I'm missing a lot of school. I'm teaching myself.'

Jack flicked through the scrapbook, frowning and avuncular. 'Mmm! This might not be the best approach.'

'Why?'

'There's no connection between these pieces. They're all over the place. No unity.'

'I have my own connections. Anyway, I need to learn new words.'

'You shouldn't put too much trust in words.'

'Why not?'

'They're unreliable. For instance, they're different in each language.'

Leila laughed but Jack was serious.

'*Rerum enim vocabula immutablia sunt, hominess mutablia.*'

'What does that mean?'

'It's Latin—dead words. I like dead words. It means, words are unchangeable, men changeable. Is there a possibility of perfect verbal expression? This belief is a remnant of a primitive faith in the inherent potency and inherent meaning of words. For example, the elaborate system of taboo and verbal prohibitions in primitive groups: the ancient Egyptian myth of Khern, the apotheosis of the word, and of Thoth, the Scribe of Truth, the Giver of Words and Script, the Master of Incantations; the avoidance of the name of God in Brahmanism, Judaism and Islam; totemistic and protective names in mediaeval Turkish and Finno-Ugrian languages; the misplaced verbal scruples of the 'Precieuses'; the Swedish peasant custom of curing sick cattle smitten by witchcraft, by making them swallow a page torn out of the Psalter and put in dough—'

Leila sighed. 'When is Zolo getting out of jail?'

Jack never minded being interrupted; he seemed to be in a

trance when he went off on a subject, and would forget it as suddenly as it possessed him. 'Are you bored?'

'I'd rather be here than at Mo's. I don't want to go to Mo.'

'Can't say I'd blame you. He's rather an ogre.'

'Can I come and live with you in your dorm until your parents come back?'

Jack looked surprised. 'It's up to your brother.'

'Then I'm done for.' Leila folded her arms across her chest and pouted.

Jack smiled. 'That's the first time I've seen you act your age. Come on, I'll get you a Coke. The awful Faz and the intoxicating and intoxicated Desiree are almost up to the bail, but they could lose again.' Jack read the blurb in front of the white tigers. 'Dear oh dear, two females. Pretty useless combination.'

'Have they got enough money to bail him out yet?'

'Zolo? I hope so. Your brother is extraordinary.'

'Everyone says that. He's always been a genius. He's mean to me.'

'Mean he may be, but he is also talented.'

'At school, he is.'

'Sure. But more than that. Do you know that a man called Roland in England is recorded as having held 110 acres for which on Christmas Day, every year, he was to perform before King Henry II—"altogether and at once, a leap, a puff, and a fart"? In fact, his descendants for about 200 years had to perform this feat to keep their land. I informed Zolo of this when we were in the Getty Museum; it is an entertainment that goes back at least as far as the Romans. There is a statue in the museum, from the first century AD, of a comedian preparing to perform this rude task. Your brother came to me the next day and did it. Believe me, I have been trying myself for years. He just did it. And can do it on command. Fifteen-year-old Zolo is an amazing man.'

'Is Zolo 15 now? Then I must be 12.'

'You don't know how old you are.'

'I haven't been thinking of dates since I got here.'

Leila and Jack both leapt while trying in vain to puff and fart. They did this a few times in front of the tiger cage.

In Orap your immediate family is all you have to gather forces against the world: your parents and your brothers and sisters. We never had a state that worked. We've tried monarchy, theocracy, democracy, autocracy, but nothing holds together because we are not so much tribal as family based.

Mo knew that we thought he was a buffoon, and he openly condemned us. Yet he understood that we were his only true reality. A call from Vegas from Zolo announcing his marriage was enough to mobilise him.

Mo slumped in the hotel lobby in his usual state of aggressive agitation and impatience. There was a Middle Eastern theme going on in the hotel. It was the latest and most bombastic on the strip. The waitresses wore skimpy little outfits but had their faces veiled. Mo sat down at a marble table in the lobby and waited for Rita to check in for them. She had done the driving, and she generally did all the arranging and booking. She carried the bulk of the luggage. She was rich and paid for everything, despite the fact that Mo was rich too, but not as rich. That evening, when she had come around to the beach house, they had rolled around on the waterbed for a while. Mo had performed his perfunctory foreplay. He stroked her coarsely and selectively, as if checking she was a woman and all the parts were intact. When he sucked her breasts, his nose dug into the soft flesh. He only ever sucked the one breast—the one nearest to him. Whether that was due to its convenient location or because once done he had no interest in moving to the next, it was never clear. Rita was 59 and had never had a good lover; she had orgasms only by mistake, usually two a decade, and never with a partner involved. She was thinking of getting a small dog. Something that quivered with excitement when she called its name.

'Honey, that's pot pourri.'

Mo had his fist in the bowl of dried perfumed leaves. He

chewed vigorously. 'This place is ridiculous. I don't like it. Can't we stay in the Bellagio?'

'The Bellagio is so old.' Rita looked about her and pointed to a man wearing a furry raccoon suit, talking to a short man with a Tigger suit. 'The Furbies are having a Vegas convention. We were lucky to get a room at all.'

'When people ask me where I stayed and I say the Bellagio, they'll know who I am. Just our luck it's full of perverts in animal suits. Let's find those horrible kids and then go to a show.' He rose and brushed off his trousers of the remaining flakes. 'That's good stuff. We should get some.'

'Honey, it's pot pourri.' Rita signalled to the porter to come for their luggage.

All the horrible kids were in their grotty motel far from the strip, watching an ancient *Planet of the Apes* on cable. It was Faz's favourite movie. When Charlton Heston bellowed out his final speech, Faz jumped up and stood in front of the TV and bellowed also: 'Oh my God. I'm back. I'm home. All the time. We finally really did it. You maniacs! You blew it up! Goddamn you! Goddamn you all to hell.'

Desiree tapped her feet off the ground, grabbed the remote. 'Are there any caveman movies on? That's all I like. Caveman movies and rodeo. Musically all I like is surf music and blues; everything else can fuck off. Oh wow, this is my favourite movie of all time.' It was her turn to jump up and perform in front of the TV, screaming along with Faye Dunaway in *Mommy Dearest*.

'No more wire hangers!' she roared.

Faz shook his head. 'This is stupid. *Planet of the Apes* is a genuine masterpiece.'

'How can you tell it's a masterpiece?'

'Because,' Faz sighed as if talking to an idiot, 'it has sequels.'

Desiree winced. 'Like you said yesterday, a restaurant is a good restaurant only if it is a chain.'

Faz agreed. 'Exactly. If there's only one of them, it couldn't be any good, could it?'

Zolo watched his wife and best friend fight as they always did. He was relieved to be out of jail and eager to get into the casino and gamble. Leila got up and went to the door. 'Where are you going, Frog?' he asked.

'There was a knock,' Leila said.

'I didn't hear it.' Zolo frowned.

'I'm not surprised,' Jack said as he put out the joint and hid the ashtray in the drawer. 'All that shouting about apes and hangers.'

Mo stormed in and ran straight for the bathroom. Rita closed the door behind her and looked at the startled bunch apologetically. 'He ate two bowls of pot pourri in a very short time.'

Zolo stood warily. No one knew what to say. They could hear Mo groan in the bathroom. He let out a wild yell. Jack offered Rita the only chair, which she gratefully accepted. 'The policeman said you were staying here. We went to the jail first. I suppose congratulations are in order.'

'For going to jail?' Zolo was surprised.

'Who is the lucky woman?' she said, smiling stiffly. They had come to admonish Zolo for his hasty decision, but that agenda had gone the way of the pot pourri.

Desiree turned away from *Mommy Dearest* and stared at Zolo. 'You told them?' she said in disgust.

Zolo shrugged. 'I guess I did.'

'Don't tell anyone else, Buster!'

'Buster?'

'To elope so young.' Rita smiled vapidly. Her eyes blinked far too often due to a botched surgery years ago. 'So romantic.'

The toilet kept flushing and flushing. Mo exited. He had intended to come in anger, but all the anger had gone out of him. Literally. Now he wanted to show off.

'Well, come on then. If you little bastards didn't invite us to the wedding, we might as well be at the reception. I'll take you all to dinner.'

Rita tried to raise her eyebrows. It was an old habit that was hard to shake despite the fact that her current forehead was immobilised by Botox.

'We'll go to La Cirque.' Mo raised a finger in the air as if he were Caesar announcing a new campaign in the senate.

'That's so expensive.'

'Expensive is good. My philosophy is Take! Take! Take!' Desiree ran to the bathroom to put on make-up. 'I'm the bride and I say let's party.'

Rita inhaled deeply. This man never once brought her to dinner, and now he was going to bring this rag-tag troupe of students to one of the most expensive restaurants in town.

Desiree came out of the bathroom. 'What's all that floating in the toilet? Did you just eat a tree?'

Mo cringed. 'It wouldn't all go down.'

'Mo flakes!' Desiree declared.

Mo laughed his booming laugh and grabbed Desiree's broad shoulders. 'I like you,' he said. Rita was ashamed at the crudeness of it all. She made sure to sit by Jack since he was the only one who seemed to have manners.

Over dinner, all Rita could see when she looked at Desiree was a big mouth devouring the world. Reducing the planet to dust, and hoovering it up those nostrils of that naturally pert nose. Even though surgery made people look better, everyone was trained to understand that it was surgery that made them look better. There was still no remedy to age. Desiree was 19 years old without an operation or injection, Rita thought bitterly. She was young and pretty and had wild red hair. She wore a camouflage T-shirt, denim overalls, army boots with no socks. There was no ring in sight. Mo was taken with this loud, brash, foul-mouthed beast. She was a match for him in sheer self-interest. Mo was a big, bald man with a hooked nose and a potbelly, laughing at all her jokes, even when they ordered a very pricey white wine and Desiree swirled it around in the glass.

'What's all this flat stuff, Uncle Mo?' She nudged him. 'Get me some champagne.'

Rita had never seen Mo like a person before. She had almost been heartened by his uniform contempt for humanity. Since she

had herself come under the umbrella of the despised, she had not
felt so singled out. If all beings were repugnant, she could not count
on an exception. Now, however, it was upsetting to witness Mo in
thrall to someone else. Especially someone young, with no influence
in the world, or credentials of any kind. That meant he was capable
of plain, unmotivated regard, and it made his heinous treatment of
her suddenly abhorrent.

Mo signalled to the waiter. 'I want a double Martini.'

'Sir, our Martinis are double.'

'What does that mean? I want double that then.'

The waiter came back with a jug of Martini and poured a glass
for Mo.

Rita was sitting between Leila and Jack. She grabbed Leila's
hand.

'Don't,' Rita said. 'You can't drink that wine.'

'Yeah, we'll get thrown out,' Faz said. 'Take it from her.'

'What's she up to?' Mo asked in irritation but, not waiting for
an answer, went on to tell Desiree about the shipment of wolf noses
arriving from Alaska. 'I'm going to cover the bedroom floor in a
leather of wolf noses.'

'Cool.' Desiree gulped her champagne and slurped an oyster in
one gulp. 'When I have a house, I'm going to have a taxidermy
lounge.'

'You should see my plans for my house in the Hollywood Hills,'
Mo enthused. 'A pyramid, and a pool that goes into the bedroom
from outside. And a control panel from the bed. And a whole play-
room that's a waterbed . . .'

'Narco-tecture!' Jack said.

'Yeah,' Desiree nodded. 'You're basically going to live like a coke
dealer.'

Mo's forehead creased in bewilderment. Rita guffawed; her six-
inch stuck-on nails speared a piece of bread. Mo fumed. 'Look at the
way you eat with those talons. They're not utensils. You may not
have had the advantage of a decent upbringing, but at least be open
to learning manners when I bring you to a high-class establishment.'

Leila took Jack's wine and downed it. Everyone looked at Rita, who was blushing and had tears welling in her eyes behind her coloured contact lenses, making her pupils look like purple frog spawn in a murky pond. 'I'm a lady,' she said.

'According to whose definition?' Mo sneered.

'According to Jesus Christ,' Rita said meekly, her eyes cast downwards.

'He was a fine judge of character. He hung out with whores.' Mo picked up the wine menu and pretended to study it. He wanted to move on. He had felt a little humiliated by the narco-tecture comment, but was now satisfied that someone at the table was feeling more humiliated.

Leila pointed. 'Uncle Mo, you have your elbow in the Martini.' They all looked. His shirt was wet and his elbow was indeed resting in the Martini glass. Mo extracted his elbow and looked at it. Everyone laughed. He was trapped and laughed too, but he felt a prickly sensation go up the skin on his back, and his throat got tight.

That night in Vegas, Mo presided at the head of the table, but he had not the dominion he imagined. All the Fatagagas men eventually became that shape—skinny limbs and bloated torso. Mo wore his trousers pulled up under his chest and tucked his napkin into his collar. No one commented on this social faux pas since there were two men in raccoon suits and one man in a panda suit at the next table.

'Everyone wants to be a raccoon it seems; have you noticed that?' Zolo asked. 'There are more raccoons than anything else.'

'Did you know that up until we are five years old, 80 per cent of our dreams are about animals?' Jack said. 'If you think of all children's books, they are about animals: Pooh, Barney, Mickey Mouse . . .'

'They cut holes in the crotch and fuck each other dressed like that,' Faz marvelled.

Mo started looking round him. 'The men do?'

'No,' Zolo said. 'The raccoons and pandas do.'

'They're all faggot computer programmers. There was a splinter group at the hackers' conference. Hacker Furbies,' Faz said. 'We should do something to them. Cut their tails off.'

'It's harmless enough,' Jack frowned. 'They're not hurting anyone.'

Leila could not take her eyes off them. 'I would like to be a wild animal more than a person.'

'Jack,' Zolo said, 'do frogs count as wild animals?'

Jack smiled at Leila. 'We are a demented species, eh, Leila? Here we are in the process of ridding the planet of wild animals, and then we run around dressed like them for sexual gratification.'

'You guys don't get it, do ya? They don't want to be wild animals.' Desiree spoke with her mouth full of lobster. 'They want to be stuffed toys.'

'Americans are crazy,' Mo said with a touch of wonder and awe.

'Orapians are crazy too,' Zolo said. 'We just aren't as organised with our free time.'

'I've heard the new government is making the women wear the veil like in Afghanistan, not like in Iran,' Mo said. 'The hardliners are complaining that they should cover up faces and eyes too. That was the government you wanted to go and fight for.'

'I got over that fairly quickly.' Zolo didn't like to be reminded of his former fidelity to the revolution.

'Good boy! Good boy! I have heard through the Orapian exile medical community that the regime is looking for doctors to clone the leader. That ugly Santa Claus of the atomic age, the one with the bad eyes. How come all our leaders seem to have bad eyes? He wants to rule for eternity. Can you imagine? The same bearded, robed, blind, fundamentalist despot again and again. I guess they don't believe in term limits. Ha! Ha! But it got me thinking. You could make a name for yourself in cloning, Zolo. It's a bit like human hacking. That would be right up your alley. Meddling with the gods. When you get your degree, you could concentrate on that side of medicine. Just become a doctor first.'

'Doctors are glorified mechanics.' Zolo poured himself more wine.

'What are you going to be? A lawyer?'

'Lawyers are glorified plumbers.'

'What's wrong with plumbers and mechanics? My daddy was a plumber,' Rita said with her eyes cast down but her tone shakily defiant. 'My uncles were all mechanics.'

'Please, Rita, just stay out of what you don't understand. What's wrong with being glorified?' Mo said. 'I'm not having this conversation. Your father and mother will come over here and get you into a medical school. That was the plan.'

'My God, there was a plan. Who would have guessed?'

Mo was not to be deflected. 'The Fatagagases have a family tradition in medicine.'

'Don't family traditions have to go back more than one generation?' Zolo asked, feigning innocence.

'When are Maman and Baba coming?' Leila asked.

'What do you care? You're having a fine time without them, believe me,' Zolo said.

'Oh, sure she is, Zolo, you idiot!' Desiree glugged the champagne. 'She leaves a refugee camp, loses her parents to come here, gets stuck in the House With No Anus, and then her first friend gets her raped.'

Leila blinked. Had she heard right? Everything went silent.

Mo was looking at Leila as if he were going to hit her. The Ick-Man was sitting at the table. Leila got up and ran.

She ran through the casino. The Ick-Man followed her at a leisurely pace but somehow always being a few steps behind. She ran through Paris, through Venice, through Egypt, through Japan. All history ends here in the Wild West as a gimmick. Men prowled in tiger suits through pyramids. Borrowed cultures, borrowed skins.

'Thus in the beginning all the world was America.' John Locke.

And in the end the world had to be America too.

Desiree had told them her secret. Blurted it out over lobster and champagne, almost as an aside. Her fleeing the table would only confirm it, would not allow Desiree to cover it up and brush it off as a joke. Leila looked for Lan. Lan had said she wanted to live in

Vegas. So now Leila searched for the small Cambodian girl. Lan would let her live with her, and she wouldn't have to go back to Mo's in Malibu.

All night, Leila searched for Lan, knowing she wouldn't find her.

At dawn, Leila found the motel, and Mo took her back with him. She told Mo her neck was stiff, and he told her he was a plastic surgeon, not a paediatrician. Rita was too mad at Mo to care about her. It was a good excuse to lie in the back seat of Rita's car and sleep. The Ick-Man was waiting for her at the Malibu beach house when they got home. He was shielding his eyes from the sun as the car pulled up. She sat in the living room as Mo listened to messages and made phone calls. It was hard for her to lift her hands. They hung by her side. Her head hung, lolling like a drooping bloom. Her stomach was nauseous; she couldn't eat for the next few days.

Zero minus zero.

Zero minus zero plus zero.

It all amounts to the same.

Her father was replacing princes' noses. Her genius brother was hacking away on a computer, wondering what to be. What to grow into. What wouldn't eat him alive. What that thing was that would satisfy his abhorrence of the mundane. Her uncle, the bad lover, was building a pyramid in honour of himself. Her mother was all on her own, with no money, no help, in an alien land, waking up every two hours to feed a baby girl.

She wanted her mother. Each night, she cried herself to sleep, whimpering, 'Maman, Baba.'

In the morning, she slowly walked out on to the deck and, slipping out of her sandals, touched the hot wood with her bare feet. Leila was sick and getting sicker. She thought she saw three sailing ships on the horizon. The *Nina,* the *Pinta,* the *Santa Maria.* Conquest.

When Mo was present, Leila stayed on the unsheltered deck in the sun. She was burned up after a couple of days. Her red face bubbled blisters, and it made it harder to move her already stiff limbs.

When Mo was absent, she read his books, feverishly gathering clippings and gluing them to the scrapbook as if preparing a case. Instinctively, she knew he would never find out what she was doing. If there was one thing that was untouched in that Malibu house, it was the insides of books.

On the third day, Leila was sitting on the couch when Mo stormed in. His hands were full of catalogues.

'I don't know what kind of prank this is, but every day for a week now, I go to the mailbox and get a load of shit I haven't ordered.'

'Is there anything from Maman or Baba?'

Mo was startled to see his niece on the couch, addressing him.

'Maman and Baba? Maman and Baba? Your Maman and Baba are leaving messages all the time on the machine, asking for money. They want money now. Your family always wants something from me. It's a black hole. No matter what I do, I have to do more. And are any of you grateful? What have you done with your face? You look like raw hamburger?'

Mo ran out on to the deck. There were stacks of catalogues on the wood planks. He scooped them up and fired them into the sea. He grabbed Leila's copy of the *Greatest Works of Oscar Wilde* and tossed it off too. Leila ran to stop him, and he swiped her by mistake. She fell back. Mo looked appalled.

'What do you mean getting in the way like that? Whose property do you think this is? Is it you ordering all these fucking catalogues?'

'No, Uncle. That was my book.'

Leila hung over the balcony, but was too late to see the book sink. That was the second time her Oscar Wilde had been thrown into the water by a man in her family. She would have to write and tell Mehrdad. She was writing telling him of everything that was happening and had happened. Everything but one thing. Mehrdad told her he was in the place where Oscar Wilde was born. Her Maman and Baba were there too. He saw them and told her he had held her little sister and she had fallen asleep in his arms.

Mo marched to the French door and swung around. 'And Zolo asks for money. I give him money. And you. Why haven't you got a job? You're not even in college like your brother. I give him money so he can follow in my footsteps. So he can continue the dynasty.'

'Was there anything in the mail for me?'

Mo rooted in his pocket and displayed a letter. He was slightly jealous of the personal mail she got. He got only bills and junk and a million catalogues. Leila snatched the letter. It was from Mehrdad.

'If that's your parents, tell them to pay their own way. I can't afford to be sending them anything. I already have their offspring on my hands. To go producing children and abandoning them. Why is it always me who has to clean up everyone's mess?'

Leila followed Mo inside the house. She wanted to ask him could she see a doctor. She felt sick. She was afraid though that if someone found out about the disease, they would all start asking questions about the Ick-Man. She lay down on the couch instead. Uncle Mo ate, with his head stuck in the fridge, out of a carton.

'What's Zolo's wife's name? Desire?' He spoke into the fridge. Leila did not answer. She closed her eyes. 'I think I'll have her over. Most interesting person I've met in years. She's a feisty one.'

Desiree came to the house at Mo's behest to inspect the wolf noses. She stayed the night with Leila on the black leather couch in the living room.

'Take me back to your house,' Leila said. 'I'm happy there.'

Desiree lay in the dark, listening to the sea.

'I'm not going back there right now.'

'You owe me for telling my secret.'

'Yeah. Gee, I'm sorry. I didn't elaborate on it though. No one really wanted the details, I can assure you.'

'The details are not what matters. They know.'

'So what? It doesn't change anything.'

'It changes everything. They see me differently. Uncle Mo can't look at me.'

'I didn't think he ever looked at you.'

'He didn't, but now he doesn't look at me intentionally.'

'You have a convoluted mind.' Desiree got off the couch and put one of the wolf masks on her face. 'I thought he'd give me one of these, but he just wanted to show me them. I think I'll take this one. How do I look?'

'Like a wolf.'

Desiree leaned her head back so the flap of wolf face would not fall. 'I'm bored. How can he live with no TV? I can't even live without cable. Plus, he's nothing to read here. All these books are by dead people. I mean, look at this one.' She held up a leather-bound brick of a book. '*Abraham Lincoln—The Prairie Years.* I mean, come on! You know he doesn't read this shit; no one does. It's like one of those books they have lying about a staged Open House, placed by the real-estate designers. And look, it's full of shredded pages.' Desiree was stunned for a moment by the cut-up book. Then she tossed it aside. 'He doesn't even have a *Guinness Book of World Records.*' Desiree rooted around and found a *Yellow Pages* by the phone. 'Thank God. At least I can read this.' She began to flip through, studying the ads with a fevered intensity.

'I want to go back to your house,' Leila whined.

'You can't.'

'Why not?'

'It's the Marth of Munch.'

'The Marth of Munch?'

'I have to get back to the school. I got momentarily bored with the experiment. But this is no fun at all.' Desiree was staring at a section in *Yellow Pages.* 'Those guys get a bit militaristic at times about their drug-taking. You'd think it wasn't leisure the way they go on.'

'What's up?'

'Zolo came up with the idea. Jack and Faz of course do everything he tells them to like the mindless groupies they are. He decided that they should experiment and see what would happen if they took three acid tabs every morning for exactly a month. So they picked this month. When we came back from Vegas on February 29th, they started the next day.'

'The month of March?'

'It soon became the Marth of Munch.'

'Are you doing it?'

'Uh-huh! I'm tripping now,' Desiree said, licking her lips. 'You know what I feel like? Eggs through a straw. Let's drink some eggs through a straw.'

Leila didn't know what acid did to you, but she pretended to understand. 'Can I go with you to the college? I need to tell Zolo I'm sick. Mo doesn't listen.'

Desiree and Leila crept out while Mo slept in the next room. Desiree looked in the fridge first; there were tiny, speckled, blue eggs in a little box. She took them with her. Mo was spreadeagled on his waterbed, completely naked. Desiree peered in the room before she left.

'You'd think he'd put some clothes on with a minor in the house,' she whispered. The Clancys were repulsed by nakedness.

'I don't go looking into his room,' Leila said, blushing. 'Should I leave a note?'

'Yeah, a note, good thinking. You're smart.' Desiree nodded vigorously. Mo stirred. He bobbed a little on the bed. Leila found a pen and wrote on a prescription pad.

'Gone to visit Zolo with Desiree. PLEASE KEEP MY LETTERS— Leila.'

Desiree stuck it on the fridge with a magnet. 'I can totally see why you want out of this dump. He must be a dick to live with. Never has real food in the fridge and no TV, for chrissake? That's just not right.'

'I haven't eaten in days,' Leila said, her voice lifting as she stood by Desiree's car. 'He keeps getting a ton of catalogues in the mail. It's driving him crazy.'

'Catalogues?'

'Like a hundred a day. Some are big and thick.'

'Wow! Where are they? I could have read those.'

'He throws them in the sea.'

Leila slept in the car as Desiree listened to the radio. It was the first deep sleep she had got since Vegas. Here, moving so fast, with someone as omnipotent as Desiree, she felt no fear. Desiree shook her awake in the college parking lot. The college was built on the mission grounds of a historical landmark. There was an old mission church from the eighteenth century still standing, surrounded by cacti and rose gardens. They padded into the mild night over the grass, past a statute of Junipero Serra, under the palm trees, and into the dorm.

'I hate this place.'

'But you're always here.'

'Yeah, but look at my home.'

'I like your home.'

'My mother drives me crazy.'

'I miss my mother. And my father was really nice.'

'You're 12; wait till you're 19.'

Jack was standing by the stairs. He wore his usual khaki outfit, but his eyes were uncharacteristically wild and flailing for meaning.

'Jack, what's up?' Desiree said.

'I just locked myself in the room.' He was looking worried.

'But you're free now.'

'On the contrary, I'm still inside.' He pointed to the shut door.

Desiree looked at Leila and grinned. 'You see what I'm talking about? The Marth of Munch.'

'All events happen together though at different points in the wall,' Jack said. Leila looked at him.

'Are you okay?' he asked.

'I'm sick,' she said.

The present has a future, but it will all become the past. The past is only a story. The past is only a way of knowing and remembering information: a shape or a pattern into which information can be arranged and experiences preserved. The past is an ancient, natural order of the mind. The past is isolated and disconnected scraps of human experience, bound into a meaningless whole.

The past is most of our lives—it is the ocean.

And Leila knew that life was just stories. She had discovered that history is memory kept in story. And memory is the wind that blows the surface and creates the waves, and the waves are what touch us. They shape the land, and the land is now, it is here, it is all we have, it is all we are left with, all that keeps us from drowning.

Leila entered the Marth of Munch.

PART VI

ORAP

Chapter Eighteen

The Marth of Munch

Faceless, marked only by our height, we are paired up and marched out of the prison. Twelve of us shuffle under the arches. Emerging from months of gloom, I crane my neck to see the tiled mosaic and beautiful intricate corners where the arches meet the wall. My eyes try to adjust to looking at something other than four walls close together. The prison is the most ancient building in Orap. The only building myriad successive regimes left standing. The façade is meticulously maintained. It remained when all else was gone. In a fluctuating, unstable society like ours, the people in the government thought more about the people in the prisons than the people outside.

I don't know what time of year it is, but the grasping bone chill of winter seems all but gone. The morning sun has an intensity that suggests Orap's early short spring. I bet it is the month of March.

For all I know, it is the Marth of Munch.

I am cuffed to a tiny woman at my side. She has to lift up her arm to be comfortable. Her hands are gloved. Mine are bare, and it actually makes me feel self-conscious and unprotected. Armed guards prowl along our flanks. Their faces are as blank as ours are non-existent. I could take this opportunity to run, dragging the tiny woman along with me, but this is not a city to escape into.

Outside the prison is a prison also.

The courtroom is across the street, and the steps are already crowded. I feel excitement build as we approach. In so many months, I have not seen a written word, an image, or had a conversation. Any break from the crush of routine would have been a thrill, but to be outside and the centre of attention is exhilarating. We all walk straighter and with purpose. We are one long narrow insect animal. In prison, it is hard not to feel forgotten. To know you are being watched is a kind of freedom.

The twelve of us, handcuffed in pairs, walk up the steps and through the door. Why did the lawyer sketch the stolen faces? Was it to distinguish who was who? I actually put my hand under my veil to touch my nose. I'm suddenly not convinced that they have left me intact. My nose is there. It is not really my nose but a nose Uncle Mo built for me after he plucked off the old, crooked Orapian nose. I was horrified when that ancient ethnic nose arrived on my face in early adolescence. I counted the days to when I could have it razed to the ground and have something more modern, more convenient, built instead. Really, I wanted a more silent nose. Life was deliciously shallow then.

Being a doctor didn't interest me as much as making lots of money and having an easy life. In fact, I considered business school or law as quicker routes to eternal stability and respectability, but my mother insisted on medicine, and I always abided by her wishes.

It was not a profession that suited me, however, and I was miserable even if I didn't recognise my misery as an aberration. I was reluctant to effect change, to plunge into people, to twist them around. I needed a profession that didn't meddle with lives, and I couldn't find one worse. Lawyers may interfere with freedom or finance, but doctoring was outrageous. I had to put my hand inside people. I rearranged them. I changed them.

Sick people disgusted me. To follow in the footsteps of my odious uncle Mo was all I wanted. When I did my residency in a ghetto hospital, I had to touch all sorts of ill-fitting people. People who smelled bad, whose feet were bloated and bruised from journeys taken to no good destinations, whose skin was that fucked-over black of black ice. Junkies, prostitutes, derelicts. Stupid people who asked stupid questions and didn't listen to the answers. These people are ruining America, I told my mother when she massaged my back and fed me Orapian stews each evening. If those patients knew how I felt about them, how touching them made me want to throw up. If they knew, I'm sure they would have preferred to die on the streets. I was racist. Like most Orapians, I aligned myself with the white people. The fact that the whites never saw us as such was something we didn't internalise. I was spoiled. An Orapian American princess. Even though I had been looking at people in pain for years, I never knew what it was.

I have time to reminiscence as they sit us down in a bare room and tell us our lawyer will be along soon. Baby Zero, let us conduct our own trial by memory. The crime will not be revealed until the sentence has been passed.

Will my mother be here? Have I put her on trial too? My mother and I used to have screaming battles. I once struck her because she bought the wrong hair dye and my blond hair went so dark I looked almost like I should have. I had beautiful hair and spent hours keeping it that way. From my father's side of the family. It is still here under my veil. My mother had stringy hair shot through with static. She kept dying it blond until it was like green fuzz. Zolo had the same hair. He let it be until it was almost an Afro. I'm not sure that Zolo ever lowered himself to look in a mirror.

Zolo never cared how others perceived him. He was free. No one ever knew why he formed the peculiar loyalties that he did. Mehrdad, Faz, Jack and Desiree. Zolo did as he pleased at all times. He was the most selfish person I have ever known, but that doesn't offend me. I always envied his liberty from other people's opinions. His drive to pursue whatever amused him at any given moment. He never said a good word about anyone, yet he never appeared disappointed. As if he knew all along that humanity wasn't up to much, but that it was entirely acceptable to him. Like Mo, he had no ideology and no loyalty, but unlike Mo he had a sense of humour.

Zolo knew implicitly that we get from one end of life to the other supported by illusions. Illusions of love, status, material goods. That was what I admired Zolo for; he was too brilliant to have sustainable illusions, yet he got through without freaking out. The strength that must have taken was immense.

The prisoners are fidgeting. We have been told not to speak to each other. I wouldn't know what to say to anybody. My only company has been my memories, putting our family history in some sort of order for you. Telling you the story.

At the beginning of this regime, the Iranians condemned the government of Orapistan for their treatment of women. You know you are in trouble when the Iranians think you treat women badly. I never hung out with women, but I used to date Iranians in Los Angeles. Medical students, of course. They were good-looking and they loved to party. I took my uncle's advice and tried to pass myself off as an Iranian with an American mother. Too bad I wasn't one and my mother was Farah.

Is Farah out there? I haven't spoken to her since her second and last visit to the prison. The taxi driver was still helping her out. She nearly spat when I said we were lucky to have found him. 'Not for free. He's charging me extra for the risk he's taking. I don't trust him. He would paint a cucumber and try to sell it to you as a banana,' she said. My mother was my maid when I was growing up. She waited on me hand and foot. She cooked for me, cleaned for me, chauffeured me and made my bed every day. She encouraged me to spend all my free time shopping and hanging out at the mall with her. As long as I scraped through medical school, she thought I could do no wrong. She dyed my hair, put on my make-up and obsessed along with me about the whole string of ridiculous pompous dates that I never allowed touch me. She trained me how to hate.

I notice something suddenly. All the women are pregnant. It's hard to tell under the voluminous black cloth but, as they shift and move, I see the bumps silhouetted. I touch my own bump. Eight months now. Are you ready? Come and join us all in this great game; truth will be checked in at the door and illusions provided for no extra charge.

My zero. My river inside.

I cup my hands around you.

Heart like a mink in a trap.

The Arabs were the first to tell us that zero is nothing, but it's where it all starts.

When I think of the future, I think of doors shutting all over the world.

What can I give you?

In my lifespan, I saw it all go up in smoke. The last wild elephants disappeared, the tigers, the koalas, the bears are gone. We have specimens in zoos—but a tiger in the zoo is not a tiger. The coral reefs are all but gone. Fifty per cent of the world's species disappeared in my lifetime. There were death announcements on TV. The last gorilla, the last giraffe, most of the insects, all the frogs. All marched into the great mountain of memory. The whale, of course. We'd been waiting for that for a long time. We stopped the countdown. Ishmael had preached to the assembled peasants in the camp that we were in the middle of the sixth great extinction. They had shrugged and thought about their families and food.

It was people like my uncle Mo with an insatiable appetite for flamingo tongues. Who liked to sprinkle ground-down rhinoceros horn in his shark-fin soup. He ushered in depletion.

The mouse, the cow, the pig, the sheep, the chicken—they are all here with us. Anything we could eat and tame, we kept. But anything that caught our eye is gone. The zebra, the eagle, the bear, the orang-utan. And we loved them, and wanted to save them, but we couldn't stop ourselves. The bear surprisingly went for his bladder— the Chinese wanted the bile. The orang-utan, man of the forest, disappeared through loss of habitat, as expected.

Can we conceive of our loss?

Nobody really liked the people who wanted to save the world. They were not an appealing cast of characters. They irked me with their single-mindedness, their chasing of causes. At times, I suspected, it was akin to fanaticism. That kind of devotion and dedication dried out their lives. But when they lost, I personally resented them for not trying harder.

Enter into this depletion. Feel what it is to be suddenly alive at the tail-end of the sixth great extinction. Come in through me. I will contaminate you with my love, just as Farah loved me. I will nurture you to leave me. And from your prison crib, you will see me smile, as all mothers do; all the love in the world will be swirling in my bottomless smile.

And my smile will be a dark hole in my face.

I know, Baby Zero, you sleep inside me now as I await my trial. I am feeding you your dreams. I am being set up. We are both helpless and at the mercy of those who have shown no mercy to this date. I keep the story going in my head.

We sit and wait. Once I would have despised my fellow inmates, but now I long to touch one of the other women. I long to catch their eyes and read how scared they are. But I can't see their eyes. The unfriendly mesh reveals nothing. This covering does not diminish us according to plan. It mythologises us. Our story is larger. We are more photogenic, more iconic. I could see the press clamour to capture our image as one snake of draped femininity. Mystery is power; we will never be ordinary like this. The slave is not ordinary in chains, and the cow is not ordinary stripped of its skin and hanging. A man enters and orders us to stand and walk in single file to the courtroom. Our trial is to begin.

The ghosts of the past are hungry. I sleep so little these nights; either the baby moves too much and lies on my bladder or the hungry ghosts gnaw through my sleep until my dreams are shredded. Days punctuated only by a guard taking my bucket and leaving food.

Everything comes through me though I am nothing. I should know. I was baby zero too.

I look at my feet; they are black, cracked, raw and swollen. The kind of feet I noted on indigent people who came into the hospital looking for my help. It was their feet that horrified me the most. I wondered how they had ever let themselves deteriorate to such a level. Parts of my feet have yellow discs of hard flesh. The skin is solidified. I stroke the sole of my foot; it is as coarse and padded as a paw.

What should I say to exonerate myself? I am an American. I merely took those women from the hospital and dumped them on the steps of the parliament building to get more medical attention for them, not to question the regime. I was doing it for the good of the women. God guided me every step of the way. If I could talk to my lawyer, I could tell him this is my defence. I was acting selflessly in the interest of others, as a woman should.

The truth is, I loathed people. The steady stream of complaining masses that came under my care probably didn't notice this. Some did. There was a black man who looked me in the eye and said, 'I am not a beast.' I looked right through him and agreed. 'Alas! There are very few of those left,' I said. But I didn't care about the animals disappearing or the fish in the underworld losing their coral beds, or the land sinking and the sea rising. I wanted to get that infernal residency over and done with and go and join my uncle in his plastic surgery practice. People who hated their outsides were preferable to people whose insides had gone wrong. If I very deliberately and intuitively existed on the outside, it was purely outsides that I wanted to deal with. I worked hard, both at the residency and under Mo's tutelage. Together we fattened up lips and vaginas, augmented breasts, clipped noses, pulled faces tight, smoothed out eyes, lifted lids, sucked fat. He was delighted with my apprenticeship, and my impoverished parents were sure he would leave it all in my hands.

We depended on him for so much. I lived with my parents all through college in a modest one-bedroom apartment in Westwood, Los Angeles. We three slept in the bedroom in the same bed. I accepted this arrangement and never expected to live in dorms or with other students. She said it was to protect my honour, but she didn't want to be alone with my deflated father. Zolo never called or came around.

My mother shaped me—she trained me to think like a hunter, to get everything. To push people around. To value money more than friendship. To be reptilian cold and murderously ambitious. To take and never be grateful. To find fault. We were very close, she and I.

Dressed in new identical burkas, we are marched into the courtroom to stand under scrutiny. There is nothing to adorn the walls of the courtroom but cracks in the green paint. There are less faded patches where portraits used to hang. Spray painted on the wall are the words, 'Orapistan, one nation under God.' And behind the judge's chair the words 'Infinite Justice' are scrawled so crudely that paint has run on some swirling letters. My mother might be able to identify me as the tallest in the group. I incline my head slightly at the audience. Men and women sit on separate sides. Do I imagine I see one of the women nod in my direction. Is that my mother? I have not felt the baby move in hours.

You will be still. You will be silent. You will be naked.

Baby Zero. How can you sleep now? We are on trial. Am I telling you too much? Revealing so many ugly things in my nature that you won't imagine me as your mother. Have I lost your sympathy? I'm only going by what Mehrdad kept telling me. And Mehrdad was the only truly good person I have ever met in my life. He kept telling me: the less we know of history, the more it controls us.

A young soldier comes out and barks, 'All rise.'

The entire assembly stands. I am comforted by the fact that we all seem to be serious about the game we are playing here; we are sticking to imported rituals of the court. But when the judge enters, hope is eclipsed eerily from my heart like the sun from the noonday sky. The judge is 15 years old. The same age as Zolo and Mehrdad were when that part of the story ended long ago. I am to be judged by a child.

We women who stand accused shiver together like one lonely trapped animal. We are thinking one thought. Children are fundamentalists and they have no mercy. Grimly, 12 of us, without a word having to be said, are marched into the featureless mountain of our fate.

For a second, I hope to see Mehrdad in the court, on a white horse, ready to scoop me up under his arm and gallop off, but I know none of the men. Their faces strain to see who we are and which one is which, faces written over with fear and hope. Again, I look to the women and search for some indication that my mother is present. It is impossible to distinguish her from the crowd of veiled women.

My mother changed her story so many times. There was no dwelling on what had gone. Rather she put forward the notion of a fully interchangeable set of stepping stones to the deserved present. She fired lies into the past like heat-seeking bullets, hoping to kill the shadows before they broke loose and floated into the present world like dark unmoored ghosts.

'America owes us this.' Maman and Baba both managed to finagle social security payments despite never having worked in the US in their lives.

'What does it owe us? Why?'

'We got here and we have no money.'

'So why does it owe us?'

'We earned what we get from the government.'

'You took it.'

'We earned the right to take it.'

'What do we have?'

We had a rented apartment in Westwood with a communal pool and a hot tub and a gym. But this was LA. Everyone had that. We had one bedroom. We had a spice rack, a dishwasher, a pedal garbage can so our fingers wouldn't get dirty. We had central air. We had cable. I watched the Style Channel, MTV and the Entertainment Channel. But if I was studying, nobody was allowed to move. My mother and father sat like statues. They neither spoke nor read. They sat in separate parts of the small living room with their hands on their laps, and I never even knew or cared what they thought of in those hours of silence. In fact, I assumed they were empty. After all, they could have gone out, but what was outside for them? Were they guarding me? Was I their jailer or was the notion of my life their jailer? I had to be the proof, to show that the past had a point. Our daughter the medical student. Even when there was no one to boast to.

We had no friends. Zolo loathed us. Uncle Mo barely tolerated us.

When Mehrdad showed up unannounced at our door in that generic apartment in Los Angeles, my father came alive as never before. He ushered him in and made him sit on the beige couch, with his feet on the machine-made rug, and put a cup of tea on the glass table under the green plastic plant.

I was in the bedroom and I heard him say, 'I was in Los Angeles for a conference, so I thought I'd look you up.'

'After all these years, young Mehrdad. My God, Farah, can you believe it?' my father gushed.

'Yes, it's good to see you, Doctor Fatagagas.' He smiled at my father, almost warmly. Then nodded more hesitantly at my mother. 'Madame Fatagagas.'

'You'll want Zolo's number. He's up in Silicon Valley making money, but he'd love to talk to you.' My father was blushing and giddy, but my mother loomed like an empty skyscraper.

'Actually, I really wanted to talk to Leila.'

I walked out to face him. He stood. His face at that moment was transformed. I thought I saw tears in his eyes. I think his hands shook, and some tea spilt on that machine-made rug.

'Leila?' he said.

I glanced at my parents; they were as frozen and tiny as the figures in the paintings. Mehrdad gathered himself inwardly and smiled, somewhat embarrassed. Intrigued, I was observing all of this. While taking note of the tears and the shake, I also took note of his brown corduroy trousers and check shirt. I didn't like the way he dressed. But he was tall, dark and handsome like the princes in the storybooks. Too bad he seemed kind of geeky.

The prosecutor is an old man of 30 with a soft voice. He wears the garb of all the men: black turban, long flowing robes and a harsh, long, tough-looking beard. He is a man who by all appearances never danced once in his life, never allowed pictures or music in his house, never laughed at a wedding. A man dulled by fanaticism, always wiping with the left hand, praying on a schedule, a man who was controlled and is controlling. Everyone leans forward in a wave to hear our crimes. I don't know why we women seem to be grouped together. Surely my crime of organising the patients in the hospital for a public protest is radically different from anything these poor creatures could have come up with.

The Boy Judge:	Where is their defence lawyer?
Defence:	Here, Your Honour.
Judge:	Are you calling any witnesses?
Defence:	There are no witnesses, Your Honour. In one case, there was another woman present.
Prosecutor:	Your Honour, one woman witness is only half a man. We need two women to make a whole witness.
Judge:	Defence, I am not interested in the individual cases. These women will be judged as a whole. Despite the media presence, this is not an important case. We have many other matters to decide today. There is a meteorite shower due to rain down on us in the hour after dusk, and I'm sure we all want to see such a sign from God. I do anyway.'

The judge smiled slightly, showing his youth. He was wearing those wooden sandals with the heel. His eyes were painted with kohl as is the fashion here. He struck me as quite effeminate.

Defence:	Yes, Your Honour. Then I will have to concede that there are no witnesses.
Judge:	Prosecutor, what is the charge?
Prosecutor:	The charge is Zima, Your Honour. Sexual intercourse out of wedlock.

Judge:	None of these women are married?
Defence:	Your Honour, these women did not consent to sexual intercourse. They were raped by prison guards. All have got pregnant since being imprisoned.
Judge:	So they were criminals to start with.
Defence:	They had been arrested, Your Honour, not charged.
Judge:	You have no witnesses. Prosecutor, do you have witnesses?
Prosecutor:	We have, Your Honour. We have the prison guards. Officials of the realm. They will tell you that these women begged for sex in prison.
Defence:	Your Honour, the guards are the ones who raped these women.
Judge:	Are the guards on trial?
Defence:	Not at this time, Your Honour.
Judge:	Then we do not tolerate such accusations. Strike that from the record.

(Everyone looks around, but it seems that no one is taking a record. Flies buzz around the eyes of the judge. He is hot and irritated. He looks to the rectangle of sky through the glassless window, anxious for his meteorite shower.)

I am confused. I have no idea why they talk of this. I thought I was on trial for what I was arrested for. That would make too much sense for these demented, ferocious children.

This trial seems to have nothing to do with me. People are shifting in their seats, and there is a lot of coughing and throat-clearing. The judge is talking to the prosecutor and defender at the bench. They motion for us to come forward. We 12 women all stand in a row before the judge, with our backs to everyone else.

'Show your faces!' our lawyer barks.

There is a gasp from the court. The judge bangs his gavel.

'Silence or I'll have the court cleared and you all flogged.'

We slowly pull up the burka and let him glimpse our faces. He scans all of them. I look at the midget beside me and realise she is a little girl.

'What age is this one?' the judge says, pointing to her.

'Twelve,' the lawyer says.

'And she's already pregnant?' The judge is staring harshly at her.

'Your Honour, you can see her brothers have already punished her. Most have been punished already by family. We see no need for further punishment.'

The face of the child has been corroded in places with acid. Her nose is burnt flat and her eyes look stuck open.

The judge stares at me with piercing eyes that convey loathing. 'This is the American?'

'Yes, I'm American. There has been a mistake—' I start to say.

'Silence.' The judge, prosecutor and my lawyer shout all at once.

'I have seen enough.' The judge waves us away in disgust. We are herded back behind a table.

'I have no choice,' the 15-year-old judge says. His moustache is soft and fine and his eyes are so young. He has tiny hands and dirty nails. 'Firstly, these women are criminals because they are in jail and therefore not good women. None of these women is married and all are pregnant. Therefore, logically, they are guilty of Zina. That is sexual relations outside marriage. It's irrefutable. The rape defence cannot be verified because there are no male witnesses. The guards will be reprimanded for giving in to the women's sexual demands. All of the women will be stoned to death as an example to Orapian women. Court dismissed.'

There are screams from the people in the court. A man shouts, 'But Your Honour, we have punished our sister. We have punished her because you asked us to. We were given the acid to pour on her face, and we did it because you said you would let her free.'

Everyone is pushing around him. Guards shove back at him. Hitting him with their rifle butts. There is so much pushing and shoving as we are pulled back into the corridor. I look for my mother, but I honestly don't think she is here. The families are yelling at the prosecutor, and the judge has come back on the stand.

'For your information, they will not be executed until they have their children. We will inform you about the fate of the children.'

It is night as we leave the court and, chained together, are marched across the street. The ancient texts described this as a beautiful city close to the Silk Road, although scholars who never believed it could be here dispute that. There are paintings somewhere of its mythical gardens and fountains and golden minarets capturing the sun. That city is long gone, gone even before our tribes swept through, gone a thousand years or more. That past is too far away to warm me as I trudge, heavy bellied, out of the court, chained to the tiny woman who is a girl child without a face. We are spooks, draped and veiled, furtively stealing glances through the mesh in front of our eyes. A corpse that was hanging from the lamppost has now been stripped of his shoes and clothes by scavengers.

Then stars begin to break down all over us. Everyone stalls and looks up to the collapsing sky.

Baby Zero, the female face is an open grave, a deadly trap. We must spare you our faces in the crowd; keep you from seeing the empty animal of our face. Bad dreams to wake to, my little baby. Hush now. No use crying inside me. I can't hear your soundless pleas. I can't comfort you. Our legacy of impotence and bovine madness will not open a door for you. Lost in our own nature. Tricked by our biologies. We know only our own stories, and we worship these stories without listening to them. We are ruined and captured. We are animals being returned to the zoo.

And I see, as I look up, a shower of meteorites in the sky, dust from a comet that passed us by 200 years ago, and I ache as they swoon, race, fizzle triumphant in coloured streaks, before disappearing for ever. The present hurts so much. I long for the past, the places in history, the times when it was all a little younger, our fate was not so sealed, depletion was not an altar, and there was less evidence of the long sacrifice. I ache for a time (was there really such a time?) when things bigger than us walked the earth. We lost them,

Baby Zero. I have nothing to show you but my own face. Little you
will gain from that.

The past is coming through and momentarily lighting our walk
under the arches and back through prison gates. They herd us on,
and we walk in a huddle straining to look upwards. The sky filled
with dust from 200 years ago, settling on this scene of small-made
sorrow.

Leila walked over to Zolo. He was wearing a white long-sleeved shirt
and black jeans. He looked serene and even smiled.

He said, 'I wish you hadn't come.'

'Zolo,' Leila said, trying to be brave and sarcastic like a grown-
up would be.

'Aw, come on,' Desiree said. 'I had to get her out of Uncle Mo's
million-dollar Malibu shack. I warned her about the Marth of
Munch.'

'I feel sick,' Leila whispered only to him.

'You are always complaining.' Zolo shrugged. 'If you hate it that
much here, make Mo send you to Ireland to Maman and Baba and
your precious Mehrdad.'

'I want to stay with you.'

'So you like California.' He paused. 'We are the inheritors; the
others are gone.'

'Zolo?'

'No, Frog. Go home.' Zolo tried to stroke Desiree's hair, but she
pulled away from him. Desiree did not like to be touched.

Outside, the palm trees held night's delicate silence between
their leaves. Suddenly the hissing symphony of automatic sprinklers
rose to a malevolent crescendo. The earth drank water brought from
far-away mountain rivers. Leila thought she could hear past voices
sounding through the mission grounds. Men from Catalonia who
came and built their big, stone, rectangular churches with noisy
bells, and the voices of Indians who were living here then. They
never knew when they swapped their gods that their children's children would not be born. 'Do not be afraid,' the priests said. 'Do not

be afraid, I am with you, I have called you each by name.' And so they came, stood within the mission walls and understood that nothing could save them.

The inheritors huddled in a room, losing their minds.

But Zolo, we are here now. Dark, undocumented refugees. We have come in the wake of it all to sit under the palms, to be mesmerised by the swamp of cloudless bitter blue sky. Aren't we blameless?

California über Alles. It was a song Desiree was playing from the computer in the room. Leila looked through her scrapbooks. She had four of them now. Three full and the last with only two pages left.

The world of the sun: warm rolling hills, parched deserts, snow peaks, ice-deep lakes, glitter of sea, a sudden mist on the mountains and the earth disappears and you are left with only yourself. It has been passed on to us. So where is the mercy? It was not shown to the first people. Should it be shown to the last?

'I almost can't bear it here,' Leila said. 'Everything is so new and clean and made up.'

The land has been cleaned of its people.

Leila felt not pity, not distant concern. It hurt so much.

'My country is history,' Leila told Zolo, and his eyes sparkled derisively.

'It's someone else's past,' Jack said. 'Don't worry about it.'

'Give it up,' Zolo said. 'I'm not in the mood.'

'She's got an Indian fixation,' Desiree yawned.

'Not just the Indians; she reads all the guidebook histories. Even the Balinese.'

'Shut her up. She never stops yammering,' Faz said.

'Leave her alone; she's a child,' Jack chided him. 'She read a book Ernie gave her, and it made a big impression.'

Leila felt the world around her. The fish were drowning in the sea. There was a hole punched in the sky. Was it conceivable that the gods were gone too? Slipped on through an ozone hole? That they too lost their heavenly habitat?

'Listen to the dry earth drink,' Zolo instructed them, and they did. When the sprinklers choked off as suddenly as they had come on, Jack implored Leila to relax.

'Forgive them, Leila. It's ours now. Please be happy to be here.'

She bent her head and tried to forgive. She tried to forgive the exuberant red-faced cowboys; she tried to forgive the Spanish priests on their mules, squinting into the sun. Those who put plaster painted statues inside the pyramids they built. Even their statues had swords.

'This country was founded on genocide,' Leila said to Jack.

'That was a long time ago,' Jack said.

'Can good come out of genocide after time?'

'We're American. We can't think of that,' Jack said. 'We came as settlers and turned the year back to zero. History starts from us now.'

'I want Maman,' Leila said hours later.

'Don't start,' Zolo said.

'But I want my maman.' Leila began to cry. Her face was flushed; there were dangerous gleamings in her eyes. 'Maman! Maman!'

'Someone take her home.'

Faz was quiet. His mouth was open and tears still ran down his cheeks.

'I think it's admirable that you are so interested in history. My name is Jack Clancy from a long line of Clancys. I can trace back our family lineage, though it gets kind of fuzzy in the twelfth century.' Jack smiled at her and shook her hand. 'I'll take you home.'

'I don't have a home. I feel sick. I want a doctor,' Leila sulked.

'Let her sleep,' Jack said to Zolo.

'No,' Leila wailed. 'Take me away from here. I can't fall asleep here.'

'In the dorms?' Desiree asked.

'No. In the Marth of Munch.'

'You can't leave, Jack,' Faz said. 'We swore we'd stay in one spot and see what happened. We said we'd stay together.'

'Rules, rules, rules,' Zolo yawned. 'Desiree left.'

'She doesn't count. She's a girl,' Faz growled. 'We men must not separate.'

Leila fled outside and sat in Desiree's car. Desiree came and found her.

'All right, kiddo. It's doing my head in, too. I'll bring you back to Malibu.'

'I want to go to the House With No Anus.'

'Good, that's closer.'

Suddenly, Zolo, Faz and Jack came running out of the dorms and got into the car with them.

The sun came up as they drove. Exhausted, Leila slept with her head on Zolo's lap. At one point, Desiree slept too. The car hurtled on down the dead-straight highway all by itself, its five occupants dreaming. No sentinel to look out for what was ahead and all around.

Leila was dreaming that she was a plucked bird in a bag.

When they reached the House With No Anus, none of them wanted to go inside. They shoved Leila out of the car. She had no clothes with her. Just her scrapbooks and Mehrdad's letters. She stood by Desiree's window and pleaded with her.

'I don't want to go in alone. Take me to the mountains then.'

'What mountains?'

Leila pointed to the blue dry mountains on the horizon.

'Oh, those? No one goes there. They're just backdrop.'

'They mightn't even exist,' Jack agreed.

'There's no road?' Leila peered into the distance. 'Lan mentioned going there. I couldn't find her in Vegas. She might be there.'

'Lan? She was evil,' Desiree said firmly. 'Forget her; she's out of the picture.'

'I miss her. She was a friend I'd made all by myself.'

'Yeah, some friend,' Zolo said, without looking at her.

Leila, darkling, nightling, blackling. Your shape cut out of the vast blondness of the desert valley, a small dark hole in the landscape.

Did you want to go to the mountains? Was that your wish before you disappeared into the house?

Because you had been looking at the mountains for ever. Extended moments spent gazing from the upstairs window when the sun set over the barren hills and liquid night poured into the parched crevices.

Did you want to stay with your brother?

Because he wasn't even looking at you when Desiree reversed the car and roared off. Because Zolo could not accept you. You were Orap to him. Small, conflicted, overlooked, unknown. Dangerous to him.

You could have walked back out into the valley. The valley between those columns of thirsty hills contained all the human hell you might need: the gloomy ranch houses, the trailer parks, the gated communities, the Mayan families in shot-gun shacks, the manicured golf courses for white people, the Indian casinos.

And you were alone. You had no more friends in the valley. You wanted to tell Lan before she left: you betrayed me, fed me to the Ick-Man, but I loved you and know why you did it, even if I don't understand.

Leila, featherless, furless, talonless, fangless, tribeless. Now the door closed behind you, and the staleness of the house greeted you with its familiar mesh of smells. If you couldn't be with your brother, this was better than living with your uncle. Patterson was watching football, and Ernie was at the foot of the stairs, petting the cat and listening to a political discussion on a small radio. Ernie smiled at you unquestioningly, and you walked up the stairs and down the corridor, with its stacks of newspapers, phone books, piles of clothes, a broken sewing machine, a heap of stuffed toys missing limbs and eyes.

You barely made it to the door. Your legs were trembling.

The door was unlocked. You lay down on the bed and rolled to the side towards the wall, and all the dreams began at once. Colossal canyons, colliding hordes, lone travellers on horseback, volumeless words, gifts of diseased blankets, broken promises, subsumed tribes, submerged worlds.

You were Baby Zero too.

And other portents at the time: such as the small potted cactus by the front door bursting out into strange golden flowers; Patterson sighting a comet as he drove home; a beached whale in the parking lot in front of the 7/11; and silent un-noted mudslides on the pathless mountains.

Chapter Nineteen

A Day That Never Was

Mehrdad and I drove to see Zolo in Silicon Valley. We wanted to know what happened. My parents were incapable of telling the truth. I had never met a man like Mehrdad. He was gentle and funny. He prayed five times a day. He carried a compass so he would know where Mecca was. I had been raised to believe that all people who followed a faith were stupid. He took my criticisms lightly. At times, he seemed elated. 'I waited so long,' he said.

Zolo laughed out loud when he saw him.

'Time has been kinder to you.'

Only Zolo could tell us what happened.

Zolo emerged from his controlled experiment that was the Marth of Munch on 1 April. Jack was outside the door. A position he had taken up early on, like a sentinel. 'April first, brother,' Jack said, and they embraced. Faz came out and hugged both of them. He had spent the last few days crying like a baby.

'Fuck! I'll never be the same again,' he gasped.

'That can only be a good thing.' Jack slapped him on the back.

'Was I hallucinating?' Zolo asked. 'Or did Leila come in all that mayhem?'

'She did. Then we drove her to my house. She had a flu or something.'

'Yeah! Shit! I'd better go and investigate.'

Zolo drove to the California high desert to see Leila. He stopped at the 7/11 for some Coke and a stick of beef jerky. He drove past the trailer park and into the suburban row of middle-class, ranch-style California houses that sat so solidly dwarfed by the valley. Automatic sprinklers, children's swings, basketball hoops, mini-vans were parked outside. All the things that need to be bought or acquired to maintain even a modest existence. The Clancys were still on holidays. The house was empty. Ernie was at work in the local tax office. Patterson had stopped coming.

Zolo found the front door open as always. He stepped inside the House With No Anus. Since the Clancys were away, Ernie had a pile of pizza boxes scattered about the kitchen counters. None of the over-packed cupboards closed any more. Zolo picked his way through the small pathways flanked by newspaper stacks and miscellaneous yard-sale memorabilia. There was a whole box of old assorted licence plates on the stairs; he walked up past them; he found a broken scratching post for the cats at the top of the stairs; the corridor was strewn with ancient, battered stuffed toys; the bathroom door was open, and a glacier of shampoo bottles, toothpaste tubes and body creams crept into the corridor. He went to Ernie's room and opened the door. He had never been inside this room before. It was dark; an American flag was nailed to the window as a curtain. There was a pungent smell in the room. Inside, he found a toy boxing ring with two dusty robots eternally facing each other, never to make battle; he found a portrait of Ronald Reagan on the wall; a small clay statue of a man squeezed into creation by a child's hand with the words 'the idiot' scratched at the base. And then he found a dead child.

Leila was so obviously dead that Zolo did not even dare to touch her or say her name out loud. Her eyes were wide open. Zolo took out his mobile phone and called Mo.

'Mo,' he whispered.

'Hello? Hello?'

'Mo, it's Zolo,' Zolo croaked louder.

'You want money, don't you? That's the only reason you ever call me, or you're in jail. If you're not in jail, you're in Vegas; if you don't need money, you're in jail.'

'Mo. Leila's dead.'

Zolo noted that Leila was lying on top of the covers. She had never felt at home enough in Ernie's forsaken room to get fully into the bed.

'Oh, Frog,' he said a few minutes after he put the phone down. 'I always wanted to be an only child.'

Leila's enormous eyes stared emptily at the cobwebbed ceiling. Her body looked muscular, amniotic: tadpole come ashore at birth. Zolo studied her as he had never studied her when she was alive. There were hours before Mo arrived, delayed by LA miserable traffic and a stop at Home Depot.

Zolo sat by her till Mo came. They carried the body to the car wrapped in the flag, and put her in the back seat. Ernie's car was pulling into the driveway as they were pulling out. He waved at them; they waved back. Mo took the lead. He drove up the blue mountains on a dusty path. His torrent of words washed over Zolo, never sinking in.

'This doesn't have to be a disaster or it might be. We could get thrown out of the US for this. My clinic is just about to open. My own clinic. I've worked hard for this day. My American passport interview is in a month; I've already done the fingerprinting. Your parents made me say you children were mine. I told them I didn't want the responsibility. I'm not into all this family stuff. They said—just say they're yours. So I did. I had to do a tonne of paperwork, get documents forged, take such risks. And you were able to come over as minors, as my children, but you're not my children. You never even listened to me. She escaped from my house; I thought she was with you. She said she had a stiff neck. I thought she was just sunburned—'

Zolo snapped out of the trance, 'Stiff neck? I had a stiff neck when I had meningitis.'

'I remember you having it. We were all so worried. But you pulled through, thank God.' Mo patted his nephew's knee hysterically. 'I brought you a space ship. Do you remember? That was the latest toy from the West. I got you all the latest toys.'

They drove for two hours through the Desert Mountains until the path ran out. Then they drove off-terrain in Mo's jeep.

'Where are we going?' Zolo said. 'What are we doing?' But he knew. Mo even had two brand new shovels in the back of the car with their Home Depot price tags on.

'Zolo. Your wonderful wife, Desiree. I admire her. You're a lucky man. She always says, what does she say? A day without a buzz?'

'A day without a buzz is a day that never wuz.'

'This will be a day that never was. Understand?'

'No,' Zolo said.

'You have to. You're not a native. You're a refugee. We all are until we get the citizenship, and even then we are. Things have to be different for us.'

'I wish there hadn't been a revolution,' Zolo said.

'Sure, sure. Don't we all? How things would have been different. One piece of advice—stay away from history. No good comes out of it.'

Mo pulled the car to a halt between some big rock piles. He closed his eyes as if he were praying. Zolo got out of the car and wished he could just walk away and never come back.

Mo took the body out of the car and laid it on the ground. He grabbed one of the shovels and threw one to Zolo. Mo said, 'The things I have to do for Ishmael. All my life. And he was my older brother. Traditionally, he should have led the way. You don't know how we grew up or why we don't talk about it.'

Zolo buckled over on to the desert floor in the dry valley. He put his forehead on the ground and began to whimper. He might have been screaming. Mo grabbed him and dragged him to his feet.

'We came from the dirt, Zolo. From mud houses and open fires, and goat herders. We came from the side of mountains. Your father and I crawled our way out of utter savagery. Do you know how savage you have to be not to succumb to savagery?'

He pushed a shovel into Zolo's hands.

'You're not making me do this on my own.'

Zolo picked the shovel up and hit the ground with it. Hard and unrelenting, the ground would not yield to him.

'Don't ruin the shovel, and keep the label on. I'll leave them back to Home Depot on my way back.'

'Why?' Zolo squinted at his uncle. 'Are you afraid the police will trace them?'

'No. No. Trace what? What do I need with two shovels? I want my money back.'

Chapter Twenty

Mehrdad Arrives in Los Angeles

Mehrdad was nearly 40 but felt like a child again when he rang the doorbell on the second floor of an apartment block in LA. The Fatagagases were such an influence in his earlier life. There hadn't been a day that had gone by without his thinking of them. He heard shuffling behind the door. Shouting from inside. Maybe he should have phoned. They probably weren't used to people coming to the door. The door opened with the chain on it, and Farah was peering through the crack. She had grown old and was wearing a dressing gown. He should have phoned.

'Mehrdad was our gardener's son in Orap,' Farah said to the young girl who had appeared and was now standing by the kitchen counter. 'You'd better go and do your study. Don't you have exams?'

'You've grown up, Leila. But you're still just as I remember you. You're beautiful?' he said, addressing the girl.

'I'm Marguerite.'

'Last time I saw you, you were a baby. I won't stay long,' Mehrdad said. He was staring at Marguerite. She might have been Leila grown up. She was tall and thin and had long bleached-blond hair. Her eyes were Orapian, huge and almond-shaped with long lashes. He was taken aback by her beauty. He felt ordinary again in front of a Fatagagas.

'You are talking funny. Like an Irish,' Ishmael said as he patted

Mehrdad on the back and motioned to Farah to get more tea. 'So you never got to America.' Ishmael was a bit smug on this point. The Fatagagases were comfortable with someone only when they found something to look down on.

'Oh, I like Ireland, Doctor Fatagagas. I got used to it.'

'And you never went back to Orap?'

'No. I hear there is yet another new regime. Another revolution. Made of the children who were soldiers for the old regime. I hear the children have taken over and are more fundamentalist and literal than the last one.'

'They're going to turn the year back to zero,' Marguerite said to Mehrdad. 'What a country. Every time there is a new regime, they turn the year back to zero.'

'It's usually in any government's interest to erase the past,' Mehrdad said.

'Yes, that's what we heard,' Ishmael said. 'My wife and I kept the deed to our house. This new regime said they'd honour the deeds that the previous regime stole.'

'I kept the deed,' Farah said in contempt. 'You kept nothing but your fantasies.'

'I was thinking if the new regime turned out all right, I could go back and set up a surgery.'

'You don't have a surgery here with your brother? I found him in the phone book and called him.'

'You spoke to Mo?' Farah tensed.

'Yes, I was asking for Leila's number. He told me to talk to you.'

'She's not here, she . . .' Farah looked at Ishmael, who looked even more deflated than usual.

'Just her phone number,' Mehrdad said. 'I won't bother her. I'm sure she's married and has kids and a job and a busy life. I just wanted to say hello to her and Zolo.'

So, I thought, he knew my brother.

'Who's Leila?' Marguerite asked.

'Marguerite, go to your room and study,' Farah barked. She had changed out of her dressing gown and was now wearing a white blouse with a lumpy bra underneath. She always wore overdecorated lumpy bras that showed through her clothing.

'I'm not 10 years old. I'm a doctor now,' Marguerite shouted back. Ishmael cowered.

Mehrdad sat with his tea cold in his hand. He had forgotten how the Fatagagases were always yelling at each other. 'Your sister,' he said. 'You don't call her Leila?'

'I don't have a sister.'

'Get out of our house,' Farah hissed.

Mehrdad stood up. He thought he knew the score. 'I'm sorry for bothering you, Madame and Doctor Fatagagas. Nice meeting you, Marguerite.'

Ishmael and Farah ushered him to the door.

'What was all that about?' he could hear Marguerite ask.

'He's a peasant,' Farah said. 'He's also a thief.'

But Mehrdad was not gone. He had come too far and wanted to know. This was his life's question. In a way, his life had been on hold for Leila. He should have come sooner, but he had kept trying to move on and forget about this wretched family. He waited outside and came up to Marguerite when she was walking to her car.

'Marguerite, I'm sorry to bother you. Did Leila do something to bring shame on the family? I know how Orapians are.'

'I don't have a sister.'

'I understand. She's been disowned. I remember from her letters: she hinted at something bad. Some man in the desert. I know this is all a bit strange, but let me take you to a Persian restaurant in Westwood. The hotel recommended it. Palace of the Mediterranean.'

You hate me now, Baby Zero. I am not Leila. The good Baby Zero. She was born the daughter of a surgeon. I am Marguerite the American. I was born in a refugee camp. I am the vain, the shrill, the materialistic, the hard-hearted Baby Zero. I am Marguerite the Fox. Although biologically from the East, I am melded with the West, as though the old antagonists, dog and cat, East and West, seem magically blended. My Eastern adaptations—lithe body, whiskers, movements, mouse chasing, tree climbing—contrast to my Western bushy tail, hole living, pointed muzzle, barking and trotting.

He handed me the card from the restaurant as if to prove its existence and thus his sincerity.

Over dinner, we decided to fly up to northern California to ask where this disowned Leila was. That is how we ended up with Zolo.

'We dug her grave and buried her out there in the high desert,' Zolo told Mehrdad and me when we visited him in Sunnyvale, California. 'Mo thought they would send him back to Orap otherwise, and he would be killed, which he would have been, no doubt. We dropped her in a shallow grave. It was barely a grave because the ground was so hard we had to pile rocks on top to cover the body. She was wearing a yellow dress with butterflies on it. There was no autopsy, of course. We just figured it was meningitis because of the stiff neck.'

'How old was she?' I asked. I had never known I had a sister.

'She would have been 12,' Mehrdad said coldly and in anger.

Zolo nodded. 'She was almost 13. I was 16 the next day.'

'Is that why you never come to visit, or never helped us out when we came to America?'

'Mo made up for me,' Zolo said. 'He paid your fare, he organised visas. He used his influence in every way. He has you apprentice with him. He'll leave you the surgery.'

Mehrdad pushed his hands through his hair. 'So, there you have it. And I thought she stopped writing to me because of the earrings. All those years. I used to walk by the statue of Oscar Wilde every day on my way to the engineering department in Trinity. I always thought of her.'

'I was born in Ireland,' I said.

'No, you were born in the refugee camp,' Mehrdad said. 'I saw you when you were a few hours old. I remember it as if it was yesterday.'

'I was never told that.'

'What were you told?' Mehrdad said.

'He never told me anything.' I pointed angrily at Zolo. 'Even now, he's telling you, not me.'

Zolo shrugged. 'Farah asked me to say nothing. She said it would only cause unnecessary pain, and there was enough of that. I didn't want to talk about it. I pretended to my friends that Leila went back to Ireland. What could I tell them? I buried my little sister in the desert when I was 15 years old. I was a fake. Mo wasn't my father. I wasn't old enough to be in college or drive or marry. You were your mother's daughter, Marguerite. I saw that from the very first time I laid eyes on you. You were six years old, and we were all gathered in the bank when Maman and Baba first came over. You said out of the blue to the teller helping us, "What happens to the money if they all drop dead? Do I get it?" That American was so shocked. Six years old, Marguerite!'

'So what if I'm my mother's daughter? Don't you love your mother? She loves you.'

'I always said Farah was base. That was the word. I said it to her all the time. Even growing up in Orap. And Ishmael always agreed. Yes, he'd say. She is base. And the few contacts I had with you— well, you seemed just like her. Aren't you? Isn't she?'

Mehrdad hesitated and stared at me.

I began to scream at him. My voice rising and rising. 'Who are you to judge? My life had no security. I don't remember any of Ireland. I only remember coming here. We went to an Afghan woman who was a neighbour. She told us where to buy cheap sausage. For years, we slept in a one-room studio on an inflatable mattress. The three of us, eating the same meal of sausage and rice. Maman was always mad at Baba. They hated each other. He never got a job to this day. She would goad him on, and he used to beat her, and I'd come between them and try to pull them apart. She used to say, 'I'm only staying with you for the child's sake.' That's how I grew up here in America. And Maman with that wretched big brown bag—'

Zolo actually laughed. 'Oh Christ! That bag.'

I nodded, looked at Mehrdad beseechingly. 'She always carried her documents—bank information, passports, the deed to the house—with her everywhere she went. She never left them in the house once. My father and I used to tease her about it. We told her she would lose it, but she never did.'

Coming from Ireland to California was like a door had opened, and I stepped from the indoors to the outdoors. I have no memories of Ireland. I had never seen light like that—golden, expansive, deep. I erroneously conjectured that my parents had come here not for dreamed-of economic advantage but to be flooded by light, to have it wash over them and make us shine. But shine we could not. We Fatagagases could not shine. Dark, argumentative, distrustful beings that we were, incapable of confidence, contemptuous of hope, remote from belief. And we saw the world prove us right.

Mehrdad left. He walked out the door. He didn't want to be with me. Zolo watched the car pull out of the drive.

'So much for the good son, Mehrdad. He's just abandoned you.'

'He'll be back,' I said. 'I have to be back at work. I'm flying back to LA this evening.'

'I don't think so. He hates us. He was always hopelessly in love with Leila. It used to amuse me,' Zolo said. 'I'll drop you at the light rail. I can't drive you all the way to the airport. I have to pick the kids and their nanny up from the mall and do the shopping.'

I could see that Zolo hated having me in the same room as him. Polluting his life and house with my presence. He went to get his car keys and came back with a cardboard box. 'These are Leila's scrapbooks and letters.'

'You kept them.'

'You can have them. If you read through them, you will realise that she was the genius of the family. Not I. I was the great impostor.'

As he talked, I stared at all the photos of his wife and his two half-Orapian, half-Chinese, American children. My racist parents would be horrified. If you marry a non-Orapian, you might at least marry a tall blonde. Why go for something even more inferior? But then they didn't even know they had grandchildren.

'Leila was obsessed with Cowboys and Indians, the story of the

West. She wrote tonnes of notes and bits of a diary. You can see in her scrapbooks she was linking the genocide of the indigenous people to the eradication of the species on earth. I think she would be happy if she saw Silicon Valley, this Wild West. The cowboys wield PhDs not guns, but they're still cowboys. And the Indians are back, but this time they're the other Indians. The ones Columbus and the Europeans were actually expecting. I think Leila would take great comfort from that.'

It was always hard to tell if he was joking or not. I could not figure Zolo out.

'Are you like the other Fatagagas men? Do you yell all the time? Do you sulk? Are you full of self-pity and bitterness?'

'Ask my wife,' Zolo said.

'I'd like to meet her.'

'No.' And then, as if that was too harsh, he added, 'She's at a conference in Baltimore this week.'

'What does she do?'

'She's an engineer, like myself.'

Zolo was pushing 40, going bald, and had a slight potbelly. He was looking very much like a Fatagagas. I saw a picture of his wife on the mantel.

'Is she American?' I asked.

'No. How would I meet an American? I studied science. No American in their right mind does that. It's an immigrant profession, like medicine. She's Chinese,' Zolo said. 'So, now you see it. Our boring suburban life in Silicon Valley.'

'I always imagined you'd be rich. Maman and Baba tell everyone you're rich.'

'And they're just the purveyors of the truth. No, I made a few bad choices. Joined the wrong companies. Never got lucky. Faz made it. He's a multi-millionaire from some stocks he had in a start-up. That idiot has a ten-million-dollar house in Los Altos hills. I wrote all his papers for him. Gave him all his results in college. He never understood a thing, but, hey, that's not what counts.' Then Zolo suddenly realised to whom he was talking. 'Okay, I'm ranting.

My wife would walk out of the room at this point. She doesn't speak English all that well, but she knows when I'm complaining.'

'How do you communicate?'

'We don't.' Zolo shrugged. 'I met her at my last company. Nothing else was happening. When you work the tech-slave hours I work, you don't get out much. There aren't exactly many hot chicks in Silicon Valley.'

I was quite shocked about the casual way he talked about his marriage. Like it was an arrangement.

Zolo dropped me off at the light rail. As I was gliding along tracks, the two-car train stopped suddenly, and the driver got out to pull some tumbleweed off the tracks. It struck me then that here, in the high-tech capital of the world, tumbleweed was still blowing across the West and tripping people up. I read later in Leila's scrapbook that tumbleweed is not a native plant but was brought to the West by Russian Mennonites by mistake. I learnt a lot from the scrapbooks.

Mehrdad was there at the airport, full of apologies for having driven away. He was distraught. We embraced and cried together, or at least at the same time. He was crying for Leila, and I was crying for myself. When he held me, I felt good. Better than I had felt in a long time. I squeezed his hand and he kissed my forehead. I could feel my long eyelashes scratching his cheek.

I didn't fly to LA, and I missed work for the first time in my life. Instead, I drove with Mehrdad down Highway 1. We stayed in a motel in Santa Barbara and became lovers.

Chapter Twenty-One

A Waste of Wolves

Mehrdad and I spent the next month piecing Leila's time together. We had Leila's letters and her scrapbooks.

We talked to all the Clancys. Jack was a taxi driver in San Francisco. Desiree was a housewife in San Bernardino. Ernie still worked in the tax office. We talked to Faz the multi-millionaire with his blonde trophy wife. Rita was living alone and happy in Palm Springs with two poodles and a Maltese called Mo.

Mo lived in a pyramid in the Hollywood hills. His house was made entirely of mirrored glass. From every level, you could see everything. The world had nothing to hide from Mo. What it saw of him was a reflection of itself.

He was easy to talk to. He had always treated me pretty well. He didn't seem shocked that I was asking about Leila.

'Where are the wolf faces now?' Mehrdad asked because he couldn't think of anything to say after the story was told.

'They all fell apart. They weren't properly tanned. It was a disgrace, a waste of wolves.' Mo paced up and down. 'I'm building a new house now. I've bought land in Greenland. Ishmael keeps telling me the polar caps are melting and soon that will be the last habitable place on earth. I remember you now. Of course, you were the gardener's son. Ishmael and I used to have your father beat you if we caught you playing with Zolo. But Zolo didn't care; he would still insist you play with him.'

'It wasn't him getting beaten.' Mehrdad shrugged.

Mo's laughter boomed out of him. 'Ishmael would never have dared beat Zolo. He was afraid of the boy. We were all a little afraid. I thought he understood about Leila. No one killed her. She was dead. She would probably have died even with care.'

'But you were a doctor,' Mehrdad said. 'You should have seen how sick she was.'

'I did not. Leila was some kind of freak accident. Who could have foretold that a perfectly healthy 12-year-old girl would just die?' Mo offered Mehrdad some fried morsel. 'Tikas?'

'No, thank-you.' Mehrdad was signalling to me that he wanted to leave.

'I am not the kind of doctor who has ever cured anyone. I do something less mundane. I change people.'

Mehrdad went to the bathroom and Mo turned to me. 'Your parents are very worried that you are with this guy. He's 15 years older than you. I know you're American and you don't quite get it, but he's beneath our family.'

'Could anyone be beneath us?' I said as I nibbled on a piece. 'What is Tikas?'

'Rat.' Mo smiled.

'Do you know where Rita is now?'

'Oh, yes. Rita! We still talk from time to time. I have her number. She was a dumbo. A born-again Christian. The dumbest kind of American. I've told you the story. What more do you want? We did what we had to do. We got your parents up through Mexico eventually. Zolo got his green card and then his citizenship and got them green cards and then they got citizenships. We're all Americans now. Americans ignore their past. It's a dirty genocidal history. You should too. Zolo tried to show me Leila's scrapbooks. He was very upset for a while. They were full of sentimental nonsense about indigenous peoples. They had to kill the Indians to enjoy this place fully. To make it their own, start from zero. What would we be doing now in the Hollywood hills with all those Red Indians galloping around scalping us? To be comfortable as an American, you have to forget. The world has never been empty, but we can pretend it has. And who wants to think about these things? That this rather banal place we live in was founded on genocide not too long ago. Forget, Marguerite. That's my advice to you.'

Mo followed us out to the car. Mehrdad wanted to get away as quickly as possible. Mo kept talking; even when we were sitting in the car and turning on the ignition, he leaned in the window. His big moustache glistening, his dark eyes gleaming, his extraordinary nose quivering with the passion of overstatement.

'The Indians had one thing right. They worshipped whatever they ate. They prayed to the buffalo, and so they hunted and devoured their gods. These modern people have contempt for what they eat—chickens, lambs, pigs, cows: no one worships them. You are what you eat, whether you be carnivore or a dreadful vegetarian. That's why you find most people are farm animals or, worse, vegetables. I try not to eat like that. I try to be transcendent in my consumption.'

'Well, he was eating rat,' I said to Mehrdad as we drove off. Mehrdad actually laughed. Maybe he could get over Leila and love me properly.

I took Mehrdad to my work one day. I showed him what I had to put up with. Assured him that I was just here temporarily to do my residency in a county hospital. That soon I would be exclusively working with Mo and wouldn't have to be subjected to the scum of the earth: the half-breeds, the dark ones, the poor chewed-up whites, the immigrants who didn't bother learning English. He said, you are the dark one, the immigrant; your skin is darker, your almond eyes browner, your black hair dyed blond. He sat in the emergency room and watched the broken people, the pain in their faces immediate and eternal. In California, we were in the most western part of the West, where everything builds up and flows back like a wave. The poor were multitudinous, a passive majority, unstoppable, violent unto themselves. Whatever you said about my mother, she had made sure we were not among them. We were not in their ranks. I would inherit my uncle's clinic. I could support my parents soon. They were broke and Zolo never sent a penny. Soon I would be able to get them health insurance. Mehrdad seemed to be withdrawing from me, but I lured him on with the quest for his beloved Leila.

I stopped the car somewhere by a canyon on the way to Palm Springs to see Rita. We moved the passenger seat right back and I straddled him, pinning him to the seat with my kisses. I unzipped his jeans and pulled them down so that they bound his thighs tightly. I took off all my clothes, and sat up straight on him. As the odd car drove past, I hoped they were looking in. We couldn't keep our hands off each other. Neither of us had much experience with lovers. I had none. But we felt natural together, and our lust was bottomless. When I had sex with him, I went into an animal trance. In the afterglow, we would lie on each other and not talk. Just stroke each other all over. Sometimes we would become peacefully re-aroused and make love in a quieter, slower way. This was out on the road in the car, and I was hoping we would be caught. I wanted to be watched.

Rita had an American flag flying from her garage flagpole. She had pictures of a blond, blue-eyed Christ all over the house. Her dogs, Mo and Jesus, were tiny and bad-tempered, but thoroughly devoted to her. She had them sprayed with doggy perfume, and they smelled awful as they yapped about, snapping at Mehrdad's ankles.

'They don't like men at all,' Rita apologised.

Rita was happy; it was obvious. Her skin was orange leather from the sun, and her house was stuffed with tiny ornaments dusted daily by Mexican maids. There was a beautiful pool that she confessed she never swam in. 'Leila. Such a sweet little thing. I never knew. I was told she went back to her parents in Ireland. Oh my Lord! What a terrible story. I feel dreadful. Yes, she was sick. She was sleeping all the way from Vegas to LA. She barely got out of the car. It was so long ago. I never thought of her really. I was very unhappy with your uncle. True, he should have done something, but Mo was incapable of thinking about anybody but himself. He's a narcocyst—is that the word? Zolo was only a child himself and a very angry, wild child. Your uncle was convinced Zolo was some kind of genius. Was he?'

'I don't know,' I said. 'Maybe he was. I'm sure my family just liked the idea that there was a genius in the family. A reflection of them.'

'Zolo. I always thought I'd read about him someday. Doing something great. Like coming up with an alternative to oil, now that it's running out.'

'Leila was just as smart, but she was kind too,' Mehrdad said.

'Mo took me to China right after that. Oh, to think he buried her in the desert. And didn't tell me. Then to go on vacation. I never saw him grieve. Dreadful. I will pray for her. Pray for us all. Jesus was watching.'

Mehrdad went off to pray at one point, and Rita took me by the arm. 'He is a lovely young man. You should marry him. He has God.'

'Not your God.'

'There's only one God. You are Muslim too?'

'I worship the buffalo actually.'

Rita looked at me oddly. 'You remind me of them.'

'Who?'

'Leila and Zolo. They were smart-ass kids.'

The truth was, Mehrdad irritated me with his religion. Religion had ruined everything for Orap and for my family. I hated religion. He was private about it. We talked about it only once, and he told me he had become religious after connecting with the mosque in Dublin when his cousin was murdered. I assumed he was looking for his identity. We all need something to make us feel special. I had Mehrdad. I could allow him to have Allah, as long as I could have him.

Rita told us about all her encounters with Leila and then, when we were walking down her driveway to the car, she stopped suddenly. 'In China, there was a restaurant that Mo wanted to go to. He told me it was to eat fried scorpions, but it was because he wanted to try that dish where they strap the live monkeys into the table and the chef opens their skull and serves their brain. They had given us the number at the Ritz Carlton in Beijing; we were searching for this place and arrived a couple of hours before they opened. We saw the chefs walk the monkeys in through the back door to the kitchen. They were hand-in-hand. These tiny monkeys and the chefs. The monkeys looked so trusting. Like parents and children. Mo was very excited to eat there, but I stayed at the hotel that night. That's when we broke up. I couldn't shake that sight from my mind. He thought I was foolish. They are only animals, he kept saying. He kept singing that song to tease me about it, "Let Me Take You by the Hand". He thought it was very funny. It was the final straw. He never loved me. I knew that. He only wanted a green card. He thought I was igno-rant because I had Jesus in my life.' She shuddered in the hot air, her eyes losing composure. But her face, held together by so many Botox injections, was taut and orange and blank. She picked up Jesus, the tiny white poodle, who was wearing a rhinestone coat with the pattern of the stars and stripes. The dog licked her on the lips and she closed her eyes. Rita had found her desert happiness, and Jesus loved her.

Jack Clancy was at his sister Desiree's house in San Bernardino. He visited often and now he was living with them. They were as close as twins. It was the closest relationship either of them had had in their lives. He was very thin and wore a seersucker suit, a boater hat perched on his head, and he carried an empty briefcase. He had an ancient camera he had found in a junk sale and went under the black hood to take a photo of Mehrdad, myself and Desiree, in her scrubby, suburban, plantless, flowerless garden. A dynamite plunger was the only decoration by a concrete wall. Desiree wore skin-tight leopard pants with a low-cut denim top. She looked worn-out sexy and junkie gaunt. They were in their mid forties.

'What an outfit,' Jack said to his sister. 'It really screams Whore!'

'At least I don't have an outfit that screams Banjo!'

'Where's your husband?' I asked her.

'He's in drunk school. He got a DUI and they make you do classes. I got my second one last year. Second one in California, that is. Jack is down here for six months to be our chauffeur as both of us have got our licences suspended.'

'What's drunk school?' Mehrdad asked.

'They send you there when you get busted. I hope my husband is doing okay. I told him to say that he's not much of a drinker. That's what I said. I kept saying it. Otherwise they trick you into more classes and guilt stuff. This guy beside me was fat and bald and had a glass eye and a horrible hairpiece. He turned to me and said, "Yeah! I'm not much of a drinker, but blackberry brandy cost me an eye!"'

We laughed and drank mudslides. I hardly ever drank. My parents never did. It wasn't really in our culture. But I was glad to see Mehrdad drink. He wasn't so rigid after all.

I was hoping his belief system could contain me.

'I wish Zolo would come down and visit. I miss him. Jack was in San Francisco but still didn't get to see him much.'

'He's busy with his kids and his work,' Jack said. Still protective of Zolo.

'Zolo was the smartest person I have ever met in my life. And your sister was something else too. They were both so strange and so smart. Zolo just said she had gone to join her parents. He kind of drifted away from everyone after that. Concentrated on his PhD, wrote research papers, and flew all over the world giving talks. Then he started in that start-up just around the time the economy crashed again. How many gold rushes have there been in Silicon Valley? Zolo was a genius, but he was never lucky.'

'He's got two beautiful children and a wife,' Mehrdad said.

'Mmm!' Jack hummed unconvinced. 'Someone of his calibre was never bound for happiness.'

'I miss Zolo. We should drive up and party with him some.'

Jack nodded. 'One of his advisors in the physics department said that one day he would win a Nobel Prize. He was marked for greatness.'

'Fucking Zolo buried Leila in the desert!' Desiree jumped off her chair. 'She died in our house in Ernie's room? That's hard to believe.'

'You were married to my brother?' I asked her.

'Actually we never got a divorce. I don't know if that counted. He was on a fake ID and under age. It got him his green card, though. I miss Zolo. He's one of a kind.'

'When did you two split up?' Mehrdad asked.

'Oh, we were never quite together. He wanted sex all the time. He was a teenage male, for chrissake. But of all my appetites, sex was never my thing. My husband now is a car salesman. We met in a bar. He never wants sex. He just wants to watch football. I'm off the hook. We go on holidays to Delaware for chrissake! I wanted to go to Vietnam. The golden triangle. Or Phnom Penh. Guns, girls and ganja. That's where Lan the whore was from. Did Zolo tell you all about her? Whatever became of her? She and Leila were real tight; dead of AIDS, no doubt; she was really quite cool, although what she did to Leila was evil. But no, we went to Delaware. The first night, I wet the bed. That's the Delaware salute, I told him.'

Desiree poured us all another mudslide while Jack rolled a joint.

'One day, I was driving to this apartment we had in LA. Zolo was paying the rent. The car spun over, and I ended up upside down. Don't know what happened. I guess I sort of crashed into myself. Anyway, I had to crawl out of there and abandon the car 'cos I was so wasted. I crawled all the way to Zolo's place. It was three in the morning, and he was asleep over some physics books. He saw my face was all scratched up, so he was worried and took me to the county hospital emergency room. We had to wait hours, and he had an exam the next morning. When we were driving home, he said, "Those nurses and doctors were so rude to me. They had a horrible attitude. They mustn't like Middle Easterners."'

'No one likes Middle Easterners,' I said.

Desiree nodded. 'I told him, "No, dude! I couldn't tell them about the car, so I said you did this to me. They thought you had beaten me up. That's why you were getting the evil eye." He was kind of pissed. Usually he had a better sense of humour. I guess it was about 6 a.m. He wasn't a morning person.'

'What did Lan, Leila's friend, do that was so evil?' Mehrdad asked.

Desiree groaned and told us all about the Ick-Man.

Jack was taking photos with another old camera.

'I'd like to get copies of these photos,' I said.

'Yeah, well you'd be lucky,' Desiree drawled. 'He never has any film in the camera.'

Mehrdad and I drunkenly lay in one of Desiree's bedrooms that night. There was a giant pink picture of Mae West on the wall and a stuffed bat in a glass box. Desiree had a huge taxidermy collection. 'You're the one going back to Ireland, leaving me.'

'I have to go next Tuesday.' Mehrdad kissed my lips. 'I can't bear the thought of not being able to touch you. I've just been a nerdy engineer for all my adult life. This is such an intense physical relationship.'

'Thanks! Only physical? What will I do without you?'

'They need plastic surgeons in Ireland too, you know,' he said.

'Is that an invitation?'

Slowly, Mehrdad and I patched it all together. I began to see that my older sister, younger than me, was as good as I was bad. I was more like Zolo; I had all his malice without his brilliance. Leila was a flower—feminine, startling, swift and strong, sharp, open. Buried in the Wild West in a shallow unmarked grave, wearing a yellow butterfly dress. Mehrdad began to see all of that too. He fell more and more in love with her as I fell in love with him. He began to draw away from me, and our brief affair looked like it was coming to an end.

One night, I made a few suggestions to him. To get porcelain caps on his teeth, and to get his ears set back more on his head because they stuck out at odd angles. His mouth was a bit too small, and I suggested making his lips fuller. It was time to start his Botox injections. I looked at this as just good grooming, like waxing your legs and plucking your eyebrows, but he was genuinely offended. Not because he was vain but because that should matter to me.

'California is the most Western part of the Western world. What starts here, like fast food, and plastic surgery, eventually goes everywhere,' I told him as we sat with my parents in our Westwood apartment where we had attempted to live out our lives.

'The West is becoming the ugliest version of itself,' Mehrdad said.

My father Ishmael was there and loved to lecture. 'Capitalism versus Tribalism. Capitalism won.'

'Go back to Orap then,' I snapped.

'No,' Ishmael said. 'The East has seized up too. Spirituality versus Fundamentalism. Fundamentalism won. We have a world where one half is preoccupied with consumerism and the other half with repression. One side of the world is sprawling, the other shrinking in on itself.'

'So what do you do?' I asked my father.

'What do you do, Marguerite?' Ishmael asked me. 'You have a Western brain in an Eastern body.'

My mother brought us tea in glasses on a silver tray. We put some sugar in them. My father sat beside us; he was always happy when I brought Mehrdad around. It gave him a chance to show off all his thinking. My mother hated it, but she felt left out by my sudden disappearances. Up to this time, I had never gone anywhere without her, or done anything without telling her. There had been nothing to tell. We had slept every night in the same bed together; we went to the bathroom together. I was 25, and I still got my mother to wipe my ass for me. I couldn't bear to touch it myself, and she didn't want me to use toilet paper like a filthy Westerner. Unwashed Asses my mother called them. How was I ever meant to fit in when I was raised to look at even the president of their country as an Unwashed Ass?

I had been a 25-year-old virgin. She knew that had changed.

'I always liked you, Mehrdad,' Ishmael said. 'You're a good boy. You had respect for your elders.'

Mehrdad smiled weakly. He was not at ease with my parents. He told me it reminded him too much of the old days. Orapian men were expected to pontificate and lecture. My father and he slotted into their old roles with alarming ease.

'Old world, new world. These are artificial distinctions,' Ishmael said. 'The world is all the same age. East and West are imaginary divisions; we divide ourselves again and again and again until we are left with populations as tiny indivisible fractions. I fear the species will die out without ever having seen its potential for anything other than mayhem. The ice caps are melting, oceans rising; there is a growing cloud over Asia. Everywhere you look there is war. This country, America, is the biggest purveyor of violence on earth for over two centuries now. America is now the most hated country on earth, and still people want to come here for the consumer goods—'

'Hush, Ishmael,' Farah said. 'He talks like this all the time. Like a prophet with nothing good to say.'

'Perhaps I do. Let us think of good things now. So, all your family are professionals,' Ishmael said. 'Did you know that, Farah?'

'All of them became doctors and lawyers, I guess,' Mehrdad said. 'I became an engineer. I liked maths.'

'You'll want to come to America now?' Ishmael said. More of a statement than a question.

'Actually, I've got used to Ireland. We're happy enough there.'

I sat, a little unsure. What was I going to do with Mehrdad if he wasn't in America? My father and I were assuming I'd marry him.

My mother looked at me and read my thoughts. My mother knew me better than I knew myself. She looked a little self-satisfied as she placed a tray of dry cookies and dates in front of us. So you whored yourself for nothing, her eyes flashed triumphant.

'You must have a job to go back to? You've been here so long.'

'The West has made the whole world alike,' Ishmael said. 'Every one is wearing the same clothes and starting to speak English. Languages have died out as fast as species. The West killed all the species with their capitalism and industry. Hundreds of years ago, every land was different: food, customs, costume. Now it's all the same. The new regime in Orap sees itself as the last stand against the West. They cannot give in. They must remain as different as they can.'

Mehrdad looked at my mother. 'I was just wondering if you had any photos of Leila and us as kids. I remember your family taking photos all the time.'

My mother's face darkened. She glared at me. My father's eyes became distant, and he removed himself from our company without moving a facial muscle.

'I'll have a look,' she said with bitterness and hatred.

When Mehrdad left, we all fought. My father punched my mother, and she pulled the lamp down and burnt his face with the bare bulb. My mother dragged me by the hair. I tried to strangle her with the cord from my laptop. This was nothing new in my life. This was how it had always been. We lay exhausted and beaten in the apartment. Each inspecting our own bruises and scratches. When I was a child, I was no match for them, but now I could give as good as I got, and they were getting weaker.

Mehrdad told me he was going home. He had been chosen from his Dublin mosque to go to Mecca and was excited at the possibility. He regretted he had no photo of Leila.

Back in his hotel room that night, as we lay together, he told me, 'All those years I wanted to come and find her. I'm 40 and my personal life felt on hold. I live with my mother. Just like you. She cooks and cleans for me. All my brothers and sisters are married with kids. I thought your parents had turned her against me because of those stupid, fucking earrings. Every time I failed in my relationships was because I was waiting for her. I have to go back and try again.'

'Can't you start again here? With me?'

'You are only 25. I'm an old man of 40. I held you the day you were born. There's the generation difference.'

'I was with you, wasn't I? I did that without my mother.'

'I don't know if you could move all the way for me. Ireland is a lot like here. Fast food, motorways, traffic, stress, shopping centres, overpriced housing, and the weather is terrible. But my family is there. My job is there. I'm too old to move again.' And he turned his back on me and fell asleep.

He was to head back to Ireland where he worked as an engineer. I summoned him once more to a motel and we had sex. The motel I chose was a generic, low-grade one by the highway. It was the motel Mo had said that Zolo and Leila had stayed in 25 years before, when I had come into the world in a refugee camp. Zolo gave me the room number. The flimsy curtains were drawn, but they could not keep out the bleached screech of Los Angeles sunlight. A light that pulled everything apart and dried it out. I was always trying to keep it from me.

Bright, bright light for the wicked.

Mehrdad was praying in the motel when I got there. He was on the floor, facing Mecca.

'Is this the motel?'

'The very one,' I said. 'Mo remembered it. Twenty-five years ago, Leila and Zolo stayed here in this room.'

They had stood outside and felt an earthquake. Where they understood that not only can a country be pulled out from beneath your feet, but the ground you stand on is in no way solid. Where Zolo left Leila alone, to get on with his life and chase his genius into all the blank walls of disappointment.

Mehrdad was taken aback by my long list of instructions. I have to be on top. I'm the only one doing the touching. The TV has to be on to one of the upper cable channels. Engineering disasters, Hollywood true stories, nature programmes, Hitler's Henchmen. You will be still. You will be silent. You will be naked. I will not remove my clothes. I was almost six foot tall, and I was lean and fit, with honey-brown skin. My bleached blond hair was long and tied back to show off my high cheekbones and perfect new nose. My eyes were dark and deep, shaped like almonds, my lids slightly hooded, lending me a dreamy, sleepy, languorous look. I was beautiful in an almost unpleasant way. He complied. I'm not sure if he was scared, but I know that I made an impression. This was the only sexual life I had ever had—Mehrdad. The string of ridiculous, pompous medical students and young empty-headed doctors I dated—I never let them touch me. For them, I was playing the role of the good Orapian girl who lived with her parents.

One man asked if I had been abused as a child. He wasn't joking.

To Mehrdad, I said my name was Leila and that meant night. He got angry. But I stood before him with my body thin like a shadow, and he complied with my request. Mehrdad's brown eyes looked clear as a child's. He had a moustache that was uneven and half grey. I approached him and began to strip him, starting with his shirt, unbuckling his belt, and noticed that his kisses were too wet, so I turned my head so he wouldn't kiss me while we had sex.

Afterwards, Mehrdad had the nerve to tell me that I had to rise above my family.

'Don't you see Zolo? He's succumbed to Fatagagas rage and bitterness. Either your family creates monsters like your uncle, or they become bitter and resentful and disconnect like your father and Zolo.'

'You're mad at Zolo because he buried Leila.'

'No. He was 15 years old, his parents were refugees in another country, his uncle was quite mad, and he had to bury his little sister in the desert. I feel sorry for Zolo. Marguerite, this has meant so much to me. I think you have so much to live for. You can't just be a plastic surgeon living in Los Angeles and worrying about your hair and your image like most of the other Orapians there, driving their Mercedes cars and dancing at weddings. You're better than that. You have to become a person of substance.'

'Why are you picking on me? I was a baby when this all happened. You've got me wrong. Sure, I have all the clothes and spend my spare time shopping or exercising, or whatever, but I have no friends. Do you know, I never had friends? You are my first friend.'

'Is that your redeeming trait? Friendlessness. Marguerite, you're something else.' He smiled and stroked my hair. Maybe he could learn to love me.

'I was pushed by my mother two classes ahead, so I didn't fit in with my peers; they never talked to me. Then I just studied and studied to get to medical school. There was no question of failure. I might look the part, but in fact all I did all my life was study while my mother watched me like a hawk and pushed and pushed. Sure, I hung around with a few people in school, but nothing deep. I never could take anyone home to my parents. My mother would have wondered what they were getting from me.'

'Marguerite, you have to be different from them.'

'Like Leila was, you mean.'

'Leila's dead,' Mehrdad said sadly, and he stood and drew the curtains, letting the wicked light flood the room.

'Leila isn't dead. She's more alive than me.'

'Oh, Marguerite,' Mehrdad said, full of useless pity, but he was leaving me.

He drove to the airport, and I had to drive back to my useless father and my horrible mother in her lumpy bras, who thought she could fix everything by returning to Orap to get her house back, and sell it, finally to have some money of her own. This was a woman whose parents were killed by one revolution. Whose brothers were killed by the next.

Farah had dedicated her life to her kids. Out of the three children Farah had, one is dead, one doesn't talk to her, one is in prison.

Leila, namesake of darkness and night, sick in a feather-coated, dusty room, lying on top of the undisturbed bed, the black hills break away and float through your fever brain, like a fleet of great ships, moving onwards, yearning, reaching.

When I found where you died, I remembered who I was, and what I had become was repulsive to the person I was. Myself created and myself imagined collided and I lost both. I became you, tried to. I imagined I was you. I pretended to be you. I vowed to become you. Mehrdad loved you and I loved Mehrdad.

I wanted you to live and I would rather have been you. I could have waited till my parents came to America, and I could have reunited with Mehrdad. I could have left the vain, shallow, judgmental, foolish Marguerite to collude away with her base mother. Utterly empty Marguerite could have gone through the motions of life like a shell, and no one would have noticed. Not everyone can shine—but Leila had.

My memory is a multi-headed, self-conjured ghost. Can I harness the smallest ghost to pull me forward, out from the rut of my fate? I did not know you, the first Baby Zero. We were sisters but separated by more than oceans and mountains; we were separated by visas, passports, and stamps, official documents, standard procedure. And those are the dreams of refugees, seemingly simple things, patterns on paper, but as elusive as happiness itself.

And I was raised to look at all others as insiders, and us as not belonging. I have no memories of Ireland as a child, only what has been told, what I can imagine; no memories except fleeting ones of the fortress-like American Embassy. I remember the attitude more that the physical place, and it triggered the hard Fatagagas bitterness that would encase me like a tough shell and seal that shell so tight that it desiccated my insides, and my internal life all but disappeared.

So what was there for Mehrdad to love? I had to become Leila. I was beautiful. I'd had work done, my nose job, my teeth capped. I was ready for romance. Did he love a ghost? Was there enough in me? I have nothing inside me, Baby Zero, but you. You are the first thing to come inside.

I would not have burdened you with the story if you had the capacity to store it. We are all forgotten. This is a bitter mercy, but there are dangers. Remembrance is honouring. Leila was bringing the native ghosts back to the land by refusing to sit comfortably on genocidal soil. And I bring her back to you, her butterfly ghost from her desert cocoon. I bring her back.

So these are the stories, Baby Zero. There are three of us—Leila, Marguerite and you. I dream that you are Leila come again through me because I imagined you so perfectly. Coming from the East from a multitude of rivers in rivers and stories in stories, Orap, Ireland, California, Cowboys and Indians, the sixth great extinction. Stories you should know built from bricks of words. Words that first came from marking animals that, tied together, made histories, religions, holy books, reasons to fight.

When humans lost the wild animals, we lost the earth. When the Indians lost the Black Hills, they had lost everything there was to lose in America. When Ishmael lost Orap, he lost everything. When Zolo lost Leila, he lost everything that made him a child.

When I lost Mehrdad, I lost my only hope of happiness

You have listened to these stories, and now you must decide if you still want to come through me.

Baby Zero. Let night be a wing and tuck you in under; let the burglar moon steal you from harm; let the red-eyed desert wind keep you warm; let the prison keep you from the hunters outside. I can hold you close, but I can't keep you safe.

PART VII

ORAP PRISON

Chapter Twenty-Two

The Night After the Trial

Condemned, we were marched from the court to the prison. They put me in with the child. She is in labour; she clings to me, and I try to pull her away from me and tell her how to breathe. I don't know what I'm telling her. I'm guessing things. I did six months in ob/gyn as training and hated it. I lie her on the bed and whisper to her. She is 12 years old, as old as Leila was when she died. An old nursery rhyme my mother used to read from a book, *rock-a-by-baby on the treetop*. She is calling out; her voice is so thick and hoarse, and she grabs on to me, clawing at my veil, I take both our veils off; we are wearing nothing beneath. It is night and the rain is coming through the slit of a window high in the wall. I strip her and hold my hands up to the rain. I place my wet hands on her belly. *Down will come cradle baby and all*. What a thing those Westerners sang to their children. The child's face is scratched off.

The baby is breach, coming fast, ass first. I squat at her legs and try to pull it into the world. She is being broken in two. Her pelvis is too small for the baby to come. Its head keeps appearing and disappearing. She pushes for hours. I hear a crack and she tears as I wrench the baby out. She is screaming. The guards, who have been scuffling outside the door, break in when they hear the baby squall. They hesitate at all the blood and shit and the naked faceless creature writhing on the bed.

'Is it a boy?' one asks.

'Yes. I need to cut the cord. Get me a scissors,' I shout.

He hands me a knife and I saw off the throbbing cord. They bundle the baby up in a dirty blanket and take him out.

'She needs a hospital quickly,' I urge them.

'No,' she screams with the last of her strength. 'I want to stay with you. Don't let them take me.'

The guards kick the door closed behind them. I cover the girl. I have nothing with which to stitch her up. Trying to stop the bleeding, I put the dirty cloth between her legs. She screams again, and this time the placenta comes rushing out too fast for me to grab the bucket and catch it. I stood through corpse dissections and numerous other medical procedures without feeling queasy, but it was always the placenta's arrival that turned my stomach. Now nothing disgusts me. I am concentrating on this child.

Baby Zero, you are moving so much. I want you to stay inside. I hold the whimpering little girl who grips me tightly.

'Tell me a story,' she says. And she sounds so much like the child she is. So I tell her the final stories that I found in Leila's scrapbooks. A picture of Sitting Bull stuck in with glue. I see his eyes looking down on us. I tell her that all we women here are the Indians. The Lakota still hunted on the Black Hills. It was Sacred Ground for them, and the US had promised to leave it alone, but gold was discovered. Sitting Bull and his people endured utter defeat. The great chief momentarily joined Buffalo Bill's Wild West Show, paraded like a relic; the money he earned he gave away to white beggars in the city streets and then went back to his people.

You, my baby, move in me. You are kicking against the back of the little girl. She has not asked for her son, but she begs me to pray with her, and I tell her the Comanche prayer Leila had stuck in her book. These are the only prayers I know. I read that scrapbook so many times.

The sun beams are running out.
The sun beams are running out.
The sun's yellow rays are running out.

The sun's yellow rays are running out.
We shall live again.
We shall live again.

I feel her weakening in my arms.

'Don't worry,' I say. 'The Everywhere Spirit is here and I am a doctor.'

'A doctor,' she murmurs, and kisses my hands.

I tell her that when Congress herded the Indians on to reservations and let them go hungry, they dreamt up one more God. The Ghost Dance. All over the West, in their despair, they gathered in great circles, singing and dancing, imploring the spirits of the dead to come and rescue them.

'And did they come?' she asks, squeezing my hand.

'They wore white robes with special symbols so the bullets could never harm them. They danced and danced and sang.'

Mother hand me a sharp knife
Mother hand me a sharp knife
Here come the buffalo returning.

The girl stirs. She turns into me, and I cradle her as best as I can against my big belly. I do not have a wall to lean on as I sit under the tiny shaft of bad air and light and rain. I didn't know it rained in Orap in late spring. My back is sore. As the Indians danced in a trance, the dead entered them, possessed them, and gave them strength. I explain to her what got me through months of solitary confinement. I had put my dead sister inside me.

'Has she gone now?'

'She will be gone soon.'

But the Americans would not allow even this dance. They were afraid of it and sent troops to march against the dance and stop it. Sitting Bull was killed. Then they went to Wounded Knee and massacred a camp of peaceful Lakota Indians: 250 lay dead, mostly women and children. They threw them in a mass grave and took photos of their battle. Leila had cut this picture out and pasted it in her book. It was the last thing she had done. White men crowding the rim of the pit and brown bodies bundled in disarray. The whites are alive and the brown ones are dead. Now they are all dead. Leila is dead too. The Ghost Dance stopped. The child is moving her lips; she is praying. The same age as Leila was when she died. Her lips are bluish and dry. I wet my finger and rub my saliva over them. I feel her tremble in contrast to your sharp kicks. She calls me doctor and she calls me mother. I am everyone for her. All her ghosts. Her family poured acid on her face, thinking they were protecting her. But they could do that only because deep down they did feel that she had shamed their family and deserved it.

I tell this child that I am a plastic surgeon. I promise her that I will restore her face. I tell this child about my family and Leila. I tell her the whole story I have told you. Every part of it. I leave nothing out. She listens and moans and holds on to me.

Gradually her grip loosens. I stroke her and kiss her, and sometime in the night she dies as I tell her stories. Small-made.

I am relieved for her. I gather her up in the night and she is all empty. We sit where the rain is coming in. We are covered in blood. In the morning, they zip her up in a bag and take her away. I hold her hand till the last minute. They take her small hand from me and shove her arm into the bag

'You see the weather?' one guard says to me.

'It is raining.'

'Acid rain,' he says. 'That is your doing?'

I am hunched, holding my ankles, in the middle of the cell where the rain comes in.

'Do you remember that cloud that was two miles long and over Asia? It is 30 miles long now, and the Americans developed a way of moving it. They moved it from their Asian allies, and now they put it over the countries they are displeased with. They have placed it over our capital.'

I am very tired. I want to cry. I miss her. I'd like to talk to her family. To find out who she was. To tell them that she was not alone in her last hours.

The guard stands at the door. He has a mop and hot water with a pungent disinfectant smell. He continues to mop at the blood on the floor. The guard looks for a moment at the hot water, so red now. He has not finished even one corner. He sighs and then gathers the bloody sheets into a bundle and throws them by the door.

'Can I talk to my mother before I'm executed?'

'Yes.'

'What are you doing with all our babies?'

'The boys we are keeping. We will raise the boys without women's influence. There will be nothing female about the new generation of men. We tried to clone boys and not have to have women at all. Pure male, no contamination. Born from the male brain. But we couldn't do it. This is a new experiment with prisoners.'

'The baby girls?'

'The families can keep them.'

'I have been here almost a year and you never spoke before.'

The young guard shrugs. 'You are to be executed as soon as your baby is born.'

My mother is sitting in the prison waiting room. We are left alone.

'Do you see how disorganised everything is becoming?' my mother whispers.

'I don't see anything in here.'

'The cloud is over us. There are already deaths from respiratory problems. Children mostly. Babies. I have to warn you, your aunt's children, your cousins, are up to something. They want to get you out. I said, "Don't go near her. She's in enough trouble because of your family as it is."'

'Maman, I'm going to be executed as soon as I have my baby. What can they do for me?'

'Cause trouble. It's not her son. It's her three daughters. They have always been activists on behalf of women here, so they tell me. Nonsense stuff, bunch of whores sitting around putting on make-up to make them feel liberated. I told them we didn't need their help. Their mother got us into this trouble.'

'What trouble are you in?'

'Oh, Marguerite, my life is so hard. I am all alone and no one comes to me. I can't leave the house because I have no male relatives. I'm starving to death. I'm so ashamed. You should hear all the talk on the street about what goes on in here.'

'How do you hear talk on the street? I thought you never get out the door. Do Baba, Mo and Zolo know I'm condemned to death?'

'It's in the newspapers over there, Ishmael said. The American government knows about your case. They're using it as an excuse to come in and bomb and get the last oil reserves.' Despite herself, my mother looked a little proud of this fact.

'Can you talk to the American Embassy?'

'There are no American embassies in this part of the world. The nearest one is in Afghanistan.'

'So the Americans know my case. They want to rescue me?'

'No. They want you as an excuse. They'd prefer to have you executed.'

'I've been thinking about things, Maman. I don't have much time. I don't want to leave my brain for eternity like an angry stone in the earth.'

'Marguerite, you're talking nonsense.'

'I want to talk about Leila.'

'They are stoning the other women in public. At soccer matches. They put them in burlap sacks, like the ones rice comes in, but bigger. Then they throw big rocks at them until they are smashed to pieces inside the bag. Listen to me . . .'

'You must have gone through all the photo albums and deliberately removed any trace of her.'

'I couldn't do anything for your sister. All the children in the camp were dying of dysentery and cholera, and the army was coming over the mountain. I thought we'd all be killed. I did the best we could. When we were in Ireland, I was always trying to get over to America. We spent our days in the Embassy. We couldn't get her to Ireland as we had said she was officially Mo's child, not ours. We had to do these things. I thought I was doing what was best.'

'You knew Mo and Zolo were incapable of taking care of her.'

'I worried all the time. I hoped for the best and the worst happened. I was 43 years old with a newborn. Your father had traded all my jewellery for opium in the camp, and he disappeared to France as soon as we got to Ireland. The only person in the world to help me was that Mehrdad, and he was stealing from me.'

'You destroyed her photos.'

'I kept them hidden. They are under the photos in our album. One on top of the other. Do you think I didn't love her? I was her mother. Your father was useless. I had to drag him around like a weight.'

'I don't blame you for her death. I blame you for not telling me. For erasing her. I thought we were so close. But you'd have done the same to me.'

'I loved you so much. I loved all of you. My children. I held you when you had fevers. I got up every night to feed you. We had nothing. You had to sleep in a suitcase.'

'And if you raise my baby, you will not tell her about me.'

'I'll tell her something else. It would not be good for a child to know she was born under these circumstances. You don't even know who the father is.'

A guard comes back in and tells me I have to come back. I follow him. In a way, trusting him more than my mother.

The guard walks me across the courtyard. They all wear face-masks to filter out air from the new cloud weapon. The grey morning only half-light from a yawning sky. I can see Heaven's tonsils, its fillings, its bad teeth extractions. I can smell the bad breath of this morning.

My breakfast is waiting for me in the cell. The usual feta cheese with tiny grubs worming on the surface. The stale pitta bread. But they have included a pomegranate on my plate. I am overwhelmed by its pink violet orange fractionated insides, tiny multitude, vivid dewdrops; it is the most beautiful thing I have ever seen. I know the whole world is in there. I want to keep it. To show it to you when you are born. But I eat it.

Chapter Twenty-Three

The Past Has an End

The night is dim. I lie here and everything is silent. The city is quiet under its cloud of punishment. The guards aren't making a sound. Perhaps there are no guards. I try the door, but it is still locked. I have a feeling they lock the doors and go home now. I believe we are all prisoners sleeping alone and unguarded. The door is thick wood, and I could not break it down even if I were not eight-and-a-half months pregnant. I wonder what you will look like. I have no conception of you. I have not seen my own reflection in a long time, and I wonder what I look like. Have I changed?

I feel my contractions. They are close together now. I catch my breath. I keep pacing. I have never felt such fear and such pain. I try to think of what will happen soon. You will be born and, if you don't kill me tonight, they will kill me tomorrow. I can hear shouting from the rooms across the courtyard. Other women in moments of mirrored terror. I think of them with their faces scratched off. I pretend to myself that we will all break loose and I will repair their faces. I could do that. I could restore the world's splendour. I could put Leila's face on every one of them. I could bring her back a dozen times over.

I am no longer two. Everything slips into the past.

Baby Zero, you came. I pushed you out. My insides were all over the cell. I was turned inside out. You were born in the East to a moth-

er who had a Western brain in an Eastern body, and you were all
Eastern. You looked Mongolian at first to me. So much so that I
looked around to see if I was really your mother. Your eyes were slant-
ed and, when I scraped off the white coating, your skin was dark as
wood. Your hair stuck up with all the juices. They had left no knife
for me to cut the pulsating cord so I bit right through it. It was like
a living thing itself. I felt like I was biting the leg off an octopus. How
can I describe birth? Your own horrible birth. There was nothing like
it. One day, you will feel it and know that there aren't words.

You were a girl.

Of course.

Baby Zero III.

The first was born to riches.

The second was born in a refugee camp.

The third was born in a prison.

I called you Leila.

$0 + 0 + 0 =$

'I heard you had an uncomplicated delivery,' my mother said
later that day in the visiting room.

'It didn't feel like that. I can barely walk. I'm lucky I'm alive,' I
told her. 'But not for long.'

'There are hardly any guards left here,' my mother said. 'Word
has it, they have taken the boy babies and gone up to the mountains
where the air is clean. So they won't die.'

My mother was holding you. She was smiling at you.

'What will we call her? Gracious, she is so dark. Darker than
you even. I was once surprised how dark you were; your father and
I were quite white-skinned. And so were Zolo and . . .'

'I called her Leila.'

My mother looked taken aback, but then she composed herself.
'Leila. Okay. Leila was white as butter when she was born. This one
looks Chinese. All my grandchildren look Chinese. And our family
was whiter than most.'

'Enough! You'd think we were Swedish, the way you go on. Give
her back to me.'

'Okay. I'll have time enough to hold her all I want soon,' she said, handing you back. You began to cry. I was squeezing you too hard. I left bruises on your arm.

My mother had brought nappies and clothes for you. Yellow and woollen. The taxi driver's wife had made them and sold them to her. We dressed you.

'How is breast feeding?'

'Sore, but okay.' I was proud. Knowing all the stories of how she had found it impossible.

'I am preparing the house for her,' my mother said.

'Who?'

'The baby.'

'And I'll be dead.'

'All the neighbours have gone. They were heading to refugee camps they heard were set up by the UN. It's a five-day walk. I can't bear it. The walk to the camp with a newborn. I am too old.'

She shuddered. 'You must forgive me, Marguerite. Now you see there will be no one for your baby if I'm not there.'

'Did Mehrdad ever contact you? Does he know what's happening?'

'He wanted only one thing, and you gave it to him, and he left you.'

'Has he contacted you?'

'I don't know why you were interested in him. He was without salt. She is so dark. Your father had some Mongolian great-grandmother. His side were Turks and all sorts of things in him.'

The night before the execution, Farah made a place for a baby. The Americans had scattered leaflets from aeroplanes in the last week, ordering people to evacuate before a bombing campaign. It was a terrible thing to be in a city waiting for an attack. The streets were empty. The last people scurrying off, loading all their belongings on old cars or donkeys and scrambling to the nearest borders. Only the very poor, the ill, the very old, the mad, remained.

Farah lived in shoddily made crooked apartment blocks that would soon be ruined. She closed the door on the narrow abandoned street. The air was layered and sooty. All windows were painted black, but no one was home anywhere except Farah. She still locked her door and whispered to herself. Orapians were nosy by nature. She had made some contacts on the streets. Some neighbours who helped her, risking themselves. She had made more connections with other humans on returning to Orap than in her whole time in California where no one talked to her. But now her neighbours were gone. They had urged her to go, but she had to wait for the birth.

The taxi driver came and said goodbye. He and his family were fleeing to a camp. He offered to bring her. She had never trusted him. Always wondering if he was a spy. But he didn't seem like a spy, with his five children and wife and parents all squashed into the cab with worried faces. He gave her his brother's number. Now she had to go to the market on her own without escorts. But there were very few revolutionary guards paying attention any more. The market had only a few stalls. Very little food. Just bags of rice and piles of overpriced rancid fruit and no meat anywhere except for a peasant selling skinned dogs. Dogs were considered unclean in Orap, and no one was allowed keep them as pets, but the wild dogs at the edge of town ran in packs, and people were desperate enough to hunt them for food. Farah crept around the market, terrified of being singled out as an unescorted woman. She was afraid of her bare hands as they reached for the bag of rice. She bought cloth nappies, which were very expensive, and she bought more baby clothes for the girl. If it had been a boy, she would never have seen it.

Farah scrubbed the house for the first time since Marguerite had been arrested. She pulled out a suitcase and padded it with blankets for the baby to sleep in. In the dead of night, she awoke and lay awake, retracing the dream, trying to get into it again and change the ending.

The dogs were barking at the edge of the empty town. She dreamt Leila was alone in a house somewhere. But Farah didn't know which house. She ran from street to street as the snarling dogs slid along beside her. Suddenly, she saw Leila's slender form in a

summer dress. Leila slipped out of one building into the other without looking around. Farah called to her, but her voice was muffled
by the cloth over her face and the howling dogs. She was afraid for
Leila. To be in this city, uncovered. They would capture her on the
spot and scrape off her face. Farah rushed to the entrance of the
building. There was no door.

'Leila? Leila?' Farah spoke out loud. She stood out of the bed
and stubbed her toe on the drawer she had laid out and padded for
the new baby. Leila had never slept in a suitcase. Farah sat at the
edge of the bed, doubled over in pain. Marguerite had slept in a
suitcase in the hostel in Ireland. She remembered so well the night
she had been convinced that her little yellow, undernourished baby
had stopped breathing. Farah looked out the window and thought
she saw the dawn. The smell of the sun on the back of the clouds.
The singed air that coated her throat and made her tongue stick to
the roof of her mouth. Tomorrow night, she would lie on her bed,
and Marguerite would be dead. Farah went to the window and saw
the reflection of an old woman. A butterfly was fluttering in frustration against the window. She cupped it in her hands and set it
free.

I lay on my bed somewhere, in the middle of the night. You were
sleeping on my chest, snoring gently. Tiny snores that cut through
me for I knew your lungs, the size of baby mice, were already black.
The guard actually said to me tonight, 'We will not be cancelled
from history like the Red Indian.' To lose is to vanish. Others will
live in your place. They will get everything, and you will disappear.
I thought I remembered nothing before I got to America, but now
my life was open like a book, and as I hold you I have no shelter
from these thoughts. I must hurry, Baby Zero, to tell you my own
memories. I spent so much time on Leila.

We were intruders in their sacred places. 'If you walk down
the street alone, the Irish will kill you,' my mother said. The first
day of school, I thought I would be killed by the white teacher.
She put me sitting by two Chinese children whose parents owned

a restaurant, and a Pakistani whose parents had a shop. Maybe she thought I would be more comfortable with them. The other half of the class was Nigerian. She was very nice to us all. Patting us on the head and smiling and giving us treats. I loved that teacher. There was an Iranian girl whose mother and father were doctors. She sat among the whites and never looked at us. 'What do your parents do?' they asked me. But I stood out. My parents weren't here for any reason; they had no business to run. We were refugees and the kids smelt it off me. My impermanence. I ran to my mother each day and told her I didn't want to go back. 'Stay away from the blacks,' she warned. 'They are animals.' She said, 'Stay away from the Chinese and the Pakistani. They are children of merchants. Vulgar people. Stay away from the whites; they will never treat you equally. They are not even Americans. In America, the whites are good.' She said to make friends with the Iranian girl. 'Her parents are doctors like our family was. They are non-practising Muslims like us.' But the girl wouldn't come near me except to say once, 'Orap? Does it exist? I've never heard of it.'

Mehrdad's family went to the mosque and became well-adjusted Irish Muslims, but we never connected with anything. We never saw Mehrdad's family once. They lived in the country. My parents told me that they were servants and thieves. The only other Orapian lived at the end of Parnell Square. He had no feet and was on drugs, and we were ashamed of him. He died of a drug overdose when I was five.

Now I even remember Parnell Square in Dublin where I spent my first six years. It was Christmas, and evenings were very dark. An African man in a long robe sold candles that smelt of Asian Spice. My father bought one, and my mother complained that he was wasting his money. There were robot monkeys with Turkish fezzes, banging drums. They all drummed on a straw mat, and a shivering Senegalese man with long, long fingers beckoned to me. All the monkeys' eyes flashed yellow like insects in a forest. When I approached, they started marching. I hid behind my mother's legs, and he smiled like the Cheshire cat. His unhappy smile hanging like a crooked moon in the black evening. We stopped in front of shop windows, and everything danced and sang and was radiant behind glass. My mother complained of the cold and the damp. Her hands were swollen with rheumatism. She showed me her fingers, which were lumpy and red. My father insisted on taking me to Santa's Grotto. My mother was unsure, but I begged and pleaded. 'I don't want her to be brainwashed by anyone's religion,' she said.

I wanted a Christmas tree to put in the window, and they argued over that. My father lit the candle in the window instead. It was to welcome strangers. My mother said the only people on the street were black rejects from dark corners of the earth. The Irish wouldn't come in if they saw who we were either, and they never walked in this area for fear of their lives. We sat, three strangers in our cramped flat, eating rice. My mother worried and possessed by escape plots to get to her son. My father resigned to ruin.

He took me that Christmas night while she slept and carried me down the stone steps to the church for midnight mass. We sneaked into a crowded church and took our place on one of the wooden benches near the back, with easy access to the door. The priests, robed resplendent, carried a wooden baby boy down the aisle to place in a manger.

'The baby was born in a stable, and his parents were refugees like us.' My father whispered the story to me. We held hands.

'Why is everyone singing and following him?' I was struck by all the important men carrying a doll so carefully.

'They are saying that every child is special. Every birth is important. Celebrated. Universal. Remembered.' My father had tears running down his face. I was tugging on his sleeve to make him stop. He was sobbing loudly now. We were intruders in their sacred places.

We were a solitary trinity up the stone steps. But even the trinity was fractures. My mother told me my father was useless. I began to look down on him. Especially after he cried in the church. It became Farah and me against the world.

My poor father. I thought as I lay in this prison, that he must have been crying for Leila. He would have known she was dead a few years before. But they hadn't told me about Leila. I remember that his sighs were like unlit tunnels that swallowed up the air around him, emptily snaking into the world. He would mostly sit by the window, the neon lights buzzing by the downstairs strip clubs. Ishmael, who strove with his brother to rise above his foreign family in Orap. Ishmael who was surgeon to the queen. He would often have his head sunk in his hands, his elbows on his knees as if he were praying; of course he was not. None of us had any God in us. Father, bereft by the window; mother cooking rice and stews, shuffling in her furry leopard-print slippers and her spidery hair crackling around her, her eyes piercing into me, rearranging my gaze. Telling me, study, study, study, study, study for us. You are all the hope we have lost.

Why was I telling you this, Baby Zero? Because nomadic people don't have histories; they have only myths and stories. This was mine.

Chapter Twenty-Four

The Night Before Execution

This was the last night. The night before my execution. There was a guard placed outside my cell; he kept clearing his throat and spitting.

He cleared his throat, punctuating the horrible hours unevenly.

I held you naked and tried to memorise every part of you. Your whole chest and tummy heaved. I could place my hand over your entire torso. My long fingers curled at your shoulders. You did not weigh much, less than the silence between each rough clearing of the throat outside. Each time he spat on the ground and it slapped off the ancient stone, I couldn't stop myself from picturing his phlegm inside my own mouth.

I didn't regret you. Because now I knew what love was. An animal thing.

Your arms were like hesitant new stems and your fingers like blind grubs writhing abstractly; your nails were tiny raindrops. I lifted your head back to look at your neck, ringed red and slightly chapped. Your comical legs curled away, fold after fold; I licked my fingers and ran them in the folds to moisturise them. I turned you over and held you in my palm, face down, hanging over my hand like a doll. Your back was fuzzy; minute hairs prickled. I patted your fleshy smooth butt, and tickled the papery wrinkled soles of your feet. I turned you over and dressed you. A butterfly got into the cell and landed on your back, bringing up goose pimples. I lifted it off. Tiny goose pimples I made vanish with my fingers: pressed them back into your flesh. Your head was open and your dreams could slip out as surely as all the gods slipped through the gaping hole we conjured in the air. Magic ozone people that we were. Outside, the guard cleared his throat and I swallowed.

Your face was beyond description: little beetle, little pistachio; words kept coming to me to whisper to you. I couldn't believe you. What would that kiss be when I gave you away? How would I suck all of you up in it to carry with me in the next dreadful steps I would have to take? And I would have put you in such dangerous hands.

We were dangerous women. You were born from it. Your multiple fathers scattered in the mountains were only children really. Your father was a rapist and your mother condemned, and your grandmother would raise you, if you could be raised. If you lived. She was a murderer. She murdered memory. I grew it back like an amputee starfish in the ocean bottom, unbeknown to her. As he cleared his throat, you stirred awake, and I put your shock of a gaping mouth to my breast. That initial tug that hurt so much, and then I caught my breath and we both relaxed. I tried not to imagine what a stoning entailed: what the stones would feel like, what size they would be, how long it would take. This second Baby Zero had reached the end of her story.

Whose life would flash before me tomorrow morning? Leila's or mine? Or yours, Baby Zero? Would I see you slide, shoot to the end of your days? Would I race into the future as fast as I sank into the past; would I try to be there to catch you at the end of your journey?

I was born daughter of a surgeon.

I was born in a refugee camp.

I was born in a prison.

Zero multiplied by zero, divided by, subtracted by, added to.

It always comes to the same.

The female Zero.

You were an infant I held in my arms this morning. You were sleeping, and this was my last time with you. There was such a place,

soft and deep between folds, compressed and moist where everything forgotten built up and coated the cracks until the cracks
turned dark. A place where all we discarded and shut out ate at the
grout of us. A place that loosened everything inside; it's what makes
us old, what dries us up and shrinks our lips, what lines our face and
shrivels our hands, what brings cancer. I won't grow old.

Farah got the taxi driver's brother, who was still in the city, to drive
her to the prison. She carried a suitcase with her. It was full of baby
clothes, nappies, her clothes and photo albums. She had spent the
morning placing Leila's photos back where they belonged.

'Wait! Stop here.' The taxi driver stopped by the river. Farah
looked out the window at the big old house by the river. Several
people were living there now. All these mansions had been broken
up into apartments. There had once been a zoo on the second floor.
What had happened to all the animals?

'That river has a river inside it,' Farah said, merely for the sake
of saying something so he wouldn't know what she was really thinking. 'Okay. Let's go to the prison.'

She told the taxi driver to wait when she got there, and he nodded. His eyes were teary. He knew where she was going.

'You can leave the suitcase here,' he said.

She hesitated. True to form, she didn't trust him. 'That's all
right. I want to show her some old photos.' Farah got out and went
to the driver's side.

'When I come out, take me to the refugee camp at the border.'

'That's three hours from here.'

Farah thrust dollars into his hand, and he nodded.

Farah marched through the prison gates and flashed her ID at
the young guard. He walked her to the waiting room, 'We will give
you five minutes. You take the baby away.' And he left.

I entered with you.

Farah did not say any thing. She leapt up, running to the door
to look. She told me to take off my burka.

'Hurry! Do as I say.' Farah ripped off her black burka, and I saw

her face for the first time in a long time. It was in her frantic organising mode. I knew that face well. Determined and machine-like.
Unstoppable and sure. She put on my ragged robes, and I put on
her clean ones. She said, 'Wait, let me look at you.'

We stood face to face. There was something sensational after all
this time to see a woman's face. I had not even seen my own since
entering prison. We kissed on the lips. She grabbed my cheeks and
her eyes were full of tears.

'You are beautiful. My beautiful child. You were always so
beautiful.'

Then we pulled our robes over our faces, and she spun me
around. The guard strolled back in with his machine-gun hanging
by his side. He gestured with the gun to me.

'Take the child and go. The execution will take place this
afternoon.'

Farah grabbed the baby and kissed it. You were crying. She
squeezed you so hard, I thought you'd die, but I let her. She pushed
you towards me and gestured towards the suitcase.

She held me again for a second and hissed, 'Outside, a taxi, go
to the camp.'

I grabbed you and the suitcase and walked from the prison. The
guard opened the door and nodded to me. He looked at the suitcase.

'You're off to the camps like everyone else?'

I nodded, afraid to speak. I had been Leila; now I was Farah.
Walking in her veil.

I walked out of the prison, on to the street. I kept walking. The
taxi driver gestured towards me, and I got into his taxi.

'That must have been hard,' he said as we drove away. So you
want to go to the camps?'

'Yes.

As he drove, I opened the suitcase. My mother was a practical
woman. Buried in the nappies were hundreds of dollars that Mo had
sent to her to get to the camps.

You were already wheezing. The world was not young; it was
not a place where lions roamed or great forests grew. There were

crow's feet spreading like river estuaries across the loose skin of each bay. The planet was a little bald and broken-hipped, but you were just stepping out into it, and you would have your life. You would take your first faltering steps in the balance of its shadows. You, and perhaps even your children—no promises, for one more life can be enough. One light is enough to steer a ship home. I loved you, Baby Zero. You would not remember any of this.

'I have to drive you fast to the refugee camp,' the taxi driver told me. 'They say the American bombing will start any minute, once your daughter is executed.'

I nodded and wondered would we make it. What would the soldiers do when they discovered their mistake? Would my mother unveil and try to get free? Or would she think that then they would come looking for me? There was no time to ask what she intended to do. A whale leaves a footprint on the surface of the water, signalling something monstrous and amazing is moving beneath.

The past has an end. It ends right here in the present. It is always ending. And this multiplicity of ends can blur right through you and swallow the future. If you don't know your history, you will be controlled by its ghosts.

That's what I was thinking of when you opened your eyes. I picked you up and we gazed at each other in the taxi.

'Leila,' I said to you. You looked at me, focusing for the first time since birth. I know you could see me. To you, I was just a mother. It was so uncomplicated. 'Farah saved us, Leila. She saved us. No one else would have done it. Farah finally came through.' It might have been wind, but I think you actually smiled at me.

Leila, in your small eyes, I see trust in all its solemnity. Hope steps from your gaze and walks across my heart.

Acknowledgements

I would like to thank the Guggenheim Foundation for the grant that enabled me to start this book. I would also like to thank the Irish Arts Council for their bursary, which enabled me to complete the book and continue as a writer. I would like to thank Geoffrey C. Ward and Stephen Ives for their extraordinary book *The West: An Illustrated History*. It was a great inspiration to me when writing this book.

Thanks to Anuj Desai, Alka Raghuram and Irvine Welsh, who gave editorial help at various stages of writing. My parents Marguerite and Eamonn, who took my family in when we fled Silicon Valley for the jungles of County Meath—and put up with the mess. Fiona and Rob Weston, who shared and lost California with us. Ciara, Kieran, Aisling, Roisín and Clodagh for giving me tea and computer rights at number 4. My brother Daragh for Australian phone therapy. Jim and Noelle Hannon, who always made New York the most welcoming city on the planet. Ferociously talented fellow banshees Imelda O'Reilly, Helena Mulkerns, Caitriona O'Leary, Darrah Carr and Elizabeth Whyte at www.banshee.info. Hillary Dully, Joe Comerford, Cassie, Dan and Tom for frequent refuge in County Clare. Marie Louise Kenny, Leanne De Cerbo, and Rosita Boland for bringing me out of my shell on all those long, dark Dublin nights. Elizabeth Quinn for a granite counter to lean on, sustenance and shelter in Rathmines. My agent, Maria Massie, and her London co-agent, Caspian Dennis, who never gave up on this book. Steve MacDonogh for having the vision to take it on. The inimitable and always quotable John and Kirsten Perry, for constant inspiration and insight into the Devil's Workshop. Finally, I would like to thank my amazing Persian-Irish daughters, Jasmine and Jade, and my husband Afshin, for keeping my mojo running.

DOUGLAS A. MARTIN
Branwell

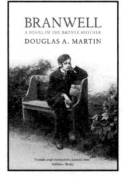

"A tender, tragic portrayal of a doomed artist."
Publishers Weekly

"Martin avoids the temptation of plunging headfirst into the gothic, instead conveying Branwell's psychic turmoil in simple, stripped-down sentences ... [He] sparsely fills in the outlines of Branwell's dissolution, a suitably phantom account of the man who painted himself out of his own family portrait."
Village Voice

ISBN 978-086322-363-1; paperback original

MARY ROSE CALLAGHAN
Billy, Come Home

"At the heart of this innocent-seeming novel lies a scathing critique of attitudes to mental illness. Mary Rose Callaghan's velvet-gloved hand wields a pen as sharp as a razor. An honest look at how we really are, this is not a novel to forget in a hurry."
Éilís Ní Dhuibhne

A thirty-year-old woman travels to London to identify a body that has been fished out of the Thames; it is believed to be that of her brother, Billy. This moving novel is about a mentally ill man and his need for a home. It is also a mystery novel, set in present day suburbia.

ISBN 978-086322-366-2; paperback original

AGATA SCHWARTZ AND LUISE VON FLOTOW (EDS)
The Third Shore
Women's Fiction from East Central Europe

The Third Shore brings to light a whole spectrum of women's literary accomplishment and experience virtually unknown in the West. Gracefully translated, and with an introduction that establishes their political, historical, and literary context, these stories written in the decade after the fall of the Iron Curtain are tales of the familiar reconceived and turned into something altogether new by the distinctive experience they reflect.

ISBN 978-0-86322-362-4; paperback original

JOHN MAHER
The Luck Penny

This engrossing novel evokes the unease of the coloniser's attempts to impart ideals and principles to a native population which does not welcome such offerings, however well-intentioned. It is a story of life and death, of loss, trauma, and recovery.

"Startlingly assured... there are echoes of Joyce, delivering not only a terrific story but a powerful display of language as well."
Pat McCabe

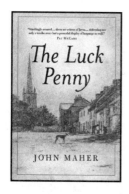

ISBN 978-0-86322-361-7; paperback original

DRAGO JANČAR
Joyce's Pupil

"Jančar writes powerful, complex stories with an unostentatious assurance, and has a gravity which makes the tricks of more self-consciously modern writers look cheap [. . .] Drago Jančar deserves the wider readership that these translations should gain him." *Times Literary Supplement*

"Elegant, elliptical stories." *Financial Times*

"His powerful and arresting narratives leave the reader in no doubt as to the fragility of the human condition when placed under the stress of political, historical and ethnic conflict." *Sunday Telegraph*

"[A] stunning collection . . . ambitious, enjoyable and page turning." *Time Out*

ISBN 978-0-86322-340-2; paperback original

William Wall
No Paradiso

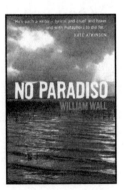

"In addition to the author's alert, muscular style, his painlessly communicated appreciation of obscure learning, his vaguely didactic pleasure in accurately providing a sense of place, many of these stories are distinguished by a welcome engagement with form. . . In their various negotiations with such tensions, the stories of *No Paradiso* engage, challenge and reward the committed reader." *The Irish Times*

ISBN 978-0-86322-355-6; paperback original

NENAD VELIČKOVIĆ
Lodgers

"Excellent... *Lodgers* supplies one of the
best examples of 'war literature' . . . More
literarily convincing and existentially urgent
than numerous current-affairs books,
newspaper reports, and travel writing,
Lodgers stands out as a poignant document
of a turbulent era." *World Literature Today*

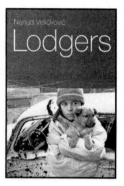

"In deploying his curious cast of 'lodgers,'
Veličković reveals an artistry that defeats
the forces of brutality with wit, indirection,
and boundless good humor." *Review of
Contemporary Fiction*

"Nenad Veličković offers a beautifully constructed account of the
ridiculous nature of the Balkans conflict, and war in general, which
even in moments of pure gallows humour retains a heartwarming
affection for the individuals trying to survive in such horrific
circumstances." *Metro*

ISBN 978-0-86322-348-8; paperback original

CHET RAYMO
Valentine

"Such nebulous accounts [as we have] have
been just waiting for someone to make a
work of historical fiction out of them.
American novelist and physicist Raymo has
duly obliged with his recently published
Valentine: A Love Story." *The Scotsman*

"[A] vivid and lively account of how
Valentine's life may have unfolded... Raymo
has produced an imaginative and enjoyable
read, sprinkled with plenty of food for
philosophical thought." *Sunday Tribune*

ISBN 978-0-86322-327-3; paperback original

KATE McCAFFERTY
Testimony of an Irish Slave Girl

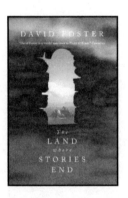

"McCafferty's haunting novel chronicles an overlooked chapter in the annals of human slavery . . . A meticulously researched piece of historical fiction that will keep readers both horrified and mesmerized."
Booklist

"Thousands of Irish men, women and children were sold into slavery to work in the sugar-cane fields of Barbados in the 17th century . . . McCafferty has researched her theme well and, through Cot, shows us the terrible indignities and suffering endured." *Irish Independent*

ISBN 978-0-86322-338-9; paperback
ISBN 978-0-86322-314-1; hardback

DAVID FOSTER
The Land Where Stories End

"Australia's most original and important living novelist." *Independent Monthly*

"A post-modern fable set in the dark ages of Ireland. . . [A] beautifully written humorous myth that is entirely original. The simplicity of language is perfectly complementary to the wry, occasionally laugh-out-loud humour and the captivating tale." *Irish World*

"I was taken by surprise and carried easily along by the amazing story and by the punchy clarity of the writing. . . This book is imaginative and fantastic. . . It is truly amazing." *Books Ireland*

ISBN 978-0-86322-311-2; hardback